it's in his arms

A RED RIVER VALLEY NOVEL

SHELLY ALEXANDER

Montlake
Romance

Text copyright © 2017 Shelly Alexander

Published by Montlake Romance, Seattle

www.apub.com

Amazon, the Amazon logo, and Montlake Romance are trademarks of Amazon.com, Inc., or its affiliates.

ISBN-13: 9781503940741
ISBN-10: 1503940748

Cover design by Damonza

Printed in the United States of America

it's in his arms

A RED RIVER VALLEY NOVEL

Also by Shelly Alexander

It's In His Heart

It's In His Touch

It's In His Smile

*To mothers, teachers, and our military—thank you
for your service and for willingly doing the toughest
jobs on earth.
To my three sons for filling our household with music,
and to my youngest son for contributing his love and
knowledge of music to this story.
And as always, thank you to my husband for loving me.*

Chapter One

"Bullshitz For Sale!"

Holding the shoebox that contained her kids' deceased guinea pig, Lorenda Lawson read the flyer that advertised the ugliest puppies she'd ever seen. She picked it off the oak dinette table and stared at the picture. Apparently, crossing a French bulldog with a shih tzu didn't produce the most attractive canine gene pool.

Did she really need more *bravo sierra* in her life?

She snorted at the code system she'd developed so the kids wouldn't know she was cussing. The military alphabet seemed appropriate since their father had been a Navy SEAL.

One thought of her late husband, and the sting of disappointment and rejection made her stomach burn.

She glanced out the window to where Jaycee and Trevor flew a remote-controlled helicopter in the front yard. Specks of morning sun danced across the property, the trees heavy with the lush green leaves of late summer.

Nope, she didn't need more *bravo sierra*, especially if she had to pay for it. Keeping up the pretense that Red River's fallen war hero had actually loved his wife and kids—totally free *bravo sierra*. Having to raise two boys on her own even before Cameron was KIA was quite enough *bravo sierra*, thank you very much.

But Jaycee and Trevor's little hearts were going to be crushed when they found out that Checkers had gone to that big spinning wheel in the sky. With the cardboard casket balanced against her hip, she stared out the window just as Jaycee crashed the helicopter into the giant cottonwood tree that shaded the driveway.

Trevor's seven-year-old face, sprinkled with light-brown freckles, crumpled. Jaycee, two years older, rushed to the crash site and seemed to be assessing the damage.

Oh *sierra*. Their beloved guinea pig and their favorite toy totaled in the same day?

She hurried to the kitchen bar and snatched her new phone off the granite counter. She held down the button at the bottom until the OS assistant's voice came through the speaker. "How can I make your day?" Minx purred like a sex kitten.

Really? Maybe she shouldn't have settled for the cheaper phone service. But it was so much more cost effective since she'd decided to add Jaycee and Trevor to the plan.

Lorenda held the phone close to her lips. "Is it possible to resuscitate a guinea pig?" She'd just found Checkers a minute ago in his cage when she went into Jaycee and Trevor's room to clean out their closet. Maybe there was a chance . . .

"Neutering a guinea pig should not be attempted at home. Here is a list of veterinarians in your area," Minx said.

Lorenda closed her eyes and tapped the phone against her forehead.

"It sounds like you're hammering something," Minx said. "Do you need instructions?"

Lorenda looked at the phone. She wasn't pushing the button anymore, so it must be malfunctioning. It was brand new! And how was it possible that an OS assistant had a voice so sultry that it made the word *hammering* sound naughty?

She heaved out a breath and tried to decide how to break the news about Checkers to the boys. Jaycee and Trevor started toward the house, their little shoulders slumped.

"Delta," Lorenda cursed.

She glanced around the open floor plan of her pretty little cottage, frantic to find a way to delay the inevitable. She didn't want Checkers's untimely death to ruin the fun she had planned. Not yet. With a new school year starting on Monday, she'd planned to drop off a suitcase full of the kids' old clothes at the rummage sale, take the kids to Cotton-Eyed Joe's for lunch, and maybe ride go-carts at the arcade.

Checkers, God rest his soul, could piss off for a few hours before he got a proper mourning.

The suitcase of old clothes snagged her attention. Perfect! Dashing to the back door, she unzipped the suitcase and stuffed the little coffin inside. The orange Nike lid slid off and made a hollow thud against the beige ceramic tile.

Double *delta*. There was no time to replace it. The zipper whizzed, concealing Checkers's brown, black, and white patchwork fur, just as Jaycee and Trevor threw open the back door.

"Mom!" Trevor howled. "Jaycee ruined the helicopter Uncle Langston gave us."

Her brother, Langston, was a lot of things—fantastic uncle, annoying brother, firefighter turned EMT, and since two years ago, a flight paramedic on a medical rescue helicopter. He spoiled his two nephews as much as Lorenda would allow. He'd probably buy Jaycee and Trevor a hundred toy helos if they asked, which she'd taught them not to do.

"It was an accident." Jaycee frowned. "You were the one that wanted me to fly it in between the trees," he said to his little brother. "If we'd taken it to the meadow like I wanted, it wouldn't have crashed."

Amazing how they both looked so much like their dad. Mocha eyes, boyish grins. Their wavy chestnut-brown hair was a mixture of her blonde and Cameron's black, and they were tall for their age, getting their height from both her and Cameron.

That was one of the things she'd loved about Cameron when they'd become high school sweethearts. They'd been friends since childhood, and when she'd sprouted into a tall, lanky teenager, he was one of the only boys who hadn't been embarrassed to dance with her because she was a little over five feet nine.

Since Jaycee was older, he was a few inches taller than Trevor. Otherwise, they could pass as twins. Funny since Cameron had an identical twin brother who never came around anymore, preferring to spend his time with his SEAL team, same as Cameron had.

She knelt and gathered them both into a hug. The feel of their little arms around her pushed out any regret about Cameron. Sure, she'd married too young, and a honeymoon pregnancy meant no more college, but those little arms around her? She breathed the boys in. She couldn't regret them, no matter the lonely price she'd had to pay as Cameron's wife.

"Hey, how about we go get a burger and a shake?" She rumpled their hair. "And then we can play some games at the arcade."

Trevor sniffled. Jaycee's frown morphed into a smile.

"Can we take our phones?" Trevor wiped a finger under his nose with another sniff, obviously trying for sympathy points.

"Nope." Lorenda tweaked his nose. "You know the rule. I got you the phones for when you're not with me. Today we're having family time without electronics."

Especially with Minx offering unsolicited conversation in a porn-flick voice.

She grabbed the handle of the suitcase. "First we need to stop by the rummage sale." She'd have to find a way to ditch Checkers. "Then it's fun, fun, and more fun the rest of the day!"

The boys tore out the door, all energy and smiles again. They yipped and yayed all the way to her Nissan Pathfinder and scrambled into the backseat. And her? She blew out a weighty sigh. For her it was business as usual.

Or should she say *bravo sierra* as usual?

Always covering. Always keeping a brave face. Always pushing her own wants aside.

That was motherhood. That was *single* motherhood.

Slinging her purse over one shoulder, she glanced at the flyer that advertised the bullshitz puppies one more time.

Hiding the painful truth from her boys had, sadly, become her specialty. If the town found out that Cameron, their hometown hero, hadn't always been so heroic, well, then the boys would find out too. There would be questions. There were *always* questions, with the way gossip traveled at the speed of light in Red River. What could she tell the kids? Their father never wanted them? Refused to come home to be a husband and father?

She wheeled the suitcase outside and locked the door.

No, she'd built a nice, sheltered life for her and the kids in this perfect little cottage-in-the-woods. She didn't need the hassle that dredging up ancient history would cause.

As she headed toward the SUV, she pushed the remote, and the trunk lifted.

She could keep up the charade that painted Cameron as a doting father forever if it meant shielding Jaycee and Trevor from the painful rejection she knew all too well. They'd been so young when Cameron was KIA, and before that he hadn't come home much. So the only mental image they had of their father was the one she created. Cameron's Trident and posthumous Bronze Star sitting right inside on the fireplace mantel was the father they needed to remember—the man Red River had on a pedestal.

And wasn't that just a bunch of bullshitz?

"We want a bullshitz! We want a bullshitz!" Jaycee and Trevor chanted over the crate of ugly puppies. The rummage sale was in full swing at one end of Brandenburg Park, and a pet adoption had the other end in a tailspin with barking dogs, hissing cats, and people either awwing over the animals or wrinkling their noses at the disagreeable mixture of pet odors.

The breeze shifted, rustling the leafy trees and blowing the offensive smells upwind toward Wheeler Peak, which loomed large over Red River.

Clifford, the maintenance man who serviced most of Red River's businesses, sat behind a sign that said "Too pooped to scoop? Doody Calls, Inc." He handed out cards along with chocolate kisses.

Lorenda would've snorted if her boys weren't shouting "bullshitz," while a teacher from the elementary school gave her the evil eye from two booths down.

Lorenda gripped the handle of the suitcase, trying to figure out how to unload the clothes at the rummage sale without the kids seeing Checkers's furry corpse. "Guys, we really don't have time to house-train a dog right now." Good Lord, she'd just gotten the boys to stop leaving the seat up.

"We'll train it." Jaycee picked up one of the puppies.

"They're all weaned and ready to go with their first shots." A portly woman with frizzy hair and wearing a "Red River Animal Shelter" T-shirt stood beside the crate.

Lorenda studied the dog as it licked Jaycee's smiling face.

Big sweet eyes. Innocent face. Loads of trouble. Puppy odors mixed with the unusual scent of rambunctious boys did not a pleasant home make. No, freshly baked cookies and homemade apple pie would better suit the peaceful, happy atmosphere she'd spent years creating.

Both boys squealed when Trevor leaned in to give the puppy a hug and got a wet willie instead.

Their laughter knocked a chip from her resolve. But really, how could she handle a puppy on top of everything else? She'd become a master at keeping her *sierra* together no matter how many piles life lobbed at her. Cleaning up after a dog might be the thing that tipped the scale.

"I don't think—"

"Please, Mom, please." Trevor's eyes glistened under the clear, blue New Mexico sky, and he stroked the dog's head. The puppy whined and licked his hand, then strained toward Jaycee to lick his face.

"Seriously, guys. A dog is a lot of work." Lorenda was about to start ticking off a list of responsibilities on her fingers when her mother shouted her name from across the park. The puppy whined. "Um, you can play with him while I talk to Grandma, but that's it."

Her words didn't seem to register.

"Lorenda!" Her mother practically skipped across the park to meet her.

Suitcase dragging behind her, Lorenda walked to meet her mother halfway. Blonde, fair, and tall like Lorenda, she looked much younger than her sixty-three years. And at the enthusiastic rate she was power walking, Lorenda was afraid she might fall and break a hip.

"Whoa, what's up, Mom?" Lorenda asked when her mother nearly plowed her over. "I thought you and Dad were spending the week in Denver?"

"We came home early." Her mother sucked in a breath and held it until Lorenda thought she might burst.

"I hope it wasn't because of the two vacation properties that just sold, because I can handle that on my own." Since her parents were mostly retired, Lorenda was the primary agent for their company, Brooks Real Estate. Selling vacation homes in Red River had been good for her and the kids financially, once she'd dropped out of college. And she did like her job. She just didn't love it.

"Of course you can handle it. That's not why we came back." A coy smile found its way to her mother's lips like she had big news and was playing hard to get.

"Okay, I'll bite. Why?" Lorenda put a hand on her hip.

"Oh, I don't know." Her mom winked. "We may have found a donor for the after-school music program you're trying to start."

Lorenda's heart skipped. "Someone wants to donate?"

Lorenda could play just about any instrument. It was a gift she'd been born with, and the reason she'd started college to become a music teacher. Starting an after-school music program at the new rec center her friends Miranda and Talmadge were building was the next best thing. She could still teach music, even if it were as a volunteer instead of a certified educator with a degree.

Her mother pretended to examine her manicured nails. "Maybe."

Lorenda tapped her foot and leveled a stern look at her mom, trying to act tough. If only she really were a badass. Or *bravo alpha*. But she was a total pushover. She knew it. She just hoped no one else knew it, because a single woman with two kids couldn't afford to be a wimp.

"Oh, alright." Her mother huffed. "The new conductor of the Albuquerque Symphony e-mailed your father about a vacation cabin on our website. They're looking at the place as we speak, and your dad is going to drop a few hints about the music program." She lowered her voice to a whisper. "When your father asked if the conductor's wife would be joining them to look at the cabin, he said he didn't have a wife."

Here it came—her mother's annoying, albeit well-meaning, quest to find Lorenda a suitable man. She fought off an eye roll, because the last time her mother had made a desperate attempt to set Lorenda up on a date, she'd ended up eating frozen pizza with Clifford the maintenance man while he discussed the best methods of cleaning a toilet. For three *foxtroting* hours.

As if Lorenda weren't already the queen of toilet cleaning, seeing as how she had two boys.

"You know I'm not in the market for a relationship. Not until the boys are grown."

"If you met the right man, the boys would benefit too," her mother argued.

"If I met the wrong man, they would suffer."

"You're young and beautiful, Lorenda. There's no need to keep martyring yourself on the sword of motherhood."

Lorenda glanced over her shoulder at Jaycee and Trevor. They sat on the ground, and the puppy crawled all over them. Satisfying warmth spread through her. They were good kids. But rambunctious and full of energy and always looking for an adventure. Like their dad and his twin brother.

Fear skated through her.

She did not want them to turn into restless, alpha war junkies like their father.

A classical musician probably wouldn't be a thrill-seeker, but one disastrous marriage was enough. She couldn't . . . she *wouldn't* chance putting the boys through that kind of turmoil. Being alone until they were grown was a sacrifice she'd decided to make a long time ago.

She shook her head. "If he really wants to help with the program, I'll take it, but not if there are strings attached. No matchmaking, are we clear?"

Her mother's lips thinned. "Fine."

Lorenda pointed to the boys. "Can you keep the kids occupied while I dump these clothes at the rummage sale?" Wheeling around a dead animal was starting to creep her out. And added to her guilt of not letting the boys get a dog. She didn't want the critter to come back and haunt her either. She had enough imaginary ghosts to live with every time she thought of Cameron.

Her mother pinched Lorenda's cheek. "Anything for my boys." Without so much as a goodbye her mother skittered around Lorenda and darted for Jaycee and Trevor.

Lorenda turned her attention to the far side of the park, her gaze skimming along the rows of rummage-sale booths. Okay, time to find one that wasn't overrun with shoppers. The park was crowded, but a few booths at the north end were vacant and . . . aha! She could slip behind one of the ponderosa pines at that end of the park and unload the suitcase without anyone seeing Checkers.

She tugged the suitcase toward the rummage sale, but a thin guy with a hoodie pulled up and draped over his forehead got in her way. His hands were crammed into the pockets of the thick hoodie like he was cold. Strange. Nights were always cool in Red River, but it was a sunny afternoon in August. "Excuse me." She tried to step around him, but he matched her step and blocked her path again, glancing at her.

His messy black hair hung in his eyes. His face was gaunt, and the look in his eyes was disturbing because it was like he knew her even though she didn't recognize him. Before she could maneuver around him again, he grabbed the suitcase and pushed her.

"Ooph!" She hit the ground, and the thief darted toward Main Street.

Bart Wilkinson, the elementary-school principal and a guy Lorenda had known since kindergarten, seemed to appear out of nowhere. "Lorenda! Are you okay?" He put an arm around her waist to help as she scrambled to her feet. Others yelled and pointed to the man as he ran with her suitcase. And Checkers.

Her lips parted. She'd just been mugged for a dead guinea pig and worn-out kids' clothes.

Wasn't the mugger going to be surprised?

As the thief bounded past Clydelle and Francine—two senior citizens who kept the locals so far up on their toes that most of Red River might as well wear stilettos—Clydelle thumped him on the leg with her cane, and Francine took a swing at him with her purse.

"Ow!" He dropped the suitcase but kept on running, only with a limp because of Clydelle's handy-dandy cane. Lorenda should get one of those. Might come in useful since she was single. But in Red River, where crime was usually less than zero, who needed weapons?

A few men took off after him, but from the side, a man came out of nowhere and tackled the mugger. The familiar build—big, broad . . . badass—made blood pound through her veins.

A crowd swarmed the mugger and the man who had stopped him.

Several of the ladies who had been milling around the park ran over to offer Lorenda assistance, but Bart hadn't let her go. His arm was still firmly around her waist.

"I'm fine," Lorenda mumbled, trying to see through the growing crowd. Trying to step out of Bart's hold. As nice as it was for him to help, she was fine, but he followed her step and stayed right at her side.

"Are you okay, hon?" Her mother darted over, Trevor, Jaycee, and the puppy trailing behind with rounded eyes.

Trevor threw his arms around her waist, which forced Bart to step back. "Are you hurt, Mom?"

"No, sweetie. I'm okay." She threaded an arm around his shoulder. She pulled her phone from her purse, but before she could get the sheriff's number typed in, blue-and-red whirling lights raced around the corner. As fast as news traveled in Red River, the sheriff had probably heard about the incident before Lorenda had even hit the ground.

"Who was that, Mom?" Jaycee said, scooping up the puppy like he was protecting it.

She shook her head. "No idea."

"Here comes Grandpa," Jaycee said around the puppy's head as the sheriff's car pulled up.

"Yay! Grandpa to the rescue!" Trevor clapped with adoration.

Sheriff Larry Lawson unfolded himself from the car. And he looked pissed. Then again, her father-in-law had looked pissed for as long as Lorenda could remember. Losing one of his twin sons to war and the other to blame and bitterness had only hardened him more. But he did love his grandsons and would do anything for Lorenda and the boys.

"Stay back, boys." Lorenda stepped in front of the kids like a shield.

The crowd around the mugger parted, and Sheriff Lawson stepped into the inner circle.

Francine used the opportunity to retrieve Lorenda's suitcase, and Clydelle tried to poke the mugger with her cane. The sheriff scowled at her and waved them both back. Through the shuffling legs of the crowd, Lorenda caught a glimpse of the man who had tackled the thief. He had the mugger pinned to the ground with one knee. Her rescuer's head was pitched forward as he held the squirming mugger in place with a hand pressing the weasel's cheek into the grass.

One of the ladies standing around Lorenda said, "Looks like you have a new hero, dear."

Lorenda wanted to roll her eyes, because heroes weren't all they were cracked up to be. She craned her neck to get a better look.

A black T-shirt stretched taut across her *hero's* wide shoulders and muscled back that angled down to a trim waist and nicely broken-in Levi's. But even hunched over, Lorenda would recognize that build anywhere. Would know the person anywhere. Had grown up with him, been sweethearts with him . . . married him.

Her hand, still holding the phone, went to her mouth, and she stumbled toward the crowd that surrounded her supposed hero until she stood at its edge.

The sheriff glowered down at both men. "Step back. I can handle it from here." But her hero didn't move until Sheriff Lawson slapped cuffs onto the thief.

The crowd whispered and buzzed.

"Is that . . . ?" someone said, their shocked whisper trailing off.

"That troublemaker is back in town," Bart said from just behind her.

Lorenda's heart contracted right along with her hero's bulging biceps, which made the familiar crown-of-thorns tattoo around his upper arm flex as he straightened. Which seemed to take about a decade, because he was tall. Six three, in fact. Lorenda knew his height, his weight. His *foxtroting* shoe size.

And like it was in slow motion, yet happening at the speed of light, he turned and locked gazes with Lorenda. No one else. Just her. And a familiar smile, the one that had won her heart when she was a teenager, then broken it just a few years later, made her heart thump and bump in an odd rhythm like it would stop at any moment.

Her head told her that it was Mitchell, Cameron's twin brother. Had to be, because Cameron was dead. Mitchell's features were identical to Cameron's, yet there were subtle differences she had always been able to pick out, even though no one else besides their mother could. But seeing him after so many years was like stepping back in time.

The bright afternoon sun grew dim, and the faces around her turned fuzzy. Except for his. His was as clear as the sky. She meant to say his name—Mitchell. But when he took a step toward her, she whispered, "Cameron."

The last thing Lorenda remembered was his smile fading along with the sunlight, and then her world went dark.

Chapter Two

So, he'd already failed his first mission in Red River—don't cause trouble.

Mitchell Lawson cradled Lorenda's long, lithe, and very limp body against his chest, bracing against her deadweight with a wide stance.

Well, hell. Trouble was something that found *him*. Snagged him like a fishing hook and reeled him in every time. At least he was consistent.

He lowered Lorenda to the ground, the grass cool and soft and so green under his knees. It was a good thing she'd fallen forward into his arms when she'd fainted, or she would've hit the ground like a nicely shaped sack of potatoes.

Adjusting Lorenda's back against a bent knee, he glanced around the park where he used to play with his brother. It had been bustling with activity when he pulled up on his motorcycle. Now, most everyone was rooted in place, either staring at him and Lorenda or staring at his father, who hauled the perp to his feet and hustled him toward the police car.

His father . . . who greeted him after six long years by commanding him to "back away."

Murmurs rippled through the crowd as recognition dawned. Whispers about Mitchell's troublemaking youth. And just as quickly as the close-knit citizens of Red River had praised him for stopping a criminal, their looks of admiration transformed to glares of disapproval.

Animosity hung on the summer breeze so thick that Mitchell could practically cut it with the SOG Desert Dagger strapped inside his boot. It wasn't exactly a ticker-tape parade for a decorated war veteran. Neither was the beautiful woman in his arms whose eyes had rolled back in her head with just one look at him.

Two little boys bounded toward them, and Mitchell froze. The resemblance to Cameron was unmistakable. For a moment Mitchell was carried back in time. Two Lawson boys who looked so much alike running through Brandenburg Park, the sweet aroma of cinnamon rolls and maple scones wafting down Main Street from the Ostergaard's Bakery, Wheeler Peak casting a quaint shadow over Red River—all transported him back to a life before sadness and death had drowned out his innocent youth.

Okay, maybe not so innocent. The glares shooting holes in his chest were evidence of that, but whatever. Nothing he'd done in Red River meant he deserved the carnage he'd witnessed during the long years of fighting a war.

"Mom!" the smaller boy hollered.

"Did Mom die?" the taller boy screamed, clutching a puppy.

A sharp sting clawed at Mitchell's gut. When death was the first thing to enter a little boy's mind, it meant something. Something wrong. He'd seen it in the villages of Afghanistan more times than he cared to remember.

An older version of Lorenda rushed forward and knelt beside them. A woman Mitchell knew well because he'd been buddies with Lorenda's brother, Langston. "What have you done to my daughter?" Charlotte Brooks demanded.

"Uh, caught her?" Mitchell said.

She looked down her nose at him like he was a smart-ass.

He *was* a smart-ass, but he'd just saved Lorenda. Twice. So the insinuation that he'd done something wrong, mixed with the murmurs from the crowd that grew louder by the second, were starting to tick him off.

So mission number two—make amends with the townsfolk for all the trouble he'd caused growing up—wasn't looking so hot either.

"Hello, Mrs. Brooks." Mitchell figured some good old hometown manners would go a long way in garnering some civility.

"Mitchell." Mrs. Brooks sniffed.

Yep. Mission number two shot to hell.

He sighed and looked past her to the boys. "It's all right, guys." Mitchell dropped his voice to a soothing lull. He had done it many times while holding the dying in his arms. Precisely why he'd vowed not to get attached to another person. It was easier to let go that way. "I promise your mom is fine." Their worried looks didn't ease. "She just fainted."

Guess seeing someone that looked exactly like your dead husband did that to a woman.

But Lorenda had been the only person outside of their mom who didn't have to ask which Lawson twin was which. She could tell Cameron and Mitchell apart way back when she was a scrawny kid with pigtails and Mitchell and Cameron thought girls had cooties.

Marry the girl who can tell you apart. That's what their mom had told them. So when Lorenda grew into a pretty young teenager, Cameron had fallen hard and eventually married her, smart guy that he was.

It hadn't occurred to Mitchell that Lorenda might need a little warning before he showed up in the flesh.

He turned his stare to the flashing lights of the sheriff's car. His father put his hand on the mugger's head and guided him into the backseat. Then his dad opened the driver's door and got on the radio to call it in, no doubt.

A short guy stepped forward, with a slight spare tire around his middle and a hairline that had started to recede. "I can take her." He looked vaguely familiar.

"And you are?" Instinctively, Mitchell's grip tightened around Lorenda.

"Bart." Small Balding Guy's tone was clipped like he was miffed. "Bart Wilkinson. We went to school together. All of our lives."

Oh yeah. An odd little guy with a doting mother who cut his meat for him until he was sixteen. Because kids could be mean, he'd been nicknamed Bart the Fart after an untimely sneezing attack in the midst of a full lunchtime crowd on pinto-bean day. Lorenda, always the nice girl, had shown him compassion and stood up for him when the other kids called him Bart the Fart. And if Mitchell remembered correctly, Bart had had a crush on Lorenda ever since.

"Thanks, but I've got her," Mitchell said.

Bart's eyes launched grenades at him.

Mitchell looked down at Lorenda. Her head leaned to the side, and long, flowing blonde hair fell across her cheek. He smoothed it back. Sunlight filtered through the rustling leaves of a large cottonwood and splayed across her smooth skin, which had turned a light bronze from the sun. Full pink lips. A tiny Marilyn Monroe mole just above her mouth. Her subtle perfume drifted up, just as soft and feminine as her.

It was probably inappropriate, but a sense of protectiveness that bordered on possessive jolted through him. Because Mitchell knew what a crummy deal Lorenda and the boys had gotten from his brother.

He gathered her closer. She was so soft. Her face so pretty. More mature than the last time he'd seen her, six years ago at Cameron's funeral. Then again, he hadn't stuck around long enough to form an opinion on whether or not Lorenda still looked like the young, pretty girl he'd grown up with, or the attractive young woman his brother married. Getting out of town had been his first priority, since his father blamed him for Cameron's death.

Mitchell was used to taking the blame. Dad had "known" that Mitchell's hell-raising had started the fire the night he and Cameron graduated from high school. Just like Dad "knew" that Mitchell had persuaded Cameron to follow him into the military.

The truth didn't matter. Never had. And why should Mitchell have to convince his dad of anything? Wasn't a father supposed to love his kids unconditionally?

He studied his nephews while Lorenda's slow and steady breaths ebbed and flowed.

There was way more at stake now than just making amends. Telling the truth to clear his name would mean hurting two innocent little boys. He glanced in his father's direction. It might also mean causing the old man to keel over, which would destroy his mother. So he'd have to find another way.

The crowd around them kept thickening, the rummage sale and pet adoption obviously on pause.

"Paramedics are on the way," someone in the crowd shouted.

Thank God. At least one person in the crowd was thinking of Lorenda's well-being instead of trying to mow him down with dirty looks. Traditional values and old grudges ran deep in a town as small as Red River.

"You want to take her hand, Trevor?" Mrs. Brooks said to the younger boy. "Maybe if she feels your presence, she'll wake up quicker."

Trevor took a doubtful step forward and knelt next to his mom.

"This is your Uncle Mitch." Mrs. Brooks introduced them, an uncomfortable edge to her tone.

The boys' eyes went wide.

Sirens blared from the direction of the fire station at the other end of town.

The elderly woman who had walloped the thief with her cane lumbered over, Lorenda's suitcase rolling behind her. "All right, people. Let's give them some space." She waved the crowd back a good distance with her cane.

Another silver-haired lady—the one who had taken a swing at the bad guy with her gigantic purse—walked up.

Ah, Ms. Clydelle and Ms. Francine. It had been awhile, but how could he not remember them? The two sisters had probably pulled far more shenanigans than he had. Which is why he'd always liked them. And made a note not to get on their bad side. They should have to register the cane and purse as lethal weapons. Maybe get a concealed carry permit.

"Aren't you the Lawson boy who took out my mailbox?" Ms. Francine asked.

Dammit. Yeah, in about tenth grade. Good to know Ms. Francine didn't show any sign of Alzheimer's. Besides, it had been Cameron's idea to play Mailbox Baseball, only he'd insisted on driving at the last minute and wanted Mitchell to swing the bat.

"How about I make it up to you?" he said. "I could mow your lawn, or fix something around your house."

"Will you take your shirt off?" Francine asked.

"Shh!" Mrs. Brooks hissed, nodding toward the boys.

Jaycee sat next to Trevor and let the puppy lick his mom's arm.

Mitchell leaned down and whispered into Lorenda's ear. "Sparky." The nickname he'd given her in junior high. Gently, he shook her, and the fond and fun memories of their friendship came flooding back. "It's Mitchell. Can you wake up?"

She groaned out a protest and turned her face into his chest. Her balmy breath seeped through his cotton T-shirt and into his chest to warm his heart. The feel of her in his arms was . . . amazing. The only perfect thing he could remember since he was a kid.

"Isn't he the one that burned down Joe's a long time ago?" someone in the crowd said without trying to whisper.

"Yup," someone else agreed.

The slam of his dad's car door drew Mitchell's attention. Without hesitating, his father started toward Mitchell with long, deliberate strides.

Aaaand mission number three—mend fences with dear old dad— just went to Afghanistan in a handbasket.

"Step away from your brother's wife." The sheriff reached them and spoke with the same gruff voice that used to have Mitchell shaking in his Converse sneakers.

Funny. Not one tremor coursed through his well-worn combat boots. Oh, the razor-sharp tone still cut into him. Just not all the way to the bone like it had when Mitchell was a kid. Not after the things he'd seen in the war. After the things he'd had to do to defend his country.

"I don't think so." His tone steely, Mitchell kept his expression blank, his stare level with an unmistakable challenge.

A hush fell over the crowd, because few people defied Sheriff Lawson in these parts.

Cameron had been compliant, submissive to his dad's authority and bully tactics. Mitchell, not so much. Mitchell had been the jagged thorn in his dad's side ever since he'd started walking and talking.

"There's room for one more in the backseat of my car," his dad threatened.

"Sheriff." Mrs. Brooks gave him a warning look and nodded toward the boys.

That seemed to stop his father.

"Sparky," Mitchell whispered into her ear again, and she shivered against him. Which, surprisingly, caused him to fight off a shiver of his own. He pulled her closer. "Lorenda, sweetheart." The familiarity of the term startled him. Not so much that he'd said it so easily, but because it seemed so perfect rolling off of his tongue.

He swallowed. "Trevor and Jaycee are worried."

She stirred, her thick lashes fluttering up, then floating down again to brush the creamy skin under her eyes.

"Mom," Jaycee said. "Wake up, Mom. Malarkey wants to see you." He shifted the dog so it could lick his mom's cheek.

She sputtered to life again, rubbing the dog slobber from her face. When her deep-blue eyes opened fully, she bolted upright and backed into Mitchell's chest to avoid more puppy breath. And damn, she felt good molding into him.

The paramedics pulled up at the edge of Brandenburg Park, and they hurried over. "Coming through." Two of them pushed through the crowd.

She turned to look at Mitchell as the paramedics went to work at her side. Instead of letting them take her blood pressure, she tugged her arm out of their grasp and pressed a soft palm to his cheek. Stared up at him like she was seeing a ghost.

"Mitchell," she whispered.

He didn't miss the almost undetectable tremor of relief in her voice, and the way she murmured his name had his pulsing humming. The thought *mine* raced through his stupid brain.

Christ.

"You okay?" He tried to keep his tone soothing but detached.

"Mommy! Can we keep Malarkey?" Trevor said about a thousand decibels louder than a RPG.

She pulled her palm away from Mitchell's cheek, and he missed her warm touch. She rubbed her head like it hurt. "Yes, I'm oka—"

Both boys cheered. "Thanks, Mom!" Jaycee squeezed the dog.

"Wait." Lorenda sat up like she was going to stand. "I didn't mean—"

"Lorenda." One of the paramedics put a hand on her shoulder. "Stay still until we check you out. Your brother will kill us if we let anything happen to you."

Her eyes went round as the boys started chanting the puppy's name. "Malarkey, Malarkey, Malarkeeeey!"

"Malarkey. A synonym for dishonesty, baloney, poppycock," spouted off a black phone lying on the ground next to her.

Lorenda's beautiful blue eyes slid shut in defeat.

She let the paramedic wrap her slender arm with the blood-pressure cuff. "My brother is an overprotective bully."

Mitchell doubted that, but there *was* a lot of bullying going around. Mitchell glanced up at his scowling father. One hand was on his hip, the other rested on his holstered gun. His khaki uniform was starched to perfection, the crisp pleat down each leg as sharp and stiff as his glare.

"Where is that no-account brother of yours?" It had been a long time since he and Langston had played high-school football and chased girls together.

Lorenda's gaze snapped to Mitchell's.

He gave her a reassuring smile, and what do you know? Her stare dropped to his mouth. And stayed there.

"He's . . . around . . ." Her gaze finally left Mitchell's mouth and locked with his. His breath caught. He'd never had a thing for Lorenda all the years he'd known her. Sure, he'd thought she was pretty, but she was like a sister to him. Literally, since his brother had married her.

Something about her was different now. Stronger yet vulnerable. Mature and . . . sensual.

Christ.

Should he make a mental list of all the reasons he couldn't think of Lorenda as *sensual*, or just pay someone to kick his ass for being an idiot?

The paramedic pressed a stethoscope to her chest and listened. Mitchell couldn't help but stare at the gentle rise and fall of her chest above her sleeveless V-neck top before letting his stare wander back to hers.

The puppy let out a yelp, and she tore her gaze from Mitchell's. "Listen, boys, we need to talk about the dog."

"We named him Malarkey, Mom," Jaycee said.

She pinched the bridge of her nose. "Let's not name him just yet."

Clydelle hobbled closer. "I have your suitcase, dear. Must be something important in here for that creep to steal it."

"It's just old clothes for the rummage sale." Lorenda's voice shook with . . . panic?

Francine shuffled up next to Clydelle and bent to grab the zipper. "Let's see what kind of clothes so we can deliver them to the right booth for you."

Lorenda shouted, "No!"

The paramedic flinched and jerked the stethoscope from his ears. He rammed a finger into one ear and wiggled it, like he was trying to shake out the pain of her scream.

Francine kept unzipping.

The crowd gasped.

A guinea pig lay lifeless and contorted in the middle of a heap of clothes. The boys let out a wail.

Lorenda fell back against Mitchell's knee like she was surrendering to an enemy. "All right, boys. Malarkey is yours." She rubbed her forehead like a headache was coming on. And muttered something that sounded like . . . *bravo sierra*? "I'm sorry about Checkers. We'll bury him when we get home."

Trevor sniffed but turned his attention to the puppy, which seemed to already fill the void of losing Checkers.

"You seem fine, Lorenda, but I have to ask if you want to go to the hospital," said the paramedic, still jiggling a finger in one ear.

She shook her head. "No. Just help me up."

The paramedic reached for her, but Mitchell instinctively encircled her with his arms. "Put your arm around my shoulder." She obeyed, and as he eased her to her feet, she wasn't just his sister-in-law anymore. She was lush and warm against him, and that warmth had his pulse kicking up dust.

"Okay, folks," Sheriff Lawson boomed, and took a step forward. "Show's over. Anyone who saw what happened needs to come by my office today. Lorenda, you'll need to come to the station and make a statement now." He puffed his chest out and inflated his large, tall frame when he turned to Mitchell. A trick his father had perfected to scare people into bending to his will. "She's coming with me."

Mitchell had perfected the same alpha move himself during the years he'd served in the military. How'd the old man think Mitchell had made it through SEAL training and survived so many dangerous missions? He beefed up his stance and stared his father down. "Lorenda, can I drive you and the boys to the station? I doubt you want to get in the same car as the jerk who just attacked you."

His father's face turned red as a beet. "He's handcuffed, and there's a glass barrier between the seats."

"Well, I—" She tried to let go of Mitchell but lost her footing again. He braced her against his side. "Sorry," she said. "I'm still a little dizzy."

"Not a problem." Without warning, he scooped her up in his arms. She squeaked and clamped her arms around his neck. "Where's your car?"

She pointed to the street that ran along the west side of Brandenburg Park. "It's the dark-green SUV."

"Boys, grab your mom's things, and let's take her to the police station."

Jaycee, Trevor, and the dog fell in behind him as he turned and strolled toward her vehicle, leaving two old women smiling, a crowd of townies gaping, and one old man fuming.

Chapter Three

Try as she might, it was kinda hard for Lorenda not to focus on Mitchell's hard chest as he carried her through the crowded waiting area, following his father to an interrogation room. Impossible not to focus on his muscled arms since he'd plucked her from the SUV like she was as light as one of the kids.

The sheriff's office in Red River didn't get a lot of traffic, seeing as how the worst crimes were rarely more than someone's dog treeing a tourist. Which was why the waiting room of the police station was standing room only at the moment.

Her father-in-law's assistant, Maureen, called to Jaycee and Trevor. "Y'all play with the puppy out here." She winked at Lorenda, her false eyelashes almost as stiff as her back-combed hair. But she was a kind woman who looked out for the sheriff. Lorenda waved the okay over Mitchell's shoulder.

"Um, thank you," Lorenda said to Mitchell when he deposited her into a black vinyl chair. "I really could've walked." Or maybe just leaned on him a little. She rubbed her aching head.

"No worries." Mitchell didn't show any sign of leaving. He stood next to her. Arms crossed, stance wide, body hot.

That hot bod was a problem. The last thing Lorenda needed was to find Mitchell Lawson attractive. He was her brother-in-law. Her pal. And worst of all, he was a man the boys were already looking at with godlike admiration. And didn't she already know how much it hurt to get *foxtroted* over by an alpha war junkie who couldn't get rid of the itch for danger and adventure?

Sheriff Lawson walked in and closed the door, shutting out the chatter of the busy waiting room. "Ready to give your statement, Lorenda?"

"Yes." She nodded, and the room swam. To make it stop, she clutched the spit-shined black-and-chrome table with both hands. *Delta.* The aftermath of fainting was as bad as a hangover. Only without the fun that usually caused it.

Note to self: remember to breathe the next time you come face-to-face with a ghost.

Mitchell put a hand on the back of her chair. "Sure you can do this now? I could bring you back later."

Her gaze locked on to the concern in his eyes, then smoothed over the light stubble that covered his squared jaw. So much like Cameron yet totally different. Different in ways that she couldn't quite put a name to. More honest? More mature? More sexy?

Breathe, breathe, breathe!

Mitchell's strong hand closed around her shoulder, and he gave it a gentle squeeze.

A flush surged through her. She hadn't had this much attention from a good-looking man, well, ever. She liked it way more than she should, if she had to be honest with herself. His strength had settled around her in the park and made her feel warm and wanted, which was totally ridiculous, because she and Mitchell had always been pals.

"No." She made sure not to shake her head. "I'd like to find out why someone mugged me." In Red River. Over a dead guinea pig and some old clothes. Why hadn't the mugger grabbed her purse? Made no sense.

Neither did Mitchell coming back to town after so many years. No one except his mother had heard from him since he'd stormed out of Cameron's funeral. The sheriff's iceberg treatment could've sunk the *Titanic* that day. His harsh words had been out of line, like Mitchell wasn't suffering over Cameron's death too. But why come back now?

The sheriff retrieved a bottle of cold water from the mini fridge in the corner, cracked the top, and handed it to Lorenda.

Didn't offer his son a thing.

She gulped down a third of the bottle.

"You can wait outside." Lorenda jumped at the sheriff's harsh tone when he spoke to Mitchell.

"Not unless Lorenda wants me to," Mitchell said.

"Mitchell needs to be here. He's the one that stopped the mugger." Lorenda laced her fingers. "So both of you sit down." She hoped her voice didn't shake the way her insides quaked. She bit her lip to keep from adding, "Please."

She returned their surprised looks with a pleasant but firm smile. Worked like a charm, because the Lawson pissing match seemed to dial down, and they both took a seat at the table.

Mitchell tugged his chair closer to hers. The rubber feet scooted over the modern ceramic tile, and a dull scrape echoed through the room. The sound raked against her nerves, because his alpha-male scent was making her pulse rev.

She gulped down more of the water.

The sheriff grabbed a legal pad and pen and took off his felt cowboy hat. He ran a palm over his graying buzz cut. "Start from the beginning, hon." His voice had lost its hard edge.

She drew in a hefty breath. "It happened so fast." One thumb rubbed the other as she verbally walked through the incident. When she was done, she said, "He could've grabbed my purse, or grabbed the suitcase and run off." She hugged herself and ran open palms over her arms. Probably nerves and not her woman's intuition, but she couldn't shake the strange gnawing in the pit of her stomach. "It might sound silly, but he pushed me down like he wanted to hurt me. Like *that* was his goal and not stealing the suitcase."

Mitchell's posture tensed, waves of testosterone pouring off of him. It wrapped around her like a protective shield.

"Do you know him?" the sheriff asked. "Maybe a tourist that's come through town? Or someone you've shown vacation properties to in the past?" The sheriff's pen scratched against the pad.

She gave her head a light shake, small enough not to set off another tidal wave inside her brain. "I'm certain he wasn't a client."

"He was targeting her." Mitchell rested a hand on the back of her chair.

"You know this how?" The sheriff's icy tone was back. His scowl deepened the lines of age around his face.

She turned to Mitchell and waited for an answer. She'd like to know too, because it gave her the creeps.

"I'd pulled up to the curb on my motorcycle." He leaned closer to Lorenda, a hand still on the back of her chair, the other arm resting on the table. "I was checking out the park. Assessing an area before I walk into it is a habit." He shrugged. "An occupational hazard, I guess."

Lorenda's heart thudded for all Mitchell must've been through.

She placed a hand over his, and his gaze snapped to hers. He blinked all emotion away. At that moment, his resemblance to his brother disturbed her on the deepest level because she'd seen the same cold, empty look in Cameron's eyes during his leaves from the military.

She yanked her hand away.

Mitchell cleared his throat. "I saw Lorenda but then noticed the guy walking toward her. He was nervous, twitchy. He moved like someone who was up to no good. Spotting unnatural movements and body language is part of my training, and this guy might as well have been wearing an orange prison uniform."

The sheriff sized both of them up, then turned to Lorenda. "Anything else you want to add, hon?"

"Nothing I can think of, but if I remember anything, I'll call you." She shifted to the edge of her seat.

He turned to Mitchell. "You'll need to be on your way out of town by nightfall."

Mitchell's grip tightened around the back of her chair, and his forearm flexed against her back. "You don't get to make that decision this time." His voice went as hard as his father's.

"Interesting that trouble started the minute you rolled into town." The sheriff stood. "So I'll take you to your motorcycle and escort you to the city limits."

Mitchell stood, drawing himself up with so much brawn he seemed a foot taller. "Interesting that it's a free country." He gave his dad a cocky stare. "So I'll be staying until I'm good and ready to leave on my own." He folded both arms over his broad chest, his biceps rippling as much as the muscle in his jaw. "And you're welcome, by the way."

The sheriff's brow wrinkled. "For *what?*"

"For it being a free country and all." Mitchell kept his composure cool and calm, but that muscle still ticked in his jaw. "I just spent the last fourteen years of my life defending your freedom. I didn't mind at all."

"Get out," her father-in-law said. "Or I'll throw you out."

"I'd like to see you try." Mitchell's voice had gone low and dangerous.

Lorenda eased out of her chair. "Gentlemen, come on." They ignored her. Or maybe they couldn't hear her over the roar of testosterone. "Sheriff, your grandsons are right outside. Do you really want them to see this go down?"

The sheriff didn't move, but a muscle in his jaw flexed and released. Like stubborn-ass father like stubborn-ass son.

She latched onto Mitchell's arm to tug him away before the situation got worse, but the door swung open and in waltzed Mitchell's mom, Becky Lawson. Affectionately dubbed Badass Becky by Mitchell and Cameron's circle of high school friends. And although those friends were now grown adults, not one of them had mustered the courage to fill her in on their little moniker. Lorenda couldn't blame them. All five foot zero of sassy attitude blazed in, sporting a newly coiffed beehive hairdo, starched Wrangler jeans, a rodeo belt buckle the size of Arizona from her barrel racing days, red roper boots, and a purse shaped like a riding saddle that everyone knew had a hidden compartment for a concealed weapon.

Her mother-in-law only wanted people to think she was packing, but Lorenda knew Becky didn't actually carry a weapon. Didn't need to. Her index finger, which she drew and turned on the sheriff, was loaded and ready to blast anything in its path.

Becky Lawson was Lorenda's hero.

"*You*"—Becky pointed to her husband—"are not going to bully our son out of town again."

The sheriff sputtered.

Her badass tone turned on a dime when she glanced at Lorenda. "I'm glad you're okay, dear. I'm so sorry about what happened in the park. It must've been frightening."

Just like that, Becky's sass was back. "And *you*"—her smoking finger swung to Mitchell, ready to keep firing; Lorenda choked back a laugh when the Special Forces war hero turned chalky white with fear—"are going to do exactly what I told you to do when I asked you to come home."

"Becky!" the sheriff roared. "You *asked* him to come here?"

"Darn right." Her finger swung away, putting her husband in the crosshairs again. "He's out of the military and here to make peace with you before it's too late."

Out of the military? Lorenda had assumed Mitchell was on leave.

The sheriff's face deepened to a frightening shade of purple and he rubbed his chest.

"Larry." Becky's tone turned fearful. "Do you need your heart medication?"

Mitchell was at his father's side with near superpower agility, a hand on his dad's arm to help him into a chair. "Dad, you need to sit down."

So that's why Mitchell was home. Larry Lawson was a god in this town because he put 250 percent effort into his work. Kept crime low and tourism high, the lifeblood of Red River's economy. It was also the reason Mitchell's finger-slinging mother was ready to serve him divorce papers. But it wasn't just about her being tired of coming second to his job. He wasn't the healthy horse he'd always been. Except, by the look on the sheriff's face, he wasn't ready to be put out to pasture yet.

"I don't need your help." Sheriff Lawson pushed Mitchell's hand away. "Becky, my medication is no one's business but mine." He turned a heated glare on Lorenda and Mitchell. "And it doesn't leave this room."

Becky's fist went to her hip.

Oh boy. At the exact same moment, Lorenda and Mitchell took a step back to avoid the blast of firepower that was sure to follow.

"It darn sure is my business, Larry Lawson. So both of you shake on it and promise me you'll try."

Sheriff Lawson snatched his hat off the table and crammed it on his head. "After all that he's done, Becky, I'll die and go to hell first."

Mitchell let out a hollow laugh and rubbed the back of his neck. He shook his head, then headed to the door. "Have a nice trip." Mitchell cracked the door. "I've been there. It was called Afghanistan."

"Mitchell Lee Lawson, you get back here this instant and give your mother a kiss." His mom's voice echoed through the crowded police station, and everyone went still.

Mitchell stopped. Put both hands on his hips and dropped his head with a sigh. Some things never changed. She could stop an armored tank with that tone of hers. He turned and gave his mother a peck on the cheek and a hug. "It's good to see you, Mom, but did you really think Dad would let bygones be bygones so easily?" Mitchell spoke so only she could hear. He'd warned her. The second she found out that he hadn't re-upped she'd started in about him coming home.

"Give it time, son. For me." His mom's salty tone turned to a plea.

That plea was the only reason he hadn't already taken the overseas job. A job with a paramilitary company that would reunite him with a lot of his military buddies—people who actually wanted him around and had his back. A job that would send him back to the war zone. Only he'd be making a lot more money for a lot less bullshit.

Lorenda came out of the interrogation room, cheeks still flushed, steps still cautious. Body still freaking gorgeous. His father trailed behind and put a hand on her back like he was offering support. Amazing how the old man could be so nice to some people and such a jerk to his own flesh and blood.

Bart shot out of a chair in the waiting room and came over. "Sheriff, I can give my statement now. I was closest to Lorenda when it happened. I helped her up after that jerk pushed her down."

"Thanks, Principal Wilkinson. Have a seat and we'll get to each one of you as quick as we can," the sheriff said.

Bart looked disappointed, but he backed away.

"Grandma!" Jaycee ran over with the puppy, and Trevor followed. "Look! We got a puppy."

The boys' excitement seemed to spur the chatter back to life in the waiting room.

"Oh." Mitchell's mom stared at the dog. The dog's snout was flat and his head was too big for his body. His hair was medium brown and short with an occasional long, black wiry strand poking through the thick coat.

"His name is Malarkey," Trevor shouted. "Isn't he cute?"

Someone from the waiting room laughed.

Cute wasn't the word Mitchell would use. From the look on Lorenda's face, cute wasn't the word racing through her mind either. When Lorenda came to stand next to his mother, his father hung back a few steps with his hands on his hips and a scowl on his face.

"Well. Sure, boys." His mom patted the dog's oversized head. "Cute."

Clydelle and Francine waddled over, cane thumping and purse swinging.

"We're giving our statements next, Sheriff. We're old and can't wait around." Francine peered over thick reading glasses. "I hit him with my purse."

"And I hit him with my cane," Clydelle crooned. "Didn't slow the little shit down one bit."

"Malarkey's a shit!" Trevor hollered.

Lorenda clamped a hand over his mouth, but then Jaycee spoke up. "No, he's a bullshitz." Jaycee seemed awfully proud of himself for correcting his little brother.

Lorenda groaned.

And Mitchell was surprised that his dad wasn't clutching his chest. His dad didn't do chaos on any level. At least not before Mitchell had joined the military at eighteen and left town.

Correction. Not before he'd been forced into the military and shoved onto a bus by his hard-ass, unyielding father as an alternative to going to juvie for arson. And just like Mitchell had taken the blame for the fire, he'd also gotten the blame for his twin showing up at the recruit depot two days later.

Life would've been so much easier if Cameron could've just sucked it up and told their old man the truth. If he had, his brother would still be alive.

His gaze coasted over Lorenda's beautiful face, her slender neck, finally anchoring to the creamy flesh where neck met shoulder. If Cam had manned up and told the truth, Mitchell wouldn't be standing in his brother's place right now, wanting to protect her. Wanting to kiss her.

Wanting her, period.

Which was a prick move by anyone's definition.

Francine adjusted the purse on her arm. "Lorenda, dear, a dog is the best security alarm money can buy."

"Oh my God!" Lorenda's hand flew to her mouth. "We didn't pay for him."

A woman in the waiting room stood up, wearing a Red River Animal Shelter shirt two sizes too small. "You can have him for free after what you went through today." She nearly had to shout over the low roar in the waiting room. She seemed way too eager to give the ugly dog away. Maybe the woman should've paid Lorenda to take it.

Lorenda's hand went to her throat, and she stared down at the puppy.

The dog wiggled, so Jaycee put him down and he loped into the waiting room. The boys followed.

"The dog's a good idea, Lorenda," the sheriff said, his hand falling to his holstered gun again. "Keep your doors locked, and I'll drive by your house every chance I get."

"Won't help." Mitchell had seen Cameron's pictures of the white-washed cottage in the woods that Lorenda had bought for them. His brother had hated it. Didn't think he could go back to Red River and live in a perfect fairy-tale house after what he'd had to do as a sniper. Didn't want to come back to his home, his wife, or his kids at all. "Her house is pretty secluded."

His dad sent a scowl Mitchell's way, but instead of resenting it, a nugget of sadness expanded in his chest. Lines of bitterness and loss ran much deeper around his father's eyes than Mitchell remembered. His hair was grayer. But most worrisome was the pale, unhealthy tint to his father's skin, which was usually deep with color from his active lifestyle.

"I can protect my daughter-in-law and grandkids," his dad growled.

Mitchell didn't bother to respond because it would have likely caused his dad heart palpitations. "Do you own a gun, Lorenda?" Mitchell asked her.

"Of course not." She glanced over at the boys just as the dog barked. As if on cue, he squatted and peed on the floor. Lorenda sighed as the sheriff's assistant hurried to a closet and pulled out a mop.

Clydelle leaned on her cane. "Can't see why Lorenda would need a gun when she's got a trained security guard right here."

Everyone including Mitchell turned a quizzical stare on the old woman with silver-blue hair.

She harrumphed as if annoyed by their thickheadedness and then waved her cane in his direction. "Mitchell can look after her."

Only if he was with her twenty-four seven. "I can't—"

"That's a grand idea!" Francine clasped wrinkled hands, her purse swinging at her elbow.

Hell no, it's not.

Trevor and Jaycee ran over, the dog loping behind. "Uncle Mitch can stay in our garage apartment!" Trevor said. "Can you teach us to shoot a gun? Like our dad? We want a BB gun, but Mom won't let us get one." He kicked the ground.

When Mitchell looked at Lorenda, her full, pink lips parted, but no words came out.

He smiled at the kids. "Guys, I don't think—"

"It's a terrible idea." His dad hitched up his pants.

The temperature in Afghanistan must've dropped below freezing, because, for once, Mitchell and the old man agreed on something. He could not live with Lorenda. His mouth was already watering every time he looked at her. Moving in with her would be like falling on his own grenade.

"Lorenda, you and the boys can stay with me and Becky for a while."

"I'm not moving out of my house." Lorenda's annoyed tone quieted everyone. "That house is . . ." She hesitated, and uncertainty flashed in her eyes. "That house is my sanctuary. It's where I belong."

"Actually, Trevor's idea is perfect," his mom said. "If Mitchell stays in Lorenda's garage apartment, that solves every problem."

The boys cheered and ran through the sheriff's office, coaxing Malarkey to chase them.

Becky flashed a warning look at Mitchell. She put a fist on her hip. And when the fist went to the hip, Mitchell and Cameron had known Badass Becky meant business. If both fists landed on her hips, it was time to duck and run for cover.

"Lorenda and the boys will be safe, and you'll have a place to stay as long as you're in town, Mitchell."

Mitchell scrubbed a hand over his jaw. Sure, he could look out for Lorenda and the kids for a few weeks. But he had a high-paying job waiting for him, and it was one of the few jobs Mitchell was trained to do. His ex-commander had recruited most of Mitchell's old team into the private security company . . . at least the SEALs who were still living . . . but the job wouldn't wait for him forever. A job like that didn't lend itself to family life. Cameron was proof of that, and Mitchell wouldn't do that to a woman or kids. So after Mitchell left . . . he glanced at his father's deepening scowl . . . which might be sooner than later at the rate things were going, who would look after Lorenda then?

Becky's other hand went to her hip, and she lifted a penciled brow.

Hell. He wanted to yell "Incoming!" because she obviously had them all zeroed.

"It's either that or *I* will move in with Lorenda until we get to the bottom of this, and Mitchell can stay with his dad." She graced them all with a sweet smile. "A little father-son time would do you two some good."

Badass Becky had damn good aim.

Lorenda's expression ran the gamut from *how do I politely backpedal out of this mess* to *what just happened?* She swallowed and turned glazed eyes on him. "I guess you're moving in with me."

And from somewhere inside of Lorenda's purse, an almost sensual voice said, "Here is a list of moving companies in your area."

Chapter Four

Lorenda held her old trumpet and a cross the boys had made with two sticks as Mitchell heaved out the last shovelful of dirt. He stood back. Rubbing a forearm across his brow, he swiped away the dampness that glistened under the sinking sun.

"Go ahead, guys," Mitchell said.

Trevor and Jaycee placed Checkers's small coffin into the tiny grave and started packing dirt over it. Malarkey sat on his haunches in between the boys and watched. The smattering of cottonwoods to the right of the front yard made a perfect burial site. A swing that hung from a tree in the center of the grove swayed gently with the afternoon breeze. They'd decided on one of the larger trees at the edge where the property opened up into a picturesque meadow on the side of the cottage.

Lorenda had left home earlier that afternoon to unload some old clothes and a dead guinea pig. How she'd ended up bringing home a new dog and a new man to live with her still had her head spinning. She wasn't sure which was worse—the dog or the man. Both were likely to disrupt the orderly life she'd carefully woven together.

A bottle of strong disinfectant and a lot of candles could solve the puppy problem. Probably wouldn't take care of the man problem, though.

Mitchell turned a bottle of water upside down and chugged it. The thick, ropey muscles in his neck flexed and released as each swallow slid down his throat. When the bottle was empty he crushed it in one hand, and the plastic popped and crackled. He lifted the bottom of his T-shirt and wiped his dewy face.

And sweet baby Jesus, those lean abs made her thirsty too. Was there such a thing as a twelve-pack? Because way more than a perfectly toned six-pack tensed and rolled as he toweled the beads from his face and neck. A feathery line of black hair started below his belly button and disappeared under the button of his jeans. A droplet of sweat trickled right down the center, and holy *charlie*, *tango*, and *foxtrot*. She'd like to get down on her knees and lick the moist glow right off with her tongue, and then—

"Sparky." Mitchell's voice was a hushed whisper, but she jumped like a fire alarm had gone off next to her ear.

He rubbed the hem of his T-shirt across his neck one more time, a small, knowing smile settling onto his lips. Something both sweet and dangerous ignited in his eyes, melting away the ice chips that had been there at the sheriff's office.

Her lungs seized. Good Lord, she'd just been fantasizing over Mitchell's abs. His divine, dreamy, drool-worthy abs.

Oh God. *Breathe, dammit, breathe.* What was the code for dammit, again? She couldn't think with him here, and it was just day one!

Mitchell let his T-shirt drop back into place, and he nodded at the boys.

Her gaze flew to them, and her eyes slid shut at the way they stared up at her. They had obviously been watching her ogle their uncle Mitch.

"Um, here." She shoved the cross at Trevor, who placed it on the smooth mound. He sniffled and put his hand over his heart as they laid

Checkers to rest under the old tree while the evening sky turned heavenly colors of purple and pink. Lorenda draped an arm around Trevor's shoulder and squeezed.

Jaycee took the trumpet from her. He puckered his lips, drew in a breath, and tried to play "Taps" the way she'd taught him. And she used the term *play* loosely.

She looked up to find Mitchell watching her with the gleam of friendly amusement that she remembered from their youth. He placed his hand over his heart too. It was meant as a gesture to pay homage to Checkers for the boys' sakes, but the crown of thorns tattoo visible just below his sleeve rippled as his bicep flexed. The same tattoo Cameron had apparently gotten after his last leave. The one Lorenda never knew about until the owner of the funeral home mentioned it. She'd insisted on seeing it in person before they'd dressed Cameron in his Navy crackerjacks.

She tried to clear the ache from her throat. She concentrated on the shoebox-sized grave and rubbed Trevor's shoulder affectionately.

Jaycee cracked an earsplitting note that had Malarkey skittering to find a hiding place with his tail between his legs. The deafening crescendo set the dog to howling as the sad song came to a close, and Lorenda clamped one hand on Trevor and the other to her side so she wouldn't give in to the temptation to cover her ears. God as her witness, leaves fell from the trees, and the moss-green shutters on her pretty little cottage shook because of the obnoxious noise. Some of the white paint may have even peeled off the new siding. She pretended to cough behind her hand to hide a laugh.

So did Mitchell. "Must be"—*cough, cough*—"something in the air." He beat his chest with a fist.

"Must be." Lorenda tapped her chest with an open palm. "Maybe I have something in the medicine cabinet for it." Like earplugs.

Try as he might, Jaycee hadn't inherited her natural ear for music. The poor kid could carry a tune about as well as her car horn.

He wiped his eyes and lowered the trumpet.

"Hey, guys, why don't you take Malarkey for a walk while I get Uncle Mitch settled in? Just be back before dark." Spending some time with the new puppy might cheer them up. Plus, it would keep the puppy out of the house for as long as possible.

"Maybe they shouldn't stray too far from the house." Mitchell did a slow three-sixty to survey the property. Tension flowed into his shoulders.

Lorenda took the trumpet from Jaycee. "How about you stay in the meadow?" She pointed to the clearing beyond the cottonwoods where bright wildflowers were scattered across the field. "Do you really think there is something to worry about?" she asked Mitchell as soon as the boys were out of earshot.

He rubbed his jaw and stared at the boys as they ran, Malarkey loping after them. "You know of anyone who might have an ax to grind with you?"

She couldn't imagine who would be that angry with her. "No."

"I think we should be careful just in case."

An uncomfortable beat went by at the way he said *we*. Like they were a family unit. *Wii* was a game system. *Wee!* was what a child screamed from a merry-go-round. *We* referred to her and the two boys. They would never be a foursome, so Lorenda had to shoot a warning over the bow, draw a distinct line, and defend her borders.

"So," Lorenda said. When Mitchell looked at her, she couldn't return his stare. The piercing brown eyes, the strong jaw, the freaking hardness of his entire body . . . well, it unsettled her. Made her body hum and shimmy in places it shouldn't. *He was her buddy!*

But he didn't look at her like a buddy anymore. Nor did he look at her like a sister-in-law. Hadn't since he'd turned around in the park and locked onto her with those mesmerizing eyes. From that moment on he'd been looking at her like a woman. Looking at her in a way that made her *feel* like a desirable woman.

Or maybe she was just projecting, now that all three of her BFFs had found husbands and were settled into wedded bliss.

"So," he repeated.

"Um, how about I show you the apartment?" So much for defending her borders. She was such a pushover.

"Let me get my stuff." Mitchell headed toward his motorcycle, which had his military-issue duffle bag strapped to the back.

He strolled away with the ease of someone who was completely comfortable in his own skin, yet his muscled body flexed and tensed with each step and his head panned back and forth like he was taking in every detail, assessing danger, and sizing up the territory.

The fact that she liked it had her wanting to rattle off the entire military alphabet. His bike parked under the shade of a ponderosa pine right next to her SUV seemed to belong. Like it had been missing all this time and now her home was complete. His watchfulness, protectiveness, and the caring way he'd interacted with Jaycee and Trevor were . . . nice. Way more than nice, actually. It melted her heart and had her looking at him like more than a buddy or childhood friend too.

He grabbed his bag and tossed it over a shoulder. She waved for him to follow and then pointed to the garage as they headed toward the house. "There's an outside staircase on the far side. I'll give you a key." She stomped her feet on the mat when she reached the front door. "It's locked, so we'll have to go through my room for now." She walked through the living room, depositing the trumpet on a chair, and started to climb the stairs. "The only inside entrance is through the master bedroom." And suddenly, her throat turned to gravel at the thought of him sleeping in the garage apartment with just a thin wall to separate them. "Um, the person who built it was an artist. They used the apartment as a studio."

His footfalls echoed through the house as he climbed the wood stairs close behind her. So close that his heat seemed to reach for her. Or was that her projecting again?

Good Lord.

She hurried up the stairs and into her room where she snatched up her purse to search for the key.

Mitchell didn't follow her inside. He stood in the doorway, shoved his hands in the pockets of the worn Levi's that cupped and hugged and . . . um, bulged in all the right places.

She redoubled her efforts to find the key and dug deeper into her purse. Where was that extra set? Her tongue slid between her teeth as she searched. Tried to concentrate on hunting for the key with a large square base that should make it easier to find. And tried not to focus on the hot and hard man who lounged against the doorframe looking cool and confident and so darned dishy that she had to keep reminding herself he was her friend. *Her childhood friend!*

And a war junkie who would get on his motorcycle one day soon and roll right out of town looking for another thrill. He'd probably leave rubber tire tracks still smoking as he flipped the bird at the city limits sign on the way out.

He wasn't someone she could count on. At least not for the long term.

But the way he looked at her and the way he'd watched over her the last few hours like he was her champion made it really, really hard to convince herself of that. Especially while they stood in her most intimate sanctuary. A lavender velvet comforter covered a king-size four-poster bed that was way too big for one person. Fancy accent pillows were arranged just so to look artfully tossed at random. She'd decorated the room for herself, accepting that she might be single for the rest of her life. Truth be told, if not for the boys, she'd have loved to share the space with someone warm and affectionate. Someone willing to show up to the party and give her his whole heart. Not just a sliver of it while the rest belonged to a desert halfway around the world.

Mitchell's mocha eyes watched her, took her in, studied her. Gave her his full attention. Something she hadn't had . . . ever. Cameron hadn't been attentive since they were high school sweethearts, because after his first tour, he'd become a different man. A man she rarely saw, except when he was on leave.

A man she didn't recognize even when he was home.

The man who had come home just long enough to marry her and get her pregnant twice had been a stranger in her high school sweetheart's body. All emotion and tenderness gone. Replaced by a distracted and distant person who couldn't hold a conversation with his own wife. He hadn't even listed Lorenda as his next of kin. His personal possessions had been delivered to Mitchell, who'd handed them to her at Cameron's funeral. Just before Mitchell had burned rubber out of town, she'd given him Cameron's dog tags.

Seemed appropriate.

Her fingertips grazed a square object. *Ah-ha! Finally.* "Here it is." She pulled a purple metallic square from the bottom of her purse.

Mitchell's chocolaty eyes rounded, then twinkled with laughter. He cracked a smile so broad a flash of white teeth nearly blinded her.

She looked at her hand. And wanted to sink into the floor, because she'd proudly produced a condom. A freaking condom. Miranda, Ella, and Angelique—her happily married BFFs—were hounding her so hard to start looking for a man, they'd given her condoms for her birthday. Which she'd thrown into her purse and never thought of again. Until now.

And she was going to throttle all three of them.

Her eyes slid shut for a beat, and blood rushed to her ears, creating a thundering roar that rattled her brain. She closed her fist around the square to hide it. As if that would help the humiliating heat burning up her neck into the tips of her ears.

Mitchell rubbed his jaw and stared at her closed fist. "Thanks, Sparky, but you keep it. I'm okay in that department."

Oh, she bet he was. She, on the other hand, had been celibate so long that her idea of a good time was setting her cell phone to vibrate, putting it in her front pocket, and calling herself from the landline. Which was why her three blissfully married friends had given her the condoms and dared her to put them to good use.

Lorenda fought for composure. Threw the damn condom that would probably stay sealed for the rest of her life back into her bag and tore through the contents of her purse. "Can you turn the light on, please?" Her tone was huffy because the room was dim, lit only by the late-afternoon sun filtering through her wooden blinds, and that didn't help the situation.

He reached over and flipped the switch. "I agree. It's always better with the light on."

Her head snapped up at the gritty tone in his voice, and she found him laughing at her. That playful smile that she remembered from their childhood and then as teenagers. It had disappeared once he'd gone into the military. Then again, she'd only seen him a few times since then because he wasn't exactly welcome in Red River.

But that full-on mischievous smile was back. And sexy as hell.

"They were a gag gift." She searched the bottomless pit she called a purse. Could not bring herself to look at him. "For my birthday. From Miranda and a couple of other girlfriends." Head still down. Cheeks still on fire. Best friends still in danger of getting a headstone right next to Checkers. Soon. She set the purse on the bed and kept the search going right along with her blathering. "They think it's time for me to move on."

Gah!

Her fingers brushed metal, and she finally found the freaking key.

When she held it up like a prize, the look on Mitchell's face made her still.

"Sparky, you should've moved on a long time ago. You deserved better than what you got."

Every drop of air disappeared from the room. He knew. *He freaking knew.* Searing anger burned through her, setting all of her nerve endings on fire. Wasn't it enough that Cameron had cut her off emotionally? That he'd regretted marrying her? He had to share her humiliation with Mitchell? That shouldn't surprise her. The twin brothers had shared everything, often reading each other's minds without having to speak a word. But if Cameron held nothing else in their marriage sacred, he could've at least protected her from the embarrassment of others knowing she was baggage he'd rather not have claimed.

She'd had his back even after he'd died, but he couldn't shield her from this one injustice.

Tears threatened.

Mitchell's eyes turned dark and raw as they caressed her face. "I'm sorry, Sparky. For everything. A woman as beautiful as you . . ." He toed the floor with his boot. "You *should* move on." His eyes lingered on her lips for a beat, then another, before locking gazes with her again. "So why have you stayed single for so long?"

She had no idea why the next thought zinged through her mind, but she bit her lip to keep it from spilling out. Blurting "because I was waiting for you" out loud wouldn't have made any sense, even though that's exactly what she was thinking. She *hadn't* been waiting for him.

But at that moment, *delta* if it didn't feel like she had.

Chapter Five

Lorenda slept in the next morning, because the puppy howling from the laundry room had kept her up most of the night. The badass SEAL sleeping on the other side of the door that separated her room from the garage apartment hadn't helped lull her into a peaceful slumber either. She'd spent hours wondering what would happen if she knocked on the door.

No. Actually she already knew what would happen. She'd spent the night fantasizing about how good it would be.

Finally, as the first blush of dawn cascaded through her windows, the howling had stopped, and she'd drifted off to sleep. But the fantasies had continued in her dreams.

And now, with late-morning sun filtering through her window, she had to drag herself out of bed and face the man . . . her buddy, her *brother-in-law* . . . with a straight face and try not to blush at the images that had flickered and floated through her dreams. Dreams that had her insides coiled tight and ready to unfurl.

She took a quick shower, freshened up, and pulled on a fitted light-pink tee, a pair of frayed jeans, and sandals. Of course the holes in the knees were from years of roughhousing with two boys, but apparently, the latest fashion designers had labeled jeans like hers "distressed," slapped on a hefty price tag, and declared them all the rage. As she walked past the dresser on the way to the door, she stopped to check herself out.

Beautiful was the word Mitchell used yesterday evening. She hadn't felt beautiful in an eternity. Although she'd taken good care of herself, it had been so, so long since a man had looked at her the way Mitchell had yesterday. It wasn't just his sweltering gaze of attraction that flipped her switch. The compassion that had darkened his eyes and knitted his brow when he told her she deserved better than Cameron's disinterest had also ignited the most erotic dreams she'd ever had until she'd woken up close to an orgasm.

She mussed her long blonde hair and snagged a tube of sheer pink lip gloss off the dresser. With two swipes, she pursed her lips at the mirror and struck a sex-kitten pose.

Okay, stop acting like a slut. She'd have to make up a code word for that.

She breathed in a deep, steadying breath and told herself to grow up. She wasn't in high school anymore, and she'd already been down the long, lonely road of marital misery with one Lawson twin. She still had the last name and the stretch marks to prove it. War-hardened Lawson twin number two wasn't an option.

He had, however, been an extraordinary fantasy.

She shivered as she drifted downstairs, her nails skimming the banister.

The scent of fresh coffee drew her to the kitchen like a salivating dog. Speaking of . . .

Lorenda checked the laundry room. Malarkey was gone. Come to think of it, the house was extremely quiet. Which caused a blaring disaster alert to go off in her mind, because the last time the house had been that quiet, the boys had decided to sneak into the garage and figure out how her car engine worked. By taking it apart. Luckily they hadn't gotten very far when she'd found them with a socket wrench and a hammer.

She hurried to the back door and opened the blind that hung over the glass panel. Her throat closed. In the backyard, Jaycee and Trevor were looking at their uncle Mitch with complete adoration. Down on one knee, he held up a treat, mouthed something to the dog, and to Lorenda's amazement, the dog sat. He tossed the treat into the dog's mouth, and everybody cheered while the dog licked and nipped at the squealing boys. Like a happy and complete family.

And the lump in her throat grew to the size of Wheeler Peak.

She fixed herself a cup of joe and headed outside. The boys had followed the loping puppy to the meadow. When she closed the door behind her, Mitchell stood, a black T-shirt stretching taut across his broad chest. It molded to hard pecs and tapered down his torso to a slim waist.

And, good Lord, did she feel a blush coming on? Because he was even hotter this morning than he had been in her dreams last night. Except for the clothes. Nope, he hadn't had a stitch on in her dreams.

Yep, either she was blushing or her temperature had just shot up to nuclear meltdown levels.

"Morning," she said, walking over to him.

"Morning," he said back.

His black hair was a little messy and revealed a smattering of gray around the temples that she hadn't noticed yesterday. The unfortunate spoils of war.

"Sorry I overslept. The dog kept me up most of the night." Her insides quivered. Hopefully he couldn't read the lie by omission on her face, because way more than the dog had kept her up last night. "Um, I hope he gets used to our house." She ran a manicured nail around the rim of the piping mug and prayed the heat in her cheeks wasn't obvious.

"He will," Mitchell assured her. "Bomb-sniffing dogs saved my unit more than once. Some of the canine handlers showed me a thing or two. I can help train him, if it's alright with you."

She looked out over the grassy meadow where the boys apparently issued the sit command, because the dog plopped onto its haunches. Jaycee held out his hand for the dog to gobble up a treat. "Looks like you've already started."

"I went to the Red River Market early this morning and picked up training treats, dog food, and a few other things."

"Oh. Well. I could've done that." She held up the coffee and took a sip. She *should've* been the one to do it, before the boys and the dog became as goo-goo eyed over Mitchell as her.

"Of course the owner, Mr. Garrett, didn't exactly welcome me back to Red River. He growled something about not getting too close to his fire alarm."

Lorenda raised both brows and angled her head, waiting for an explanation. More than one of Mitchell's pranks had been misconstrued as vandalism back in the day.

He kicked the ground with one boot and then looked up at her with a twinkle in his eye that said he was kind of ashamed but not really. "Cameron thought it would be funny. So of course I had to find out for sure." He rubbed the back of his neck. "Wasn't really all that funny. At least not to the owner, my dad, the fire department, or any of the customers who happened to be shopping in the store that day."

She put a hand on her hip, and Mitchell followed the motion. His eyes darkened, and one side of his mouth curled into a smile.

His gaze found hers again. "To make up for it, I offered to stock his shelves once a week while I'm in town. He's a miser, so he didn't hesitate to take me up on the free labor." He laughed. "And I didn't mind getting the dog supplies. I've got little else to spend my money on. Besides a leave here and there, most of my military pay has accumulated in the bank." He shoved his hands in his pockets, and the crown of thorns flexed and rippled.

She really, really liked the flexing and rippling. But she really, really needed to keep her goo-goo eyes to herself.

"Least I can do since you're giving me a place to stay."

Right. He *was* living with her now. Right on the other side of a very thin door. Which she should nail shut and booby trap ASAP before her *vajayjay* tried to thank him for all the help.

Okay, a different subject might help. A safer subject that didn't make her girl parts go rogue.

"Are you staying in Red River for good?" The thought of him being around forever sent a zing of electricity prickling over her arms to settle in her breasts, where her nipples proceeded to stand up and salute.

She wrapped an arm across her chest.

He shook his head, and his gaze trekked to the boys in the meadow. "I came back because Mom asked me to." He rubbed the back of his neck. "Wants me to make peace with Red River, because that will help make peace with the old man." He chuckled. "You saw how well that's going."

"I didn't know about your dad's health." Lorenda let her coffee mug hover at her lips. A big part of her father-in-law's stress came from Mitchell's rebellion as a kid. A rebellion that Larry Lawson believed had led to Cameron's death.

Unfortunately, no amount of atonement would bring Cameron, the favored son, back.

"I know you just got out of the military, but have you figured out what you're going to do?"

"I've been out for a year." He stared at his boots.

Her lips parted. "And you're just now coming home? Mitchell, where have you been?"

He kicked the grass. "Here and there."

Ah, the years of military life had instilled that same wanderlust spirit in his brother. The same unsettled sense that he didn't belong. Anywhere. Lorenda suspected that if Cameron had lived, he wouldn't have stayed in Red River. Wouldn't have stayed with her and the boys. And wouldn't have wanted them to follow him.

"Why now?" She'd asked Cameron to leave the military after his second tour was over. He wouldn't, claiming that Mitchell planned to stay in and wanted Cameron to stay too. Cameron didn't want to leave his brother over there alone. It was a twin thing. An inseparable bond that he couldn't break.

"I'm thirty-two. That's getting to be an old man in SEAL years. I figured it was time." He turned his attention to the house. "While I'm here, I can help around the house and yard." He pointed to the small stack of wood on the far side of the garage. "If I split that thinner, it will burn better. And I can haul in another cord so you'll be stocked up when winter hits."

"That would be . . . nice." It would be great, actually. Having some help around the house would give her aging father a break, and Lorenda could focus on the music program instead of the constant to-do list that plagued her as a single parent. "You'll need a more practical vehicle than your motorcycle." She gave the closed garage a thoughtful look, the nail of her forefinger tapping against the mug with a chink, chink, chink. "I never got rid of Cameron's truck. I'll give you the keys."

"I'd . . ." Mitchell seemed a little choked up, and he shoved his hands deeper into his pockets. "I'd love to drive Cameron's truck. Thanks."

The dog yelped, and they both looked to the meadow where the boys played with Malarkey. "I can teach the boys how to take care of him while I'm here, because it doesn't look like your cozy house is ready for a pet." He gave her a cocky smile. "At least not a live one."

She grimaced. "Yeah, cleaning up after two boys is enough for me. I didn't think I could handle a dog, but I was in a tough spot yesterday at the park, so I caved."

He laughed. "Getting caught red-handed trying to dispose of pet remains would do that to any parent."

Her lips hovered above the rim of the mug. "Yeah, it's all fun and games until there's a dead guinea pig in the suitcase."

His laugh faded to a gentle smile. "Maybe I can even take the boys fishing."

She stilled because his suggestion was breaching the danger zone. Chopping her wood was one thing, but being so kind to her boys, well, that revved her pulse into overdrive, just like when he'd called her beautiful. "I . . . I'm sure they'd like that." They'd freaking love it, but none of this was a good idea. "I don't want to put you out, though. We're fine on our own, Mitchell." No, not really. A part of her would love to have a man take her boys fishing, go on the Wilderness Scouts campout, maybe even throw a ball around the yard with them. Just not someone hardened by war and too restless to stay in one place for very long. The other part of her wanted to protect the boys from the disappointment if it didn't work out. "We're not the people you need to make up with. You should focus . . . on other people instead of us."

A crease formed between his eyes. "Okay. Sure, Sparky."

Her gaze darted away, because *sierra*, she wasn't sure she could keep looking at him while he used that gravelly tone that made her nether regions hum like a tuning fork. Her insides went all mushy when he called her that cute, familiar nickname he'd given her in junior high after her science experiment went terribly wrong and nearly blew up the science lab.

She stared down at the caramel-colored liquid, trying to shake away the old memories that set her sleep-deprived nerves even more on edge. She should've thrown in some whiskey instead of cream. She took another sip. "Mmm." Her eyes drifted shut, and she let the liquid gold slide down her throat. "This is so good. Nice and strong."

Her eyes fluttered open, and how about that? Mitchell's stare dropped to her lips for several beats. Which made her self-conscious about putting on the lip gloss. And glad.

Gah!

Uncertain what to say next, she bit her bottom lip. And Mitchell's eyes clouded over, his lips parting.

"Mom!"

Lorenda startled when Jaycee called out to her as he ran toward them.

"Mom, look what Malarkey can do!" The dog chased and hopped behind Jaycee. Her oldest threw a stick and Malarkey lit out like a ball of fire after it.

"You've done a good job with them, Sparky." Mitchell's voice was low. Almost tortured.

She took a deep breath. Gazed at her boys. "Yet they've never looked at me like they were just looking at you."

That broke her heart, because their uncle Mitch would only be around long enough for the boys to grow attached and then be crushed when he left.

And she knew how much it hurt to be left behind by a Lawson.

Chapter Six

"Take a deep breath and blow across the top of the mouthpiece," Lorenda said to Andrea, the tenth student she'd fitted for an instrument that day for the after-school music program. The third day of school had ended an hour ago with a ring of the bell and a din of backpack-wearing kids jacked up from the rush of seeing their friends again.

She scooted her chair closer to Andrea's and took the old silver flute. Lorenda twisted the mouthpiece to make sure it was properly attached and handed it back to the little girl who had walked into the gym with a skip in her step and determination in her eyes.

Getting the music program started would also give Lorenda something to think about other than the sizzling-hot man who was sleeping a stone's throw from her bed. She could throw the sealed condom in her purse at that smokin'-hot guy and hit the target if the door were open.

Precisely the reason she hadn't gotten a good night's sleep since he'd moved in five days ago. Of course, the howling dog in the pantry hadn't helped her fall asleep either. Mitchell finally offered to let Malarkey sleep in the garage apartment so she and the kids could get some rest. Didn't help.

No, she couldn't blame the dog for her sleepless nights. She could only blame her fantasies and the electrical current that buzzed through her every time she saw Mitchell. His brooding deep-brown eyes followed her as their paths crossed in the yard, in the driveway, at the table when he ate dinner with them every night.

She smiled as Andrea kept trying to make a sound.

Lorenda hadn't missed Mitchell's body going tense every time a car rumbled past her secluded place. The way he went still, listening until every noise was identified. Or the way his eyes never stopped scanning her property when he was outside.

Especially after the sheriff stopped by her house yesterday with news that the mugger had been moved to the county jail where he'd be charged but probably released on bail. The mugger also wasn't talking. No ID on him, no hit on his fingerprints, and no form of transportation that could be found, which only deepened the strange mystery of why he would mug her in Red River of all places.

Lorenda adjusted the flute against Andrea's little lips and nodded for her to try again.

"I told her to take piano lessons instead." Andrea's mother sat on the bleachers and crossed her arms over her middle section. The determination in her daughter's hazel eyes faded.

Andrea wrinkled her freckled nose, and her light-brown pigtails swished around her shoulders when she shook her head. "I can't do it." Her face fell.

"Sure you can." Lorenda gave Andrea a reassuring smile. "This is your first day. We're not trying to be Mozart yet; we're just trying to make a sound. If the flute doesn't fit your embouchure, we'll try a different instrument." Of course even if Andrea did manage to blow a note, the wood floors, high ceilings, and school mascot banners on the walls instead of acoustical panels would probably make it sound more like a foghorn than a flute.

And that was the least of her problems. The rickety instruments and flimsy music stands she'd been collecting at garage sales and pawnshops every time she visited the city were just this side of pathetic. Kids didn't need the best instruments. But it did help for them to have instruments that could be played in tune should the kids actually show some musical ability.

But the point was to get the students started. In the beginning they'd probably sound like a foghorn no matter where or what they played. The program would move to the new rec center as soon as it was finished in the spring, where Red River's famous "green" architect was designing an acoustical room for programs like Lorenda's.

Better instruments, on the other hand, seemed so far out of reach they might as well be on the moon. Which was why she needed a donor. A sponsor who saw the potential in teaching kids the love of music at a young age. A supporter who understood that, out of the hundreds or even thousands of kids that filtered through a music program, only a few would show long-term interest or the natural talent to stick with it, and those few would be worth the investment of time and money.

Andrea's mother tapped her foot. And sighed. A big, loud, heavy sigh that said she was running out of patience and Lorenda was running out of time.

"Let me show you." Lorenda cleaned the mouthpiece and played a perfect B flat.

Andrea's eyes widened, the determination reignited.

"Instead of blowing into the mouthpiece"—Lorenda cleaned the shiny silver again—"blow across it." She grabbed an empty glass Coke bottle from under her folding chair. That's how her private teacher had taught her when she was Andrea's age. Lorenda's parents had driven her all the way to Santa Fe once a week for lessons, since the Red River Independent School District didn't have a music program. On top of the drive, music lessons were expensive. So providing an opportunity to learn music free of charge right here in Red River had been Lorenda's dream since that first day when she was Andrea's age and her teacher showed her how to blow a B flat with an empty soda bottle. "Like this." Lorenda blew, and a hollow sound echoed through the gym. "Now you try."

Andrea lifted the flute to her lips, copied Lorenda's effort to a T, and bingo.

A shaky B flat honked out.

Andrea's little freckled face lit with a smile brighter than the Northern Lights.

After Lorenda showed her a handful of basic notes and gave her a beginner's songbook, Andrea asked, "Can you play something for me before I go? I want to see what I'll sound like in a few years."

Lorenda loved that spunk. That determination. That confidence that Andrea could be good at music. *Would* be someday.

So Lorenda raised the flute to her lips, lifted her elbow to the correct position, sat up straight so that her diaphragm could work to full capacity, and, by memory, played Mozart's Flute Concerto no. 1 so beautifully that it would've made Wolfgang Amadeus himself weep. And really, she didn't just play. She closed her eyes and let the music take her, *creating* the music instead of blowing a string of notes.

She followed the crescendos, flowed with the cadenzas, and felt the long vibrato notes to her soul, just the way Mozart's musical genius intended. The way he must've felt it when he wrote it.

When she was done, she opened her eyes to find Andrea's eyes wet and her mother's posture no longer stiff and unconvinced. And *that* was why the music program was something Lorenda *had* to do. Music wasn't just something she enjoyed. It was woven into her DNA. She'd given up her dream of becoming a music teacher for marriage and motherhood. Getting married at twenty years old and having kids right away had required a lot of sacrifices. Required Lorenda to put just about everything in her life on hold. Now, for once, she wanted this one thing for herself. Music filled a hole in her soul like nothing else could. She needed it as much as she needed food and water and oxygen.

As much as she needed ice cream when she had a sucky day. Because music and ice cream were steady and constant and never let her down. On those sucky days when she needed someone to lean on—someone over four feet tall who was her equal and didn't sleep in superhero pajamas—she could climb into her comfy bed with a pint and a spoon and snuggle up with Ben, Jerry, and Beethoven. They were the only three men likely to enjoy the fortune she'd spent on eighteen-hundred-thread-count Egyptian cotton sheets.

Someone clapped behind Lorenda, and a dog let out a small yelp.

She whirled to find Mitchell standing there. Watching. Waiting. With Malarkey on a leash, and a look in his eyes that said he didn't just appreciate the music. This look was dark and cloudy and filled with something she was afraid to put a name to.

He leaned against the painted cinder-block wall, legs crossed at the ankles, thumbs hooked into the pockets of another pair of worn-to-perfection jeans, that thorny tattoo drawing her gaze. And just as she had since first seeing Cameron's identical tattoo six years ago, Lorenda couldn't help but wonder if there was a meaning behind it. Malarkey's leash dangled from one hand, and the dog sat obediently at Mitchell's side.

"Um, Andrea." Lorenda tore her gaze from the impossible mirage that lingered at the back of the gym. "Practice as much as you can this week." She packed the old flute into its beaten-up case and handed it to Andrea.

Andrea threw her arms around Lorenda's waist and hugged her. Then she ran to her mother who mouthed "thank you" with so much awe that Lorenda knew this was the start of something good. Something meaningful. Something so much more rewarding than selling vacation cabins to well-off out-of-towners, because Red River was such a wonderful place that the vacation properties practically sold themselves.

Lorenda looked over a shoulder. The sexy-as-hell man standing at the back of the gym, who happened to be living with her and was technically still her brother-in-law, now *that* was the start of something altogether different.

Lorenda just wasn't sure what.

"Hey," Mitchell said to Lorenda as she ambled toward him with a soft, almost shy smile that made her look like an angel.

He didn't want that perfect, peaceful look that she obviously got from playing music to vanish. He had no choice, though. His dad had stopped by the cottage to deliver news. The perp who'd attacked Lorenda had made bail. So until this mystery was solved, Mitchell needed her to see that moving in with his parents was the safest solution for her and the boys.

Now that Mitchell had decided to leave town immediately.

His father hadn't liked it one bit when he was greeted on Lorenda's driveway by his rotten offspring. Mitchell had held his tongue so the old man wouldn't keel over right there in Lorenda's front yard, but he'd made up his mind. Time to abort the impossible mission to make up with his dad and report to the new job that was waiting for him. His mother would be mad as a hornet, but his presence here might actually make his dad's heart problems worse.

Lorenda kept coming toward him. White jeans molded to every inch of her mile-long legs. Her painted toes peeked out of sparkly sandals. A feminine sleeveless top swayed around her waist with each step and drifted up to reveal creamy skin and a sweet-looking belly button when she reached to tuck a lock of blonde silk behind one ear. She was even more beautiful than the music she'd just played.

And that was pretty beautiful. He wasn't an expert on classical music. He wasn't even a musician, but he was moved by the sheer emotion in the way she played. Amazing, considering how he'd forced most of his emotions so deep to keep his edge and bury the pain of war and loss that he wasn't sure he'd be able to bring them to the surface again.

His presence seemed like sandpaper against her soft, velvety world.

He forced his gaze to meet hers and knew the pink in her cheeks was probably from him ogling her. Because he had been. Every time he was around her. Which was why he'd spent time with the boys and helped train Malarkey outside when she was busy inside, and why he'd gotten out of her house as soon as dinner was over each night.

He didn't do attachments. Or feelings. He didn't do them very well, anyway. And he especially couldn't do either with Lorenda, who had already been through so much, thanks to Cam.

"Sorry to interrupt," he said.

She shook her head. "That was my last student." Long, wavy hair flowed around her bare shoulders. A beautiful and sexy contrast to her sun-kissed skin.

Sun-kissed? Wouldn't his SEAL team give him nine kinds of hell for using a word like *sun-kissed.* He shifted, trying to fight off the chain reaction that started in his brain, moved to his gut, and had now dropped below his belt.

She gave him a soft smile that revealed the tips of her pearly whites.

That smile ignited the chain reaction to nuclear fission capacity. He clasped his hands in front of his crotch in a cool, casual stance that said, *I'm just getting comfortable and not at all trying to hide a hard-on.*

"Before you left this morning, the boys told me you'd be here after school." He left out the part about the kids asking him to come to their Wilderness Scouts meeting, since most of the other kids' dads had volunteered.

She came to a stop in front of him, and her brow crinkled. "Is everything okay?"

Malarkey didn't whine for her attention the way he did with the boys. It was like the dog sensed that out of everyone Lorenda was the one who could take or leave him. Preferably leave.

"I was washing my clothes in your laundry room this morning, and the water heater isn't working." He scrubbed a hand over his jaw. He didn't want the news he was about to deliver to upset her. So he kept rambling about house maintenance like an idiot. "I relit the pilot, but I have a feeling you need a new unit."

"I'll call Al's Plumbing on Main Street and have it replaced," she said.

"No need just yet. I bought a few parts at McCall's Hardware to see if I can fix it." He scratched the back of his neck. "Of course, Mr. McCall wasn't all that happy to see me. He said something about me shooting out his storefront window with a high-powered pellet gun when I was in junior high."

Lorenda's brow rose.

Mitchell shrugged. "Cameron bet me I couldn't outline every letter in McCall's Hardware with a pellet. I had to prove him wrong."

That's the way it had always gone with him and Cameron. Cameron put him up to something, and Mitchell did it. It wasn't until years later that Mitchell realized it was because Cameron never wanted to take the blame.

"I offered to clean his windows for free once a week while I'm in town to make up for it." Mitchell smiled. "Something tells me he'll make sure they're plenty dirty before I get there each week."

A soft laugh slipped between Lorenda's lips. "Glad to see you're trying to smooth things over. It'll make your mom happy."

"That's me, winning friends and influencing people. Listen, there's news—" Malarkey pulled free from Mitchell's grasp and disappeared behind the portable risers that served as spectator stands.

"Come on, boy." Completely ignoring the command, Malarkey sniffed his way under the bottom of the risers, and all except his butt disappeared. "Obviously, we haven't mastered the *come* command yet."

Lorenda's face went up in flames.

Well, hell. He hadn't meant it like *that*. But that blush was sweet.

Malarkey's butt disappeared under the risers. "Malarkey, come." He glanced at Lorenda's hot-pink glow and fought off a smile. "Come here," he added. The dog ignored him. "Hold on." He squeezed between the wall and the risers.

"Mitchell, you're . . . um, kind of a big guy to fit into such a small space," Lorenda said. "Want me to try?"

"Nope," he grunted out, and then went down on his knees, disappearing behind the risers. "I'll get him." He called to Malarkey again, and a flattened snout appeared with a lunch-size bag of Fire Hot chips clamped between his teeth. Oh wow. Spicy human food probably wouldn't sit well with his delicate . . . uh, constitution. The training treats were already doing a number on him, and Mitchell wasn't sure the mistress of the house could handle the odor.

"Come on, Malarkey." Mitchell clicked his tongue. The dog gave a little puppy whine— without dropping the chip bag, of course—and tried to obey, but his leash snagged on a corner of the risers. Mitchell snaked his way through the small space and unhooked the leash.

As he started to back out, leading Malarkey with him, the gymnasium doors slammed open. The sound of very unhappy boys grumbled through the quiet gym. Jaycee and Trevor.

"Mom!" Jaycee said.

"Ouch!" Trevor cried out. "He's hurting my arm!"

Mitchell tensed all the way from the hair prickling on the back of his neck to the toes of his leather combat boots.

"Stop with the theatrics, Trevor." Mitchell didn't recognize the male voice. "I was giving his arm an encouraging squeeze when he wrenched away. No harm done," the man tried to explain to Lorenda.

"What's going on, Principal Wilkinson?" Lorenda's voice pitched high.

Bart. Mitchell's dad had called Bart "Principal Wilkinson" in the park. It hadn't registered in Mitchell's brain at the time, but now

Mitchell pieced it together. Bart had grown up, gone to college, and become a teacher.

The thud of feet came to a stop somewhere in Lorenda's vicinity. "Nothing to worry about, but they were disrupting the Scouts meeting." That voice raked over Mitchell's patience. "It wasn't fair to the other boys."

"We didn't do anything," Jaycee groused.

Slow and quiet so he could hear, Mitchell backed toward the opening.

The man gave a condescending chuckle. "I'm sure they don't think they did anything wrong, Lorenda. They don't have a lot of fatherly guidance. And I've told you to call me Bart."

"They have their grandfathers." Lorenda's voice was polite.

Mitchell kept easing backward, Malarkey following him nose to nose, still holding the bag of chips in his mouth. And Christ, Malarkey's silent-but-deadly gas picked a bad time to make an appearance. Mitchell fought off a gag and waved a hand in front of his nose while trying to eavesdrop on the guy who was obviously making Jaycee and Trevor unhappy.

"Grandparents have a way of spoiling kids. They mean well, I'm sure." The insinuation grated on Mitchell's nerves. Jaycee and Trevor were a little rambunctious and curious, but wasn't that normal for kids? They didn't seem spoiled to Mitchell.

Malarkey's collar snagged on a nut and bolt. Mitchell reached down to free it.

"You should reconsider my offer." On the last word, Bart's voice dropped low. "After the incident in the park, having a man around more would be good for them. And good for you."

Every protective instinct in Mitchell's body dialed up to imminent-threat level.

With brute force, he pushed the riser forward, shot to his feet, and stepped out into the open. Malarkey dropped the chips and strained toward the boys with a whine. Mitchell gripped the leash so tight his knuckles hurt.

Trevor and Jaycee didn't run to their mother. They ran to Mitchell.

As much as that made his chest swell, the look of hurt and worry on Lorenda's face confirmed that Mitchell's decision to get on his motorcycle and gun it out of town was the right thing to do. She didn't need him disrupting the family life she'd built any more than he already had.

Malarkey pawed at the boys' legs, whining for a scratch. Jaycee picked him up.

Bart made sure to stand closer to Lorenda than Mitchell. "Lawson." He kept his tone friendly, but his eyes frosted over.

"Bart," Mitchell said.

Something about Bart chewed at Mitchell's gut. Like a rat gnawing at a piece of cheese.

"How long will you be here?" Even though Bart spoke to Mitchell, his gaze slid back to Lorenda.

"I'll be here as long as my family needs me." Mitchell put a hand on Jaycee's and Trevor's shoulders and guided them a few steps to his right to close the space between them and Lorenda.

Something in Bart's eyes flared.

"Pets aren't allowed in the gym." Bart widened his smile.

"I hate him. He's mean," Trevor whispered.

Bart narrowed his eyes at the kids, but his smile didn't waiver.

"Trevor!" Lorenda corrected him, and Trevor folded both arms over his chest with a pout. "You apologize this instant."

Trevor stayed quiet and burrowed into Mitchell's leg.

"I got the same treatment in the Scouts meeting while I was trying to demonstrate how to tie a proper knot," Bart said. "That's why I pulled them out."

"He was tying it wrong. Uncle Mitch showed us how yesterday." Jaycee held up his wrist where a black nylon rope was twined into a bracelet. "He said a piece of rope and a good knot could save our lives someday like it did his in Afghanistan. So he made us these survivalist bracelets out of rope."

"Oh." Her expression blanked, and her blue eyes locked onto Mitchell. "That's so . . . scout-ish."

Mitchell wanted to smile. Who could argue with that? Or compete with it?

Bart's face turned red, but he kept that thin smile planted on his pasty lips. "Lorenda, I'm sorry to say their behavior is becoming an issue both in the classroom and in the Wilderness Scouts. Trevor's teacher has already had to send him to my office, and the school year just started."

He put a hand on Lorenda's elbow, and Mitchell wanted to hold Bart the Fart in a headlock until he learned his lesson about putting his hands on a woman.

Mitchell's woman.

And that thought almost made his head explode.

"I want them to stay in the Scouts," Bart said. "The structured environment will help keep them in line."

Mitchell had heard that before. The day his dad gave him the choice between juvie and the military. It didn't sit well with Mitchell that the same words were already being used on his nephews.

"You should consider my offer and try to get them to follow my leadership." Bart's smile was encouraging, like he had the answers to all of her problems.

Mitchell's special-forces training had taught him to read body language, voice tones, and even the subtle twitches of facial muscles. He already liked this SOB about as much as he liked having a root canal. Without anesthetic. And he trusted him even less.

"I apologize for my son's rudeness." Lorenda shot a scolding look at Trevor, who turned his face into Mitchell's leg. "And for any problems they're causing. The music program will only be here in the gym until next spring." She gave Bart a patient smile. Shifted her weight so that she pulled away from Bart's touch and closed the small space between her and Mitchell. Their arms brushed, and he could swear she shivered. "Then we'll be out of your way."

Something flashed in Bart's eyes that made the hair on the back of Mitchell's neck rise again. But the little rat bastard kept smiling at her, like he was her best friend.

"A program with so many kids might be more successful if it stayed here at the school. Some of the teachers could help." His voice practically dripped with honeyed helpfulness. "It could be a community effort with you in charge. I can probably find money in the budget for the program, but the school board will only approve it if it stays on the school grounds."

Lorenda's smile widened. *Oh good God, gag me.* Did she not see he was a weasel? A weasel who was playing her as well as she'd just played the flute.

Bart's smile broadened too, like he thought he'd hit all the right notes.

Mitchell's fist clenched.

"That's a generous offer"—she hesitated like she was torn—"Bart."

Hell. Lorenda was sharp as the knife he carried in his boot. How were Bart's tactics not registering on her bullshit radar?

"If their behavior doesn't improve, then maybe I should pull them from the scouts. They can stay in the gym while I work with the music kids." Her hand closed around Trevor's shoulder and overlapped Mitchell's hand. His pulsed revved, and she drew in a sharp breath. Shot him a bewildered look and pulled her hand away.

"But we want to go on the Scouts camping trip!" Trevor protested. "All of our friends are going."

Bart just kept on smiling at Lorenda, which was really pissing Mitchell off. "Then you boys need to show respect for leadership so your mom will let you stay in the Wilderness Scouts."

Mitchell was guessing the leadership would be Bart, of course.

Lorenda looked from the kids to Bart and back to the kids. "If their behavior is such a problem, I don't want them to ruin it for the other ki—"

"You could go, Lorenda," Bart said, his eyes dilating. "Mothers sometimes volunteer as chaperones when the dads can't be there."

Oh, hell no. The thought of Lorenda and the boys on a camping trip in the middle of nowhere with this joker made Mitchell's skin crawl, even if other kids and parents would be there.

"Please, Mom, please?" Trevor begged. "I'll be good, I promise."

"Well . . ." Her tone and the guilt in her expression told Mitchell she was about to cave.

He needed to keep his mouth shut. Any number of grown men could go on that camping trip. Mitchell's dad; Lorenda's dad; her brother, Langston—anybody but Mitchell. He needed to stick to the plan, get on his motorcycle, and get out of town. Get on with his no-attachments life and go back overseas where he could make some real money for a change. It was a good, solid plan.

A plan was everything going into battle. Until the battle actually started—then the plan usually turned to shit.

"I don't know much about camping," Lorenda said.

"No problem. I'll take care of everything for you and the boys." The triumphant gleam in Bart's eyes made Mitchell's fist clench again, and that sealed the deal.

He let out a heavy breath. "I'll go on the camping trip. I've got practical experience." He already regretted what he was about to say. "And I've got the time." He doubted the private security company waiting for him to report for duty would agree.

The boys cheered.

Bart's eyes flared again.

Lorenda turned beautiful blue eyes on Mitchell that said she was grateful for the support. He shifted closer so that his arm brushed hers, and this time he was sure a shiver raced over her. He had to dig deep to find self-control because he wanted to put his arm around her slender shoulders so she'd know he had her back.

One side of Lorenda's full mouth quirked up into a shaky smile, and whatever he'd seen in her baby blues a few moments ago turned to something he'd seen many times in mud-hut villages.

The unmistakable glint of fear.

Her stare darted to the kids, and Mitchell understood. The boys were already getting attached. The admiration in their expressions grew with every hour Mitchell had spent with them the past few days.

He knew exactly how Lorenda felt. His life was all about protecting and defending, but he usually did it without personal attachments. Attachments meant emotions, and emotions were dangerous in his line of work.

If he let himself care about someone too much, it meant getting hurt when he lost them.

But what choice did he have? Cam had abandoned his post. Left his wife and kids exposed. Mitchell had felt crummy about Cameron's decision to keep fighting a war but not keep fighting for his family. His brother's family needed him now, and maybe Mitchell could be the next best thing. At least for a while.

Chapter Seven

After hauling all of the music equipment to the parking lot, Lorenda meticulously arranged and rearranged the instrument cases in the trunk of her SUV. Jaycee and Trevor played with Malarkey over on the empty playground, and she tried to shake off the tingle that rushed up her arm every time Mitchell handed her another case and their fingers brushed.

Busy.

She needed to keep busy. Busy was her friend when something was seriously wrong, and the thing that was seriously wrong was helping her load the car. Had just invited himself on the boys' campout, even insinuating that she and the boys were his family. Well, technically they *were* family, but she and the boys weren't the family Mitchell was really here for.

Healing his relationship with his dad for his mother's sake was Mitchell's priority, not Lorenda and her boys.

She moved a trumpet over to squeeze a flute into the small space. He handed her a trombone next, and she placed it toward the back of the trunk.

What was even more seriously wrong was that she'd liked it when he'd sent the silent territorial vibes that she and the boys belonged to him. At least that's how it had felt at the time. Couldn't have been her imagination, because Bart's eyes had widened with surprise for a fleeting moment.

And her kids had run to Mitchell instead of her, like he was their father.

Seriously. Wrong, wrong, wrong.

"Hand me the French horn." She pointed to a large case, and Mitchell picked it from the pile of instruments. "Thanks." She didn't look at him when she took it, but her hand brushed his, and she fought off a shiver.

The same shiver that had lanced through her when he'd acted all alpha protective in the gym. *Gah!* She didn't need alpha! And she didn't need her boys becoming devoted to Mitchell as their father figure. They were already halfway to calling him Dad . . . or Zeus . . . or Jesus . . . if their looks of hero worship were any indication.

She shuffled the cases around some more and finally yanked one out. "I need to unload them all and start over." Yes, busy, busy, busy.

Mitchell's hand closed around her arm, and he turned her to face him. "I came to give you the news about the mugger. He got out of the county jail." Mitchell's thumb caressed her arm, and he gave his head a small shake. "Still hasn't talked." Now all five fingers moved against the bare flesh of her arm, making it pebble. "I'll be here until this is solved one way or another."

Him being here was precisely the problem. She and the boys already liked him being here way too much. But the look of bona fide concern in his eyes, like he'd stand in front of a speeding truck for her and the kids, made her mouth go dry and her resistance go soft.

She was such a cream puff.

So she tried to suck it up and stay strong. "Look, Mitchell. Maybe you should stay with your parents."

Several creases appeared between his eyes.

"I mean, I really like having you around." Something flashed in his eyes, and she wished she'd left off the "really" part. "The kids love it, actually, but you see, we're not your responsibility, you know, and, well, um. Yeah."

He took a small step and closed the gap between them. His breath smoothed across her cheeks, and she stared up into his mocha-latté eyes. Some coffee chain should really name a drink mocha *hotté* with a picture of his eyes on the cup, because women would stampede the doors first thing every morning. It would be just like Black Friday every single day. Sweet baby Jesus, the color was so smooth and delicious that she wanted to drink him in . . . and then kiss the hell out of him to get a taste.

He reached for her hair and pulled free a tiny piece of lint that must've come from a cleaning cloth she'd used on the instruments. He flicked it away and then went back for more, his fingers lingering against her skin.

"Bart seems interested in you. He was kind of a strange guy in high school." His hand floated at her ear for another moment like he didn't want to move it.

She chewed her lip. "I've always felt kind of sorry for him. Kids weren't very nice to him when we were growing up, and he was so henpecked by his controlling mother."

"Want to tell me about the offer he mentioned?" Absently, like her mouth mesmerized him, Mitchell gently swiped away something from her cheek. His calloused fingers, rough against her ear, sent a shock wave of desire rippling from her earlobe all the way to her toes. Which curled against the flat, bejeweled sandals.

"He's been asking me out for a while. His wife left him."

"Really," Mitchell deadpanned. "Someone married him?"

"She's Russian . . . or Ukrainian . . . or something." Lorenda shook her head.

"Did he order her online?"

Lorenda arched a brow. "Now *you're* not being very nice."

"Unfortunately, I'm serious." He let his hand fall away, but not without letting his fingers brush against the length of her hair.

She wanted to grab it and put it right back against the sensitive flesh beside her ear . . . or maybe against her cheek . . . or maybe thread his fingers through her hair before guiding it down to her—

"Lorenda."

She jumped at the intimate way her name rolled off his tongue. Deep and husky like he could read her mind. Her lips parted, but nothing came out except a small gasp when his head dipped and his handsome face hovered so close to hers, his gaze flowing over every inch of her face before their eyes locked.

"What was he talking about?"

She swallowed. "Well, um, he seems to think he could mentor the boys."

Mitchell's jaw tensed, his shoulders almost curving around her protectively.

"He's trying to help, but I think he wants me and the kids to be a package deal."

Mitchell's eyes dilated, and at that moment there was no doubt in Lorenda's mind that he was lethal when facing an enemy during battle.

"I've said no," Lorenda rambled, because by the look on Mitchell's face he might march back into the school and teach Bart a new meaning for the word *mentoring*. But Bart really was harmless, albeit a little pathetic.

"If he's bothering you, why are you setting up the music program here?" Mitchell rasped out.

"He's not bothering me. He's just a little persistent. And nowhere else in town is available after school until next spring when the rec center is finished."

"Then wait until next spring to start the program," Mitchell said.

She shook her head. She'd considered that. Truth was, if she didn't start the program now, she was afraid she'd never get around to it. She'd put this dream on the back burner for Cameron and the kids. It was now or never. Plus, she liked the idea of spending more time around the school because Trevor's teacher had sent a note home about his behavior.

"I think it would help Trevor if I'm here more. He's a lot like you, Mitchell." She chewed her lip. "The boys don't have a father to keep them hemmed in. I know you're trying to help, and I appreciate it more than you know, but it could also backfire if they start thinking of you as a father."

His heavy exhale cascaded over her cheeks and neck, and the muscle in his jaw flexed. "Sparky." The affectionate way he said it made a balmy glow wash through her. "You're an extraordinary woman. I don't know why my brother lost sight of that."

An ache seeped into her chest and squeezed her heart.

"The way you look out for Jaycee and Trevor is amazing. The same goes for the way you want to share your love of music like it's a gift that should be given away without asking for payment in return."

Lorenda couldn't have been more bowled over if she'd been a pin at the end of an alley.

Her throat closed. "Oh" was all she could croak out.

Mitchell saw in a matter of days what Cameron couldn't see in all the years he and Lorenda had dated and been married. Maybe it was lack of maturity because they'd married so young, or maybe it was lack of time spent really getting to know each other as adults. Whatever the case, Cameron hadn't completely ignored her talent, but he hadn't totally appreciated it either.

"Music *is* a gift that can't be assigned a monetary value. It's priceless." She twirled her grandmother's antique ruby ring around her finger, because she'd stopped wearing her wedding ring years ago. "It's . . . I don't know . . ." She twirled the ring again and looked at the blue sky. "It's sort of like my duty to pass it on to others."

He gave her a smile so soft, so full of heart, that she felt it to her soul. "I can relate," he said.

She knew he could. Protecting others had been a gift that he'd seen as his duty since he was a kid.

"I especially want to share it with kids because they can learn it so much quicker than adults. Like speaking another language."

That sweet smile faded a little. "I'm sorry my brother enlisted. I'm even sorrier that he wouldn't come home for good when you had the boys." Mitchell's gaze raked over her face. "I tried to talk sense into him when you were pregnant with Trevor, but he wouldn't listen. I should've tried harder."

A block of ice formed in her chest, and she pressed a hand to her heart. "You tried to stop Cameron from re-upping?" The same coldness around her heart threaded through her words, because Cameron had said the opposite.

Her confusion must've shown on her face, because Mitchell reached up and gently smoothed a thumb across her forehead like he was trying to smooth out the worry lines.

"What is it, Sparky?"

"I begged Cameron to get out of the military when I found out I was pregnant again so soon after having Jaycee." Her voice dropped to a vacant whisper. "He said you asked him to stay in. You needed him, and the Lawson twins always had each other's backs."

Mitchell's expression turned even more sorrowful, and he gave a small frown of disappointment.

He didn't defend himself. Neither did he throw his brother under the bus. It's how she knew Mitchell had been telling the truth. Cameron hadn't stayed in the military for his brother. He'd stayed in for himself.

The familiar chill of rejection, abandonment . . . loneliness skated over her.

"All the more reason I'm sticking around until I'm sure you and the kids aren't in danger," Mitchell said. "I . . ."

Lorenda stilled, waiting for him to finish, because for a moment she thought he might say, "I want to stay because of you and the kids. Not because of my brother."

And didn't it just suck that she *wanted* him to say those things. That she was tired of being alone. That she yearned for someone to touch her and kiss her and just *talk* to her. It sucked that she couldn't risk opening herself up to more rejection because Mitchell would make an inevitable exit from their lives. And it sucked that she certainly couldn't risk exposing the boys to that kind of pain.

It all sucked. Hard.

What didn't suck was the way Mitchell looked at her like he *did* want her. Like he *did* care about her. But she doubted he'd ever say it or act on it, because of whatever complicated bro code men lived by.

Against every sound argument she'd just run through in her head, Lorenda reached up, intending to cup his cheek with the palm of her hand. She wanted the light stubble along his strong jaw to tickle her fingers, but she hesitated. Let her hand hover there so close that she could feel the heat of his skin.

All the emotions that had been flickering through Mitchell's eyes collided at once and ignited into desire. And that was her undoing. She placed a knee on the inside of his, so his legs framed hers, and she leaned in. Went up on the balls of her feet until their noses grazed and his hand found her waist to pull her closer. His expression told her he was hungry for her kiss and her touch. And anything else she was offering. But just before she touched her lips to his, a car pulled into the parking lot, and Malarkey let out a string of barks from the playground.

She pulled away, and so did Mitchell, putting an arm's length between them. Thank God, because kissing him would've been foolish, and what if the boys had seen them? The car pulled through the parking lot and disappeared behind the school.

"My failed relationship with Cameron wasn't your fault." She picked at a cuticle. "You don't owe me and the kids anything." She rubbed her arms with both hands like she was trying to warm herself.

It was seventy-five freaking degrees out and she had goose bumps.

Her gaze darted away to the school building. A small crack in one of the blinds covering the windows snapped shut, and uneasiness slithered up her spine.

"Look." Mitchell drew in a deep breath, weighty with concern and determination, like he was trying to figure out how to solve world hunger, or how to cure the common cold, or why fruitcakes were so popular for the holidays when *nooooobody* liked them. He leaned his weight against the frame of the trunk. Bent a knee, which brushed against Lorenda's again, and there went that ripple that rocked her world. "I understand your concerns about the boys. The last thing I want is for them to get hurt. But, Lorenda, I *am* their uncle. I can't stay away from them forever."

She bit back the urge to say, "You've done a pretty good job of it since Cameron died."

"I've got a bad feeling, Sparky. Sometimes safety trumps emotions."

She tilted her head and gave him a quizzical look.

He ran fingers through that thick mane, and her mouth went dry.

"If you and the boys are in some sort of danger, then there's no way I'm leaving you alone. Your safety is too important, even if the boys are a little disappointed when I leave town."

A little disappointed? Disappointed didn't begin to describe what they'd be if Mitchell lived with them much longer and then left. He'd been living over the garage for a few days, and the boys were already playing SEAL Team 5 in the yard. Their father had been assigned to SEAL Team 8. Mitchell had been a member of SEAL Team 5.

He studied her. Seemed to read her mind.

"If you kick me out of your garage apartment, I'll just pitch a tent across the street and camp out." He chuckled. "Trust me, it would be an improvement over some of the missions I've been on."

True. Not to mention Lorenda would be eaten up with guilt if she forced him out of a warm apartment that would otherwise sit vacant and he moved into a tent like a homeless person. And her boys would likely try to move into the tent with their uncle Mitch and think it was all fun and games.

She sighed. Heavily.

Yep, she had the spine of a marshmallow.

He smiled like he was close to victory. "Can I see your phone?"

"Why?" She plucked it from her purse but held on to it.

"Do you trust me, Sparky?"

Yes. She did trust him. She just didn't trust herself if she had to live with him much longer. She handed him the phone.

After a few minutes and a lot of tapping on the screen, he handed it back to her. "I downloaded a safety app so we can track the kids at all times. We'll all be in a *family circle* on the app. If any one of us has an emergency, we just hit the "Panic" button and every phone number in the circle will sound with an alarm. I'll come over tonight and teach the boys how to use it on their phones."

She stared down at the phone. She should be grateful. Really, she should. He was trying to help. Trying to look out for her and the boys.

Instead she was scared *sierra*-less. Because all it would take was a few more looks like he'd just given her, a few more touches of her hair, or a few more attempts to play knight-in-worn-denim-armor for her and the kids, and she'd be lost. Or at the very least, beating down the door between her bedroom and his apartment.

She tried to focus on loading the rest of the equipment. She pointed to a case. "Hand me the sax."

"Did you mean sex?" Minx purred from her phone. "Because I'm not that kind of girl."

Mitchell's brow rose.

Lorenda's racing heart nearly pounded through the walls of her chest. Teeth gritted, she said, "I'm just trying to finish loading my SUV."

"STDs can be prevented by abstinence or condoms," Minx informed her.

Throaty laughter rumbled from deep in Mitchell's chest. When he showed no sign of stopping, she crossed both arms over her midsection and waited for him to finish.

Finally, he wiped under both eyes. "As I recall, you're all set in the condom department, Sparky."

Lorenda sure as heck was, thanks to her BFFs. She still owed all three of them a throttling for the embarrassment their little gag gift had caused.

Unfortunately, if Mitchell touched her hair or stared at her mouth again, she just might put those gag gifts to good use. And because it had been so long, if Lorenda ever did open that door, the handful of condoms in her purse wouldn't be nearly enough.

Chapter Eight

"Go wash up for dinner," Lorenda hollered to the boys, who were playing with Malarkey in the den. She pulled a pan of lasagna from the oven and replaced it with a baking sheet of buttered garlic bread.

She wanted to celebrate the launch of her dream. Today had marked the end of the first week of school and her music student's first week of rehearsals. They were already making progress, and it never ceased to amaze her how fast kids learned.

With tongs, she tossed the salad in a large wooden bowl and set it on the table along with the lasagna.

A spark of anticipation coursed through her because, about this time every evening, Mitchell came over for dinner. Of course he had to be included in the celebration. He was family. He lived over her garage.

He had also been the first person to zing through her mind when she'd left rehearsals and decided to prepare a special meal tonight.

Just two days ago, Mitchell had vowed to be her protector. Promised to stay in Red River, not only to try to repair his relationship with his father but to guard over her and the boys. In just the week since he'd moved in, they'd started to function like a family. She'd actually hurried home after music rehearsal to make dinner, setting the table with nice linen placemats, fine china, stemware, and candles.

Things she never got the chance to use—why would she with just her, Jaycee, and Trevor in the house?

While the garlic toast was browning, she lit the candles, then hustled into the den and flicked the remote until the entertainment system landed on a nice jazz station. Her dream date would involve dressing up in a pretty dress, strappy heels, and going to a jazz bar in the city where she could cuddle with her date in a corner booth, drink a glass of wine, and listen to music.

She looked down at her flirty crepe skirt—beige with a soft plum floral print—paired with a beige gypsy top and a brass chain-linked belt that hung low on her hips. Strappy heels. Upswept hair.

And suddenly she felt very, very silly. Oh, dear Lord, she'd subconsciously dressed up like she and Mitchell were going on a date. Like a real couple. She needed to change clothes! Put on sweats, and maybe even socks with a pair of flip-flops, because she looked ridiculous dressed up for a quiet family dinner with two little boys.

If she hurried, she could pull it off before Mitchell arrived and she died from embarrassment. She tore off one of her heels and limp-ran to the dinette table to blow out the candles while trying to take off the other heel in the process. She was puckering to blow out one of the flames when Mitchell tapped on the glass of the back door.

Oh *sierra*. Bent over the candles, one shoe off, and cheeks puffed out, she froze. All except her eyes, which moved to the back door to find Mitchell looking through the glass pane right at her. He lifted a brow.

She straightened, let out a deep breath, left the candles burning, and put on a smile to wave him in.

"Smells good." He stepped inside and closed the door behind him. His gaze slid over her.

She smoothed her skirt. Hid the high-heeled sandal dangling from one hand behind her back as if he wouldn't notice her wearing only one shoe. "Thanks." Her voice had gone all croaky.

Good God.

"You clean up nice, Sparky. What's the occasion?" Was his voice huskier than it had been a second ago?

She chewed her lip until she realized she'd probably end up with pink lip gloss all over her teeth. Her eyes slid shut, and she ran the tip of her tongue over her front teeth.

"I just, um, wanted to celebrate the music program getting off to a great start, and, well, I sometimes do this for me and the boys because"—she waved a hand down her outfit, then across the table, which was perfectly set with the best of everything she owned—"you know, it's good for them to learn formal manners, and it's a good example to dress up once in a while." *Liar, liar.* She brushed a hand across her bottom to make sure it hadn't caught on fire. Good thing she wasn't wearing pants. "And, um, yeah." She fell silent.

"I see." A wrinkle appeared across his forehead. He sniffed the air. "Is something burning?"

Delta. She limp-ran into the kitchen and threw open the oven door. Smoke billowed out. She grabbed an oven mitt off the counter and pulled out the baking sheet filled with bread. Only it didn't look like bread anymore. More like lumps of coal.

She waved the oven mitt around in the air trying to swish the smoke away. She coughed. Who messed up garlic toast? So much for the tasty and tempting scent of roasted garlic and Italian food.

Mitchell turned and put his hand on the doorknob. "We better let some of the smoke out before it sets off the—"

The smoke detector screeched to life, filling the entire house with a defending alarm.

Malarkey howled from the den.

Jaycee and Trevor came running.

With all the waving and sputtering, a chunk of Lorenda's hair came loose from its up-do and fell across her face.

Mitchell's expression filled with laughter. He opened the back door and flipped on the ceiling fan. "Let's clear out some of the smoke before the fire department shows up."

She tossed the bread into the sink, pulled off the other shoe, and grabbed a bottle of wine from the fridge. "I need a drink."

Mitchell came over and took the bottle from her. "I'll do the honors." He went right to the drawer where she kept the wine opener, because that's how comfortable he'd become in her house. Knew right where everything was.

"Boys, go let Malarkey out," she said.

They went into the den but came clambering back to the kitchen with rounded eyes.

What now?

She didn't ask. Just walked to the den and dropped her head back in defeat.

One of her throw pillows wasn't exactly a pillow anymore. It was in shreds, the stuffing scattered from one end of the den to the other. Not to mention the round yellow spot on the carpet.

"I'm guessing that's not lemonade?" Mitchell came up behind her, and his presence both soothed and unnerved her. He placed a hand on both of her arms and gave her a reassuring squeeze. An electric tingle shimmied through her. "The alarm must've scared him. The wine is on the table. Go sit down. The boys and I will take care of this," he said.

She tossed her shoes onto the stairs as she passed, took a seat at the table, and knocked back the entire glass of wine. Then poured another one.

By the time Mitchell and the kids were done and washed up again, the wine had settled her nerves, warmed her insides, and made her disastrous attempt of a celebration-turned-subconscious-fantasy-date seem a little less pathetic.

She dished up the lasagna and salad while they sat down. "Thanks for cleaning up."

"Thanks for cooking," Mitchell said.

"I'm not sure I'd call it cooking exactly." She poured cherry Kool-Aid for the boys.

"Bread is overrated, and everything else is perfect." His gaze swept over her, and so did a flush of heat. "Boys, doesn't your mom look nice?" He forked up a mouthful of lasagna.

"Why are you dressed up, Mom?" Jaycee asked. "Are you going out?"

"Well, no." She stumbled over the words. "I wanted to spend the evening with you guys."

"But you never dress up when we eat at home."

"We're celebrating," she said through gritted teeth.

"Is that why the table is so fancy?" Jaycee asked. "Because we never use the fancy stuff either."

"Of course we do. You must not remember." Lorenda plastered on a smile and leveled it at Jaycee. Who promptly got the message and clamped his mouth shut.

Mitchell looked up at her from under hooded lids, and a hint of a smile settled onto one corner of his mouth.

Hell. Forget code. She wanted to rattle off real cuss words because she was so busted.

"Uncle Mitch," Trevor said. "Could you come to my class for parent career day and talk about being a war hero?"

Wait. Trevor hadn't asked *her* to come talk about being a realtor. And Mitchell wasn't a parent.

Mitchell's expression darkened at Trevor's request, and he stared at his plate.

"Guys, it's not fair to ask Uncle Mitch to do that."

"I'm not a hero." Mitchell picked at his food. "I was just a guy doing my job."

Obviously, he didn't want to talk about the war. Cameron certainly hadn't. They'd had a don't-ask-don't-tell policy in their marriage.

"Uncle Mitch isn't your parent. I am, so I'll do it." She reached over and ruffled Trevor's hair, but he pulled away. His face fell in disappointment.

Gee. Lorenda felt so special. But having Mitchell around had obviously made their lack of a father figure glaringly apparent to the boys. Probably why Trevor was acting up at school.

Jaycee spoke up. "When I was in Trevor's grade, Grandpa Lawson came and talked about being the sheriff. It was so cool, and he wasn't our father either."

Mitchell kept moving food around on his plate.

"Why can't you be our dad?" Trevor asked. "You live with us, and your last name is the same as ours."

Lorenda's stomach did a flip.

Mitchell's head popped up to study the boys, his expression unreadable. "I could never take your dad's place."

Lorenda had never expected Mitchell to take Cameron's place. So why did his words knock the air from her lungs and make her want to double over?

"Guys, Uncle Mitch is just staying here for a little while until the guy from the park is . . ." She didn't really know. "Until we're sure he won't cause any more trouble."

"And then you're going to leave?" Jaycee asked.

Mitchell slid a look at Lorenda. "I'll have to go eventually." He rubbed the back of his neck. "There aren't any jobs here in Red River for me."

Lorenda fought off the urge to plant a hand on her forehead. Of course he needed to go back to work. He couldn't hang around Red River forever just to be her bodyguard. A man who had lived the kind of life Mitchell had, never putting down roots, living off the adrenaline rush from missions and combat training and war, would get bored in Red River.

And he's not my husband. Not my boyfriend. Not even my friend with benefits. But guarding her body is exactly what she wanted him to stay here and do. Even though she knew it was foolish, she couldn't control the way the body in question responded to him. Couldn't stop it. It was like a locomotive steaming down the tracks at full throttle, and there was no way to put on the brakes.

"You could still be our dad," Trevor said, all innocence and naiveté.

Jaycee nodded. "Our real dad was never home either."

Lorenda dropped her fork, and it clattered against her plate. "Boys. Eat."

She shouldn't be doing this. Setting her kids up for disappointment. Setting herself up for more pain. Yet here she was, dressing up and messing up over a man who could never be hers.

The squeal of sirens pierced through Mitchell's sleep. He rolled over in bed and tried to push the misty dream of Lorenda's smoke alarm out of his brain. His mind searched through the foggy blast of deafening sound, trying to reclaim the dream he'd had earlier of her in that flowing skirt that teased him by revealing just enough thigh to make his imagination go wild.

The siren kept wailing, and Malarkey barked.

Mitchell bolted upright.

He sprung out of bed and snatched his phone off the nightstand. The screen flashed Jaycee's name. It wasn't the smoke alarm. Jaycee had hit his panic button.

Wearing nothing but black boxer briefs, he charged to the door that led to Lorenda's bedroom and pounded on it. She yanked the door open in a panic. Bedhead and all, she looked just as good in lacy panties and a spaghetti-strap tank as he imagined she would.

"What happened?" He hurried into her room without an invitation. If there was an intruder, Mitchell wanted to catch the son of a bitch before they had a chance to escape.

"I don't know," she said.

Mitchell headed for the stairs. "Stay here."

She was right on his heels.

"Lorenda!" he whispered. "I said stay here."

"No." She pushed at his shoulder so he would start down the stairs again.

He didn't have time to argue. When he reached the bottom floor, he said, "Then stay behind me." He went straight to the boys' bedroom, pushed it open, and scanned the room. Nothing but darkness.

"Oh my God." Lorenda's hushed tone cracked. "They're gone!"

"Jaycee," Mitchell said, his voice still low. Malarkey bound into the room and went straight for the closet. He pawed at the closed door.

Whispers came from inside, so Mitchell went to it—Lorenda still at his back—and gently slid the door open. Both boys were huddled at the bottom of the closet.

She sagged against Mitchell. He reached behind to give her hand a reassuring squeeze, but his fingers found the side of her thigh instead. Even better.

"What happened?" She pushed Mitchell out of the way, went to her knees, and gave Jaycee and Trevor hugs, showering their little faces with kisses.

"Someone tried to break our window." Trevor's voice wasn't frantic. Not even all that scared.

Mitchell had seen enough frightened children in the Middle East to know what real fear looked like in a child's eyes. He wasn't seeing it in Trevor's and Jaycee's.

He snatched a comforter off one of the twin beds and draped it around Lorenda's shoulders. "*Now*, stay here."

He went to the window. It was cracked but not shattered . . . and unlocked. Mitchell was pretty sure he knew the identity of the burglars, and neither had hit puberty.

"I'll be right back." Mitchell pulled a flashlight from a kitchen drawer and eased outside. The night air was cool against his skin, since he was nearly buckass naked. The soft grass under his bare feet reminded him of playing outdoors with Cam when they were kids.

Mitchell stood still and listened. Listening was a skill. It was one of the first things he'd learned in the military because it saved lives. As he stood there, the sounds of the night crowded in on him. Crickets, bugs, even an owl hooting from one of the cottonwoods in front of the house. Nothing that didn't belong.

He had a sixth sense about danger, and there wasn't a threat on Lorenda's property. To be safe, he flicked on the flashlight and examined the perimeter of the house to make sure it was secure. All was well, until he got to the boys' window. The ground was slightly wet, even though everywhere else was dry and Red River hadn't had rain in weeks.

He bent at the knees and examined the spot closely. Several foot-prints were clear and visible. And less than half the size of his. He scooped a little mud onto his finger and sniffed. The sweet scent of cherries tickled his nose. He doubted many criminals drank cherry Kool-Aid while breaking and entering. Just so happened the boys had red Kool-Aid for dinner.

Mitchell rubbed his eyes with a thumb and forefinger.

He didn't want to get the boys in trouble, but he couldn't let Lorenda go on thinking that someone had tried to break in either. For the first time, he understood how hard parenting must be. And how frustrating it must be to see your kids mess up. This was a minor thing. Almost funny. He'd get a big laugh out of it if it weren't for the fact that the boys were obviously trying to find ways to keep him from leaving. If something this small caused his gut to twist with worry over their future, then Mitchell must've made his parents' lives a living hell.

He went back inside. "All clear." He turned on the lamp. "You guys can get back in bed. No one is out there." He should tell Lorenda. Out Trevor and Jaycee right then before their shenanigans grew to the point of his and Cameron's and one or both of them ended up in the military. Or worse.

"Should we call the sheriff?" Lorenda asked as the boys scrambled back into their beds.

Mitchell shook his head and gave her a look that communicated, *let's talk in private.*

She tucked them in, left the lamp on, and followed Mitchell into the den.

When he turned she was right in front of him, so close he could hear her breaths, still a little heavy from the rush of adrenaline.

"I . . ." He ran a hand through his hair.

"What is it, Mitchell?" Panic rose in her voice again.

"It's nothing to worry about." Not true. She'd been right. The bond that had so quickly and naturally formed between him and the boys was going to devastate them when Mitchell left. Him just as much as Trevor and Jaycee. "I think the boys set us up."

"What? Wait. What?" Her tone was confused.

He explained the whole mess. When her breaths grew heavier and an angry expression replaced the lines of worry, he ran both hands down her arms. "Don't come down on them. This is my fault."

She let her eyes slide shut for a moment. "Mitchell, you can't take the blame for everything. Stop being a martyr."

"Maybe you were right about me not living here, but I'm not leaving you alone."

"This whole mugger thing could take months or even years to go to trial. I won't let this turn my life upside down for that long. I'm staying here where I belong." She stood her ground, and the look in her eyes said she wasn't backing down.

Neither was he.

"Then I'm staying too, Sparky."

But first thing tomorrow he was going to see his dad to find out how long it'd be before the trial took place. The sooner the better—before Mitchell destroyed two little boys in the process. The same two little boys he was trying to protect.

Chapter Nine

Mitchell offered to take the boys by his mom's house the next morning while Lorenda showed a few properties to a client. Perfect excuse to visit his mom and have a word with his dad to offer an olive branch for Lorenda and the kids' sakes.

Badass Becky's pointing finger was smoking when Mitchell got there because his dad was at the office on a Saturday. Had refused to hire a new deputy or two, claiming no one was qualified, and was working twenty-four seven because of it. The one thing that seemed to have his mom blowing off the smoke from the tip of that finger and holstering it was Jaycee and Trevor.

So he left the boys in good hands and headed for the sheriff's office. A row of small houses lined the road on the other side of the street, and he passed two kids flying a kite in one of the yards. Mitchell looked up.

The bright-red kite and its long colorful tail were stark against the blue sky, and it gave him a sense of comfort. A sense of home. So did the woman, two kids, and ugly dog he was currently living with.

Too bad no one else in this town made him feel so welcomed. If not for his mother, he wouldn't have come back at all. If not for Lorenda and the kids and the pull they had on him, he wouldn't be staying.

But Mitchell's gut wouldn't stop sending an SOS signal to his brain that something wasn't right with the whole situation surrounding Lorenda, so he had to stay at least a little while longer. Maybe if he kept approaching his dad with Lorenda and the kids' safety in mind, the old man would finally listen.

Hell, who was Mitchell kidding? His father—so levelheaded, so fearless, so beloved by the community—had been blind to Mitchell's strengths and Cameron's weaknesses since they were little boys. Just because Mitchell wouldn't walk the sheriff's rigid chalk line. Cameron had followed all the rules, at least when everyone was watching.

Mitchell pulled up to a four-way stop behind another truck and waited his turn.

Cameron's good-twin façade was partially Mitchell's fault. He'd been happy to accept the blame for Cameron's screwups as soon as Mitchell was old enough to realize that their mischief caused ripples in the nicely starched fabric of their hard-nosed father's world. His dad's inability to accept that Mitchell wasn't his carbon copy, his insistence that Mitchell never quite measured up the way Cameron did, had made Mitchell want to goad his dad all the more during his stupid youth.

Apparently Cameron had used Mitchell as an excuse to stay in the military rather than come home to his family. Which was just one more reason for Dad to resent the less-perfect son. Especially when Cameron finally did come home in a box with a flag draped over it.

Mitchell dialed his ex-commander's personal cell number and put the phone to his ear. He'd postponed it long enough, and after last night's phony break-in, it was time. The car in front of him pulled away. With a wrist flung over the steering wheel, Mitchell rolled forward to the stop sign.

If Mitchell had made Cameron take responsibility for his own crap, he might still be alive to look after Lorenda and the boys.

Then again, maybe Cameron would've come up with another excuse to stay away, because he'd made it clear he wasn't much interested in coming back to Red River or his family. His reasons still had Mitchell stumped. He understood better than anyone that war changed a person, but Cam had become an empty shell. A robot.

Now that Mitchell saw the kind of woman Lorenda had become—so beautiful, so feminine, so different from the callous soldiers Mitchell was used to—he couldn't imagine wanting to be anywhere else if he'd been the lucky one married to her.

On the fourth ring, Mitchell motioned to the only other vehicle left at the four-way stop. The driver, an older gentleman wearing a camo billed cap, frowned at Mitchell as he meandered past. An older couple, obviously out for a stroll on such a beautiful day, stopped at the intersection and waited. Mitchell waved them through. They studied him for a second, and then one whispered to the other and pointed.

Mitchell smiled at them and waved. They kept the same stony look on their faces and didn't lift a finger to wave back.

Mitchell pinched the bridge of his nose while the phone kept ringing and snatched his aviators off the dash to hide an eye roll. He doubted giving the locals more attitude, like he had growing up, would help win back their trust. One of them would likely be on the phone to the sheriff before Mitchell hit the next intersection. Or worse. They might call Badass Becky.

Mitchell shook off a shiver and then punched the accelerator.

He'd rather keep driving right through Red River. Right out of town. The job he was about to give up would've put him right back in the only profession he was qualified for. A job that would make him top *dawg* for a change, in charge of his own team. With people who actually liked him. People who didn't hold mistakes against him but appreciated the years he'd spent serving.

He turned left onto Main Street just as Allen Carson's voice mail answered. Mitchell waited for the beep.

"Allen, it's Mitchell. Listen, buddy." Mitchell paused. Was he really this stupid? He exhaled. Yep. He really was. "I'll have to take a rain check on the job. I've got family stuff to deal with."

He scrubbed a hand over his jaw.

Coming back to Red River because his mother asked him to was a good reason, but staying to protect Lorenda and the kids was his duty. Protecting is what he did. The only thing he'd ever done well. And since Cameron hadn't gotten the job done even when he was still alive, Mitchell couldn't help but feel responsible, at least on some level.

Wasn't it in the Man Rules? Or the Bible?

Unfortunately, a rule against coveting another man's wife was too, and Mitchell was already breaking that one every time he laid eyes on Lorenda.

"Call me when you get the chance, and we'll talk." He disconnected before pulling into the sheriff's office parking lot.

At the front glass doors, Mitchell pulled off his sunglasses and hung them from the front of his shirt. Maureen sat behind the reception desk wearing a red T-shirt that said, "If at first you don't succeed, reload and try again." A pencil was inserted into her backcombed hair to rest behind her ear.

"Is my dad in?" Mitchell shoved his hands into his pockets and waited for the usual cold-shoulder response he got from most of the residents of Red River. Especially from those close to his dad.

Maureen studied him like a protective momma bear, and Mitchell had to respect that.

Not one strand of her big hair moved when she finally nodded. "Let me see if he's available." Code for *I doubt the sheriff wants to see you.* She directed him toward the waiting room with a pointy red fingernail. "Have a seat."

"Yes, ma'am." Mitchell flashed a smile at her, because it didn't hurt to score points with the old man's assistant. During many of their phone conversations, Mom had mentioned how much influence Maureen had over his dad. A fact that Badass Becky worked to her advantage by enlisting Maureen as an ally when it came to his father's health and stress level.

Maureen's raised brown eyebrow told him her BS radar had just caught him doing sixty in a thirty-five.

He parked his butt in one of the plush waiting-room chairs, while she disappeared down the hall.

He looked around his father's brand-new digs since he hadn't been able to pay much attention when he'd been here the day of the mugging.

Nice. Quite a step up from the old office that could've doubled as Sheriff Taylor and Deputy Fife's station. A lot of chrome, a lot of black and white, a lot of glass. Way too modern for his father's taste.

A man as rigid as his dad didn't take change well, and Mitchell couldn't help but wonder if the new office had contributed to his father's stress. Maybe the modern decor was a sign that his father couldn't keep up with the changing times.

Maureen reappeared, her fair skin more red than before. "He's . . . indisposed."

Indisposed. Right. Mitchell sat forward. "Tell him it's about Lorenda and the boys. I'm sure their safety is just as important to him as it is to me."

Maureen's brown eyes narrowed like she wanted to ask him to leave. Or throw him out at gunpoint if the T-shirt were any indication.

Mitchell lounged back in his chair and crossed an ankle over his thigh. "I can wait here all day until he *is* available."

She folded both arms over her sizeable chest and tapped a foot.

Ah hell, go big or go home. He grabbed *Field & Stream* off the table and thumbed through it like he really did intend to wait as long as necessary.

With a huff, Maureen disappeared down the hall again.

As he was right in the middle of reading last hunting season's rut report, Maureen reappeared.

"Down the hall to the right." She turned her back to Mitchell and pulled open a filing cabinet drawer. Head down, she flipped through the contents, and Mitchell made his way to his father's office.

"Make it quick." His father never looked up from the paperwork on the black lacquered desk. Matching bookcases lined the walls directly behind the desk, a folded American flag sitting encased high on one of the shelves.

Mitchell didn't have to ask where it had come from. Or why his dad displayed it so proudly. Lorenda had given it to the old man the day they'd laid Cam to rest with a twenty-one-gun salute.

Mitchell drew in a pained breath. Since his dad didn't offer one of the black leather-and-chrome armchairs, Mitchell kept standing. "Is there any way to keep tabs on Lorenda's mugger?"

"Not unless he doesn't show up for his trial." His dad scribbled something on a form and flipped the page.

"How long will that take?"

His dad didn't answer. Just kept scribbling and flipping.

"In the meantime, is there anything we can do?" Mitchell asked.

"Not legally. I'd have him watched at a distance if I had the manpower." His tight mouth turned down in a frown, and his writing faltered for a second. "But I don't. I had to fire a deputy last month, and the other quit to make more money in a bigger city. I haven't found a replacement with the skills that go with the job."

Mitchell studied the top of his dad's graying hair. His badge. His clean and crisp uniform.

An idea flickered to life. "Deputize me. I'll do it for free."

For the first time since Mitchell had walked in, his dad's head lifted and he looked Mitchell in the eye. "You've got to be kidding."

"Why not? I've got more than enough training."

"With your reputation in this town?" The sheriff's tone was patronizing. Belittling. The same tone he'd used every time the much younger Mitchell had expected his dad to give him the benefit of the doubt. "That's the most ridiculous idea I've ever heard."

A sharp sting settled in Mitchell's chest. That tone held all the rumors and sins that had long since caused the court of public opinion to find Mitchell guilty. He fought to keep his anger in check.

If it were just about him and his already broken relationship with his father, he'd get up and walk out without so much as a backward glance. But it wasn't about either of them. It was about at least trying to keep his promise to his mother to make amends. And it was certainly about looking out for Lorenda and the boys, something all of the Lawsons owed her.

"Just until the guy is convicted. After that I'm leaving town anyway, so what do you have to lose?"

His dad's fist closed tighter around his fancy ink pen. "You're seriously going to ask me that after all that you've cost me?" His tone held more disbelief than disgust.

Mitchell's anger bubbled closer to the surface, but he beat it back. "The whole situation is wrong. I just know it, and I'm better trained than anyone else in this town."

"Stay out of it and let me handle things." His dad went back to his paperwork. "You can see yourself out."

Mitchell strolled to the door and stopped with a hand on the doorframe. "I'm going to watch out for her, Dad."

His dad's scribbling stopped, and he slowly raised his gaze to meet Mitchell's. For a moment the hardness in his father's eyes softened. And Mitchell caught a glimpse of the youthful dad he remembered from before their personalities started to clash and their relationship turned into a complete clusterfuck. Maybe because his father had the same ingrained protective instinct as Mitchell, which was both his biggest gift and his biggest weakness.

"She deserves that much," Mitchell said. "She shouldn't be alone in the first place."

And just like that, his dad's stone-cold stare was back. "No, she shouldn't. Are you so hell-bent on hovering over your brother's wife out of loyalty to Cameron or for some other reason? I saw the way you looked at her. Don't you feel the least bit guilty?"

Mitchell should feel guilty. Lorenda had stirred something deep inside that had been locked away so long he couldn't even label which emotion it was.

But, no, he didn't feel guilty. Cameron was the one who should've felt guilty for tossing away the best thing that had ever happened to him. There wasn't a shred of doubt in Mitchell's mind that being here for Lorenda now was right. Leaving before the mugging mystery was solved would eat him up with guilt.

"I'm going over to the house to visit Mom. Just thought you should know so you can avoid me." He glanced up at the flag. A flag both he and Cameron had proudly served with their whole hearts. "And Lorenda's last name might be Lawson, but she's not Cameron's wife anymore, Dad. It's time you accept that."

His father's lips thinned, the tension lines around his mouth deepening.

Mitchell walked past Maureen with a tip of his head and a "thank you, ma'am." He left before his smart mouth got away from him and sent his dad to an early grave. Or at the very least to the hospital with chest pains. For his mother's sake, Mitchell didn't want to shatter his father's illusion of Cameron. But that illusion had somehow morphed into a delusion over time.

An evening glow lit the sky, and Main Street was quiet. He reached his brother's old truck with long strides and climbed in. Mitchell had accepted that Lorenda wasn't taken anymore the moment she'd fainted in his arms. Couldn't help it, because nothing had ever felt better than when he was holding her.

What he hadn't accepted yet was how perfect the feeling had been. And how much he wanted to have her in his arms all over again. Only conscious. And naked. And all his.

Chapter Ten

The following Saturday morning Lorenda's schedule was just as busy as it had been the previous weekend—she was showing more vacation cabins to the same client, Albuquerque's newest symphony conductor. Her parents had lined up the appointments and had conveniently forgotten to mention the client's identity.

She rushed into the bathroom, already running late, and flipped on the shower to let the water heat up.

Mr. Daniel Summerall had seemed like a nice guy and a great catch. Professional. Good looking. More a gentle kind of guy and really well dressed in a trendy sport coat and dress shirt left unbuttoned at the top. All the things Lorenda should want if she were looking for a relationship.

But she hadn't been the least bit attracted to him.

A fact her mother hadn't stopped harping on all week. "Give it some time. Get to know him," her mother had said. Over. And over. Every day since last Saturday.

Lorenda stuck her hand under the running shower only to jerk it back when the icy water bit into her skin. She turned the knob labeled "H" wide open. All that came out was freezing water.

Sierra. Mitchell had tinkered with the hot water heater last week. As nice as it was to have someone around the house to do the heavy lifting, it looked like she'd still have to give Al's Plumbing a call. *Delta.* No time for that today. She had to meet Mr. Summerall at the first listing in less than an hour, and she was all sweaty from a morning run. She couldn't be late, and she couldn't show up smelling like a gym. She wanted that sale, because she could use a small portion of it for her music program.

Plus she hadn't mustered the nerve to bring up the music program during her last appointment with Mr. Summerall, even though her parents had already laid the groundwork for her. She was such a chicken.

She skittered across the slate tile and grabbed a plush moss-green towel off the rack, wrapped it around her, and darted through her bedroom and down the stairs. Trevor and Jaycee were spending the day with her parents, so with virtually no knowledge of how water heaters or plumbing worked, she tried the boys' shower.

No luck.

Next she tried the kitchen sink. Again, freezing. She'd hose off outside if it meant getting at least enough lukewarm water to rinse the sweat off.

She cracked the door and peeked outside to see if all was clear before checking the water temperature from the hose. And thank the shower gods, Mitchell's truck was gone.

She chewed her lip. The apartment had its own water heater, which meant a hot shower was waiting. Calling to her. Daring her to finally open the door that separated her bedroom from Mitchell's private quarters.

It was rude to invade Mitchell's privacy, even if she did own the place. But it was her last option before she was stuck washing off with as much class as the dog.

She charged back inside the house, up the stairs, and straight to that door. The door she'd wanted to open for days. The door she'd dreamed of busting through. The door her brain told her to barricade shut just to keep herself from the temptation. One hand rested on the brushed nickel knob, and the other held the towel in place at her chest.

She probably shouldn't. But she couldn't spend the day with a client without a shower, especially since she'd run an extra mile this morning.

Her body heated in places it shouldn't at the thought of opening that door. Like she'd be crossing a threshold and there would be no going back.

Gah! That was stupid. Mitchell wasn't home.

With a turn of the knob, the lock clicked open and she walked in. Napping on the old sofa, Malarkey's head popped up and he whined.

She came to a halt with a skid.

Huh. Mitchell usually took the dog with him. Which meant he would probably be back soon.

That spurred her into motion. If she hurried, she could grab a quick shower, then hightail it back to her side of the door before Mitchell got home from wherever he'd gone. She crossed the small apartment, rounded the corner, and hustled through the open bathroom door.

Right into a hard, wet wall of muscle.

"Oof!" She collided with Mitchell, and every last drop of air whooshed out of her lungs. She tried to blink away the black spots in front of her eyes, because, holy mother of God, all that male hotness was darn near blinding. He was naked except for dog tags and a white towel draped around his waist. Nope, no water heater problems here, because steam swirled around the bathroom and right off of Mitchell's rock-hard body. Thousands of droplets slid over his sleek build and sparkled under the light. She tried to pull back, slipped on a towel that was on the bathroom floor, and stumbled.

The ceramic sink rushed up at her, so by instinct—or idiocy for being in Mitchell's apartment to begin with—she let go of the towel to keep from cracking open her head.

Quick reflexes and all, Mitchell did the exact same thing. His towel dropped to the floor along with hers as he caught her and hauled her against his firm, slick body. Oh, she really liked firm and slick. Had forgotten how much she liked it.

She slipped a forearm over her breasts just before she landed against his chest. "Oh my God, I thought you were gone!" She should step away. But then he'd see her naked from head to sweaty toes instead of just the up-close-and-personal angle above her forearm.

"I pulled Cam's truck around back to change the oil." His arms settled around her waist, calloused hands causing a tidal wave of lust to riot through her entire body.

Dear Lord.

They were completely naked. At the same time. In the same room. With the light on!

Panic mushroomed through her chest, squeezing her lungs so tight she was afraid to take a breath. But instead of scrambling for her towel, she whispered, "The water heater went out in the house."

"I figured it would." His voice turned to gravel, and his eyes darkened. "Your plumbing needs some attention. Mine's just fine."

Obviously. *Everything* looked just fine here. And how could he make plumbing sound so sexy?

Unless that lusty tone in his voice was just her imagination . . . or her fantasy. Maybe she should slap herself to see if she was dreaming.

Because he looked even better in his real-life birthday suit than he had in many, many of her dreams. The *plumbing* that was pressing into her belly and growing firmer by the second was solid and fully functional. All hot-blooded male flesh. All hers, if she wanted it.

Grab the towel and run!

Her feet seemed to be glued to the floor because they didn't move. When she pulled a lip between her teeth, the generous firmness against her belly turned to granite, and he moaned. *Moaned!*

Which caused her to forget the towels pooled at their feet. Instead, she uncrossed her arm and let her needy nipples—which matched his granite plumbing in firmness—press into him. At least they were on the same page.

Like it was the most natural thing in the world, she sank both hands into his damp hair and pulled him into a red-hot, openmouthed kiss. With tongues and everything. And, oh God, his taste, his touch, his heated breath washing over her as she angled her mouth against his to give him better access was so, so yummy.

She deepened the kiss and pressed her full length against him. That produced another moan, this one so deep his chest rumbled against her breasts, and Lorenda thought she might orgasm right there.

His roughened hands caressed up her back until she did a little moaning too. Okay, a lot of moaning, because, holy *sierra*, Lorenda loved being in his arms. So strong, so dependable, so safe.

So talented at the moment.

She broke the kiss to nip at the wetness on his neck. When she let her tongue slip through her swollen lips to lick at the small space where his corded neck met a muscled shoulder, he growled. Pushed her back a fraction and leaned forward to cover one of her peaked nipples with his hot mouth. Anchored his hands to her hips and guided her backward to the sink. Then both of his large palms slid down and around until they cupped her ass.

Without warning, he lifted her to sit on the edge of the counter. She squeaked as he stepped between her legs, his shaft pressing against her throbbing center.

"Sparky," he rasped out. "I need to get protection." He tried to step away, but she pulled him back, clamped her legs around his firm, perfectly formed butt, and held him tight.

"Not yet." She trailed soft, sweet kisses across his chest, and his breath hissed out.

"You keep that up and we won't need protection," he said through gritted teeth, one hand pressing into the small of her back like he wanted to melt their bodies together skin to skin.

"Kiss me again." She wanted to feel his warm mouth against hers, feel his hot body wrapped with hers for a little bit longer before they . . .

He wound a handful of hair into his hand and angled her head so that they fit together like two pieces of a puzzle. Perfect together.

Her hand brushed over the metal dog tags hanging around his neck, and the coldness of the metal and all they represented seeped into her fingers. A chill sliced bone deep, even though the air was thick with steamy heat.

Her head snapped back, and she tried to blink the glaze from her vision. "Mitchell." She swallowed, staring up into his chocolaty eyes. His were just as glazed over with lust as hers must've been.

She couldn't do this. He was everything she didn't need. Everything she didn't want. But her girl parts were screaming for more. And his muscled chest, and handsome face, and sultry eyes, were drawing her in until she didn't think she could let go. Couldn't let go of what his body could do for hers. Couldn't let go of the need in his eyes that matched the need spiraling through her body. Couldn't let go of him.

This was insane!

The doubt must've shown in her expression, because Mitchell's eyes softened. He pressed a gentle kiss to her forehead and stepped away to snatch up his towel. The crown-of-thorns tattoo undulated over the tension of his muscled bicep, then he turned his back and draped the towel around his waist.

"Go ahead and shower. I've got errands to run." He stopped. Looked over his shoulder like he wanted to say something but couldn't. "See you later, Sparky." He drew in a breath and walked out, leaving her to stare at a closed bathroom door.

Leaving her wanting him more than ever.

"This is one of our newer listings," Lorenda said to Daniel Summerall a little over an hour after she'd been naked with Mitchell. Discussing their *plumbing*.

She forced her toes to uncurl from the tips of her designer black pumps. One of the things Lorenda loved about her job was being able to dress up once in a while. Trade in Red River's standard dress code of jeans, thermals, and hiking boots to be a girly girl. Clothes, shoes, lingerie, and the way she decorated her cottage were all feminine and frilly and just for her. It was the way she filled the void of being single.

"It just came on the market earlier this week." She tried to sound personable yet professional. That was her job. She'd show him cabins for as long as it took for him to find something that felt like *his*. And somewhere in the process she had to work up the nerve to bring up the kids' music program.

She studied him as he wandered around the open floor plan. The brand-new cabin was built out with expensive rustic wood trim still rich with the woodsy scent of newness. Daniel was tall and slender, with sandy-blond hair, and he was dressed smart-casual like he'd just stepped off the cover of a men's fashion magazine. Perfect.

For someone else.

She guided him through the lower level, then over to the wooden staircase that led to a large loft and master suite. "Construction was recently finished. Never lived in."

"It's gorgeous," Daniel said, following her up the stairs.

Lorenda felt oddly self-conscious that he was eye level with her rump and resisted the urge to splay both hands across her butt to hide it from view. Her mother seemed to think he was very interested, and she had all but insisted that Lorenda throw herself at the man. Of course Mom had also fixed Lorenda up with Clifford the maintenance man.

Always nice when a gal's mother tried to pimp her out.

"The cabins I showed you last week were smaller and not as new." Lorenda reached the upstairs landing and turned left into the open loft.

"They didn't seem to meet your needs. I wanted you to see this one so you could compare the two price ranges."

This cabin was more expensive. Larger than most, and on a generous parcel of land. She didn't like upselling her clients, but if it worked for him, then it was a win-win. The client would be satisfied and happy with his purchase, and she'd get a nice commission. The portion she planned to use for the music program would barely make a dent toward the cost of better equipment and supplies, but it was a start.

"A place like this is even more beautiful when trimmed out with the right furnishings. I can steer you toward some interior decorators who specialize in decorating vacation cabins to look artful and rustic at the same time." She led him into the master suite.

He followed her into the large bedroom, which had a stone fireplace nestled into the corner. "Hiring a decorator would be my choice. I don't have a lot of time, but I do have the budget to pay someone to do it for me. I'd want it decorated with quality furnishings for entertaining guests."

Wow. Every girl's dream. A man with money who was a sharp dresser and appreciated home furnishings. Too bad she couldn't stop thinking about the naked alpha guy whose standard wardrobe consisted of combat boots, worn Levi's, and plain black T-shirts that came in packages of three.

She opened the large walk-in closet while Daniel checked out the bathroom. When he rejoined her in the bedroom, she said, "It's a lot of square footage and a lot of acreage for the money, if that's what you're looking for."

He leaned against the wall, bent one knee, and sank both hands into the pockets of his expensive-looking dress pants. The top two buttons of his pinstriped dress shirt were unbuttoned, revealing the hint of a slender but toned chest.

"I like it. It's definitely closer to what I'm looking for." His appreciative gaze drifted over her.

She swallowed.

His stare darted to the double French glass doors that opened onto a large redwood deck.

Great opportunity to change the subject. "The view from this room is spectacular."

"It certainly is." His gaze darted back to her.

She ignored the tightening in her stomach and motioned for him to follow her onto the deck. "A purchase like this is a big commitment. You may want to think about it." She shrugged. "And look at it a time or two before making a decision."

Was she actually trying to dissuade a sale of this magnitude? What in God's name was wrong with her? Stupid question, because she knew exactly what was wrong. She didn't want to give the man the wrong impression. The impression that she wanted more than to be his realtor. The impression that she might be available. The impression that she wasn't already developing feelings for someone else who happened to share her house and her last name.

Obviously, she needed to keep her impressions to herself, because she was sounding a little pathetic.

He turned back toward the doors and propped himself against the railing, crossing his legs at the ankles.

"Your parents tell me you're a musician, Lorenda," he said casually.

"Um, yes. I am." She moved to the far side of the deck.

"And you're starting a free music program for children?"

"Yes."

"So why haven't you brought it up? This is our second meeting." His gray eyes locked onto hers.

"Well, I—" she stammered. Drew in a breath, and decided to go for honest. "I wanted to keep it professional."

He let a few moments of silence go by like he was thinking on that. Finally he nodded. "I understand."

He did? Oh thank the Virgin Mary she wouldn't have to explain that he wasn't her type. Even though he should be.

Gah!

He brushed a fallen leaf aside with a posh leather dress shoe. "Music programs of any kind aren't cheap. My biggest concern is your lack of experience."

He wasn't the only one. Bart had pointed out that she might need help.

"But your willingness to do this on a volunteer basis demonstrates your love of music, and I like that."

Now they were getting somewhere. Her innate, soul-deep love of music was the reason she needed to do this. She held her breath and waited for him to finish.

"So I'll tell you what."

What? *What!*

"If you can put together a written plan explaining how you intend to build the program and allocate funds, then pull together a concert for the kids using the equipment you already have, I'll consider putting my support behind your program."

"Seriously?" She didn't mean to sound that unsure of herself, but she couldn't very well help it.

He chuckled. "Seriously."

"Then let me write this down." She pulled her cell from the pocket of her soft pink linen blazer and typed his instructions into the notes app.

"If you really impress me, I'll do one better. I've got a lot of connections in the music world. I'm sure I can line up other sources of support as well."

Holy cow. She'd done it. Well, actually she hadn't done it. Daniel Summerall and her parents had. She hadn't been able to bring it up because she was scared. Scared he'd get the wrong idea. So she'd kept it all business, and he'd brought it up for her.

"You have four weeks."

Four weeks? She'd need more like four months to pull off what he was asking and do it right.

"In the meantime—" He looked up at the bright-blue sky, one of his eyes narrowing against the glare. "I'll probably make another trip up here to look at the cabin again. I do need to think about it." His gaze slid to her again. "And it'll give me a chance to get to know you better."

Well, *sierra*. So much for professional.

"Lorenda." He straightened. "I don't believe in coincidence. Meeting your parents"—he smiled—"and meeting you, everything seems to be falling into place like it was meant to be. I believe things happen for a reason to bring life into balance and create harmony in the world."

Her lips parted, but Lorenda didn't know what to say. How to tell him she was taken.

Maybe because she wasn't.

"Here is a link to eHarmony, the world's most trusted online dating site." Minx purred to life with her sex-kitten voice. "I hope you find the person you're looking for."

And so much for good impressions.

Chapter Eleven

After Lorenda finished up with Daniel, she swung by the office to get some paperwork in order. Staying busy was the key to happiness. Or denial. She wasn't sure which, but did it really matter? Until a few weeks ago, her life had been virtually Y chromosome free. Trevor and Jaycee didn't count because they shared her DNA, and they weren't old enough to shave. Now she had more adult Y chromosomes vying for her attention than she knew what to do with.

Bart was dropping in on her rehearsals every day after school. Try as she might, she'd still given a client the wrong idea about her availability. And she'd been skin to skin with Mitchell just hours ago. Which was why she'd retreated to her office instead of going home. She wasn't sure if she could face him again after almost shagging him in his bathroom this morning.

Before she knew it, it was late afternoon, and she hadn't looked up from her desk. Her phone rang, and her mother's number popped up.

"Hi, Mom." Lorenda saved her work and shut down her computer. "Sorry, I didn't realize it was getting so late. Ready for me to pick up the boys?"

"Absolutely not. They're fishing with your father, and I'm making dinner. They can stay the night and go to church with us tomorrow morning."

In that case, Lorenda could see if her three BFFs, the four of them affectionately dubbed the mommy mafia, wanted to meet her at Joe's. While she was there, she could try to solicit help for the concert. If she got organized, stayed focused, and suckered enough people into assisting her, she might be able to pull it off.

"*Sooooo*, how did it go with Daniel?"

Lorenda chose to ignore the obvious—her mother wanted to know if things were getting more personal with Mr. Summerall. "It went well. He liked the cabin but wants to think about it. Understandable, considering it's more than he'd planned to spend. We talked about the music program." She rubbed her eyes. "I've got some work to do before he decides on that too."

"*Aaaaaand* did he make another appointment with you?"

"He said he'd probably want to look at it again before making a final decision."

"Yes!"

Lorenda could practically hear the fist pump in her mother's voice.

"He's going to ask you out, I'm sure of it," her mom said.

Lorenda rolled her eyes. "Exactly how are you sure?"

"Why else would he keep making appointments to see you?"

Lorenda eased back in her plush leather executive chair and let her head fall back. "Um, to look at real estate?" Lorenda glanced at the huge glass window of their storefront that had "Brooks Real Estate" scrawled across it. "That's typically why people make appointments with realtors."

"Nonsense. Men are hunters. If they see something they like, they make a decision to buy it right there on the spot. No browsing. No waiting around for something better to come along. Just *boom*"—her mom made the sound of a gunshot—"they're done."

"Mom, he's a really nice guy, but he's not my type."

"Oh pishposh," her mom argued. "How would you know what your type is? You don't date."

"Why are you trying so hard to find me a husband?" Her mother's matchmaking efforts used to be cute. Until two weeks ago, give or take, when they had become just plain annoying.

Lorenda told herself the timing was a coincidence and had absolutely nothing to do with the smokin'-hot SEAL who had moved in with her about the same time.

"Maybe I want more grandchildren." Her mother sniffed.

"I've already given you two. Go put some pressure on Langston." Lorenda pushed back, pulled off her pumps, and propped her feet up on the desk.

Her mother scoffed. "Like that's a possibility."

True. But still. Langston should have to shoulder his share of the parental nagging.

"How long is Mitchell going to be staying with you, honey? Letting a single man with a bad rep move in with you won't help your love life."

"I don't have a love life, Mom," Lorenda ground out.

"Exactly!"

Oh for God's sake. Lorenda was not discussing her love life with her mother.

She decided to change the subject. "Do you need me to bring any clothes by for the boys?"

"No, I've got some extra pajamas here for them, and I can throw the clothes they're wearing in the wash after they take a bath."

"Good, then let me know when I can pick them up tomorrow."

"Okay, sweetie," her mom said, and Lorenda was thankful that the topic of men was closed. "When you see Mr. Summerall again, make sure to wear that pink sundress. You know, the one with the white belt. It shows off your figure."

Lorenda banged her head against the chair. "*Mom.*"

Her mother acted oblivious. "And your dad is going to follow up with him tonight. He may mention that your housemate is your brother-in-law, and nothing more."

That was true. Sort of.

⎯⎯⎯⎯⎯⎯

"Hey, Dylan." Lorenda slid onto a barstool at Cotton-Eyed Joe's. She'd arrived a few minutes before the rest of the mommy mafia so she could ask Dylan McCoy to help with the concert. He was Joe's nephew, head bartender at Joe's, second-in-command of Red River's favorite watering hole, and most everyone speculated that Dylan would take over when Joe retired.

"Hey, Lorenda." Dylan filled a frosty mug at the tap and set it on a tray so the server could deliver it to its rightful owner. His chestnut-brown hair was a little longer than Red River's norm, and the small diamond stud in his ear sparkled under the dim lights. He wiped his hands on a towel as he came to stand in front of her. "What can I get you?"

"Um . . . how about a beer? My usual."

"Coming right up." Within a minute a cold, longneck bottle was sitting in front of her on a coaster.

"That all?" Dylan asked.

"Um, well . . . you're a musician." She snagged a peanut from the bucket and peeled off the shell. "And you used to write songs for some pretty famous bands, right?" Okay, stupid. *Eeeeverybody* knew Dylan had been a professional songwriter, because several of his songs had been hits. And everybody also knew that Dylan didn't talk about whatever had gone down that caused him to leave Los Angeles. In fact, he hadn't had anything to do with music at all since he'd moved back to Red River.

"I guess." Dylan's voice turned guarded. "Why?" He tossed the towel over a shoulder and checked the ice machine behind the bar.

She explained the situation in one long breath before she lost her nerve.

"Wish I could help you out, but I can't."

"I'm asking for the kids, not for myse—"

"No." His tone was flat and final. His expression was firm.

She'd obviously struck a nerve, so she backed off out of respect for his boundaries. "Thanks anyway." She lifted her bottle. "Start a tab. It's ladies' night out."

His boyish grin returned. "You got it."

She turned to find a table, because it was dinnertime on a Saturday night, and the restaurant was starting to fill.

"Lorenda," Dylan said.

When she turned back to look at him, his expression had gone softer. Sad, almost. He hesitated. Looked away with a muscle ticking at his jaw. "I'm sorry," he finally said.

She shook her head. "It's okay, Dylan. I had to try, though."

She claimed a booth against the right wall, and one by one, each seat at her table filled with either a pregnant or nursing woman. Hence the mommy mafia nickname. Lorenda loved each one of them like sisters.

"Let's order," said Miranda, finally over the first trimester blues and barfs from pregnancy *numero uno*.

"I'm with you, sister," said Ella, who was growing round with her second bun in the oven.

Angelique, bleary eyed from nursing her first bundle of colicky joy, flagged down a waitress, and they each rattled off an order. When Lorenda ordered another beer, every last one of them gave her the evil eye.

"We haven't seen you in a few weeks." Ella's tone was teasing. "Guess you've had your hands full, Lor."

Did she ever. Especially this morning in Mitchell's bathroom.

She lost her concentration. Cleared her throat. And drained the rest of her longneck.

Desperate situations called for desperate measures, and the mommy mafia was just the right group of ladies to help with both of her problems. "I have an offer you can't refuse," Lorenda said like a mafia foot soldier. She set the empty bottle to the side with a thud. "Right after I kick your asses."

"You're enjoying delicious cold beer right in front of us, knowing we can't have any, and you want to kick *our* asses?" said Angelique.

Lorenda's back was to the door, but she knew the moment Mitchell walked in. A sixth sense caused her posture to go rigid and the spot between her thighs to go hot. Sure enough, Mitchell walked past with Talmadge and Langston.

Talmadge stopped to give his wife a quick kiss. Miranda grabbed him by the shirt collar and stared into his eyes. "It's your fault I can't drink during ladies' night out for the next several months." She rubbed her baby bump.

"You don't drink, babe, but I'll make it up to you anyway," Talmadge said in a sensual tone, then glanced around the table. "When you're not with your hit squad."

"Darn right you will." Miranda gave him another kiss and let him go.

He winked at them. "You ladies do realize you're a little scary when you're all together, right?"

"There's power in numbers," Angelique said. "And in hormones."

He shook his head and joined the other guys in a booth at the back of the room. A table of hotties—with the exception of Lorenda's brother, because *eww*—but no one except Mitchell existed as far as she was concerned. Every table and barstool had filled, but the cavernous restaurant/saloon/honky-tonk dance hall might as well be empty. All Lorenda could focus on—besides the mommy mafia who looked like they might stab her with a fork every time she took a sip of beer—was the gorgeous, badass ex-SEAL.

As if he could read her thoughts, he swung his gaze on her, and his expression turned brooding. She squeezed her thighs together and looked away.

Their waitress delivered their food and plopped a fresh bottle in front of Lorenda. Angelique's black Italian eyes stared longingly at it. "It's three against one. I think we can take her," she said to Ella and Miranda.

Lorenda snorted and took another exaggerated pull from the bottle. "We can take it outside after I'm done with my *beer*."

"Honey, with our raging hormones pooled together and all the healthy food we consume, your skinny blonde ass wouldn't stand a chance," Angelique said, all alpha female. Her smile broadened like a somewhat friendly variety of barracuda.

Ella twirled a long red lock of hair around one finger with an absent gaze resting on Lorenda's beer. "We can totally take her, but first I want to know about her offer."

"So what's up, Lor?" Angelique asked, stabbing at her salad.

Lorenda glanced at Mitchell and drew in a breath. Held it when he lifted a frosty mug to his lips and that thorny tattoo flexed.

Meow.

Lorenda jumped when Miranda snapped fingers in front of her face. "Oh. Um, right." She swallowed. "I need help organizing a concert."

"We're in," Ella said.

Lorenda blinked. "I haven't finished."

"We're still in, you know that," Miranda said.

"Well, at least hear me out." Lorenda waved a hand in the air. "I need to wow a potential donor. He's in charge of a big symphony and wants to see the program in action, among other things. I have four weeks to get the kids ready. Miranda, could you take care of hors d'oeuvres for a large crowd?"

"Consider it done." Miranda picked at her salad like it was gruel.

"Angelique, can you help me come up with a mission statement for the program, and a potential budget, goals, and participation guidelines geared for a kids program like this? I have no idea where to start."

"Sure thing." Angelique stabbed a piece of asparagus like she wanted it to suffer.

"And, Ella, your husband is on the city council now, right?"

"Kicking and screaming about it, but, yeah, Coop is a councilmember," said Ella.

"Could you ask him about a permit so we can do it in the park? Maybe around the gazebo with chairs set up for an audience?"

"I'll do one better." Ella bared her teeth at the glass of plain ice water she lifted to her lips. "I'll make sure it's decorated up with lights and flowers and whatever else we can find to make it festive and pretty."

Lorenda's eyes misted. "You guys are the best. He wants to be impressed." Possibly in more ways than one.

She held down the button on her phone until Minx purred to life with her sex-kitten voice. "How can I make your day?"

Lorenda held the speakerphone to her lips. "Minx, can you give me a list of shops in my area that sell a wide variety of party favors for kids?" Rewarding the kids for their effort couldn't hurt.

"Here is a list of shops in your area that sell large panty sizes," Minx purred.

Everyone at the table next to them turned to stare.

Lorenda clamped a hand over the speaker. As if that would help.

All three members of the mommy mafia raised a brow.

Lorenda switched her phone off and stuffed it in her purse. "I'll Google it at the office."

"Let's make sure Felix Daniels from the newspaper covers it too," said Miranda. "He did wonders with the publicity for the new gazebo and the Hot Rides and Cool Nights Festival when I was chairperson."

Lorenda didn't have to look to know Mitchell's eyes were on her. Her body responded to him on some sort of crazy mystical level. When he walked into a room, she felt his presence before she saw him, and his gaze heated her from the inside out.

She tried not to look.

She did.

But his stare drew hers like it had some freaky magnetic pull.

Their eyes locked. His darkened, and she hoped her face wasn't as red as it was hot, because it was heated enough to fry an egg. The desire in his look was unmistakable. And darn near irresistible.

One of the mommy mafia cleared her throat, but Lorenda had no idea which. Slowly she turned her attention back to her BFFs and tried to bring them into focus. Not easy with a pinup-worthy SEAL looking at her like he wanted to have her for dessert instead of Joe's famous peach cobbler à la mode.

"And the ass-kicking part?" Miranda asked.

"Those condoms you gave me for my birthday caused me a lot of trouble." She left out the part about how they'd almost come in very handy too.

"Hopefully the kind of trouble that's long and satisfying." Ella laughed.

"Nothing like that, I assure you." But almost. She glanced over at Mitchell's table again. He, Langston, and Talmadge clinked frosty mugs in a toast, and something tingled in Lorenda's chest. Seeing Mitchell here in Red River, reconnecting with the people who had been close to him since childhood unlocked a warmth deep inside her soul. "Which is why I should kick your asses. I thought I was pulling the garage apartment key from the bottom of my purse"—she leveled a stare at each one of them—"with my new tenant standing there watching and waiting."

Miranda's eyes widened, and she stopped cutting her chicken. "*No.*"

Lorenda lifted a brow. "Imagine my surprise when I pulled out a shiny purple square instead of a key."

Angelique's mouth fell open, and her fork clattered against the glass plate. "The grape-flavored one?"

Ella snorted, then clamped a hand over her mouth. "Sorry." She glanced over her shoulder at Mitchell's table. "He's really nice looking."

He wasn't just nice looking. He was hot as hell. And all wrong for Lorenda and the kids.

Angelique picked up her fork and started to move veggies around her plate. "From the few glimpses I've gotten of him around town, he's got a really great body."

Yep. Lorenda could vouch for that after this morning. Her nipples hardened at the memory of his tight butt and sculpted back when he'd turned to get his towel.

"Judging from his way with girls back in high school, I'm sure he would know exactly how to make the most of those condoms," Miranda said around a mouthful of grade-A beef.

"Which brings me to the other reason I need your help," Lorenda said, and snagged a fry from her plate to pop into her mouth. "I can't get involved with Mitchell. I had one alpha man with the last name Lawson. I don't need another one." Even if she did want him. Needing and wanting were two different things, and a responsible mother had to make sacrifices for the sake of her kids. "You three can hold me accountable. Or slap me around if I start to cave."

"Lorenda's husband and Mitchell were identical twins," Miranda informed the two BFFs who hadn't grown up in Red River. "Looked just alike."

Lorenda picked at a cuticle. "They didn't look anything alike," she mumbled.

Ella and Angelique slid a look at each other that said they knew there was more to that story than Lorenda cared to explain.

Miranda smiled. "No one could ever tell them apart but you." She turned to the others. "Mitchell and Cameron used to play tricks on the teachers at school by pretending to be each other."

They certainly didn't act anything alike either. Mitchell just didn't let most people see his soft side. The deep well of compassion he'd hidden under layers of teenage rebellion and then buried deeper because of the horrors of war.

"The boys are already head over heels about him. I've gotten a call from Trevor's teacher every week since school started because he's acting out. I suspect it's because he knows Mitchell will leave eventually, and the kids are already so attached to him." She twisted her beer bottle in a full circle, already feeling the sting of that loss in her chest as well. "They've been trying to throw us together. Two nights ago they put a garter snake in my bed. It wasn't pretty."

"Did it work?" Ella teased.

"I screamed so loud, Mitchell nearly beat down the door trying to get into my room."

"Smart kids. You've got a regular *Parent Trap* going on at your house." Angelique laughed.

"My point is it's going to be hard enough on the kids when Mitchell leaves town without me mooning over him too."

"What can we do, since you're already living under the same roof?" Miranda asked.

Ella gave her head a decisive shake. "Can't do anything. Coop and I lived under the same roof as mortal enemies, and I still ended up like this." She pointed to her baby bump.

"Just make sure he keeps his shirt on," Angelique warned, pointing her steak knife at Miranda. "We warned Miranda about letting a gorgeous man take off his shirt in front of her. Talmadge did, and look what happened to her."

"I feel so sorry for all three of you," Lorenda deadpanned. "You're all madly in love with husbands who adore you."

"Okay. Repeat after us," Miranda said. "No. Bare. Chests." She fisted her fork and tapped the end of it against the grainy wood table. "No. Bare. Chests."

Angelique and Ella joined in the quiet chant. "No. Bare. *Chests*. No. Bare. *Chests*."

Well, hell. A little too late for that. She pulled a lip between her teeth and chewed.

The mommy mafia went quiet, and Angelique let out a long whistle. "Too late, isn't it?"

Lorenda chewed harder until she was sure she tasted blood. The mommy mafia stared and waited, until finally, Lorenda collapsed back against the seat. "I sort of saw him naked this morning."

All three of her BFFs turned to gawk at Mitchell. He must've sensed the attention, because he stopped talking to Langston midsentence. His expression blanked when he saw the mommy mafia staring.

Angelique was the first to turn back around with a hopeless look. "If he looks as good undressed as he does with clothes on, you're screwed. Literally."

Lorenda might as well wave a white flag. "He looked even better when he dropped the towel he was wearing right after a shower."

All three BFFs leaned in like she better give up all the details or they really would use a piece of flatware as a weapon.

"The hot water heater gave out, and I was going to have to hose off outside."

Three sets of brows scrunched.

"So I ran to the garage apartment because I had to meet a client, and Mitchell's truck was gone, so I was going to use his shower, but he was in the bathroom all wet and steamy, and I slipped and let go of my towel, and he caught me before I broke my neck, so he let go of his towel too, and then I kissed him." Lorenda waved a hand in the air, not sure what else to say. Because, really, didn't her rant kind of explain how *foxtroted* she already was? "And I kind of licked him too."

Ella's mouth fell open. "Nice. I remember *kind of* licking Coop. I think it led to this." She pointed to her stomach.

Miranda gave Lorenda's hand a pity squeeze.

Angelique fell back against the booth with a thud. "You're toast."

They had no idea.

"You don't have a choice," Ella said.

It was almost like Miranda read Ella's mind because she finished the sentence with, "Sex is going to happen. You might as well sleep with him and see where it leads. It's your only option."

If only she could. But not only could Lorenda not take her relationship with Mitchell to the next level because she had to protect her boys, she couldn't because she also had to protect herself.

"Not gonna happen." It was Lorenda's turn to stab at her plate. "Dinner's on me, ladies." At least they had her back when it came to the music program. But why did she even try to enlist their help when it came to men with muscled arms, strong thighs, and a killer smile? Every one of the mommy mafia had taken a hit, and ended up happily married and pregnant.

Mitchell Lawson had a lot to offer. Just nothing to offer Lorenda except maybe great sex, loneliness, and a broken heart.

She'd had enough of the last two. The first, not nearly enough.

Mitchell turned his frosty mug in a circle and tried to follow whatever Langston and Talmadge were talking about. He'd asked his old high school buddies to join him for a beer so they could catch up, and to glean any clues to Lorenda's mystery mugger. Instead, he'd spent the evening daydreaming about her sitting naked on his bathroom counter.

The waitstaff hustled to tend to the bustling crowd. Chatter grew to a low roar as a three-man band set up next to the long bar.

"What do you guys make of Lorenda getting mugged in Red River?" Mitchell refused to look in Lorenda's direction again. Refused.

Fuckin' A.

He looked. Took in the silky blonde hair that framed her smooth cheeks and cascaded over slender shoulders to brush against nice, full breasts. The very ones that had been pressed against him, begging to be kissed not more than seven . . . he glanced at his G-Shock underwater watch . . . make that eight hours ago. His mouth turned to gravel, and he tried to wash it away with a drink of beer.

Langston shrugged. "Probably a freak isolated incident. I can't imagine it being anything else here in Red River."

Mitchell wished it were as simple as that. Unfortunately, his gut told him otherwise.

"I'd still like to break the guy's arms, though." Langston looked across the room at his sister, and the brotherly love and protectiveness in his expression was something Mitchell knew well. Too well, really.

"Anything weird happen lately? Even something small?" Mitchell kept digging.

"Why?" Talmadge polished off his beer and started on the fresh one already sitting in front of him. "What are you thinking?"

Mitchell shrugged. "Just asking questions."

"Do you know something we don't?" Langston asked.

"Nope." Mitchell shook his head. "But my dad said he doesn't have the manpower to watch the guy now that he's out, so I figure the next best thing is to keep an eye on your sister twenty-four seven." Mitchell had been unable to do anything else every time she was in view.

The band struck up a fast C&W song, and the dance floor filled.

"Langston, when you're not pulling a shift on the helo, maybe you can check on your sister and nephews? Her house is fairly isolated. I won't be staying in her garage apartment forever."

If his ex-commander had anything to say about it, Mitchell would've already been on his way to the Middle East. The friendly telephone cuss-out session his CO had given him for "wussing out" on the best job he'd ever find had nearly busted Mitchell's eardrum. Just before he'd said "love you, man" and then told him to wise the hell up and get on a plane to DC so he could be prepped for deployment.

Langston gave Mitchell a smart-ass grin. "You know you're an asshole, right?"

Mitchell did know that. Hard to say which reason Langston referred to, though. There were so many. Seeing as how Langston was Lorenda's brother, he was probably referring to the fact that Mitchell had been undressing Lorenda with his eyes all night.

Mitchell nodded. "So I've been told. By just about everyone in this town."

"You don't come home for years, and you're already planning your exit strategy after two weeks," Langston said.

"That's Mr. Asshole to you, and why should I stick around when not many people but you two want me here?" Mitchell waggled a finger between Langston and Talmadge. "I'm surprised Joe hasn't thrown me out yet. He's been shooting suspicious looks at me since I walked in."

Talmadge spoke up. "I warned Uncle Joe we were coming. He said he was fine with it as long as there weren't any problems."

"I don't plan on causing problems. In fact, I'm trying to rebuild some of the relationships I ruined during my hell-raising days. Turn over a new leaf and all that BS. I made a list of names."

Langston snorted. "I bet it's as long as a football field."

Mitchell rubbed the crease of his nose with his middle finger, and it was just like the three of them were back in high school.

He had to admit, being here with friends and family felt pretty good. He glanced at Lorenda. The need to bolt that usually set in about an hour after he stepped into Red River's city limits still hadn't fully formed like it always had.

"I've been cleaning windows at the hardware store once a week." Mitchell rubbed his jaw. "I swear to God, Mr. McCall is throwing dirt on those windows before I get there just to make me work harder."

His buddies laughed.

"I've stocked the shelves at the market once a week too. I don't mind stacking soup cans and produce, but Mr. Garrett is just being a mean prick. The women's aisle has been completely empty both times.

No way are there enough females in Red River to use that many feminine products."

"No way." Langston's expression turned to fear.

In the middle of a sip, Mitchell pulled the mug away from his lips to nod and swallow. "I kid you not. After the first week, I got suspicious. So this week, I stopped in late the night before I was scheduled to work for him again. The aisle was full. Next morning when I arrived"—Mitchell sliced his hand through the air to make a point—"totally empty. Try having Ms. Francine ask *you* to go find lubricant in the back storeroom." He leaned forward and dropped his voice to a whisper. "And what the hell is a douche bag? I thought that was teenager slang for asshole."

Talmadge and Langston laughed so hard Mitchell wanted to flip them the bird for real.

Mitchell cleared his throat. "Joe is on my Suck-Up List too." Mitchell had been avoiding him like a chickenshit teenager. "What can I do to break the ice with him?"

Talmadge shook his head. "Uncle Joe's a good guy. He'll come around eventually. Just stay out of trouble."

Trouble was Mitchell's middle name. Didn't matter if he was looking for it or not, because it always came looking for him. Which drew his attention to Lorenda again, who was laughing it up with her friends until she caught him staring at her. She blushed a deep pink and gave him a shy smile before looking away.

Double trouble.

"This asshole moved back for good." Langston hooked a thumb at Talmadge. "Don't see why you can't do the same, Mitch."

"Be careful what you ask for," Mitchell said. "If you think we were assholes gone, we're twice as bad in person."

Talmadge snorted and lifted his mug to toast Mitchell.

"What the hell." Langston lifted his mug too. "If you can't beat 'em, join 'em." They all clinked mugs and took a swallow.

"Maybe we could teach Lorenda how to shoot." If Mitchell could enlist Langston's help, Mitchell might be able to talk Lorenda into buying a weapon to defend herself, since his dad was running short on personnel.

Langston belly laughed. "No way is my sister letting a gun anywhere near her house or her kids." He sobered like he'd said too much. "She's kind of had enough gun-war-alpha crap—her words, not mine." Langston picked at a groove in the table. "Sorry."

And Mitchell knew Langston was talking about Cameron not coming home alive. What no one else in this town knew was that Cameron hadn't wanted to come home at all. And it appeared that Lorenda had done a good job of keeping it a secret.

"No, *I'm* sorry," said Mitchell. Much more sorry than Langston could possibly imagine, because Cameron's absence from Lorenda and the kids' lives was largely Mitchell's fault.

The boot-scootin' couples slowed with the music, and the dance floor cleared. Now that the bar was in full view again, Sandra Edwards, a girl with enough cleavage to make a man go blind, straddled a stool at the long bar and wiggled four fingers at Langston. She'd been around the block with Langston in high school. Several times. Had lapped the block so many times with different guys that she could've qualified for the Indy 500. Her red cowboy boots and denim miniskirt that stopped just shy of her kill zone told all three of them that she was ready to take Langston out for another spin.

"That, my friends, is my cue to leave." Talmadge pushed Langston out of the booth and stood. "I'm going to snag my sexy, pregnant wife and take her home. With all the hormones she's got going on, I'll either get lucky or get castrated. Not sure which, but wish me luck." He winked and walked over to Lorenda's table.

When Miranda slid out of the booth, Talmadge laid a kiss on her that had every woman in the room sighing. The other two ladies at Lorenda's table put a hand to their chests, then grabbed their purses and dashed for the door like maybe they were going to hunt their husbands down too.

Lorenda sat back down. Alone. Looking wistful and sad, and so damn gorgeous that Mitchell wanted to take her home and make her feel lucky tonight.

"You're both single, ya know."

Mitchell jumped at Langston's words.

Langston eyed him. "Just don't hurt her, or you'll wish you never left Afghanistan."

"I know what she's been through just as well as anybody." Mitchell knew far more about Lorenda's hardships and disappointments than anybody else.

Langston gave him a sad smile, because he'd been Cameron's friend in high school too, and they'd all grieved when Cam was KIA. "I know, buddy."

Langston didn't actually know the half of it. If Lorenda didn't see fit to tell him how badly Cameron had let her down, Mitchell wasn't going to either.

"I wouldn't do anything to hurt her." Mitchell wanted to do the opposite. He wanted to protect her and make her world right again. Which was why he couldn't get involved with Lorenda. "She's my friend. Has been since we were kids, just like you." Mitchell returned Langston's level stare.

Langston drained his mug and slammed it to the table. "Uh-huh. Well, I'm your friend, and if you looked at me the way you've been looking at her all night, I'd kick your ass." He slid out of the booth. "I think I can find better company tonight than the likes of you." He gave Mitchell a slap on the back and headed toward Sandra.

Mitchell twirled his beer around a few times and glanced at Lorenda again. She chewed her lip like she always did when she was nervous. *What the hell?* They were in a public place with lots of people around.

Nothing could happen that they'd regret. At least nothing nearly as tempting as what had already happened this morning in his bathroom.

He snatched his beer and walked to her table. "Hey."

"Hey," she said, already blushing. As though she knew her skin was turning colors it shouldn't, she ran a hand over her cheek, down her slender neck, and rested it on the bare *V* of skin that showed above the buttons of her silk shirt.

Mitchell couldn't tear his eyes from the quick, steady rise and fall of her breasts. They'd been so tasty and tempting when he'd had them in his mouth. "Mind if I join you?"

Before she could give him an answer, the band's lead singer started talking into the microphone. "I've got a brother in the Army, so the next song is to honor our veterans." He plucked out a few slow cords. "So come on, folks. If you're with a vet, drag them out on the floor and tell them how much you appreciate their service. I want every vet dancing." The rest of the band joined in, and their soothing ballad caused the dance floor to fill again. "Especially tell them how glad you are that they made it home."

Lorenda squared her shoulders like she'd made a decision. Like she was being brave. Her lip pulled between her teeth told Mitchell that she was still nervous. She stood and hooked her arm in his. "Looks like I'm your dance partner for this one." She led him onto the floor and stepped into his arms.

"Sure you want to do this, Sparky? I'm not exactly Red River's favorite person." He pressed a palm into the small of her back, and heat skated up his arm. "A lot of these folks dislike me. A lot. It might rub off on you."

"Then we can be equally disliked, because you heard the man. Every vet has to dance."

It had been a long time, but he fell into a smooth two-step. Her subtle perfume relaxed him, and he pulled her closer. She molded into him, so soft and sweet. Heat seared through his clothes everywhere she touched.

"I appreciate your service," she whispered against his ear, and a spark of desire thrummed through him. His eyes slid shut for a beat, because even though she believed she was a widow because of him, she was still being kind. Too kind for her own good.

That was so her.

Her hand resting on his arm slid up his bicep and over his shoulder.

"You're welcome, Sparky." He concentrated on the steps instead of the warmth that radiated off of her and charged the air around them.

"I'm especially glad you're home safe." This time she turned her lips into his ear so that her warm breath fanned the spark of desire to a full-blown flame.

He had no idea how much alcohol she'd had, but obviously she was past her limit. Because she released his hand and circled it around his neck. Melted into him like they were lovers. Or like she wanted them to be lovers.

His hands tightened against her waist. He would not thread his arms all the way around her like he wanted to. It would be foolish and unfair to both of them.

She tilted her head back and stared up into his eyes. The slight hint of alcohol scented her breath. "It doesn't surprise me that you didn't ask Cameron to join up with you, or that you didn't ask him to stay in either. That's not who you are."

His throat closed.

She saw him. The *real* him. Not the hell-raising rebel that everyone thought he was. For the first time since he was a kid, he admitted to himself how much he really did want people to acknowledge the good in him. Pride rocketed through him. Circled his heart and closed around it until it shook loose the emotions he'd locked away for so long.

It was all Mitchell could do not to kiss her right there in front of the entire town. So instead he did exactly what he'd promised himself he wouldn't do. He let his arms slip around her waist, and he held her tight. She drew in a sharp breath when their hips connected, because his reaction to her was impossible to hide.

He dipped his head so that their noses almost touched. She swallowed, her green eyes glassy with just a tad too much beer and a truckload too much lust. "Thank you, Sparky."

Her eyes misted over. "I suspect you didn't start the fire at Joe's either."

A tank might as well have fallen on Mitchell's chest, because her words knocked the wind right out of him. Mitchell shook off a stab of pain in his heart, because even though Cameron had faults like everyone else on the planet, he was Mitchell's brother. His *twin* brother with a bond that went beyond human and stretched into the supernatural. And just like Mitchell took the blame for the fire, he would've taken that bullet for Cameron if he could've.

"It's time you stop covering for Cameron so you can salvage a relationship with your father." Lorenda's eyes dropped to his mouth, then traveled up again. "If you don't tell your parents the truth, then I will."

Had to be the alcohol talking. "It would hurt a lot of people, Sparky. Especially Trevor and Jaycee."

"They wouldn't have to know. No one has to if you want, except your mom and dad."

It was too late. Too much time had gone by, and there was enough water under that bridge to form an ocean. He wouldn't destroy his mother all over again with the truth or put more strain on his father's weakening heart. But another truth that had been pounding at Mitchell's heart was that Cameron had willingly let Mitchell take the blame. Something Mitchell could've never done if the tables had been turned.

The music slowed to a stop.

"Don't you dare, Sparky." His tone was low and hard as steel. "Or I'll put Red River in my rearview mirror and no one in this town will ever see me again." He set her away from him and played the only trump card he had in his deck. "Including my mother."

Without so much as a goodbye—because his jaw was locked down too tight—he walked out on the best woman he'd ever met. Just like his brother had.

Chapter Twelve

Still trying to process Mitchell's rebuke, Lorenda punched her pillow and turned onto her side. The soft glow of a half-moon streamed through the cracked blinds to cast a silvery hue over her lavender velvet comforter.

After she'd made her brother be the designated driver and bring her home a few hours ago, Mitchell's vehicles were in the drive and his lights were still on. She'd been tempted to pound on his door. She didn't because he'd been right to warn her not to spill details to his parents.

As wrong as it was for him to take the blame for so many things that had been Cameron's doing, it still wasn't her story to tell. Hell, she was still covering for Cameron so her boys wouldn't be disappointed by the truth. She didn't have much room to tell Mitchell not to do the same.

But darned if she still didn't want to knock on the door—panties and spaghetti-strap tank top and all—and talk sense into him so that he really could mend relationships in Red River. So that maybe he would stay.

If she had to be honest with herself, she wanted Mitchell to stay and see if they had a future together. All of the arguments she'd made to the mommy mafia about why she shouldn't get involved with Mitchell were more to convince herself.

Hadn't worked. And that scared the hell out of her. She'd spent too many years fixing problems caused by one Lawson man who wouldn't let her inside his heart or his head to help him and wouldn't even try to help himself. She did not want to go down that long, lonely road with another Lawson.

Never mind how hard it would be to explain *that* family tree to people.

But the current that stirred the air around them was getting stronger every day. Harder to resist. It wasn't just her either. It was in his stare, his body language. It was in his arms, spiraling around her and encircling her when they'd danced.

The outside door to Mitchell's apartment opened and slammed shut again with such force that the windows rattled. Lorenda couldn't help but wonder if Mitchell was as frustrated as her, or just pissed off. The stairs leading down to the drive creaked under his quick descending footsteps, and within a few seconds, his motorcycle roared to life and sped away.

Lorenda stared at the ceiling, and a light scratch sounded at the door. She ignored it.

Scratch, scratch, scratch. A little louder this time.

Still ignoring it. She threw an arm over her eyes.

A few minutes of blissful silence passed, and she snuggled deeper into her pillow.

Scratch, scratch, followed by a whine that tugged on her heartstrings.

With a hefty exhale, she threw back the covers and went to the door. Malarkey bounded in and sat in front of her. Stared up at her with giant, pathetic eyes, waiting for her command.

His dander was almost as unpleasant as his looks. She went to the bathroom and knelt to search through the cabinet for some baby powder to mask the smell. Malarkey followed her and sat watching her obediently. Under the sink she found a can of disinfectant spray and snatched it up. Looked at the dog. Back at the can, then at the dog again.

Maybe he would live.

"Oh for God's sake." She was outnumbered by all the testosterone in her house. She tossed the can back into the cabinet and went back to bed.

She patted the mattress. "Okay. You can get in bed with me just this once."

"Sorry, but I don't do one-night stands," Minx purred from the phone on Lorenda's night stand.

She rolled her eyes and patted the space next to her again. Malarkey rocketed onto the bed like he was scared she might rescind the invitation. Once he curled into a tight ball and snuggled against her, not a muscle so much as twitched.

Lorenda couldn't believe she was sleeping with a dog. It wasn't exactly the kind of companionship she'd hoped for at this stage of her life. Then again, she hadn't exactly hoped for any companionship until Mitchell had shown up and she'd fallen right into his arms.

She stroked Malarkey's wiry coat and resumed her staring match with the ceiling. For a long, long time, until she fell into that awkward state somewhere between sleep and consciousness.

Her Mozart's Magic Flute ringtone pierced through her dream. Mitchell's wet body, glistening dog tags, and draping towel evaporated into mist, and she grabbed for the nightstand, patting around for her cell.

"Hello?" Her voice was muffled with sleep.

"Lorenda, I'm sorry to wake you." Badass Becky's voice streamed through the phone, filled with panic.

Lorenda bolted upright.

"What's wrong, Becky?" Fear splintered in her chest, because it must be bad for her mother-in-law to call in the middle of the night. "Are the boys okay?" Wait. The kids were staying the night at Lorenda's parents', not the Lawson's.

"I'm sure your boys are fine, hon." Becky's voice shook. "My boy isn't."

Oh God. Had there been an accident? Just the way Mitchell slammed the door when he left earlier had sounded angry. And he'd been on his motorcycle instead of in the truck.

Every muscle in her body tensed with fear. She swallowed, reliving an even deeper gut-churning terror than she'd experienced six years ago when the call about Cameron had upended her life.

"What's wrong, Becky?"

"It's Mitchell." The shake in Becky's voice turned to a full-blown cry. "He's being questioned. Can you come to the station?"

Lorenda clamped her eyes shut. *Thank you, God. He's alive.*

Lorenda threw off the covers, which sent Malarkey skittering off the bed, and grabbed the first thing she could find out of her dresser—leggings and a pullover compression shirt. "On my way." She hopped on one foot trying to pull on the leggings, the phone pressed between her ear and her shoulder. "Why is he being questioned?"

Becky sniffled and then let loose another sob.

Lorenda stilled, one leg in the pants and one out. "It'll be okay, Becky. Take a deep breath and tell me what's going on."

Becky's heavy exhale caused the phone to crackle as though she were standing in the middle of a windstorm. "For *arson!*"

Lorenda's lungs went on lockdown. *Not again.*

"Okay, Becky," Lorenda said as she grabbed a pair of flip-flops, her purse, and her keys and flew down the stairs with Malarkey on her heels. "I'll be there in a sec, okay?" She shut the dog in the pantry and was already out the door and pressing the button on her car remote. The lights on her SUV blinked and it chirped.

Becky, a woman who could intimidate a charging bull with just one point of her index finger, burst into tears again. She'd already lost too much because of a stupid fire. The fire that had burned down Cotton-Eyed Joe's so many years ago and had forced one son into the military. The other had followed and came home in a box. And the lie behind that fire was still driving a wedge as wide as the Grand Canyon between a grown man and his family. All because of Mitchell's misguided sense of honor and loyalty to his twin.

"I'm hanging up now so I can drive." Lorenda climbed in and fired up the SUV, kicking up a storm of dust as she sped out of the drive.

Becky mumbled something that sounded like "yes," and the line went quiet.

Lorenda knew a mother's love. How it consumed a woman, filled her with pride and peace and fierce protectiveness all at once. And she hoped to God this was a big misunderstanding, because she didn't know if any of them could live through the same thing again.

Lorenda held down the button on her phone and Minx purred to life. "How can I make your day?"

Lorenda rolled her eyes. "Minx, call Angelique." When her buddy's sleep-strained voice answered the phone, Lorenda said, "Ang, meet me at the sheriff's office. Mitchell may need a good lawyer."

Angelique didn't hesitate. Didn't ask why. Lorenda figured that as one of the best criminal-defense attorneys in the Southwest, Angelique didn't care why.

"I'll be there," Angelique said. And that was that.

Lorenda had broken every traffic law in the county by the time she hit the Red River city limits.

Fire trucks still surrounded the construction site of the new rec center. Smoke poured from the building, but no flames were visible.

Lorenda motored past and pulled into the sheriff's office parking lot.

As soon as Lorenda walked through the front doors, Becky ran to her, arms open, eyes red. She threw her arms around Lorenda. "My husband suspects Mitchell for a fire at the rec center."

Lorenda gave her a hug and then motioned her into a chair in the waiting room. Oddly, Badass Becky sat without an argument and blew into a tissue, while Lorenda went to find someone who could tell her what had happened.

"What's going on, Sheriff?" Lorenda stepped into her father-in-law's path as he emerged from the hall.

"I'm questioning the suspect, that's what's going on." He tried to step around her.

She moved in front of him again and tried to muster a resting bitch face. She darn well wanted some answers, and until she got them, she wasn't playing nice. Playing nice hadn't gotten her much in life except heartache. "Do you have other suspects?"

The sheriff tapped the file in his hand. "No. A motorcycle was seen leaving the scene, and I caught up with Mitchell driving a motorcycle on his way back to your place. In the middle of the night."

"So?" Lorenda said. "Lots of people drive motorcycles."

The interrogation room door jerked open and Mitchell stepped out. He stilled when his eyes locked onto Lorenda.

"Mitchell has a history of this kind of behavior, as you well know. No one else in town does." The sheriff spoke like Mitchell wasn't in the room.

"What are you doing here?" Mitchell asked Lorenda.

"I called her." Becky ran over.

"I got here as fast as I could," Lorenda said as his eyes slid down her body. She realized how she must look. Hair a mess. Sleep still in her eyes. Black leggings, flip-flops, and a fitted black shirt that left nothing to the imagination, especially the fact that she wasn't wearing a bra. She crossed both arms across her chest.

"I'm fine." He shot a look at his mother.

He was just as stubborn-assed as he was badass. So Lorenda ignored him.

"Mitchell's history consists of a fire that happened well over a decade ago and was an accident, Sheriff," Lorenda said.

"It was irresponsible and could've cost lives. Like I said, it establishes a pattern."

But Mitchell's involvement . . . or lack of involvement . . . could easily be cleared up.

And it was time.

"Maybe the point here is that things aren't always as they appear on the surface. Maybe if Mitchell finally explains exactly how that fire at Joe's accidentally got started, it will clear some things up." She tried to return Mitchell's stony stare until the muscles in her face started to ache. Because, dammit, a resting bitch face wasn't as easy as it seemed. Being a hardass wasn't at all natural to her the way it seemed to be for the Lawsons.

"There's nothing left to say." Mitchell's tone was low and granite hard. "I think you should leave," he said to Lorenda. "There's nothing you can do."

Yeah, not going anywhere.

The sheriff studied his son for a second, then turned his attention to Lorenda. "Mitchell doesn't want you here because you can probably hurt him more than you can help."

Mitchell crossed both arms over his chest and let a deadly silence hang between him and his father.

"Larry, he's our son!" Becky teared up again.

The sheriff's expression softened. "Do you think I enjoy this, Becky?"

Mitchell cleared his throat as if to say *he* sure thought so.

The sheriff's look went hard again. "Because I don't. Never have, but I've got a responsibility to the badge I wear. I don't turn a blind eye for anyone. It's a promise I made to this town when I first ran for sheriff, and it's a promise I've stood by for darn near forty years."

A riot of sobs overtook Becky.

The sheriff tapped the file again. "Mitchell doesn't have an alibi for tonight. Says he hiked up to Middle Fork Lake. Alone. In the middle of the night."

"I did hike up to Middle Fork Lake in the middle of the night. Alone."

"Lorenda, can you tell me when Mitchell left your premises?"

"Um . . ." This was so not good. She glanced at the clock on the wall, and her heart fell to her feet with a thunk. It had been hours since she'd heard Mitchell leave the apartment, and that made the situation far worse than she'd thought.

The sheriff crossed his arms, mimicking Mitchell. He didn't look the least bit smug. The lines around his mouth ran deep with exhaustion and sadness.

"You're going to have to make a statement sooner or later, Lorenda," the sheriff said.

"He's right." Mitchell's stare didn't leave his father. "You might as well tell him now."

Lorenda drew in a shaky breath. She had to two choices. Door number one—lie about the time, but the sheriff would know she was lying and that would make Mitchell look guiltier. Plus, lying had already screwed up this family enough. Door number two—tell the truth and confirm that he had no alibi, which might lead to his arrest.

Where the hell is Angelique?

There was no doubt in Lorenda's mind that Mitchell wasn't responsible. She couldn't allow more blame to be laid at his feet for something he hadn't done. An idea flickered to life in the back recesses of her mind. There might be another way, albeit drastic. Something she'd heard Angelique talk about once.

Foxtrot.

"Don't you have more to tell your parents first?" Lorenda gave Mitchell a chance to make this right and save them both from door number three.

"No. I don't." His voice turned gritty. "But you can tell them everything about tonight." He emphasized the last word like it was a silent warning not to talk about the past.

Damned stubborn Lawson men. He wasn't going to save himself this time any more than he had the last. She'd have to take door number three and all of the uncertainties that waited behind it. It was the only solution that bought Mitchell time.

"Your spouse doesn't have to do any such thing, Mitchell." Lorenda ignored his look of confusion and stepped to his side to hook an arm in his. She flashed a bright smile at her in-laws. "Because we're getting married."

Mitchell covered a sputter with a fist like he was coughing.

Becky's expression blanked.

"It's called spousal privilege." She probably should've waited for Angelique before sacrificing herself on the altar to see that justice was done. "A husband and wife don't have to incriminate each other."

As if on cue, the front door flew open, and Angelique blew through it. Her shark-like expression announced to everyone in the room that she was ready for a fight.

"Don't say another word," she said to Mitchell. No hello, no smile. Just a look and a tone that had Lorenda thanking the heavens that she and Angelique were on the same side.

"They wanted to interview me about Mitchell's whereabouts, but I, uh, just invoked my right of spousal privilege." Lorenda gave Angelique a look that said *play along.*

Angelique didn't miss a beat. "Then my client should be free to go, unless you have sufficient evidence for an arrest, which I'm assuming you don't, since he's not cuffed."

The sheriff frowned. "At this point it's circumstantial."

Mitchell took a step toward the door, and Lorenda stayed right at his side, her arm still hooked through his.

"Not so fast," the sheriff said.

Mitchell stopped dead with a heavy sigh, causing Lorenda to stumble.

"They're not married yet," the sheriff said to Angelique. "Spousal privilege doesn't count for crimes that occur before the marriage."

Delta.

Lorenda tried to keep a cast-iron expression like Angelique's. Wasn't happening. She so needed to take lessons or something.

"You're not going to stop until you find a reason to send me to prison for real, are you?" Mitchell said to his father, but the sheriff ignored him.

"We'll be getting married in a few days," Lorenda blurted. Mitchell tensed, but she kept her arm hooked through his and stroked his bicep.

Angelique kept a steady stare trained on the sheriff. "My clients have nothing more to say. And for the record, spousal privilege as it pertains to adverse testimony counts for matters that occur before and during the marriage."

Thank God. Lorenda let out the breath she'd been holding.

The sheriff's gaze shifted from Angelique to Lorenda, then to Mitchell. "Only guilty people lawyer up."

"Or people who are being treated like they're guilty without sufficient evidence," Angelique said.

Lorenda cleared her throat. "We'll be in touch with the details," she said to Becky. Hopefully before the authorities found something that could be used against Mitchell. "No sense waiting when you know it's right."

"Lorenda, do you know how much trouble you can get into for hindering an investigation?" The sheriff's frown deepened.

"When you have enough evidence to arrest Mitchell, let us know." Angelique said. "Until then, we're done here."

"Can we go?" Lorenda asked, all innocence. "I have wedding plans to discuss with my fiancé."

Mitchell stiffened, his eyes clouding over.

Becky's stunned look slowly turned to a smile. "Well, what do you know? I get a wonderful daughter-in-law all over again."

The look on Sheriff Lawson's face told Lorenda they weren't just in-laws anymore. She and Mitchell had just been declared outlaws.

"Thanks, Angelique," Mitchell said once the three of them stepped into the parking lot and were alone. Dawn colored the sky pale purple as both he and Angelique turned their attention on Lorenda.

Who started to chew a plump lip.

"Spousal privilege?" Angelique said. "Really?"

Lorenda shifted from one Nike flip-flop to the other. "Um—"

Angelique held up a hand. "That wasn't actually a question. And since you've invoked the right, I suggest you two actually become spouses as quickly as possible." She pulled a set of keys from her purse and pointed the remote over a shoulder at her Lexus. It chirped, and she backed toward the car. "Call me later with the wedding plans. As my wedding gift, I'll take care of the cake. If the Ostergaards can't do it on such short notice, I'll have my mom and grandma drive up from Albuquerque and we'll make it ourselves."

"Thanks, Ang," Lorenda said.

"What the hell was that?" Mitchell asked Lorenda as soon as Angelique pulled out of the parking lot. He hadn't expected to walk out of the sheriff's office without cuffs. Walking out with a new fiancée was an even bigger surprise.

He took the driver's seat without asking Lorenda's permission. If he was expected to be the man of the family, then he was damn sure going to act the part.

She stared straight ahead at the side of the brick building and chewed her lip.

"Do you know what you've done?" He threw a wrist over the steering wheel.

"Saved your ass?"

Well, hell. Besides that.

He scrubbed a hand over his stubbled jaw. "I'm already the town outcast. Now they'll want my head on a spike and probably yours too." He couldn't let that happen.

"The people here have been my friends and family since I was born. I have more faith in them than that. Red River looks out for their own. Even if they have doubts about you because of your past, they'll trust my judgment."

He pinched the bridge of his nose. "Sparky, you haven't been on the receiving end of their grudges. They do look out for their own. That's my point. They don't see me as one of their own."

Lorenda gave her head a stubborn shake. "I don't believe that."

"We're going to wait an hour and then announce to *everyone* that it was a misunderstanding. That we're still just friends." Not to mention in-laws. Thank God there wasn't an audience in the waiting room like the day of the mugging.

"Oh good. If we wait an hour, that will give you plenty of time to tell your parents the truth." Lorenda stared him down. That stubborn female look in her eye told him she wasn't backing off.

That kind of look was fairly new, coming from her. He liked it when it wasn't directed at him. But when it was, it sucked.

"The truth will hurt the boys." Bingo. Pulling the mother's-guilt card worked because her lip chewing commenced.

"We don't need to tell anyone but your parents. They have a right to know what really happened to Cotton-Eyed Joe's on graduation night. You and I have been covering for Cameron too long."

And now he couldn't follow through on his threat to leave Red River if she spilled the truth. His father had issued a warning for him not to leave town during the investigation.

"When did Cameron tell you that he started the fire?" Mitchell softened his tone.

She turned a sad look on him. "I loved Cameron, but I can't tiptoe around his faults anymore. Not with you, Mitchell."

Right. Cameron hadn't told her. Taking responsibility wasn't his MO. She'd figured it out some other way.

"Then how did you know?" To his surprise, his words came out in a whisper.

"That night he climbed up to my window like a scene right out of *Romeo and Juliet*." She chuckled. "At least that's how a teenage girl would see it." One of her thumbs worked furiously against the other. "He was nervous. Upset and scared, I think, but he wouldn't say why. When I hugged him, he smelled like smoke. I didn't want to believe it, but as time went on . . ."

She looked away, because they both knew that as time went on, Cameron's behavior formed a pattern.

Silence hung in the air.

Finally she asked, "The three of us were good friends since we were little kids, but do you know why I fell for Cameron and not you?" She laughed. "I mean, besides the fact that you weren't in the least bit interested in me beyond being buddies."

"It had nothing to do with not being interested, Sparky. Hell, I was a guy, and you'd grown into a knockout, but Cameron was clearly head over heels, and there's a bro code I couldn't breach. So when he finally worked up the nerve to ask you out in high school, I accepted that you and I would always be friends."

"Oh," she whispered, her eyes round.

"But now I'm curious since you brought it up," Mitchell said.

"Cameron was Red River's golden boy. Everybody loved him. I thought he was the safer bet. Turns out I was wrong, and that night was the first clue. I just chose to ignore it." Her sigh was heavy with sadness. "As time went on, I just knew in my heart that he was the one who had started the fire and not you."

He let his head fall back against the headrest, and relief washed through him. Relief that someone he could trust finally knew the truth. Knew he was an upstanding guy who not only didn't start that fire but also hadn't ratted out his only brother.

"It was an accident." Mitchell propped his elbow against the door and rubbed his eyes. "We were all goofing around that night, drinking and acting like eighteen-year-old idiots. We set off some fireworks behind Cotton-Eyed Joe's. Joe came out and ran us all off. Everybody left, but Cameron forgot the lighter so he went back for it alone."

He stopped. It wasn't necessary to tell Lorenda that Cameron had decided to set off the last of the firecrackers before running away, just to get back at Joe.

Lorenda put a hand over his, her warmth making his heart ache with regret. And need.

"Let me guess," she said. "Someone saw Cam running away and everyone assumed it was you."

Mitchell nodded in silence, because he was too choked up for words.

"And you never told them otherwise."

And neither did Cam.

He leaned over the console, taking in her silky hair that was just messy enough to make his brain go haywire, her full lips that were just plump enough to make his mouth go watery. Her black outfit that was just tight enough to make his prick go hard.

He smoothed down her cheek with the back of one finger. "Why, Sparky? Why are you going to such lengths to help me?" Because no one else had ever done so except maybe his mom, and the solution Lorenda had come up with wasn't in her best interest.

"I can't let you take the blame for something else you didn't do," she whispered.

He wanted to take that plump bottom lip between his teeth and nibble. Instead, he said, "You've kind of got me by the balls, Sparky. Is there any way I can talk you out of this?"

She gave her head a small shake and swallowed as his finger slid down her neck. "Not unless you're willing to set the record straight with your folks."

It was Mitchell's turn to shake his head. "Can't do that. It would destroy my father. He might have a heart attack on the spot, and losing him would crush my mother. That's a chance I can't take."

He pulled away just enough to let his eyes wander down her length, and if he hadn't been sure that she was braless inside the station, he sure was now. Her perky breasts strained toward him, forming two nice peaks that he'd like to see without that tight-ass shirt. Sexy as it was.

"I could do worse than having you as my wife." He said it like it was a warning. A very sensual warning loaded with as much innuendo as he could pack into so few words.

Her lips parted. Her eyes dilated. And he thought for sure she was going to cave.

A pink tongue slid out to wet the seam of her mouth. "I've been through worse in my life too."

Dammit. She'd been through far worse.

He retreated in his mind just long enough to launch a counter assault. He had one more shot at getting her to surrender.

"What about Jaycee and Trevor?"

Her eye twitched.

"I'm a mother, Mitchell. I'd want someone to help them. Especially if they were too bullheaded to help themselves." Her thumb kept working fiercely against the other. "Let me ask you something." She stared at her fidgeting fingers. "Do you care about my kids?"

Mitchell had to keep his head from snapping back. "You know that I do."

"Then promise me something."

"Anything, Sparky." He covered her hands with one of his to still them.

"I know that helping you is the right thing to do. The boys already care about you so much. They'd be completely crushed if you got arrested and they couldn't see you anymore. So promise me when this is over you'll always be a part of their lives. Even if you're not around physically, you can visit, and there's Skype, e-mail, video chat, or whatever."

He took her hand and rubbed the ruby ring on her finger. Since he'd been back in Red River, he hadn't seen her wear the diamond wedding band Cam had given her. Of course Mitchell had been the best man and kept the ring in his pocket until the reverend asked for it on the altar. Mitchell would've never guessed in a million years that someday he'd be the one sliding a different wedding ring onto Lorenda's finger, even if their marriage were just for show.

"I'm crazy about Jaycee and Trevor. I couldn't walk away from them."

"That's all I ask, Mitchell. I'm asking for them."

He kept fiddling with her ring. "So what now, Sparky?"

Her lush, pink lips curved into an uncertain smile. "We get married."

Chapter Thirteen

The next evening, Lorenda took the boys for ice cream. She wanted a little time alone with Jaycee and Trevor so she could give them the news in her own way. Mitchell agreed and left them alone to make a few stops of his own.

And because she was nervous . . . and suffering from a severe case of guilt . . . and, okay, feeling selfish too, she'd gotten them an extra scoop. And bought them a new video game.

Whoever said bribery was poor parenting obviously hadn't had two kids in as many years and then had to raise them alone.

They ambled down Main Street with Malarkey on a leash, and all three of them licked at their dripping cones. When they approached her SUV, she didn't stop. "How about a Sunday-evening stroll in the park before we go home and do homework?"

"Sure," Jaycee mumbled around a lick.

Trevor nodded, a chocolate ring around his little mouth.

The park was busy, so Lorenda found a shady spot under a tree where they could have some privacy.

"What would you guys think about us helping Uncle Mitch out of a tough spot? A really, really tough spot that could get him in a lot of trouble when he doesn't deserve it."

Jaycee stopped licking. "Aren't you always lecturing us to help each other because that's what family does?"

Lorenda's took in Jaycee's serious expression and responsible words. When had he started to sound so grown up?

She cleared her throat. "The kind of help he needs would change our life at home, at least for a while."

"How?" Trevor said between licks.

"Um, well. Your Uncle Mitch and I would have to get married."

"Uncle Mitch is going to be our dad?" Trevor yelled.

Lorenda's head shot around to see if anyone had heard. Stupid, since the news had probably already circled the state. Twice.

"Well, technically he'd be your stepfather," said Lorenda.

Trevor let out a shriek.

Malarkey squatted and relieved himself, his typical reaction when a loud noise scared him.

Delta. Maybe she should find a bathroom too, because her nerves were getting the better of her. She rubbed her temple. She'd known the boys would be happy. Their adolescent pranks to scare her so Mitchell would stay hadn't eased up, including a letter to the tooth fairy asking for a raise so they could buy a high-powered slingshot for protection.

Wondering how they would take it when the marriage ended had her insides tied in knots.

"I guess what I'm trying to say, boys, is that we may not stay married."

Jaycee and Trevor both frowned.

"Why not?" Jaycee asked.

Lorenda stared at her melting cone. "It's complicated—"

"Can we call him Dad?" Trevor got on his knees and bounced with so much joy that Lorenda was torn between seeing them excited and feeling guilty for the fact that Mitchell wouldn't stay their stepfather forever.

Which would make him their uncle, stepfather, and ex-stepfather all in one. And *that* would make her a pathetic excuse for a mother. The thought made her brain stutter.

"Um, why don't you keep calling him Uncle Mitch for now." So they could all have time to process the new family tree.

Jaycee took a few more licks of his cone, looking deep in thought. "The way I see it, we never got to know our dad because he died when we were little, but he's still our real dad, right?"

"*Yeees.*" Lorenda wasn't sure where this was going.

"But Uncle Mitch is alive, so does it matter if he's our uncle or our stepdad as long as we still get to see him and talk to him?"

"I guess it doesn't matter." Much. She gave her cone another nervous lick and then shut one eye against the brain freeze that speared through the center of her head. Honestly, she wasn't sure if it was from the ice cream or from anxiety, because her entire body had broken out in a cold sweat. "Do you guys think you can keep this just between us?"

They both nodded.

Malarkey curled up next to Lorenda. She leaned away to escape his unfortunate odor.

"There's one more thing." Lorenda bit into her cone and tried to find the right words. "Sometimes kids say things that aren't very nice."

"You mean like when Mattie Welsh called Billy Reynolds a toad and told my whole class that if they touched him, they'd get warts." Trevor was totally serious.

"Yes, exactly like that," Lorenda said. "You shouldn't listen to such things. It's hurtful. If anyone at school says anything mean about your Uncle Mitch, I want you to ignore them, okay? He's a good person and hasn't done anything wrong."

"Why would anyone say mean stuff about him?" Jaycee finished off his cone.

Because they don't know him like we do. She blew out a breath. "Your Uncle Mitch has sometimes been . . . well, misunderstood by some people in Red River." Okay, by most people in Red River. And the stuff he pulled as a kid wasn't exactly misunderstood. He had been *trying* to cause trouble and had excelled at it.

That was in the past, though. He'd grown up, and he'd certainly paid his dues in the military.

"I'll beat them up," Jaycee announced.

"Me too." Trevor's expression said he thought defending his uncle was a grand plan.

Lorenda thought it sounded like an alpha-male plan, and that's precisely the influence she'd been trying to shelter the boys from their whole lives. So she'd gone and insisted on marrying another alpha war hero because falling for a man who was more beta would apparently be too easy.

"No!" Lorenda tried to calm her voice. "No, you're not going to beat anyone up. You're going to ignore it and walk away."

Jaycee fiddled with a blade of grass like he hadn't heard her.

"Jay*cee.*" Lorenda delivered a clear warning in her tone.

Jaycee rolled his eyes. "Mom, sometimes you have to let us handle things like men."

Her lips parted. He didn't sound at all like the little boy who used to sit in her lap and suck his thumb.

A sting started behind her eyes.

After all the years she'd spent as their role model, it had only taken a few weeks with Mitchell around for her little boys to start changing.

"Fighting doesn't make you a man," Lorenda argued.

"But Dad and Uncle Mitch fought a war, and that made them heroes." Jaycee gave her a dead-on stare like his statement had explained the key to manhood.

She pinched the bridge of her nose. "Your dad and your uncle Mitch were in the military. That's a very different kind of fighting. You two are not to use your fists at school. Use your words." God knew they certainly had no shortage of them. "That's final."

Malarkey let out a comfortable exhale and shifted to rest his big head in her lap. She gave him a scratch, then frowned at the shedding hair left on her hand. Ah hell. Why not be his pal, even if he were a little gross? She scratched all the way down his back. Her boys were growing up. Would leave home one day, just as they should. And Lorenda was marrying a man who had made her no long-term promises. Malarkey might be the only male in her life that would actually stick around for good.

While Lorenda spent some time with the boys, Mitchell caught up to Talmadge at his office on Main Street. He pulled open the glass door that read "Talmadge Oaks—Environmental Architect. Building Clean & Green." There were a lot of things Mitchell had taken the blame for without setting the record straight. Setting fire to a friend's community building project wasn't going to be one of them.

The bell tinkled, and Talmadge emerged from the back room.

"Hey, what's up?" Talmadge held out a hand for a handshake, and the angry hornet's nest in Mitchell's stomach settled.

"Thanks for taking my call." Mitchell shook his hand. "Sorry to bother you on a Sunday."

Talmadge waved him to the back office. "No bother. I'm just getting some paperwork in order before tomorrow."

Mitchell followed him into the office and took a seat in front of Talmadge's desk. The office was small but beautifully designed, efficient, and modern.

"I didn't set that fire," Mitchell blurted. He scrubbed a hand across his jaw.

Well, at least he'd gotten that off his chest quickly.

"Never thought for a minute you did." Talmadge plucked a brown bag off the credenza behind him and set it on his desk.

"Really?" Mitchell wasn't sure why he'd been so worried. Even after the fire at Joe's, Talmadge had remained a faithful friend. Maybe Mitchell had been worried because so many others had developed a habit of judging him without hearing his side of a story. Admittedly, that was partially his own fault.

"Really." Talmadge pulled a six-pack from the bag. "I walked down to the market after you called." He popped the tops off of two beers. "The fire at Joe's was an unfortunate accident, but you claimed responsibility and have been paying for it ever since. I know you well enough to know that if you had started the rec-center fire, it would've been an accident too, and you would've fessed up."

Mitchell almost choked on the irony.

They bumped bottles in salute and took a long pull.

"So you and Lorenda," Talmadge said.

Yeah. Him and Lorenda. Not much more he could add to that statement. So he took another drink and nodded.

"Mind if I ask how long you two have been"—Talmadge raised a brow—"you know?"

Mitchell did mind because he and Lorenda hadn't been *you-knowing* at all, but if her plan to get married was going to work, then everyone had to think they were *you-knowing*. "It's a fairly recent development."

"Let me get this straight." Talmadge rubbed his chin with a smart-ass smile on his face. "You're marrying your good buddy Langston's sister, a girl you grew up with and who is also your sister-in-law, and you're the uncle to her two kids?"

Mitchell pursed his lips and nodded. "That about sums it up."

"Is that even legal?" Talmadge needled him. "Because I'm pretty sure that might be illegal in most states. Except Nevada. I doubt much is illegal in Nevada."

"Should I tell you to go to hell now, or after we've finished the six-pack?" Mitchell delivered the barb with a smirk.

"What do both of your parents say about it? It's got to be a little weird with your family history." Talmadge took a big swallow and chuckled.

Weird didn't begin to describe the situation. "We'll work it out." Maybe.

"Here's to recent developments." Talmadge lifted his bottle.

Mitchell finished shooting the breeze with Talmadge and left to find Lorenda and the kids. He walked down Main Street with her parked SUV in sight. The streets were fairly empty since it was getting late, so Mitchell slowed his pace and enjoyed the cooling late-summer climate.

He stopped at a side-street crossing and closed his eyes for a second, breathing the crisp, clean air into his lungs. It was good to be home.

His eyes popped open, because he couldn't remember thinking of Red River as home since he was a kid. The few times he'd come back to visit while on leave, he'd been revved to leave again within a few days. Or hours.

It was different this time. He was different. And Lorenda and the boys had a lot to do with him feeling more grounded and connected to Red River than ever before.

A Jeep full of teenagers slowed as they passed him, rolled down a window, and shouted, "Jerk!" at him.

Too bad his contentment with being back in Red River wasn't mutual.

He crossed the street and rounded the corner of the historic business district, which brought him to the edge of Brandenburg Park. He slowed to scan the area until he found Lorenda sitting under a tree while Jaycee and Trevor played with Malarkey across the park under the gazebo.

He headed straight for her, passing a few families and couples in the park. He nodded to each, and every single group snubbed him in return.

He drew in a gritty breath.

"Hey." He eased on to the cool grass next to Lorenda. Knees bent, he balanced a forearm over each knee and watched the boys.

"Hey yourself." Lorenda's long, slender legs were stretched out in front of her and crossed at the ankles. She leaned back with both arms braced against the ground.

"How'd they take it?" Mitchell asked, nodding at the boys.

"They're thrilled." She stared at the boys with a wistful look. A gentle breeze shifted a strand of silky hair across her lips, and Mitchell wanted to brush it away. "I think they like you better than me."

He chuckled. "No, they don't, Sparky. They just missed out on getting to know their dad, and now I'm the next best thing." He shrugged. "Or so they think."

"When did you become an expert on kids?" she asked.

"Last night. I read an article online." He winked at her, and she swatted his shoulder.

"Seriously." She turned a soft, almost sad expression on him. "How are you so good with them when you've never had kids?"

Mitchell figured she was comparing the way Mitchell interacted with the boys to Cam's complete lack of interest.

He let his gaze wander over her face. Her creamy skin, deep-blue eyes, and slender neck. And those lips. Pink. Plump. Perfect. He leaned into her, his shoulder brushing hers, and the pulse where her neck met her shoulder quickened.

"I was a boy once. I figure treating them like I wanted to be treated by my dad is a good strategy."

She swallowed. "Not everyone figures that out, yet you make it sound so simple."

"You make being a parent look easy, Sparky, but I know it's not." His voice went hoarse.

She lifted a shoulder. "I'm too much of a softie. I'll admit it."

"You're tougher than you think." Her lips formed a subtle curve, and Mitchell went back to eying her mouth. A mouth like that was worthy of a few fantasies. "If you weren't, they wouldn't be such great kids."

Her lips parted, and she leaned in. Just a breath away, the loose curls that framed her face grazed his cheek. Just before their lips touched, his phone rang.

She shot to her feet, brushing off the back of her jeans. "I'll go round up the crew. We should go home and do homework before it gets too late."

Mitchell pulled his phone from his pocket, and Allen Carson's number popped onto the screen. He waited for the voice mail to beep, then listened while Lorenda met the boys at the gazebo. Malarkey jumped on her, and she actually gave him a hug instead of her usual barely-a-touch pat on the head.

Allen's message started with a cuss-out session. Then he turned serious. "Come on, Lawson. A guy like you can't stay still for long, especially in that small Podunk town you're from. No one is better suited for this job than you, so get your head out of your ass and get back to work so you can stay out of trouble."

Precisely why Lorenda had insisted they get married. To keep him out of trouble.

If they were in a bigger city where law enforcement consisted of more than one overworked sheriff, their plan would've likely already been outed. In Red River, there wasn't much the understaffed sheriff's office could do.

The crummy thing was, Mitchell was letting Lorenda do it, even though there wasn't much in it for her. Seemed like a Lawson family trait. He shouldn't. He just couldn't bring himself to hurt his mother and cause his father's health to go further downhill. And Mitchell sure wasn't ready to walk away from Lorenda. Not yet, when she might still be in danger. Even though walking away was exactly what he should do.

Chapter Fourteen

In Red River, the line between gossip and truth often got muddled. When the last school bell rang on Monday and only half of the folding chairs for the music program filled, Lorenda knew the rumor mill had already tried and convicted Mitchell. She might as well have put on her prison orange too because she was about to marry him.

Hence, the empty chairs. She needed to find a way to inspire confidence in the parents so they'd let their kids stay in the program.

"Okay, kids." She gave them a dazzling smile of assurance from behind her director's stand, which she so did not feel. "Let's close the gaps and form a tighter group."

While the kids stacked the empty chairs to the side and rearranged their seats and stands, Andrea came over with her eyes glued to the floor. "My mom said I might not be able to stay in the band."

At this rate, Lorenda wouldn't have to worry about a place for rehearsals. The entire adolescent orchestra would fit in the bathroom by the end of the week.

"Tell you what, hon." Lorenda put a hand on Andrea's shoulder. "Let's practice our hearts out today, and then you go home and tell your parents that a professional musician is going to be helping out from now on."

Sierra. There was only one professional musician in town, and Dylan McCoy had already given her a resounding no.

"And tell your parents that we'll likely be getting better equipment soon because a conductor from a big city symphony is so excited about this program that he plans to sponsor us."

Ouch. That would be news to Daniel Summerall. His sponsorship was a big *if* and depended on the concert. Which was already falling apart. A band concert would be a little difficult if there were no students left to perform.

Plus, Lorenda was getting way too good at manipulating the truth. And for a second, she saw how easily it had been for Cameron to slip into that pattern of covering his ass. It was easier than disappointing people. "So chin up, okay? We've got a few weeks to practice for our concert, and then everyone will see how great this program is."

They rehearsed "Hot Cross Buns" until a dull throb started behind one of Lorenda's eyes. Principal Wilkinson walked in and stood at the back of the gym. Wearing a short-sleeved dress shirt and a tie that she would swear was clipped on, he crossed both arms and waited.

Aaaand the throb escalated to a full-blown migraine that seared the center of her brain like someone had jabbed her in the eye with a hot poker.

"That's it for today, kids. Practice the next song in your book for our next rehearsal." She released the kids and gathered up her music.

Bart joined her by the bleachers.

"Are Jaycee and Trevor in the Wilderness Scouts meeting?" She stuffed sheet music into a satchel.

He nodded. "I haven't had a lick of trouble with them since our last run-in. I think they're responding to my leadership."

No. They just wanted to go on the campout. For someone whose career centered on children, Bart didn't actually understand much about them.

"Do you really think Mitchell Lawson is the best influence for your boys, Lorenda?" Bart's voice was calm but had an unmistakable edge of concern.

"I'm sure you mean well, Principal Wilkinson."

His lips thinned. "We're friends, Lorenda. Call me Bart."

"Bart." She smiled.

He smiled back.

"Please don't speak that way about my fiancé, especially if my kids are around." She folded up a music stand and stacked it on the bleachers by her purse and satchel.

He stayed quiet for a beat. "I'm afraid I can't allow Mitchell to go on the campout. Word is the fire chief has officially ruled the rec center foul play. Parents don't want their kids around an arsonist."

Lorenda bristled. "He is not an arsonist. He's never been convicted of that or any other crime. In fact, he's a war hero. Does anyone in this town remember that?"

Bart shoved a hand in his pocket. "I've already gotten a few calls from concerned parents." A thin smile formed on his lips. "I'm sure you understand that, when kids are involved, parents become extra cautious."

"Mitchell hasn't even been charged, and he never will be." She hoped and prayed. "Because he didn't do it." She stacked another folded music stand.

"I have a responsibility to the kids going on the campout and their parents. Under the circumstances, it's best for Mitchell not to go. Of course, you could still be a chaperone, and I'll be there to help you." Bart's smile broadened. "We've changed the date to this Saturday. I gave flyers to the boys today with all the information."

Her wedding was the night before. "Not possible, but thanks for offering."

"Jaycee and Trevor are doing so well, it might be nice for you to see how they interact with me and how they follow my lead."

She stacked another music stand and faced him. "I'm getting married Friday night."

"I'm aware." His eyes darkened.

"I know you're trying to help, but I don't think Jaycee and Trevor will be able to go on the campout this year since you've changed the date."

She'd have to take the boys on a separate campout. Right after she kicked her own ass all the way to Nebraska. Now she had to break the news to her boys that they were no longer going camping with the Wilderness Scouts because of her rushed marriage.

Bart's stare was void of emotion.

Something prickled at the back of Lorenda's neck.

Finally his usual friendly smile returned. "The school board isn't sure we can continue to accommodate the music program." He rubbed his jaw. "A shame, seeing as how the rec center's opening will be delayed because of the fire. I'm going to bat for you, though."

She relaxed. "I appreciate that, but you should go to bat for the kids in the program. I'm doing this for them." That wasn't totally true. Teaching music was as much for her as it was for the kids who wanted to learn. That's why she was willing to do it for free.

"Yes, of course. For the kids," he said absently. "Lorenda, I'm just worried about you." He hesitated. "And about Jaycee and Trevor. This marriage is so sudden. Maybe you should take some time to think about it." He shrugged. "Just to make sure your judgment is solid. I'd hate to see you and the boys disappointed."

She gathered up her things from the bleachers. "You're very kind, but I know what I'm doing."

She so did not.

Bart studied her. "Well." He sounded cheerful, but his eyes didn't reflect the same emotion. "I'm sure you do." He took a step back. "If you need to talk. Or need anything at all, you know where to find me." He backed away. "I'll send Jaycee and Trevor to meet you in the parking lot."

Lorenda hurried out to her car, ticking off the mounting list of problems that her decision to marry Mitchell had caused. And *foxtrot*. Bart's concern may be misplaced, but he was right about one thing. Marrying Mitchell might end up disappointing everyone in the end.

———

After the boys piled into the SUV, Lorenda headed over to Cotton-Eyed Joe's. She had the boys sit in a booth, then claimed a stool at the long bar, hoping to convince Dylan McCoy that the after-school music program needed him. That he alone could save it. That little kids in Red River would be starved of the chance to learn music and would remain forever one-dimensional if he didn't help out, and how could any real musician allow that to happen?

Okay, so that approach might've been a little dramatic, but Lorenda was desperate. And she wasn't beneath playing the guilt card if it meant saving the music program. The program itself could open a whole new world to the kids of Red River.

Since it was early afternoon, he was busy drying glasses with a hand towel and cleaning behind the bar to get it ready for the dinner crowd.

"Hey, Dylan." Lorenda forced herself not to chew her lip.

"Hey, Lorenda. Congratulations."

She deposited her hobo-style purse onto the bar along with her phone and keys. "Thanks! I'm really, um, excited, and we're, um, very happy." She couldn't help it. She pulled her lower lip between her teeth and gnawed.

He dried another glass and lined it up with the others. "What's up?"

"I, um . . ." Her eyes squeezed shut, and she lowered her forehead to the bar. She sucked at trying to make people feel guilty. "I need a huge favor. I'm getting married in a few days, and parents are already pulling kids from the music program, and teaching music is my dream, so I thought that you helping might give the parents more confidence in the program, and I promised some of the kids that a professional musician would teach along with me, and that professional musician is you because there isn't anyone else I can go to with the necessary skills and—"

She lifted her head just enough to peek at Dylan. Several creases had formed between his brows, and his boyish grin, which made him look nineteen instead of twenty-nine, was gone.

"And, um, yeah." Her forehead hit the lacquered bar with a thud.

"Anything else?" he asked.

When she straightened, he'd folded both arms across his chest, and a hint of a smile played across his lips.

"Um, no. That just about covers it."

One of his brows raised a notch.

"Okay, so we may not have a place to rehearse after this Friday." Because that's when she and Mitchell were getting married, and the school board was obviously holding that against her at the expense of the kids.

"Did you say hearse?" Minx purred from Lorenda's phone. "I'm sorry for your loss."

Oh for God's sake. Lorenda snatched up the phone and punched the power button.

"I see." Dylan nodded, and Lorenda waited for him to say no. "Sounds like a challenge."

He had no idea.

She slid off the barstool. "Look, I'm sorry to bother you with my problems—"

"Count me in." Dylan flashed a million-dollar smile.

"Seriously?" Because she must've sounded as crazy as the young girls who threw themselves onto the stage while famous rock-and-roll bands played his tunes.

"Seriously," he said, and the smile disappeared. "I've been thinking about your program since you first brought it up. I haven't played or written music in a long time. Maybe teaching kids will bring back the fire."

Lorenda hopped onto the footrest of the bar, pulled Dylan toward her by his shirt, and kissed his cheek.

He cradled his cheek and gave her a teasing look. "I'm never washing my face again."

She rolled her eyes. Dylan was used to young, pretty girls offering him a whole lot more than just a peck on the cheek. "Thanks, Dylan." She hopped down again. "I owe you big."

Lorenda called for the boys. They scrambled out of the booth and followed her as she left with a bounce in her step that hadn't been there before. One problem solved. Only a thousand more to go.

<hr />

"Am I doing the right thing?" Lorenda asked Miranda the next morning after explaining the whole faux-marriage arrangement. A bag of fresh cranberry-pecan scones and four strong cups of coffee from the Ostergaard's Bakery filled Lorenda's real-estate office with a mouthwatering aroma.

The mommy mafia was stopping by to work on the concert. The least Lorenda could do was bribe them with scones and coffee, but she'd asked Miranda to arrive early so they could talk in private.

Besides Mitchell, Miranda was the only person on earth who knew how empty Lorenda's marriage to Cameron had been, and there was no one she trusted more. Her head was telling her that marrying Mitchell was a mistake she might live to regret.

Her heart and her body were shouting something entirely different.

She handed Miranda a cup. "Yours is decaf." Then she spread napkins on top of her desk and pulled the scones from the bag.

Lorenda had kept Cameron's secret about the fire at Joe's. Had kept his coldness and disinterest toward her and the kids quiet. Yes, keeping his secrets had spared her public humiliation, but she'd done it more for the boys, her in-laws, and for a town that worshipped Cameron's memory. It was time for someone to show Mitchell the same compassion and consideration. It seemed that someone had to be her, because no one else was willing.

As reckless as marrying him might be, Mitchell needed someone in his corner. Needed someone to save him from the suffocating web of lies that had started the night he and Cameron had graduated high school and was still threatening to choke the life out of him.

Cameron hadn't stepped up, but Lorenda could. So she'd spent the last twenty minutes spilling the whole mess to Miranda—at least the parts she didn't already know—starting with the night Cameron and Mitchell had graduated.

Miranda's jaw hung open.

Lorenda waved a scone under Miranda's nose, hoping it would shake the glaze from her eyes. Her look remained almost catatonic.

Lorenda held up the scone. "Should I stuff it in your gaping mouth, or do you have something to say? Anything. Yell at me. I don't care, but say something."

"I'm speechless." Miranda reached for the scone.

"Gee, that's so helpful," Lorenda deadpanned. "No wonder you're my bestie."

Miranda bit off a healthy portion, chewed, moaned with pleasure, then washed it down with coffee. "Sounds to me like your mind is already made up."

"I've got everything I've ever wanted." Lorenda sat back in her chair and sunk into the plush leather. "I've created a good life for me and the boys. Structured. Ordered. I've got friends, family, and now a music program." Or at least what was left of it. "Why am I screwing with my own happiness?"

The majority of Red River was giving her the same cold shoulder they'd always given Mitchell, and it hurt. She was starting to understand why Mitchell hadn't come around much, and she was bringing it on herself with a marriage that wasn't even for real. Screwing with her own happiness was an understatement.

Miranda shrugged. "Maybe because there is one important ingredient missing from that recipe for happiness you just named off—love. Since Cam, you've refused to date at all."

"It's not just about me. I have the boys to think about." They were far more sure about her marrying their uncle Mitch than she was. Mitchell, being the stand-up guy that he was, offered to take them all on a family camping trip when he found out they couldn't go with the scouts. That had eased Jaycee and Trevor's disappointment and cemented Mitchell's superhero status.

Since they weren't taking a honeymoon, they were set to go camping at Middle Fork Lake on Saturday. The day after the wedding.

"True, and I admire that. But you also don't want to care about someone, then have them push you away again." Miranda polished off the rest of her scone. "So you've been playing it safe by being alone."

"What's wrong with playing it safe?" Lorenda waggled her chair back and forth.

"Nothing if you want to wake up one day when your kids are grown and realize that you're still alone." Miranda dusted off her hands and took a sip of coffee. "You deserve some companionship too, Lor, and I think you want that companion to be Mitchell." Miranda's eyebrow formed a high arch. "There's certainly enough chemistry between you two."

"Really?" Lorenda said. "I hadn't noticed." She so *had* noticed. She just hadn't realized everyone else was noticing too.

Miranda snorted. "Sure you haven't." She wiped her mouth, wadded the napkin, and aimed at the trash. Sunk it with a swoosh. "The electric charge in the air when you two are together could power this entire town. Maybe that's why you're finally willing to take a risk."

"There's no guarantee he'll want it to be permanent." Lorenda's head fell back and she stared at the ceiling. "The kids and I will both be hurt if and when he leaves once this whole arson mess is cleared up."

"Marry him. Don't marry him. I don't know the right answer, but I do know that you and the kids are already invested. At least if you're married and don't have to make a statement against Mitchell, it might give you more time to see if you do have a future together. By the time the real arsonist is caught, Mitchell may not want to leave Red River." Miranda gave Lorenda a sympathetic smile. "He might want to stay with you." Miranda arched a brow. "Plus, you'd have the benefit of sleeping in the same bed without having to hide it from the kids."

"It won't be like that." Lorenda pulled two more chairs in front of her desk so there would be enough for the rest of the mommy mafia.

Miranda helped her with one of the chairs. "With any luck, it'll be exactly like that. And since you have to keep up appearances, I'm giving you the honeymoon suite at the inn Friday night. Consider it a wedding gift."

"You, Ella, and Ang are already throwing the reception for me at the inn. I can't take advantage." Lorenda settled into her chair again and sipped her coffee.

"You should know you can't argue with a pregnant woman. We always get our way. It's a rite of passage because of what pregnancy does to our bodies. End of discussion." Miranda took a seat, rubbing her baby bump.

As if on cue, Ella and Angelique tapped on the glass door once, then threw it open.

"Oh God." Ella closed her eyes and breathed deep. "Tell me that's decaf, so I can have some. Otherwise I might commit a violent crime."

Angelique pushed past her and stared at the cups and bag from the bakery. "I'd offer to represent you, but I might need to get my own attorney if whatever smells so good isn't for me."

"I'd be scared not to get enough for all of you." Lorenda passed out the coffee and handed them each a scone.

Lorenda tried to shift gears and concentrate on the preparations for the concert by getting out a list of items they needed to cover. But the benefits Miranda had just been talking about had Lorenda's mouth watering far more than the scones and coffee. The possibility . . . the anticipation of sharing a bed with Mitchell every night and waking up with him every morning was the very thing that would make it even harder when their temporary arrangement came to an end.

Chapter Fifteen

"I'm not changing my mind, Dad." Lorenda and her father waited in the foyer of the Red River Lutheran church for the wedding march to begin. She wanted to get through this as quickly as possible before she really did change her mind.

"All I'm saying, sweet pea, is my car is parked right out front." Her dad gave her a peck on the cheek.

Langston came over and wrapped her in a bear hug. "You look pretty, sis."

She pulled him to a corner for privacy, and slipped the ruby ring off her finger. "Can you give this to Mitchell? He'll need a ring to put on my finger."

Langston frowned. "He didn't get you a ring?"

"Um . . ." Probably not since it was a rushed faux wedding, but she couldn't very well say so to Langston. "It all happened so fast that he may not have had time to go shopping. Just take it to him, okay?"

Langston took the ring and left to find Mitchell.

Lorenda rejoined her father and picked at the white lilies in her bridal bouquet, the fresh scent drifting up to settle her nerves. She spun the titanium wedding band she'd gotten Mitchell around her thumb, the steel gray a stark contrast to the white lilies.

Lorenda's first wedding had been extravagant. This time around she'd kept it simple with a bouquet, a pianist to play "Here Comes the Bride," and a new stylish cream halter dress that revealed more cleavage and thigh than Lorenda was used to.

What the hell? A girl only got married the second time once.

She held back a snort and tried to get a grip.

At least her parents were being reasonable enough to give her away. After the near riot over her wedding announcement finally subsided.

Her mother ran over. "It's not too late. I can still make an announcement that the wedding has been cancelled."

Aaaand, so much for being reasonable.

"Mom," Lorenda said under her breath.

"Oh, alright," her mom huffed. "I just don't see any reason to rush into things. You and Mr. Summerall have so much in common; I think you should give him more of a chance." She studied her nails.

That was never good.

"*Mom*? What have you done?"

Her mother adjusted her corsage. "I may have hinted that you wanted him to ask you out."

"Mother!" Lorenda whisper-hissed.

"Well, why *are* you rushing things with Mitchell?" her mother complained. "Is it so you can have sex? Because you know it's the twenty-first century."

Her dad stepped away and started to hum.

"Really, sweetheart." Her mom leaned in. "Have intercourse with him. You have my permission, but don't get married until the accusations against him are . . . um, cleared up one way or the other."

Lorenda's eyes slid shut. Someone should put her out of her misery.

"And don't marry him just because he looks good." Her mom glanced at her father pacing on the far end of the foyer and dropped her voice. "Looks don't last forever. Someday he'll look like your father."

Before Lorenda could respond to her meddling, matchmaking mother, Langston reappeared and drew her into another hug. He pressed the ruby ring into her palm so their parents wouldn't notice and whispered in her ear. "Mitchell said he's got it covered."

Her pulsed spiked. He'd gotten her a wedding ring?

"Got to go find a seat," Langston said.

She slid the ruby onto her finger. The right hand this time.

The piano struck its first cords and the rest happened in a blur, like Lorenda was floating through a dream that was happening to someone else. Her parents walked her down the aisle with her friends, the faithful few who were still speaking to her, looking on. With teary eyes and a croaky voice, her dad gave her away again, this time to Mitchell. The reverend spoke. A lot. But the words seemed to run together, because a current of anticipation pulsed through the air around Lorenda and Mitchell until her insides were as hot as a humming teakettle and her ears buzzed.

Mitchell looked down where her hand rested on his forearm. For a few perfect moments, the reverend, the soft music, and the audience melted away and it was just her and Mitchell. She followed his stare and found that her fingertips were gently stroking the white twill fabric of his dress shirt. His gaze drifted to hers and flooded with something so sweet, so sexy, that it almost made Lorenda believe the whole pretense was real.

A few songs played during the short, informal ceremony, she repeated the vows when the reverend cued her, and before she knew it, she was placing the steel-gray ring on Mitchell's finger. Just like him, it was made of strong, hard stuff and looked super badass.

When it was Mitchell's turn, he pulled an elegant wedding band from the breast pocket of his shirt. The diamonds, set into brushed platinum, glittered under the dim, nuanced lighting. Lorenda's gaze shot to his, and the corner of his mouth curved as he slid the ring onto her finger.

It was exquisite. He'd gone to a lot of trouble for a wedding ring that represented a farce.

He repeated after the reverend, and his deep, throaty voice rumbled through her and settled in the most delicious spot. The fire in his eyes as he spoke those vows sent the same fiery heat ricocheting through her chest and her mind and her girl parts. Then it penetrated her heart and she knew she was lost, because she wanted to believe his words more than she'd ever wanted to believe anything.

The ring in place, he caressed her finger with his thumb. Gently brushed back and forth with feathery strokes.

Lorenda's throat closed, because Mitchell didn't seem the least bit scared or uncertain. He seemed . . . choked up.

"I now pronounce you husband and wife." The reverend grinned. "You may kiss your bride."

His words startled her, and her lips parted as Mitchell took her in his arms and laid the softest, most sensual kiss on her. Nothing else had ever compared. At that moment, standing at the altar in his arms, she couldn't remember why marrying him couldn't be real, when nothing had felt more so.

"Kiss the bride!" Langston yelled as soon as Mitchell and Lorenda sliced into the wedding cake in the dining room of the Bea in the Bonnet Inn.

Oh yeah, Mitchell definitely wanted to kiss the bride. All over. Because that kiss on the altar had unlocked something deep inside him that he'd thought was long gone. Emotions were a tricky thing, and his had been bubbling to the surface lately. Mitchell wasn't sure how to deal with that. Wasn't sure he wanted to deal with it, especially since those emotions threatened to erupt once he'd seen her walking down the aisle to him in that fucking dress that he wanted to peel off one stitch at a time.

The fact that she'd looked at him like she really wanted to see him naked too didn't hurt either.

A few camera flashes went off from the small group that gathered around the table, and he slid an arm around Lorenda's slender waist to pose for the camera phones pointing at them. Her hand lay on top of his, keeping the knife firmly in the cake. He supposed she'd done this before and knew the ropes, so he followed her lead. When she snuggled into his side, he wanted to moan. Her silky hair was up in one of those elegant knots at the nape of her neck. Loose curls framed her face and brushed her bare shoulders right where Mitchell wanted to put his lips. And his tongue. Definitely the tongue.

His new mother-in-law stood with an arm around both Trevor and Jaycee. She tried to mask her disapproval with a smile, which only made her face look more pinched. Charlotte Brooks had been good to Cam, but Mitchell couldn't blame a mom for looking out for her only daughter. Lorenda could do better than marrying a suspect in an arson investigation.

Mrs. Brooks led Jaycee and Trevor over to flank them for a family picture. Lorenda stepped in when they pushed each other for the spot closest to Mitchell.

And that nearly ripped Mitchell's heart in half. If the look on Lorenda's face was any indication, he'd guess her guilt was tearing into her heart too because her expression said, *what have we done?* Her soft body stiffened like a plank of wood at his side.

He caressed her hip, his fingertips sliding over the smooth, delicate fabric like it was glass. Her tense gaze found his, and he wanted to kiss the worry away.

He wasn't exactly sure why he'd agreed to the whole thing, except now that he had, he wanted to take things further with Lorenda. If he had to be honest with himself, he wanted to stick around and see if the bond they'd developed would lead to something more. Like maybe a future with him a part of this family for real and not just an occasional stop-in to take the boys fishing or a weekly Skype conversation from a war-torn country.

Not to mention that he wanted to explore the attraction that zinged between him and Lorenda every time they were in the same room together. At the moment, the lust swirling around them was so thick he could probably cut it with the fancy cake knife someone had slapped into his hand.

Mrs. Brooks called the boys away after everyone seemed to be satisfied with their photos.

"Step up and take your medicine," Talmadge said. "I want to see wedding cake on your face." The rest of the men laughed.

Lorenda seemed to know the drill. She took the knife and cut off a small slice of cake. She handed it to him, and her lush lips parted, pink lipstick shimmering under the antique chandelier.

A thrilling rush of heat scored his insides.

"Mitchell," she whispered, and the rush of heat went straight to his groin as her lips moved. "Put it in my mouth."

Holy shit. Mitchell nearly lost it right then and there.

She took his hand and guided the cake to her mouth. Took a bite, and then licked her pouty pink lips.

She cut another slice and held it up for him to taste. He took in the whole piece of sugary heaven and swallowed. Before she could pull her hand away, he grabbed her wrist just like she'd done and guided her fingers to his lips. He had no idea what possessed him, except maybe pure, unchecked lust, but the moment was so perfect, so potent, that he couldn't let it just end.

Slowly, he wrapped his lips around one of her long, slender fingers and suckled the icing off. Those perfect lips parted again, and she drew in a sharp breath that communicated her surprise. Her eyes, on the other hand, clearly showed her excitement.

So he moved on to the next frosting-covered fingertip and did the same.

As his tongue smoothed over her finger, the tip of her tongue slipped out to trace the seam of her lips like it was a reflex she wasn't aware of. The muscles under the creamy skin of her neck worked as she swallowed, and her eyes dilated.

One of their guests let out a low whistle that said they were putting on a show.

Were they ever. In more ways than one.

His buddies cheered him on, and some of the women awwed. Lorenda blinked several times, fast and sharp like she was blinking away a mesmerizing fantasy.

Mitchell wondered if it was the same fantasy he was having.

And didn't that just make him a contender for the Asshole of the Year Award? He glanced around the small circle of friends that he and Lorenda had left. He'd stayed in Red River to protect Lorenda. Instead, he'd just made her situation worse. Her marriage to him had caused her to lose support from most of Red River, along with its sheriff—the one person who really could help her.

His father's absence and the very small crowd in attendance were proof that she was guilty by association. And no matter how much misplaced blame Mitchell had willingly shouldered in the past, he really was to blame for the tough spot Lorenda and the kids were in.

He had a chest full of medals that meant nothing to him. But somehow being the front-runner for the Asshole of the Year Award meant everything, especially if his help ended up hurting her in the long run.

Lorenda stepped out of the honeymoon suite bathroom to spend her first night as a newly married woman wearing one of her more conservative gowns—a silk floral number with spaghetti straps and a matching robe that tied at the waist. She'd considered wearing sweats since she'd be sleeping with a man who couldn't enjoy her taste in lingerie. But old sweats weren't exactly how she wanted to spend her wedding night, faux marriage or not.

Only a French boudoir lamp lit the cozy room from a bedside table, casting a rich glow across the quilt-covered four-poster bed, the vintage wood floor, and the lovely man who relaxed on the antique fainting couch. Eyes closed, hands laced behind his head, and legs crossed at the ankles, Mitchell still wore black dress pants that molded to solid, muscled thighs. His shoes were kicked off, and his shirt was untucked and unbuttoned halfway down his incredible mouthwatering chest, which rose and fell in steady, even breaths.

She crept across to the bed, trying not to wake him, but a board creaked under her foot, and he stirred.

"Toss me a blanket, Sparky." He nodded to the quilt that was folded at the end of the bed. "I'll sleep here."

She ran her fingers over the soft, worn quilt made into a double wedding ring pattern from lavender, moss-green, and pale-yellow fabric. "Mitchell, you can't possibly get comfortable on that thing. You're too tall for it."

"I've slept in far worse conditions. I'll be fine." His stare grazed down her entire length, and her nipples gave a sharp salute.

She sighed. Always the stand-up guy. He obviously couldn't help himself. "Your feet already hang off the end, and you're not even lying down." She walked around to the other side of the bed and pulled back the fluffy covers. "You're not on a mission. Plus, I'll feel guilty if you're uncomfortable all night. It's a big bed; you can have that side. I'll stay way over here." She patted her side of the overstuffed mattress.

With a deep, ragged exhale, Mitchell got up and worked the rest of the buttons until his shirt fell open and the light glinted off his dog tags. His rock-hard abs were drool-worthy, and her gaze followed the thin line of dark hair that disappeared under the waistband of his pants.

"Is my fly unzipped?"

Her stare snapped to his. Laughter, and maybe a little pride, glittered in his eyes.

"Um, no." Unfortunately. But the view was just fine as it was. Heat climbed up her neck and settled in the tips of her ears. She whirled around and discarded her robe, then slid between the sheets.

Mitchell shrugged out of his shirt while Lorenda stared at the ceiling and tried not to look. Until the sound of his fly unzipping for real made it impossible not to look.

And oh. My. Lord. The man was freaking gorgeous. Every inch of him. Of course she already knew that, but getting a bird's-eye view of all that skin and rippling hotness was like sitting on the front row of a Chippendales show . . . not that she'd ever been to a Chippendales show. But good God, this had to be better, because when his pants slid to the floor, revealing very nice, very formfitting boxer briefs, Lorenda was tempted to stuff a twenty in the elastic waistband. Or tug them off with her teeth.

Asking him to sleep in the same bed without climbing all over him may have been an overcommitment.

When he reached under the fringed lampshade to switch off the light, his crown-of-thorns tattoo flexed and flowed with the movement.

The light went out and Mitchell climbed into bed, the mattress dipping under his weight. They both lay in the darkness with only the gleam of moonlight filtering through the lace curtains.

Mitchell threaded his hands behind his head again, but he wasn't asleep. Or even relaxed anymore. Tension flowed off of him as much as it did her.

Finally, he said, "Why didn't you ever go back to school to finish your teaching degree?"

Mmmmkay. That one took her by surprise. "I had my hands full raising two boys alone. I figured I would when the time was right." She shrugged and snuggled deeper into the plush pillow-top mattress. "The time was never right, I guess."

"It's not too late. You could still go back to college. You were half done with your degree when you quit, right?"

True. But it was a dream she'd had to let go, and now it seemed like it would be too hard to make it work.

"Real estate pays well. I've never had to worry too much about making ends meet for me and the boys." It wasn't her dream job, but she had never been in a position to be choosy.

"You're so gifted, Sparky." He rolled onto his side. "Seems a waste of God-given talent."

"That's why the music program is so important to me. I don't want it to become another unrealized goal like my college education. If I don't start it now, I may never get around to it. Or worse, if I have to shut down the program before I can really get it off the ground, then I'll never get it started again."

Except for the pounding of her heart, his easy breaths were the only sound for a few moments.

"I'm sorry our friendship is making it harder for you."

She let her head roll to the side so she could look at his shadowed face.

Friendship. Is that what it was? Because she hadn't made a habit of exchanging rings or wedding vows with any of her other friends, and she sure didn't fantasize about them, dream about them, or share a bed with them.

"Mom said some of the parents pulled their kids."

Thank you, Becky. Lorenda hadn't planned to mention that some parents had lost confidence in her because of her decision to marry Mitchell. As important as the music program was to her, she hadn't lost confidence in him.

She angled onto her side to face him. "The parents will come around." She hoped. "Enough about me. Tell me something about you I don't already know."

He chuckled. "What do you want to know, Sparky? I'm not that interesting."

Like hell. That was like saying he wasn't absurdly good-looking.

She rose onto an elbow and rested her temple against an open palm. "You're more interesting than you think, especially to someone like me who hasn't traveled much. You've seen places most people only dream of."

His laugh rang hollow. "I've seen places no one should have to see."

She couldn't help but reach out and touch his bicep, tracing the thorny pattern with the tip of one finger. The air around them grew thick and sultry.

"What does the tattoo mean?"

His breaths quickened. "What makes you think it has a meaning?"

"Because Cameron had one too. Just like yours. I didn't know about it until . . . well, after."

Just when Lorenda had given up hope that he would answer, he said, "When we were kids, we'd play-fight with swords. We tied towels around our necks for capes and wove branches into crowns. We were kings defending our kingdoms." He blew out a gusty sigh, and Lorenda knew he was smiling at the memory. Could hear the warmth of fond memories in his tone. "One time we got into Mom's prize-winning rose garden and cut off some of the longer branches."

"Oh my." Becky protected her roses like a momma grizzly protected her cubs.

"You got that right." Mitchell laughed. "After she finished doling out enough hard labor as punishment to make the Gulag look like a nursery school, she told us we should be ashamed." His voice grew wistful. "Cameron *was* ashamed for disappointing her."

"And you?" Lorenda's finger trekked in the opposite direction and followed another bramble.

"Not in the least. I figured they'd grow back, so I brushed it off and found some new trouble to get into."

This time she chuckled.

"Cameron and I met up for a weekend during his last tour. We tied one on and ended up at a tattoo parlor with an artist smoking opium from a hookah and a trained monkey who spit peanuts out of its butt."

She pushed Mitchell's arm playfully. "It so did not."

He grabbed her hand. "I swear it really did." Laughter threaded through his words, and he drew her hand to his lips and kissed it like it was the most natural thing in the world.

A shiver ricocheted through her.

His kiss must've been a knee-jerk reaction because, just as fast, he tried to push her hand away. She wouldn't let him.

He fell silent for a beat.

"When Cameron saw this design he wanted it. He brought up that incident when we were kids and said the crown of thorns was symbolic for outcasts like us who give up so much to save others and suffer rejection and shame for it. It's the reason we have a hard time coming home to normal life again."

And Lorenda knew they weren't just talking about normal life anymore. Cameron had been talking about life with her and the kids. A life he couldn't comprehend anymore.

For the first time, she realized Cameron might not have been rejecting her and the kids. Maybe he felt like the one being rejected because Lorenda couldn't relate to what he'd been through.

"I was too young to understand that war changes a person. I expected him to slide right back into his old role." She could see it now that she had more experience in life. "How should I have helped him?"

Mitchell exhaled again. "I don't know, Sparky. We all handle it differently. Cam was a people pleaser. He cared a lot about what people thought of him. I don't think he expected to feel like a monster for doing a job that earned him medals."

Cameron had been the golden child, set high on a pedestal by his parents, Lorenda, and most of Red River. Lorenda couldn't imagine how

Cam had felt, coming home where everyone might see that he'd fallen off that pedestal and had hit the ground hard.

"And you?" Her fingertips brushed over the tattoo again. "Does rejection and what people think of you really bother you so little? Especially when their low opinions are based on incorrect information." Lorenda doubted he brushed it off as easily as he pretended.

"I was already used to being the screwup, so the things I had to do as a soldier didn't affect me as much as Cam."

She pressed her hand to his chest and flattened it over his heart. The rhythmic beat pulsed into her palm. Her mind said to back away, but her body ignored the command and leaned into him until their lips were just a breath apart. "I'm sorry for both you and Cam."

His fingertips found her cheek. Caressed along her jawline, and his thumb smoothed over her bottom lip. A prickle of anticipation raced through her. "I'm sorry for Cam too. He missed out on the best thing of his life." His words whispered over her, and her skin pebbled.

But instead of dipping his head to kiss her, he tugged her hand from his chest and dropped a soft kiss at her fingertips.

"Get some sleep, Sparky." His voice had gone flat like he'd flipped the emotion switch to off. "We've got a couple days of camping ahead of us, and roughing it in the woods doesn't seem like your style. Rest will do you good."

He rolled away. Her heart beat in a sickly rhythm. Because Mitchell wasn't the first Lawson man to climb into bed with her as though she were a stranger and leave her staring at his back.

Chapter Sixteen

Mitchell spotted for Trevor and then Jaycee as they dove into Middle Fork Lake the next day. Jaycee's head broke the surface and the three of them treaded water.

"Do Mom! Do Mom!" Jaycee shouted.

Mitchell sputtered out lake water.

He totally wanted to do Lorenda. So badly that he had to hold on to the dock for a second to stop from inhaling a lungful of water when Trevor joined his brother for another shout of "do Mom!"

"Your mom is still changing into her swimsuit." Mitchell tried to change the subject to stop thinking about doing Lorenda, but then his stupid male brain started fantasizing about her taking off her clothes in the tent. Right that very moment.

Spending the entire night in bed with Lorenda without being able to touch her had been agonizing. Not exactly how he'd pictured spending his wedding night. After all the *camping* he'd done in the military, he hadn't pictured spending his honeymoon in a tent either.

Then again, Lorenda obviously didn't want the "real deal." Trying to provide her own wedding ring even after she'd bought one for him was proof of that.

At least it was a beautiful little lake surrounded by giant pines and willowy aspens, and just small enough that a strong swimmer could swim across. Mitchell's only request was no phones and no electronics. He wanted the boys to enjoy the experience the way he and Cam had growing up.

"Boys, see that buoy?" He pointed to the center of the lake. "Your dad and I used to race to it when we were your age."

Trevor and Jaycee stared at it in awe.

At that moment, the joy of Mitchell's carefree youth and the special bond he'd had with his brother came rushing at him. The good memories of what a great person Cam had been in spite of his mistakes.

Mitchell had made so many of his own, he couldn't throw stones. Especially not at Cam. Maybe Mitchell could pay Lorenda's help forward by giving the boys a little part of their father. By helping them get to know who Cam really had been before war had morphed him.

Jaycee kept staring at the buoy like he was trying to imagine his father. "Can we race to it now, Uncle Mitch?"

"Let's wait for your mom," Mitchell said.

"What's taking her so long?" Trevor was getting impatient.

"Ladies need a little more time than us guys do, and we've got her seriously outnumbered, so give her a break." Mitchell splashed the kids to keep them occupied, and they shrieked.

Trevor obviously couldn't wrap his little mind around why women were so different from men, so he yelled, "Mom! Come on. Uncle Mitch wants to do you!"

Lorenda darted out of the tent wearing a black bikini that gave Mitchell a boner right there in a mountain glacier lake. He forced himself to wave casually, and her stance relaxed. She turned around to grab a collapsible camping chair and a book, dropped the book, and then bent over to pick it up.

And sweet Jesus, he redefined the phrase *pitching a tent.*

Malarkey barked at the edge of the lake, unable to work up the courage to jump in, and Lorenda walked to the end of the pier to get comfortable, the dainty bows at each side of her swimsuit bottom moving with the sway of her hips.

"Mom!" Trevor yelled. "Watch! Uncle Mitch taught us to dive." He scrambled up the ladder that attached to one side of the pier and dove off headfirst. Mitchell spotted for him, and after a few seconds his little head popped out of the water.

A crinkle appeared over her brows. "Is it deep enough to dive?"

"It's way over my head," Mitchell assured her.

"Mom!" Jaycee hollered. "Let Uncle Mitch do you!"

Her face went up in flames along with the patch of skin between her breasts, which was revealed by the plunging neckline of the swim top that tied behind her slender neck.

Mitchell couldn't hold back a grin. He'd definitely love to do Lorenda. Turning away from her in bed to hide his obvious attraction had been the only way to keep his hands from pulling the thin silky straps off her shoulders, kissing every inch of her creamy skin, and making love to her until she moaned his name during one of the many orgasms he'd wanted to give her.

Because, hell yes, he'd laid awake most of the night fantasizing about each one.

"This is a family camping trip, Sparky, so come get in the water."

The boys cheered, and Malarkey loped down the pier to be closer to them.

Lorenda ignored them all with a smile, slid a sexy pair of glamorous sunglasses off her head and onto her nose, and opened her book.

"Okay, boys, swim over to the bank and rest for five minutes, then swim back," Mitchell said.

They splashed off, and Malarkey doubled back along the pier to follow them.

"Hey, you," Mitchell said to Lorenda.

She lifted her nose in the air and pretended not to listen.

So he splashed her with water, at which point she pulled her sunglasses down a notch to glare over the top like a movie star.

He laughed. "Yeah, you, with the small bikini and the big attitude."

One of her silky golden brows lifted.

"Come get in the water."

"Do I know you?" she asked.

Treading water with one arm, he scratched his chin thoughtfully. "I'm pretty sure you're the one that gave me this last night." He held up his left hand and thumbed the smoky gray band until it circled his finger.

She ignored him.

Since she was being so difficult, he decided to give her a taste of her own medicine. He lowered his voice so the boys couldn't hear. "Plus, I've seen you naked, so, yeah, I think we've met."

Her eyes widened. "That was an accident! I slipped and dropped my towel."

Yes, Lorenda dropping her towel in his bathroom had been an accident, but every contour and curve of her lush body was burned into his memory for all eternity. He shrugged. "Still saw you in the buff."

She pushed her glasses back up. "I'd rather read." She crossed one long leg over the other, and Mitchell's mouth turned to cotton. "And I'm not one of your subordinates that you can order around." Her foot started to kick like she was nervous, but her lips twitched like she was holding back a smile.

"Really? Because I distinctly remember you promising to honor and obey me just yesterday. And I was smart enough to bring along witnesses, so jump in. I'll catch you."

"I don't want to get my hair wet." She twirled a blonde lock around one finger. "There's no plug for my hair dryer." Her foot kicked faster. "I'll just read and soak up some sun while you boys swim. I could even read out loud so you can enjoy the story too."

She held up her book to block him from view. "The brutish knight, hardened from years on the battlefield, thought himself a near god and expected everyone should jump to do his bidding with a mere snap of his calloused fingers." She read like one of his teachers from high school.

"Your book's upside down," he said.

"Is not," she said around the side of the book. But slowly turned the book right side up and continued her invented story with a clear of her throat. "But the intelligent princess refused to bend to the brute's will."

"Get. In. The water."

"Aren't you tired yet? You've been treading water for a long time." Her voice lost that teacher's edge. "Maybe you should take a break."

"Sweetheart, I had to tread water for a lot longer than this to become a SEAL. In BUD/S training they tied our hands and feet together and threw us in water over our heads."

Obviously Cameron had never shared the details with her because her lips rounded into a shocked *O*.

"Isn't the water cold?"

"As ice," he said. "It'll get your blood pumping and give you lots of energy." Too bad all of his blood was pumping to the same spot.

"So you enjoy torturing innocent women, then?"

She was joking, but that one still stung. "The media would have you believe so, but no, I actually don't get off on torturing innocent women and children." He braced both arms on the pier's edge and hauled himself out. Her lips parted as her gaze took in his every movement.

He had to admit that he liked it. Liked her attention on him. Liked that she obviously liked what she saw, because the tip of her tongue slipped out to wet her bottom lip and her cheeks pinked even more.

"I do, however, enjoy torturing my new wife." He took his time walking toward her so she could get an eyeful. "Especially when she's too prissy to get her hair wet."

"No!" She closed the book and pointed a finger at him. "You stay away from me."

He shook his head and gave her a cocky smile. "No can do, sweetheart. If you wanted to be left alone, you should've married one of those Air Force lackeys."

She shrieked when he gathered her into his arms and lifted her out of the chair like she was a feather. Her book clattered onto the wood planks, and she pulled off the glasses and tossed them onto the chair.

And holding her against him in that skimpy bikini that showed off legs that stretched from here to heaven and a body just as divine—even after two kids—didn't help the stiffening going on beneath his trunks.

"Cover your nose, darlin'." He walked to the end of the pier.

She shrieked again but clamped a fist over her nose.

Jaycee and Trevor splashed back into the lake screaming, "Uncle Mitch is doing Mom!"

Mitchell jumped in with Lorenda still in his arms, and those long, sexy legs and arms went in every direction. When he came up, she'd managed to keep the top of her head dry, but water starred her lashes and she gasped for air while wrapping herself around him.

Nice.

Her silky skin smoothed against his and made the water seem much warmer than it had a few minutes ago.

"Happy now?" Her tone was huffy.

Thoughtfully, he studied the dry top of her head. "No." He dunked her under the water just enough to douse all of her hair this time, and she came up sputtering.

"Now I'm happy."

She splashed him, and he laughed. Held up his hand to block the spray of water.

"You're not a frogman, you're a toad." She ran a hand over her face to shunt off the wetness. Her tone was irritated, but she wrapped both arms around his neck again and hung on so he could keep both of them afloat.

Super nice.

Jaycee and Trevor reached them and splashed around, trying to get Malarkey to jump in.

"They're good swimmers," Mitchell said.

She nodded. "I took them to lessons every summer. They swim like fish." She locked gazes with him, the blue of her eyes even deeper in the bright afternoon sun. Her starred lashes shimmered.

"Or like frogmen," Mitchell said.

Her expression went serious. "I hope not. I'm a mother. I don't want that life for them."

"I hope not too, Sparky." His voice sobered as much as hers.

His gaze raked over her face, and he wanted to kiss that sweet mouth.

"Okay, frogman, I'm in the water. Take me for a swim."

He turned so she could latch onto him from behind. "Let's go, boys. Last one to the buoy is a rotten airman."

And damned if it didn't make his chest expand that they really did act like his family, welcoming him in like he finally belonged. His only regret was that it wasn't for real.

———

Lorenda pulled on a warm change of clothes and left the tent to see if Mitchell and the kids wanted to eat the picnic she'd packed. Mitchell wasn't kidding when he said the icy water in the high mountain lake was rejuvenating. Of course, it hadn't felt all that cold while she was rubbing up against him. That felt pretty hot. But as soon as she'd climbed up onto the pier, her teeth had nearly chattered right out of her mouth.

When she stepped out of the large tent that could hold all four of them, Mitchell and the kids had changed into fresh clothes too. They stood at the edge of the lake, the kids and dog flanking Mitchell as he stared through a pair of binoculars.

"What's up?" She walked up behind them.

He moved so that she could wedge in next to him, kept staring across the lake with narrowed eyes, and handed her the binoculars. "The Wilderness Scouts. I thought they were camping along the river above Bobcat Pass."

She took the binoculars and brought the bustling campsite across the lake into focus. "That's what the flyer the boys brought home said. Must've changed the location."

She lowered the binoculars. Trevor was close to tears, and Jaycee, a little older and more mature, just looked disappointed. She couldn't blame them. They'd wanted to camp with their friends. It hadn't seemed like such a blow when she told them Uncle Mitch was taking them on a family campout. But with the troop right under their noses, in full view, the boys were probably feeling left out.

"Only one person could make that decision." Mitchell hooked both thumbs in the pockets of his jeans and kept staring, his expression darkening.

Right. The troop leader. But Bart wouldn't have done something so callous on purpose. It wasn't his style.

"Funny he moved the location here. Where probably everybody in Red River knew we'd be camping," Mitchell said. "Gossip moves too fast in this town for him not to have known."

Trevor's pout deepened, and Lorenda gave his shoulder a squeeze. She lifted the binoculars again and zeroed in on Bart. She slung the binoculars over one shoulder. "I'm sure it wasn't intentional. He's not that much of a *foxtrotter*."

Mitchell's brow crinkled, but a corner of his mouth lifted.

"It's code cussing," she whispered.

His handsome face cracked wide open with a full-on smile. He shook his head. "You're one hell of a woman, Sparky."

She widened her eyes at him. "That's one *hotel* of a woman in front of the kids."

He nodded, but his smile didn't dim. "Has anyone seen my dog tags? I left them in my duffle bag when we went swimming. I can't find them."

She shook her head. So did Jaycee.

"Can I wear them? *Please?*" Trevor begged.

"Sure thing, buddy. But we have to find them first. Boys, stay close to the camp unless I'm with you."

Lorenda frowned at Mitchell. "Hey, guys, can you feed Malarkey and get him fresh water? His bowls and food are around the back of the tent." When they were out of earshot, she said, "I'm pissed at Bart's thoughtlessness too. It's a crummy situation for my kids, but they aren't in danger. What gives?"

"I don't know, Sparky, but I can't shake the strange feeling I've had since you were mugged in the park. Something's off, and I'd rather be safe than sorry."

He shifted his weight and closed the small space between them. His shoulder grazed hers, and a shiver lanced over her. A response she'd had a lot since Mitchell had showed up in Red River and so quickly become an important part of her life.

"Sparky, I have a sixth sense when it comes to dangerous situations." Lines of sadness tightened around his mouth. "It's why I'm still alive."

She knew Mitchell was looking out for her and the boys, even if his suspicion toward Bart was overkill.

"There's an estuary a few miles in that direction." He pointed to the woods behind them. "If we take the boys there to hike and fish, they won't have to look at the scouts all day and feel excluded."

She curved a hand around his arm, and he went still at her touch. "Most people wouldn't have thought of the boys' feelings."

His mocha eyes caressed her face. "I know what it's like to be ostracized. It's not fun, and I don't want them to feel like that."

So rejection really did bother Mitchell more than he let on.

"You're a good man," she whispered.

His expression turned smoky with lust, and that sent the rest of her meager restraint crumbling to her feet. That look of raw desire pushed out every reason why taking her connection with Mitchell beyond friendship had been foolish and would likely leave her and the kids with aching hearts. The pull he'd had on her since they'd locked gazes at the park overrode any sound reasoning.

Maybe lack of sex did that to a woman. Because that look of his was the only thing that had made her feel like an attractive woman in far too long. Getting compliments from her father didn't count. Neither did attention from Clifford the maintenance man.

She leaned in and kissed Mitchell. Pressed her lips to his and hoped he'd respond instead of turning his back to her again.

He did respond. Took control of the kiss without hesitation and caressed her lips with his, his breath going heavy. His warm mouth made her sigh, and his tongue traced her lips until they parted. When she took his lower lip between her teeth and nipped, he let out a growl. He eased her to him with a strong arm around her waist and the other hand at the back of her head. Gentle but completely in charge.

And holy thigh-clenching moly, she melted into the kiss as his tongue found hers and explored. She let out the breath she'd been holding and ran both hands up his toned back, over the contours and angles and planes of his exquisite male form.

His hand did some exploring too. Under her shirt, his fingers traced up her spine. His rough fingertips sent a storm of need spiraling through her until her toes curled into her suede hiking shoes.

"Damn, Sparky," he whispered against her mouth. It sounded sweet and a little desperate and made Lorenda's pulse sing, because it was as though he'd lost the last shred of his self-control and was asking her to step up with some resistance for the both of them.

Wasn't happening.

She dropped one hand to the most spectacular male ass she'd ever seen and cupped it.

He groaned and trailed sweet, hot kisses across her temple and down to her neck. He made out the same way he lived the rest of his life—like a rebel who broke all the rules. He was as passionate as he was protective, and right now his touch and his kiss communicated how much he wanted her.

"Mitchell, I can't help wanting you," she murmured against his mouth all breathy and just as desperate as him.

He didn't answer. Just dropped a hand to the small of her back and pressed her hips into his. And, oh baby, he obviously wanted her too, because that wasn't a piece of firewood pressing into her belly.

She let out a little gasp, which seemed to urge him on. He took her from desperate to crazy with a gentle grind of his hips. Amazing that she was about to orgasm right then and there, and they were still completely clothed. And he hadn't done much except kiss her because the kids were just on the other side of the tent.

The kids . . .

She let out a sigh of disappointment against his lips and then deepened the kiss to get one last taste of him before forcing herself back to the reality that she was a mother of two young boys who didn't need to see their mother making out.

"Ewww!" Jaycee said, and Lorenda nearly jumped out of her skin.

The boys disappeared behind the tent giggling.

Mitchell leaned his forehead against hers and blew out a small laugh. "You ready to go?"

Oh yeah. She was ready to go. Could go off with just another touch and maybe another kiss. She tried to pull out of his embrace, but he tugged her back.

"We'll finish this another time." His words sent a thrill of anticipation rocketing through her, and the tingle that had her nipples tightening turned to a full-on burn of unfulfilled desire.

Mitchell released her, her girl parts sighing with disappointment, and he called the boys over to gather up the fishing gear. Before Lorenda joined them, she held the binoculars to her eyes one more time, and the hair on the back of her neck prickled.

Staring back at her from across the lake was Bart Wilkinson.

Chapter Seventeen

Lorenda wrapped the boys up like sausages in their sleeping bags, and Malarkey curled at their side between them and her. She snuggled into her bag and tried to zip it, but the zipper wouldn't move. Mitchell opened the flap on the ceiling and climbed in next to her for a good night's sleep.

No way was that happening.

The grazes of his hand against hers when he offered to steady her during their climb up a rocky hill, his hand pressed to the small of her back when he helped her cast a fishing line into the river, and his sultry looks had her body humming by lunchtime. By dinner, he could've grown a third eye and she'd still be utterly fascinated by his mouthwatering body and the natural way he handled the boys.

Just like the father they'd always wanted. Just like the father she'd always wanted for them.

No way could she actually float off to sleepyland with his muscled hotness sizzling so close to her that she might spontaneously combust before the night was over.

Especially since he seemed so content. So at peace. Not the war junkie who was too restless to come home that she'd always thought him to be.

"I'll close it later to keep some of the cold out." Mitchell turned onto his side to face her but stared up at the sky.

They'd had a full day of more fun than Lorenda could remember in . . .

She stared through the opening in the ceiling and tried to count the years. Actually, Lorenda couldn't ever remember having so much fun as a family. Sure, she and the boys had had lots of good times. Had made lots of great memories. But on top of raising them, laundry, cooking, cleaning, working, and worrying, she'd often turned them over to her brother or her parents or their Grandma and Grandpa Lawson for this kind of fun.

They'd roasted weenies and made s'mores over the campfire after the sun disappeared behind the mountains. Now they were tucked into sleeping bags made for subzero temperatures to fend off the cold that settled over the Rockies every night.

"See the three stars lined up and angling down?" Mitchell pointed up at the millions of sparkling dots blanketing the velvety sky like diamonds. "That's Orion's Belt."

"I see it!" Jaycee said from his side of the tent.

"I don't see a belt," Trevor said.

"It's right there." Jaycee's tone held a thread of impatience. Lorenda smiled into the dark, because Langston had used that tone with her more times than she could count when they were little. Still did when she tried to boss him around.

"And there's the Big Dipper!" Jaycee said.

"Good job." Mitchell's warmth penetrated both sleeping bags and wrapped around Lorenda. She snuggled closer to him.

"I don't see that one either!" Trevor was obviously getting disgusted at his inferior stargazing skills.

Lorenda leaned over Malarkey so that Trevor could follow her finger, and she pointed up. "See, the handle angles down, and the cup is square."

Trevor went quiet until he finally yelled with delight. "I see it!"

Malarkey let out a whine at Trevor's high-pitched squeal, which, surprisingly, humans could also hear.

"Bet you guys can't guess which constellation is my favorite," Mitchell said. "There's a prize for whoever guesses the right one."

The tent went quiet.

"Gemini." Lorenda's tone was hushed, because she knew without a doubt she'd guessed right. She rolled her head to one side. His face was shadowed, the moonlight outlined his form.

"Good guess, Sparky."

It wasn't a guess. Red River was a small town with a small school. And since she, Cameron, and Mitchell had grown up together, they'd taken field trips together too. She remembered an overnight school trip to Albuquerque when they were little kids. Their group had visited the planetarium, and she'd never forgotten Cameron and Mitchell's reaction when the constellation of the twins, Castor and Pollux, had been pointed out by the teacher.

"Was that our dad's favorite too?" Jaycee asked.

"It was." His voice held the slightest tremor. "When we went on campouts with your grandpa, we'd find as many of the constellations as we could. Your dad was better at it than me. When we were overseas, we weren't always on the same base." He hesitated. "We had a deal that we'd find each other in the stars every night, like when we were kids."

Lorenda's heart thumped. She'd spent so many years focusing on her own pain from Cameron's rejection, she hadn't considered how lost he must've been. How lonely he must've felt. And she hadn't known how to reach that part of him to help make it better.

"You look just like our dad's pictures," said Jaycee.

Mitchell exhaled, slow and steady. "Your dad was a good guy." The pain in his words sliced through Lorenda's heart.

She found his hand and squeezed. Whether Cameron was good or bad had somehow stopped mattering to Lorenda in the past few weeks. Why, she wasn't completely sure. Maybe because he'd been flawed but so had she. Maybe because he was still Mitchell's brother and the kids' father, and that counted for something. *That* was what mattered to Lorenda now. Not how Cameron had disappointed her.

She laced her fingers with Mitchell's. He brought them to his mouth to lay a tender-sweet kiss on the tips.

A thrum reverberated in her chest.

A band of locusts cranked up a tune. As if on cue, crickets joined in.

Mitchell rubbed the back of her hand against his cheek, the day's stubble causing her skin to pebble.

"Want to know a trick from the military?"

"Yes," Trevor said on a yawn.

"Sparky, you'll like this. Listen." He stared up at the sky and went quiet. "Really listen."

More insects joined in until an entire orchestra played a concerto. A gentle breeze stirred the trees into a dance, and they swayed in rhythm with the insects.

"It's almost like they're in tune with each other, like a band. It's so loud," Lorenda said. "But still peaceful."

"Exactly. When we were on a mission, sometimes we'd have to sleep outdoors."

"Like a campout?" Jaycee's voice was fading.

"Yep. Just like a campout. We learned to savor the sounds of nature because they were much more peaceful than the alternative."

Lorenda bet they were. The sounds of war probably messed with a person's head as much as the death and destruction that came with it. The thought caused another ripple of sadness to crash through her heart.

Mitchell scooted closer until the full length of his body pressed to her side. "The company on this campout is infinitely more pleasant." Laughter mingled with his words.

"Okay." Lorenda's voice was hushed. "Let's get some sleep."

Obviously the boys were either asleep or almost there, because neither protested.

Mitchell closed the ceiling flap and crawled in next to her again. "You better zip the bag, Sparky, or you'll get cold. The temperature will drop pretty low during the night, especially since summer is almost over."

"It won't zip. I tried." She snuggled in deeper.

"Come here." He opened his sleeping bag wide, so she could get in with him. "My bag is oversized."

"But you're so big." Lorenda couldn't help but chew her lip.

"You sure do know how to compliment a guy, Sparky," he teased.

She was glad the tent was dark to hide the heat that crept into her cheeks. "I'm serious. There's not enough room for both of us."

"Then I'll give you mine." He started to get up.

"No." She put a hand on his chest to stop him. She couldn't let him go all night in the cold. She scooted into his bag until they were front to fantastic front, pressing against each other from head to toe.

The zipper whizzed as Mitchell closed them into the thermal cocoon. "Comfy?" His warm breath caressed over her cheeks.

"Yes." *Heck yes.* And that was the problem, wasn't it? What was she doing with a man whose future was as unsure and unstable as his turbulent past? A man who could upend her life before moving on to another state. Or to Leavenworth. Because if the authorities were able to find one shred of evidence to implicate Mitchell in the rec-center fire, she'd be visiting him in jail.

At least she wouldn't be the one to seal his fate with damning testimony if he was ever arrested. She'd never forgive herself, and she certainly wouldn't want to have to explain it to her boys because of how much they loved their uncle.

So she'd married him without a real promise of forever.

Her breath hitched. She'd spent most of her adult life building a structured and secure life for herself and the kids, only to toss it away on a whim. Because Mitchell wasn't a sure thing. He was far from it, even with a license that said he was legally required to stick around.

Hadn't she learned that a marriage license didn't mean much to Lawson men if they got the itch for something different?

Mitchell threaded a hand around her waist and pulled her into him. She meant to push him away, because her boys were asleep just two feet over. Instead, her palms smoothed up his chest.

Delta her wandering hands.

She swallowed. "This probably isn't a good idea," she whispered. "The boys are right here. What will they think if they wake up?"

"We're married, Sparky. They'd probably think it was weird if we didn't sleep close together." He caressed the small of her back through the thick fabric of her thermal shirt. "We've got clothes on, and we're just sleeping. That's all."

Okay. Good. As long as they were on the same page.

"For tonight," he clarified like he couldn't make that promise stretch any further into the future.

Her girly parts went nuclear.

"So about that prize I owe you." His voice turned to a tease again. "Can I give it to you another time?"

"Um, sure."

"When we're alone." Sleepiness murmured through his words.

A hum of electricity zinged through her and settled between her thighs. "Well, um, what is it?" Did she really want to know? Her brain said no, but her tingling girl parts said, *give it to me, baby!*

"I'll think of something . . ." The last word trailed off, and his breathing grew thick and heavy as sleep overtook him.

And wasn't that just great? The deep rumble of his voice, the closeness of his hard body, and the promise in his words made her feel more alive, more like a woman than she'd felt in her entire life. Caused her core to heat to a rolling boil, turned her insides to liquid fire, and then he drifted off to sleep while she laid awake all night trying to put out the flames.

Something wet and slobbery drenched Mitchell's cheek and his dream of being a real member of Lorenda's happy family faded like mist. He woke to the smell of a campfire and beads of sweat trickling down his back. Malarkey whined at his ear. Mitchell's eyes popped open and he lay still, listening in the darkness.

Something was wrong. Seriously wrong.

The campfire outside flared and cast a glow across the tent.

A shot of adrenaline exploded in his chest and shot to the tips of all four limbs.

"Sparky." He shook her awake. "Something's on fire."

She bolted upright, but he put a firm, comforting hand on her shoulder. "Don't panic." Panic caused mistakes. "Put your shoes on to protect your feet. Make sure the kids get their shoes on too." He grabbed his hiking boots and was on his feet and moving toward the door.

Malarkey barked a warning, his dog senses obviously aware of danger, but Mitchell stepped outside anyway. The heat from the woods burning down the hill made his head snap back. He choked on the dense smoke, his throat stinging.

He did a three-sixty, looking for a way out. Opposite the fire was a mountain ridge that couldn't be scaled without rock climbing gear. The lake boxed them in on one side, so that left only one escape route.

He jerked aside the flap, which hung in front of the tent's door. "Come on!"

Lorenda and the boys stumbled out of the tent, and tears streamed down Trevor's little face. Mitchell bent and took him by the shoulders. "Being brave doesn't mean you're not scared."

Trevor sniffed.

"I need you to help me get your mom and Malarkey out of here. Can you do that for me?"

Trevor nodded.

Mitchell turned to Lorenda. "As fast as you can, go that way toward the stream we fished in today." Mitchell pointed. "I'll go last to make sure we don't lose anyone in the dark."

When they got to the stream, Mitchell had everyone hold up. Smoke thickened the air, and the heat from the fire had turned the cool night as hot as a desert. He swiped the sweat from his brow with the front of his shirt. Lorenda's chest heaved from the fast pace. Mitchell took off his underwater watch.

"Give me your arm, Lorenda."

Still panting, she held out her wrist. He strapped the watch on and pushed a button on one side. "Here's the light. And there's the compass." He pointed to the red arrow on the face. "Go west until you hit the highway. You'll have to double back along the road to find the truck where we parked it at the base of the mountain, or flag down the first vehicle that passes—"

"Mitchell, no." She grabbed his arm. "We're not leaving you here."

"Sparky, listen to me." This time he took both of her arms in his hands. "I wanted to make sure you and the kids got out safe. If you do what I say, you will. There are two dozen Wilderness Scouts camping on the other side of the lake. The fire is spreading fast, and I can't just leave them."

"*Mitchell.*" Lorenda's voice was desperate. "You can't leave *us*! What if you don't—" She stifled a sob with her hand.

He framed her face between his hands. At that moment, all he wanted in his sorry excuse for a life was to be there for his family. To become the husband and father Lorenda and the boys needed. In his selfish need to goad his father, he'd talked himself into believing it was okay to take responsibility for Cameron's mistakes. That had been the first domino, and they were still falling all these years later, ruining the lives of people he cared about. Most of all ruining Lorenda's life. That was hard enough to live with, but if he didn't help the scouts, he wouldn't be able to live with himself at all.

"Sweetheart, you know I have to."

Moonlight shimmered against the wetness in her eyes. She nodded, inhaling on another sob. "I've lost one husband. I—"

He smothered her fearful words with a kiss. Then he pulled back and brushed her nose with his. "I'm coming back. I promise. Just get yourself and the boys out of here and get word to my dad. He'll know what to do."

He pulled her into another urgent kiss, then set her away from him.

"Boys, stick with your mother and make sure she's safe, okay?"

"Yes sir," they echoed.

As soon as they turned to walk down the hill, Mitchell took off toward the lake in a dead run. When he broke through the woods into the clearing around the lake, the fire had gotten much closer. It was almost to the scouts' campsite, so he quickly ticked off his options. He could go around, which would take longer, or he could go across.

He broke into a run toward the pier.

They don't call 'em frogmen for nothin'.

He didn't slow when he got to the end, but dove headfirst into the water and swam toward the other side. He splashed onto the bank, ready to bark orders to the scout leaders and piggyback as many kids out of there as he could carry. Fiery heat licked over him as he turned full circle looking for any sign of life.

Every tent was gone, and the campsite was empty.

Mitchell walked around the site. Called out in case anyone was left behind.

It took time to get that much equipment torn down and packed up. They'd been gone for a while. Strange, since they'd just gotten there that day.

He walked past the fire pit and the blaze glinted off something metal. He bent, picked it from the ashes, and wiped it off.

That feeling, the one that told him something was terribly off, dialed up so high that blood pounded through his veins.

How did his dog tags get across the lake and into the Wilderness Scouts camp?

By the time Mitchell made his way to the highway, the Forest Service had arrived, along with the Red River Fire Department and what must've been every volunteer firefighter in the county. Everyone except the two people he needed to find the most—Lorenda and his dad.

He ran through the crowd of scrambling first responders and their vehicles looking for Cam's old truck and the sheriff's car.

"Whoa, buddy." Langston came out of nowhere and blocked Mitchell with an arm. He yelled to one of the firefighters that Mitchell was accounted for and told them to call it in to the chief. "A search team is looking for you up there." He pointed up the mountain, which burned bright and lit up the night sky that had been so peaceful just a few hours ago.

"I need to find Lorenda and the kids." Mitchell tried to push out of Langston's hold, but his buddy wouldn't let go.

"She's home safe and sound."

Mitchell's eyes slid shut for a beat, and the knot in his chest loosened.

"She drove straight to the fire department and then wanted to come back here after dropping the kids and that ugly dog of hers off at my parents." Langston led him to an ambulance. "I told her it wasn't safe." He was clearly annoyed. "But do you think she listened?"

Hell no, and Mitchell wanted to give her a lecture about putting herself in danger since she had two kids to think about. Had him to think about too, because he didn't want to lose her. Not after it had taken him so long to find her.

The thought knocked the wind from his lungs.

After he finished lecturing her, he wanted to kiss the daylights out of her. The only other people who had cared enough about him to try to save him were his SEAL Team. And Cameron, who'd followed Mitchell into the military, even if he couldn't own up to the fire.

Langston kept complaining about his sister. "The guys manning the roadblock called me on the radio and said she was trying to slip through. She was blubbering about how she had to get back here to find your sorry ass." He shoved Mitchell down, and he landed on the bumper with a thunk. Langston didn't seem to notice and slapped an oxygen mask over Mitchell's face.

"Nice bedside manner." Mitchell moved the mask aside. "Bet your patients love you."

Langston shoved the mask back into place. "They do, actually. I only treat assholes like this." He strapped a blood-pressure cuff on Mitchell's arm.

Mitchell moved the mask again. "I already told you, that's Mr. Asshole to you. And why are you here? Aren't you supposed to be working on a helo helping to rescue people or some such bullshit?"

"My next shift doesn't start for a few days, and the Red River Fire Department still calls me in when they need extra help." Langston folded Mitchell's arm across his chest and pressed a button on the cuff. It started to expand. "Obviously, they needed me to save someone named Mr. Asshole."

Mitchell used his free hand to squeeze Langston's shoulder. His buddy, who used to play football with him in high school, and now happened to be his brother-in-law, stilled and dropped the pissy look for a second. "Thanks, Lang. I owe you, buddy."

Langston pounded him on the back, then went back to his sibling rant. "Damn straight you owe me. That wife of yours was causing such a ruckus at the roadblock, I had to call your dad."

Oh wow. Mitchell would've paid money to see that fireworks display.

"And would she listen to him?" Langston's voice turned to disgust.

Mitchell smiled and felt it spread through his entire body.

Langston read the numbers on the cuff and stripped it away. "Hell no, she gave him shit too. He had to threaten to arrest her before she finally left. And then he still had to follow her home and take her keys away to keep her from coming back and barreling through the roadblock."

No one in this town could get away with talking to his old man like that except his mom and Lorenda. If anyone else had tried to stand up to him, he'd likely have them brought up on charges of treason and shipped them off to Gitmo.

Or the military.

Langston shined a light in Mitchell's eyes. "Okay, you're fine. But I still have to offer you a ride to the hospital."

Mitchell flipped the mask off and tossed it inside the ambulance. "Hospitals are for pussies."

"Right." Langston rolled his eyes, put the equipment away, and pulled a phone from his pocket. "Here." He shoved it into Mitchell's chest. "I figured you'd be asking to use it. Lorenda said you made everyone leave their phones at home, so go call your wife."

Mitchell walked away for some privacy and dialed Lorenda's number. She answered on the first ring, and he let out the breath he was holding. The sound of her voice sent a wave of relief flooding through him.

"Sparky."

"Mitchell!" Her voice shook. "Are you okay? Did all the scouts get out okay?"

"I'm fine, but the scouts were already gone. You and the kids are good?"

"We're great thanks to you. Just terrified." She hesitated. "Until now."

Mitchell wanted to reach through the phone and kiss her. "Thanks to Malarkey. He saved us. I might not have woken up in time if not for him."

"Mitchell." Her voice was almost a whisper. "Come home. The kids and Malarkey are with my parents."

There was a promise in those words. One that he hoped would start with a hot shower for two, include several shouts of his name, a shout or two of hers, and end with enough empty metallic squares to build a fort.

"I'll be there soon. I just need to talk to Dad first." He looked around the bustling crowd. "If I can find him."

"I told him it couldn't have been you."

Mitchell's stomach tightened. Cameron was already dead because of the lie they'd kept from his parents. If it came out now and made his father's heart condition worse, it would be the last straw of guilt on top of an already staggering load of regret that would break Mitchell in every way possible.

"Sparky, you didn't—"

"I only talked to him about tonight. I told him there wasn't a minute where either me or the kids weren't with you." She let a beat go by. "You should know that he was relieved. I mean, he was really, really relieved, Mitchell." She hesitated.

Something shifted in Mitchell's chest.

Because, hell. Didn't that just top off the adrenaline rush and emotional overload from the night. He'd figured his dad would want it to be Mitchell's fault, because dear old dad seemed to like blaming Mitchell for every problem on the planet, especially if fire was involved. Mitchell was surprised his dad hadn't blamed him for global warming and the price of oil too.

Admittedly, Mitchell brought some of that on himself, but the old man did seem to enjoy jumping to the conclusion that Mitchell was guilty. Every damn chance he got.

And speak of the devil, here came his dad's car with the lights whirling. Just the person Mitchell needed to see. He wanted answers. And he wanted them now, because someone had just tried to fuck with his family. He smiled for the first time in hours. No one tried to *foxtrot* with his family and got away with it.

But at the moment, there was a beautiful woman on the phone, inviting him over for a slumber party. The kind where not a lot of slumbering actually went on.

"Come home, Mitchell."

He raked a hand across his jaw. "Sparky." He couldn't believe what he was about to say. Too many close calls with RPGs must've scrambled his brains. "Are you sure about this?"

"No. I'm not," she said.

His entire body deflated. Not just because of the physical letdown of missing out on the very thing that had occupied his fantasies for the past few weeks, and not because she still had doubts about him. But because she had every reason to have doubts about him. He hadn't exactly been a go-to guy the last several years, at least until the past few weeks. Why she'd married him to save his worthless hide still boggled his mind.

Maybe after tonight he could change that.

"But it's what I want, Mitchell. And for once in my life, I'm going to let it be about me."

His eyes slid shut. "I'll be there soon."

He tossed the phone at Langston as he walked past, heading straight for his father. "You here to arrest me?"

Deep lines framed his dad's mouth. "No, son. We can talk tomorrow." He pointed to a highway patrol car. "There's your ride. Go home and get some sleep. You need it after the night you've had."

Huh.

Not what Mitchell expected, but he'd take it.

His dad pulled car keys from his pocket and handed them to Mitchell. "These are Lorenda's."

Mitchell took them, running a thumb over them for a moment. "I'll see you tomorrow, then." He was going home to his wife. And once he got to her, he'd make sure it was totally and completely about her. She deserved it, and so much more.

Chapter Eighteen

Lorenda waited at the window until car lights pulled into the drive and wound around to stop in front of the house. She peeked through the wood slats in the den as Mitchell climbed out of the car.

Relief washed through her, and tears stung the back of her eyes.

Mitchell was home. He may not know it yet, but Lorenda was sure that he belonged here. In Red River with her and the boys. Her only hope was that he would figure that out somehow, and it would overpower his desire to hit the road again and put this whole experience behind him.

And didn't that shave a few more points off her IQ, because she'd spent years keeping the home fires burning and hoping for the same response from a different Lawson twin, only to be left lonely and then completely alone.

Logic and reason told her not to take the step she was about to take with Mitchell. Getting into bed with him would only make her all the more vulnerable. But somehow in the depths of her soul, she knew that her decision to sleep with Mitchell was right. Mitchell wasn't Cameron. Not even close, and it wasn't fair to keep comparing them.

With one hand on the top of the car and the other arm slung over the open door, he dipped his head to speak to the driver, then slammed the door and patted the top of the car, signaling it to go. Red taillights glowed as it did a U-turn and rolled down the drive.

She threw the door open and ran to him. No inhibitions. No shyness. No doubts.

Okay, maybe a few doubts. But she'd almost lost him, and she'd rather have doubts than regrets. She launched herself into his arms and got lost in the deep, demanding kiss the moment their lips connected and his strong arms closed around her.

She molded herself against his hard and hot body, melting into the most incredible thigh-clenching kiss. A sigh escaped from deep inside, her hands sliding up his chest and into his hair.

She broke the kiss and tilted her head back to look at him. "You're safe."

"You're beautiful." His eyes burned as hot as the fire had.

That was all it took for Lorenda to wrap herself around him again and smother him with another needy kiss.

Talking was overrated.

One of his hands dropped to her ass and flexed. He tugged her hips tight against his, and a rock-hard bulge made her moan against his mouth. He moaned in response and slid the other hand to the back of her head, angling her so he could deepen the kiss.

When she made a sensual noise that communicated how much she thoroughly enjoyed his touch, both of his big hands slid to her ass, and he rocked his hips into hers. Need crashed through her, and she trailed her swollen lips across his jaw, over to his ear, and breathed a hot sigh against it.

She squeaked when he swept her into his arms and carried her inside, kicking the door shut with a boot. He took the stairs two at a time, his eyes never leaving hers, and headed straight into her . . . *bathroom?*

"Let's finish what we started in my apartment the other day." He set her on her feet.

Oh. Well. In that case. "I could use a shower." Her eyes stayed locked onto his, and her fingers worked the top button of her shirt.

"Don't move." His eyes fell to her fingers as another button fell open. "Except for that. You can definitely keep doing that."

One side of her mouth curved up, and her fingers released the last button. He turned on the water and was back in front of her faster than she could say *what the hell am I doing?*

He reached behind his head and pulled his long-sleeved thermal off with one hand. His muscled chest drew her hands, and she traced over the contours, shadows dipping into the swell at the center. So hard yet so smooth at the same time.

Lorenda's fingertips found the edges of her open shirt, and she pulled it off. Sheer desire showed in his expression. He closed the small space between them and ran both hands up her arms to slowly peel off one strap of her bra and then the other.

"You're so sexy, Sparky." He slipped those powerful hands that were being so gentle at the moment around her back. With the twitch of his fingers, her bra unhooked. He gently eased the silk fabric away, leaving her bared.

She actually blushed. His heated gaze licked over her and burned a trail across her skin.

Steam filled the bathroom and swirled around them as thick as the cloud of lust that smoldered in his eyes.

Slow and gentle, like he was savoring every moment, he unbuttoned her jeans, inserted his hands between her skin and her pants so that his palms molded against her flesh, and slid them down. Her breaths quickened as the fabric descended and grazed across her skin right along with his gaze. He left her panties in place, like he was unwrapping a package, slowly, gently, savoring each little bit he revealed before peeling back another layer. His movements were controlled like he was in complete command of his self-restraint. Only the lightning-fast pulse at the base of his corded neck gave away the war that was going on inside of him.

He stepped into her, blanketing her with his strength and engulfing her in his heat. And she was happy to let him. She'd waited so long to feel like this. Waited so long to be wanted.

He buried one hand in her hair and slid the other under her panties to cup and knead. He took her mouth with his, delivering a punishing kiss that told her his self-restraint was an act. He was as desperate for her as she was for him, so she found the inviting bulge at his crotch and did a little cupping and kneading too. Nipped at his bottom lip, then blazed a trail of hot kisses across his jaw. She worked her way down the ropey muscles of his neck, suckling and nibbling.

He let out a deep moan that rumbled inside his chest. It drove her on, and she flicked open the button, lowered the zipper, and had him in her hand before he could move away. Not that she thought he would. He seemed content to stay right where he was with her circling and massaging his length.

"Jesus, Sparky," he growled against her mouth as he slid a powerful thigh between her legs.

He scorched a trail of hot, wet kisses down her neck and took one of her aching breasts into his mouth. *Finally!* He suckled her nipple into a throbbing peak, then took the tip between his teeth with just enough pressure to cause her to toss her head back.

Eyes closed, breath heavy, she leaned back and braced herself against the counter. He took full advantage and moved to the other breast, working it with his teeth and tongue until she whimpered.

With the tip of his tongue, he traced down between her breasts and sank to his knees, his hands burning a trail over her ribs, his tongue blazing a path over her stomach, around her belly button, and lower.

"Mitchell!" She speared fingers into his hair.

His warm, moist breaths reached through her panties, heating her center as silk slid across her most sensitive spot with the movement of his tongue.

"Oh God, Mitchell," she panted out.

"I've dreamed of hearing you say my name just like that," he breathed against ground zero. "I plan to make sure you say it several times tonight." He bit into her flesh through the panties, and a current coiled low in her belly. "And again in the morning." The coil tightened. "And any time of the day you want."

She thought she'd unfurl right then and there. She hung on for dear life.

He moved her panties to one side, and his breaths grew even hotter against her pulsing center. Nothing prepared her for the electrifying jolt of ecstasy that blistered every nerve ending in her body when he covered her throbbing nub with an openmouthed kiss. His incredible tongue stroked in rhythm with his lips that moved and suckled and massaged, coaxing her to the edge.

He slid two wonderful fingers inside and reached deep before flicking his fingers back and forth.

"*Mitchell!*" she screamed, and he smiled against her before giving those amazing fingers one more twitch.

She saw stars as she splintered into a million tiny pieces, his incredible mouth and hands and fingers milking her orgasm for as long as possible.

When her breathing started to slow, she wrapped both arms around his head and cuddled him. He buried his face in her abdomen, in the sweetest, most intimate way. So touching that it reached into her soul.

It wasn't the action of a hardened soldier. Wasn't the gesture of a man who could no longer feel. It was soft and sexy and so, so loving.

They stood there for a long time, before Mitchell rose to kick off his pants. She watched his every movement, watched every muscle of his beautiful male body move and shift until he was completely naked, except for protection, and reaching for her again.

Another rush of sexual heat bucked in lady land.

His gaze took a nice long trip from her mouth all the way to her curling toes, and the corner of his mouth tipped up.

"Nice panties," he said.

"Thank you." She gave him a shy smile.

"Yeah, not really." Before she could protest, he took a hand full of silk in each fist and ripped them in two.

He smothered her gasp with another commanding kiss and backed her into the shower. "Let's clean up before the hot water runs out."

Fine by her.

She could think of worse things than soaping up Mitchell's hard body. He stepped in after her and wrapped all six feet three of pure man around her. And Al the plumber just became Lorenda's hero for replacing her water heater. The hot water rolled over them, but her skin still pebbled as Mitchell dropped a spray of quick, sexy kisses over her neck and shoulder. Lorenda snuggled into the nook of his neck and nipped.

As if Mitchell hadn't already rocked her world enough, he backed her against the shower wall and hooked one of her knees over his thigh. Bracing one hand next to her head, he entered her with one long, scorching thrust, which sent a storm of pleasure thundering through her. She arched against him, her head banging against the ceramic tile as she cried out an incoherent shout of approval.

He gave her a second to adjust. Or maybe he was adjusting, because he leaned his forehead against hers. "Christ, I'm one lucky SOB."

She let out a chuckle. "I don't have a code for that one."

He laughed too and drew her bottom lip between his teeth. "How about"—another nip—"Geronimo?" This time instead of a nip, he moved to her earlobe and sunk his teeth in just enough to cause a shiver to race from the top of her wet, tangled hair all the way to her tingling toes.

"Geronimo was a lucky SOB?" She laughed again as he started to move inside of her. Even under the steamy water, she shivered, and her nipples tightened to hard peaks.

"He was misunderstood." Mitchell's mouth closed around the beating pulse at the base of her neck, and his tongue smoothed over it while he suckled. "A misunderstood warrior who just wanted to defend his family like me." His hand found her breast and massaged it into a molten mound of aching flesh. His strokes grew quicker and more demanding as he drove into her over and over.

She dug her nails into his shoulders. "Then it doesn't fit, because I'm understanding you just fine." Her words came out like a desperate whimper.

"Baby, the fit is perfect from where I'm standing," he said with a gritty voice. Then to prove his point, he reversed the movement of his hips, adjusted his weight just a smidge, and bingo. He hit the spot that made her body sing like a bird.

She tightened and undulated around his generous flesh, and he followed her chorus in perfect harmony. He devoured her mouth with his as his crescendo throbbed inside of her.

Somehow they ended up in her bed. And lucky Geronimoette that she was, they were just getting started.

Yes, Lorenda definitely understood Mitchell better than anyone else he'd ever met.

He moved on top of her, already hard and ready to hear her say his name again. He didn't care how—a whisper, a shout, a moan—as long as she said it in the midst of him pleasuring her.

"Oh my," she gasped when his hardening prick pressed against her scorching hot folds.

"I promised you'd say my name several times tonight." He guided her hand over her head and placed her fingers around the bedpost. "You should probably hold on."

He should probably hold on too, because Lorenda had become far more important to him than he'd planned. It wasn't about making up for his and Cameron's lie that had screwed up everyone's life, especially Lorenda's. It wasn't about keeping her safe anymore. It was about keeping her.

He kissed his way to one of her lush breasts and found her sweet spot with his thumb.

"*Mitchell*," she said on a gasp.

"There's one more," he murmured against her skin as he kissed down her rib cage. "Only a hundred more Mitchells to go."

Her soft skin against his was just as velvety as the girly comforter on her bed.

And just like that, Lorenda, with her pink lip gloss, sparkly sandals, and feminine clothes, used the full force of her body to flip him onto his back and straddle him.

He didn't offer up any resistance.

And God bless girly comforters. It was soft and smooth and sexy against his back as she ground against him and ran her dainty hands up his abdomen, across his chest, and over his shoulders. Drank every inch of him in and made him want her even more. He rose up and took her soft mouth in a kiss, wrapped her up in his arms, and held on tight because she felt so perfect pressed against him, naked and needing more.

"Okay, Geronimo, maybe *you* should hold on to something." She pushed him back, a wicked gleam in her fiery eyes.

The soft lamplight cast a glow over her creamy skin. Her pouty lips parted as she skimmed them across his, then slipped her tongue inside his mouth for a long, languid kiss. And then used those same sweet lips to spray kisses over his chest, over his abs . . .

Christ. He hissed out a breath as her lips closed around his shaft.

And if he hadn't already thought he was one lucky SOB, he sure did now. Her hand moved everywhere her lips couldn't reach, and that mouth . . . holy hell, that mouth was pure heaven.

When he couldn't take it another second, he grasped her arms and hauled her up to consume those beautiful lips with a hot, hard kiss. She barely gave him a second to grab protection before she lifted her hips and slid all the way onto him. Her eyes slammed shut as a shudder racked her body.

He framed her face with his hands. "You look so beautiful like this."

She braced both hands against his chest. Her gaze locked onto his, and she lifted to his tip and slid down again until he was buried to the hilt and pressing into the deepest part of her. She did it again, and the fires of desire burned bright in her eyes. Her speed increased, and she never looked away. Never broke that intimate bond that passed between them as her stare held his.

Of all the fantasies he'd had about her, this wasn't one of them. He'd dreamed of making love to her, bringing her to one orgasm after another while she enjoyed each one more than the last. He hadn't considered that she'd be the one trying to please him.

That was so like her, though.

Her full breasts bobbed in a sexy, mind-blowing rhythm as she circled her hips against him. So he lifted enough to take one nipple into his mouth, and a sexy little sound whispered through her lips.

Her breathing increased right along with the speed of her thrusts, until she was panting and wrapping her arms around his head again. She buried her face in his neck and kept riding him, her body tightening around his length until he thought he would explode.

The feel of her muscles starting to quiver and close around him again made his mind go blank. Until finally he started thinking clearly again as her heat built to a mind-altering level. She had welcomed him into her life, her family, her body. And for the first time in his life he belonged. He thought he'd found acceptance in the military. But the brotherhood he'd formed there was only a replacement for not being welcome in his town, his home, and his family.

He'd finally found his true home, and it wasn't a house with four walls. His home was Lorenda. With her wrapped in his arms.

A thrill raced through him and wound around his heart.

With one fluid movement, he flipped her onto her back again and buried himself inside of her.

"Oh!" she moaned, arching into him.

"That's it, baby."

She wrapped her legs around his waist, and he drove into her. Over and over until his name rolled off her tongue, and her orgasm contracted around him, making him follow her into that dreamy state of complete satisfaction.

He collapsed on top of her, crushing her into the soft velvet comforter. Afraid he was too heavy, he tried to move, but she wrapped her arms and her long, sexy legs around him and held him in place.

"Don't move," she whispered against his ear.

He never wanted to move from that spot. So he braced both elbows on each side of her head and gently threaded his fingers into her silky hair. His temple rested against the bed, and he nuzzled her ear.

It took a while for their breathing to slow and his mind to shift out of overdrive. He lay there covering her, listening to the ebb and flow of her breaths, and letting the pounding of their hearts mingle and twine together. They were one now—husband, wife, lovers. She was half of him. The better half, and he had a lot of changing to do to live up to the standard she deserved.

Finally they crawled under the covers, and he pulled her into his arms. Her cheek rested against his chest, her fingers sketching over his skin.

"I was so scared, Mitchell. I was physically sick until you finally called and I heard the sound of your voice," she whispered against his chest.

He caressed her hair. "I had to go back and try to help those kids."

She nodded. "How do you think the fire started?" Her warm breath prickled his skin.

He drew in a weighty breath. "Good question. Tomorrow I need to talk to my dad." Mitchell also planned to find out why the scouts had disappeared in the middle of the night. It was time for Mitchell and his dad to work together, whether they wanted to or not. If they couldn't put their differences aside and compromise for the greater good, someone was going to get hurt.

That someone might be Lorenda or one of the boys. And that was something Mitchell couldn't let happen.

Chapter Nineteen

The next morning—after enjoying coffee in bed and another hot shower for two—Mitchell toweled off his hair and decided to bring up a touchy subject with Lorenda. Maybe with her being all naked and vulnerable and satisfied, she'd actually listen to reason.

"So I was thinking, Sparky."

A towel wrapped around her, she stood in front of the mirror and brushed through her wet hair. She turned to look at him, still brushing the ends.

"I know you think Bart is harmless." He ran the towel over his chest, and her eyes followed.

Ah. Not a bad strategy. Maybe she'd agree to what he was about to propose. He ran the towel over his arm, then down the other, making sure to flex his tattoo at the opportune moment. Worked like a charm, because her eyes hung on that ink. The brushing stopped, and the tip of her tongue traced the line of her mouth.

"But I'm not so convinced." He toweled and flexed some more.

"The scouts showing up at the lake and then disappearing does raise some questions." Her eyes moved from Mitchell's ink to his chest. Then lower. "But I can't imagine that Bart arranged all of that on purpose or had anything to do with the fire."

Mitchell draped the towel around his waist. "Remember how my dog tags went missing? I found them at the scouts' campsite."

Her forehead crinkled. "We swam to that side of the lake before the scouts showed up. Maybe you dropped them."

He shook his head, and droplets of water sprayed his shoulders. "They disappeared from our tent. Had to have."

She started brushing again. "No one could've gotten into our tent without us seeing them. I'm sure there's an explanation."

Yeah. The explanation was that Bart was much creepier than anyone suspected, and why Lorenda couldn't see it bothered Mitchell.

"It's entirely possible Trevor snuck them into his pocket and dropped them. He wanted to wear them pretty bad."

Mitchell hauled in a breath. "You should put the music program on pause until you find another location." He flexed his ink again, proud at the way he stressed the word *pause*.

She pulled her gaze away from his tattoo, and her eyes narrowed. "I'll try to help you find another place. I'll even—"

"No." She turned back to the mirror.

"Sparky." He stood behind her so they both faced the mirror. "It would be temporary."

"No." Her voice was even firmer that time.

He ran open palms up her arms, and her soft skin pebbled. His head dipped and pulled a sweet earlobe between his lips for a taste. "It's for your own safety," he whispered against her ear, then planted a soft, openmouthed kiss behind it. She shivered, and her head fell back against his chest.

She melted back against him and rubbed her magnificent ass against his crotch.

Christ.

"The answer's still no," she said, eyes closed. Voice breathy.

"Bart's got something to do with this. I know it, Lorenda." He rarely called her anything but Sparky. Hadn't since they were teenagers, but this was serious.

Her lids popped open. "You're overreacting. Yes, he's a little peculiar, but in a pathetic, harmless kind of way." She stepped away from him and started brushing her hair again. "But even if what you say is true, I'd rather be at the school where I can be close to the kids."

Mitchell had considered the kids, and he couldn't come up with a solution because it was the only elementary school in town.

"I can't let the music students lose momentum when they have a concert to get ready for." She put a hand on her hip and stared at him through the mirror.

"Damn it, woman. You're willing to put yourself in danger for a free after-school program that is meaningless to most of the town?"

Probably a poor choice of words. But every instinct he had told him to stay on alert.

First, her eyes flew wide. Then she slowly lowered the brush. Next she turned to face him with a look as hard as granite.

"That came out wrong." He tried to explain.

She held up a hand to silence him. "Don't start pulling your alpha-male-warrior crap with me."

Definitely could've chosen his words more carefully.

"I've put my dream on hold long enough. I've been on my own my entire adult life." Her voice escalated, and her usual easy-going, softie demeanor evaporated. "You are not going to start making decisions for me on day two of our marriage, which is not even for real anyway."

Well, hell. It *was* only day two of their fake marriage, and they were already having their first fight.

He stepped in front of her. Fingered the edge of the towel that was tucked and holding the whole thing in place. "Last night was very, very real, Sparky. At least it was for me."

Her eyes flared, turning a deeper shade of blue. But it shut her up, which was fine by him. He'd gone and ruined a perfectly good sex marathon by opening his stupid mouth and making her dream seem trivial. Which was not at all what he'd meant.

He flicked the tucked piece of terry cloth free, and the towel fell away. He stepped into her, then put one hand at the small of her naked back and the other in her hair to pull her against him. "It doesn't get more real than this." He smothered her mouth with his.

Not only did that distract her from the awkward turn of their conversation, but she completely lost track of time. They went back to bed and stayed there for a long, long while.

When they finally got dressed, Mitchell dropped Lorenda off at her parents' where the kids had spent the night. He needed to see his father. Alone. So he drove over to the sheriff's office.

He pulled into the sheriff's office parking lot and slid out of the truck, every muscle in his body aching from the most incredible sex he'd ever had. It hadn't just been him wanting to go all night. Lorenda couldn't seem to get enough, and he'd been more than happy to oblige.

Least a man could do for his wife. A smile spread across his face. A soul-deep contentment went with it because Lorenda was his. At least she'd felt like his until she'd gone and reminded him that it wasn't for real while wrapped in nothing but a towel.

He'd done his best to remind her otherwise by taking her back to bed.

He walked in to the sheriff's office and leaned against the reception desk. Maureen had obviously come in on a Sunday because his dad needed the help. Every light on her multiline phone flashed red.

Maureen held the phone to her ear. "Sheriff Lawson will catch the person responsible, I assure you. The fire chief is investigating, and the state troopers have gotten involved since the sheriff is shorthanded."

She went quiet, listening. Then her eyes flitted to Mitchell for the briefest of moments, and she blushed. Like maybe the person on the other end of the line was talking about him.

"The sheriff is following every lead."

She waved Mitchell toward the hall. With a hand over the phone she mouthed, "Your father said to send you right in."

Mitchell made his way to his father's office and leaned against the doorframe. His dad faced the back wall, talking on the phone. The top of his graying military cut showed over the back of his chair.

"There's no hard evidence. It's all circumstantial, and I guarantee you I'll get to the bottom of this." His dad drew in a breath, obviously exhausted. "I can't arrest anyone until we have sufficient evidence. You're the mayor. You know that as well as I do." More silence. "I've got people leaning on me too, Harold, but Mitchell's wife said she was with him the whole night." His tone held an edge of anger.

Mitchell's pulse kicked.

"I'll hire new deputies as soon as I find someone who is qualified. Until then, I've asked the state troopers to take the lead on the investigation." Garbled yelling streamed through the receiver so loudly Mitchell could hear it too. "I've devoted my life to public service just like you, Harold, and—" His dad drew the phone away from his ear. The mayor had obviously hung up. His father spun to replace the receiver.

He startled when his eyes landed on Mitchell.

"Tough day?"

"You could say that." Deep lines creased the tanned skin around his father's eyes.

Mitchell shoved his hands in his pockets. "Let me guess. They're wanting you to arrest the most likely suspect." Which would be Mitchell.

His father didn't answer. Just ran a hand over his face and then rubbed his eyes.

"Why not give them what they want?" His dad hadn't had a problem accusing Mitchell in the past.

"Because you didn't do it, that's why," his dad said. "You know me well enough to know that if I thought you had done it, I wouldn't hesitate to lock you up."

Mitchell did know that.

"Have a seat." His dad pointed to the armchair in front of his desk.

Mitchell sank into the black leather, his edginess relaxing. He hadn't realized how much he'd actually wanted his father to believe in him. He'd spent years burying that need for approval deep, because he didn't think he'd ever get it. Now that he had it for once, he wasn't sure what to do with it.

He toed the ground, unable to meet his father's gaze. "Anything you can share about the investigation?"

"The fire chief and the forest rangers are sure it didn't start on its own. Same as the rec-center fire."

"Anyone come forward from the Wilderness Scouts?"

His father's expression turned dark. Worried. "As a matter of fact, yes. And they're not keeping their mouths shut about it either. I've been getting calls all night." His fingers drummed against the desk, a sure sign he was bothered.

"My attorney would kill me if she knew I was here," Mitchell said.

His dad exhaled. "Off the record, Angelique is one of the best. You were smart to retain her. Even with Lorenda vouching for your whereabouts, everyone is convinced that it was you because you were there.

They think she's covering for you. And now that she's made a statement about this fire, it looks bad that she won't make a statement about the rec-center fire."

Mitchell gave his dad a pointed look. "What do you believe?"

"My gut tells me it's all too conveniently pointing to you." He returned Mitchell's stare with a softer look in his eyes. The worry lines around his mouth deepened. "Which is why I asked the state troopers to take the scouts' and chaperones' statements. The troopers are going to each home as we speak. It seemed like a conflict of interest for me to do it since I'm your father, and I don't believe you should be arrested."

Mitchell blinked. Maybe they should join hands and sing "Kumbaya." When Mitchell finally recovered, he asked, "What do you know about Bart Wilkinson?"

His father's brow wrinkled. "Not much. Seems like an okay guy. His mother's a real piece of work, though, and he's never been able to cut the apron strings. Why?"

Mitchell rubbed the back of his neck. "I can't quite put my finger on it. He's definitely interested in Lorenda and doesn't like it now that I'm in the picture. Something's off about him." Mitchell explained about the scouts showing up at Middle Fork Lake when they were supposed to be camping several miles away. "Maybe the troopers should ask Bart why the location was changed and why the entire troop disappeared just a few hours after setting up camp." He pulled the charred dog tags from his pocket and held them up. "These were left behind in the Wilderness Scouts' camp last night. They disappeared from my tent yesterday."

Instead of taking them in hand, the sheriff picked up a pencil and scooped them up. He punched the intercom button on his phone. "Can you bring me an evidence bag, Maureen?"

"Sure thing, Sheriff."

Well, hell. Mitchell hadn't thought of the dog tags as evidence. He probably shouldn't have touched them.

Maureen popped in, opened the bag, and the sheriff dropped them in.

"Anything else?" Maureen asked.

The sheriff shook his head, staring at the bag of evidence.

When Maureen was gone, his dad asked, "Isn't Lorenda holding music rehearsals at the school?"

"Yep. She was planning to move it to the rec center until it caught fire. Who knows when it will be ready now? In the meantime she's stuck at the school."

"Another convenient coincidence." His dad leaned back in his chair.

Mitchell's thought exactly.

"Maybe she should shut the program down until this blows over," his dad said.

Mitchell shook his head. "Don't go there with her. Trust me." For being such a pushover, she could be hardheaded when she wanted to be.

"I'm hearing rumors that you're reaching out to folks to make up for some of the things you did when you were young," his dad said.

Mitchell bounced one leg. "I figured it couldn't hurt. Mom wanted me to make amends. I'm calling it my Suck-Up List."

His dad frowned. "I see you're still a smart-ass."

Mitchell couldn't deny it. "Any way you can help me repair things with Joe? He'll be the hardest." *Besides you.* Mitchell stilled his bouncing leg. He and the old man had been in the same room for more than five minutes and hadn't threatened each other yet. Had to be a record. So if Mitchell could start making inroads with his dad, surely he could find a way to reach out to Joe.

His dad leaned back in his chair. "I'll see what I can do, but you keep a low profile for a while. Stay away from town. I don't need more trouble right now."

Obviously the Kumbaya moment was over. "I'm not trying to cause trouble." Mitchell's voice was a little louder than it should've been. "I'm trying to protect my family."

"It doesn't matter." The sheriff's voice raised a few notches too. "Trouble happens wherever you go."

True. But his dad saying so still pissed Mitchell off after the almost-warm-and-fuzzy moment they'd just had. He pulled himself up to his full six feet three just to make a point. His posture inflated with a rush of defensive adrenaline as if he were about to engage the enemy. A move he'd learned from his dad.

Slowly, his dad stood too. Struck the same pose, as if they were mirror images of each other. And that pissed Mitchell off even more because he was not like his hard-ass dad.

Mitchell wanted to yell. Get up and storm out. Slam the door and pull out of the parking lot with the wheels squealing. Same way he'd always handled confrontation with his father. But for the first time, Mitchell realized how adolescent that behavior had been. How it had only made the problem worse.

He pinched the bridge of his nose. "Okay. I'll try, but I can't guarantee I'll stay away from everyone. Red River isn't big enough to hide forever."

His father studied Mitchell. Not scrutinizing. Not looking for fault. But more like he was seeing Mitchell for the first time as a man, not the hell-raising kid he'd been. A few silent beats went by.

"Fair enough," his dad said. "Whoever did this put my grandkids in danger, and I won't rest until they're behind bars." His dad's jaw hardened. "Any lunatic who will go to those lengths won't stop until he gets what he wants. I want to catch the son of a bitch before anyone gets hurt. I'll pay Principal Wilkinson a surprise visit. See if I can scare him and get him to slip up. I hope to God you're wrong because he's got full access to Jaycee, Trevor, and every kid enrolled at the elementary school. Arson is a lot more serious than most of the crimes I deal with in Red River. Usually I can straighten people out with just a subtle warning and a hard look, but this is different."

"It worked for me." Mitchell blew out a gust of laughter.

"No, son, it didn't." His father's voice held a tone of regret.

Mitchell shoved his hands in his pockets. "It did more than you know. I was just too much of a rebellious punk to let it show." Mitchell smiled at his dad. His father didn't smile back. Hadn't since Mitchell was a boy. And he had to admit, he hadn't really given the old man much reason to. But a hint of peace glinted in his dad's eyes, and that was enough for the moment.

Chapter Twenty

Monday afternoon Lorenda was in the gymnasium, waiting for the last bell of the day to ring. Chairs lined up, music stands filled with sheet music for "Greensleeves." And Mitchell—all six feet three of hard muscled man—was sitting on the bleachers reading a motorcycle magazine.

Like she needed a babysitter. Which was getting on her nerves, because she'd been on her own a long time before he'd come back to town. And she'd be alone again if he got restless and left.

Unless he meant what he said about them being real. Of course, he'd been talking about sex, and she knew all too well that it took much more than sex to make a marriage real.

The bell rang, and a blur of backpacks, Vans sneakers, and chatter shuffled past the open doors that connected the gym to the school building as the kids poured out of the classrooms.

And there she was, standing in front of her stand. Staring out at empty chairs.

Dylan blew through the side door, his boyish grin in place. "Sorry if I'm late. I had an influx of customers at the end of my shift and no one to cover for me." He and Mitchell gave each other the silent dude nod, and Dylan came over to stand by her. He looked at the music.

"No worries." She put on a brave face and smiled, but worries were exactly the thing winding around her gut to settle in her stomach. The hallway chatter ebbed with the receding tide of students, and not one of the empty chairs filled.

She glanced at the clock hanging over the door.

The ticking of the second hand seemed to echo through the gym, even though it wasn't audible. It was the ticktock of failure that filled the silence. The click-clack of defeat pounding against her hopes. The rap, tap, tapping of disappointment weakening her confidence and belief in the people of Red River who had been her network of support since she was born.

"You okay?"

She jumped at Dylan's voice.

His expression filled with sympathy like he understood the emotions that scratched at her heart.

Mitchell gave her a worried look over the top of his magazine, but he didn't say a word. Didn't come over. She couldn't blame him after the way she'd bitten his head off when he'd suggested shutting down the program. Tears stung the backs of her eyes. "Sure. I'm fine."

"Gossip can suck." Dylan gave her a friendly nudge with his elbow.

"People don't have to believe it."

"But they usually do." He took the beginner's music book and thumbed through the pages. "I'm in your and Mitchell's corner, and so are your close friends."

"I don't know why I've stayed in this little town." She glanced at the clock one more time, and with a weighty breath, started to break down the music stands.

Dylan started stacking chairs. "Because it's your home, just like it's mine. People gossip everywhere, Lorenda, no matter the population. It doesn't hurt any less when it's happening in a big city."

She stuffed music into her satchel. "I'm sorry I wasted your time."

"Music is never a waste of my time," Dylan said.

Mitchell stepped off the metal bleachers and gathered up an armful of music stands. "Help me carry these to my truck?" he asked Dylan.

"Sure, man." Dylan gathered up an armful too.

When the gym door slammed behind them, the silence became almost deafening. Which made no sense because Jaycee and Trevor should've been there already. They knew to come straight to the gym after school.

She bent over the bottom step of the bleachers to dig through her satchel. She pulled out the contact list for every kid in the program. She'd call each one of the parents, visit them in person, maybe offer a kidney if she had to.

Footfalls sounded behind her. Good. Jaycee and Trevor were there and they could go home. She turned to greet her boys and came face-to-face with Bart.

She took a step back, but the bleachers stopped her and she almost tumbled backward.

He grabbed her arms to catch her. "Whoa. You okay?" He helped her find her footing.

"Thanks. You startled me." She smoothed her hair.

"I came to check on you. I've been worried. Must've been traumatic to have your boys in harm's way. I'm just glad you got out safely." He sounded genuinely concerned, and she relaxed.

"I'm glad the scouts got out too. Mitchell went back to help, but you were already gone."

Bart's eyes dilated, and a chill slithered up Lorenda's spine. *Oh for God's sake.* This was Bart! She was not going to buy into Mitchell's overprotective alpha-macho crap.

Something was niggling at the back of her mind, though. Had been since she'd lifted the binoculars and found Bart staring back at her from across the lake. "I'm curious . . . um, Bart." She smiled. "Why was the campout location changed?"

He slid both hands into his pockets and rocked back on his heels. "Loggers were clearing a parcel of land close to our original location. I had to make a command decision, and I felt it would be safer to move the campout."

Makes sense. Her mind stopped niggling. Niggling was silly. Bart was harmless.

He glanced around the empty gym. "No one showed up today?"

She shook her head, fighting off tears.

"I'm sorry, Lorenda. I managed to get the school board to let the program stay here for now, but it doesn't look like there's a program left." He took a step closer. "Is there anything else I can do to help?"

"Well." She chewed her lip. If she accepted Bart's help, it would likely upset Mitchell.

"Anything at all, just name it," Bart said.

What could it hurt to let Bart help if it meant the kids being able to learn music?

"Some of the kids were showing real promise. Maybe if you called their parents, they'd let their kids continue in the program." She waved a hand across the bleachers. "The parents are welcome to sit and watch if it would make them feel better."

Did Mitchell really need to know that she was taking help from Bart? Shame coiled in her chest, because she'd resented Cameron for skirting the truth. Now she was doing the same thing.

"Consider it done, and I'll even give them my assurance that I'll be at every rehearsal with you. That should regain their confidence."

Oh dear. Mitchell would be at every rehearsal too, she could almost guarantee it.

Bart placed a hand on her arm and gave it a gentle squeeze. "I know things are hard right now. If there's anything at all you need, just let me know. We'll work this music problem out together, okay?"

The front doors of the gym slammed open. Lorenda jumped as high as she had when the mommy mafia had caught her eating a gooey cinnamon roll from the Ostergaard's Bakery after she'd agreed to go on a postpartum diet with them.

She'd paid her dues after two pregnancies with no husband around for support. Dieting was for suckers.

The scrambling of small feet that she was sure belonged to her kids made her turn toward the door to greet the boys. But it wasn't just Jaycee and Trevor. Mitchell stood in the doorway too. Stance wide. Fists clenched. Stare lethal.

Bart's hand fell away.

Jaycee and Trevor snatched a basketball from a bin and started tossing it toward the hoop.

"I've got paperwork to do," Bart said. "I'll be sure to make those calls."

"Thank you, Bart," she said, but he was already taking long strides toward the hallway.

"Come on, boys." Lorenda slung her purse over one shoulder and picked up her satchel. "Put the balls away and let's go."

Mitchell's cast-iron stare didn't waver as she walked toward him.

"Was he here to rub it in that no one showed up today?" Mitchell asked when she got close enough.

"No. On the contrary." She chewed her lip.

The boys barreled out of the gym toward the car. She was right behind them.

"He had his hand on your arm, real friendly like, and it's not the first time I've seen him do that to you. I would've had a little talk with him about personal space if he hadn't scurried out of here so fast."

"I don't think he was scurrying. He had work to do."

When they got to the SUV, Mitchell opened her door so she could climb in. He loomed in the open door, hovering over her. "Cockroaches scurry less."

She snorted. He didn't.

"Can you blame him, Mitchell? He's not a big guy. But you"—she waved a hand down the length of Mitchell's ripped body, all the billowing testosterone distracting her for a second—"you're spectacularly intimidating."

One side of his mouth turned up.

An object flew from one side of the backseat to the other, and an argument broke out between Jaycee and Trevor. Lorenda didn't care at the moment because of the spark that had just flared to life in Mitchell's eyes. She knew that spark. Had experienced all that came with it several times over the last few days.

"Let's go home. I'll make dinner." She glanced to the backseat where Jaycee and Trevor were still arguing. "Since they aren't behaving so well, they can go to bed early."

Mitchell's smile went full-on, and he shut the door to walk around to the driver's side.

Lorenda stared straight ahead as he got behind the wheel.

With any luck, Mitchell wouldn't get arrested for assaulting the school principal. Because if he did, it would be her fault.

Mitchell had made it through the most grueling military training on the planet. He'd faced brutal enemies on foreign soil. He'd been on missions where the chances of his entire SEAL team making it back in body bags had been better than good.

Damned if mowing the lawn for two little old ladies who carried a loaded cane and a high-powered purse didn't scare the shit out of him.

Mitchell parked in front of the old powder-blue Victorian house late Friday morning so he could mark another person off his Suck-Up List. Francine and Clydelle were waiting for him on the wraparound porch, both sitting in the swing with a glass of lemonade.

He'd gotten restless staying around Lorenda's house. His dad had asked him to keep a low profile, but Mitchell wasn't exactly a low profile kind of guy. So while Lorenda was putting in some hours at her real-estate office, he got out his list and started making calls.

Following through on his promise to make up for his hell-raising days might win back some confidence from the townsfolk and squelch gossip. Problem was, the first two people he called hung up on him.

When he got to Ms. Francine, she'd said she was happy to have him come over and mow the lawn, since it was a warm day.

No idea what that meant, because the outside temperature was nice now that the seasons were starting to change.

"Morning, ladies." He strolled up the concrete walk and pushed his aviators farther up onto his nose. "I promised to make up for ruining your mailbox." Sixteen years ago.

Ms. Clydelle pointed her cane at him. "Took you long enough, young man. We've been waiting since that day in the park."

"Uh, well, I've had a lot going on since I got back into town."

Ms. Francine studied him over thick glasses perched on the end of her nose. "I'd say."

He tossed a look over one shoulder at the overgrown lawn. "Looks like your grass needs to be cut. I could start there." He gave the graying sky a once-over. "Good day to mow since it looks like rain is coming."

"Mower's out back along with the gas can," said Ms. Francine. "And if you get hot and sweaty, feel free to take off your shirt."

"I'm sure I'll be fine, ladies."

"Oh, you already are, hon. That's why we want you to take off your shirt." Ms. Clydelle waggled bushy gray brows.

Without answering—because really, what could he say to that—he stumbled around the house and found the work shed in the backyard. Ten minutes later he had the mower fired up and was cutting a trail back and forth through the thick grass.

The two old sisters sipped their lemonade and gawked at him like mowing the lawn was a spectator sport.

A few minutes later, Ms. Clydelle picked a long stick-looking thing off the tray.

Mitchell did not want to know. He didn't.

She snapped open an old fashioned accordion fan and started fanning herself like a regular Southern belle.

Mitchell was sure his groan could be heard over the mower's motor.

It wasn't hot. It was the middle of September. In the Rockies. And it was overcast.

Ms. Francine waved for him to cut the engine, so he did.

"Sure is hot out, Mitchell," Ms. Francine said.

He pulled the cord again as though he hadn't heard. He was not taking his shirt off.

She snagged another fan off the tray and snapped it open like her sister.

Jesus.

He killed the mower. "Not gonna happen, ladies. I'm taken."

A thrill rushed through him. He *was* taken. In every way possible. For the first time in his life. He'd been in relationships, but none had ever lasted long because of his rush to get back overseas to the brotherhood of warriors where he thought he belonged. Now all he wanted to do was stay here in Red River with Lorenda and the kids, because that's the only place he felt at home.

Too bad not many people in Red River agreed.

"My wife might get jealous if you ladies keep ogling me, so I could come back when you're not home if you'd like?"

Ms. Francine harrumphed.

"Oh, don't get your boxers in a twist." Ms. Clydelle waved her cane at him. "You can join us for a glass of lemonade when you're done."

"Only if I can stay fully clothed." Mitchell wanted to establish the ground rules because he'd heard stories about these two. They seemed to be as unruly as he was, but they got away with it because of their age.

"Fine." Francine agreed, albeit with some reluctance.

He finished the lawn, put the mower away, and climbed onto the porch to join them. He took a seat in a wicker rocking chair, out of reach in case they decided to cop a feel. Which he wouldn't put past these two old rascals.

"Your house could use a coat of paint," he said.

Ms. Francine handed him a glass of lemonade.

"We live together now that we're both widows," Clydelle said. "And we don't have a lot of help."

"I'd be happy to do it." He took a sip of lemonade, and, God in Heaven, it was laced with vodka. He sputtered and wiped his mouth with the back of his hand.

"That's our version of afternoon delight." Francine smiled. "It's all we have to look forward to at our age."

Clydelle lifted her glass. "This and engine-washing day at the fire station during the summer. Those nice firefighters are so fit." She lifted her nose in the air. "They do take their shirts off when it's hot."

Mitchell nearly choked. "Okay, let me be perfectly clear. I'd be happy to help out if you two will behave." Only in Red River would he be lecturing two old women about sexually harassing him. He couldn't make this stuff up if he wanted to. Which he definitely did not want to.

"Well," Francine said. "I guess that's fair. But I don't want you to start if you can't finish. A half-painted house is worse than an unpainted house."

He pulled his eyebrows together.

"A lot of people in this town want you to either go to jail or go on your way." Clydelle's porch swing moved back and forth at a slow, lazy pace.

"I can't just leave this time. It's not that simple." Nothing about his situation with Lorenda was simple, and he had no idea how it was all going to work out. Especially in a town that mostly disliked him to the core, and where those grudges were bleeding over to Lorenda and the kids. "It didn't solve anything when I let myself be chased out of town years ago. It only created more problems and more heartache."

"Because you didn't have the decency to die too?" Ms. Clydelle said.

Mitchell's stare snapped to her. All the lewd teasing was gone, and she was serious.

"Survivor's guilt is a difficult thing, dear." Ms. Francine swayed with the rhythm of the swing. "My Henry had it bad when he came home from Korea. I'd imagine it would be a lot worse losing someone as close as a twin."

Heaviness settled in Mitchell's chest. Maybe that was the problem—Mitchell didn't have survivor's guilt.

He missed his brother. Every day. But he didn't feel guilty about surviving when Cameron hadn't. He felt guilty that he and Cameron had set the whole thing in motion graduation night and never manned up. Cameron had died for it, and Mitchell was still cleaning up the aftermath all these years later.

Grief bubbled up from the depths of Mitchell's soul.

"That wife of yours is a special one." Ms. Clydelle refilled her glass. "So are those two little boys. Marriage and raising a family are commitments, just like painting a house. Once you start, you can't give up."

Mitchell's heart knocked against his chest. That's why he was here, allowing himself to be objectified by two elderly women. Cameron had given up on Lorenda and the boys, but Mitchell wasn't going to. Making amends in Red River wasn't just for his mom or his dad anymore. He wasn't sure when it happened, but it had become about Lorenda and the kids and giving their future together a chance.

Not true. He knew the precise moment the goalpost had changed—when she'd fainted and landed in his arms in the park. From that moment forward his ship had been sunk, and he was all hers for as long as she wanted him.

He just wasn't sure if being with him was in her best interest. Or in her long-term plan.

"Leaving a house half painted just isn't right." Francine kept swinging.

The rocking chair soothed him while he weighed her words.

"You know, you'd look right smart in a police uniform." Francine tapped her chin. "Think you could wear one the next time you mow the lawn?"

Christ. These two obviously had a thing for first responders, which was breaching the creepy zone. "I told you two you had to behave."

"I'm being serious," said Francine, and Clydelle nodded in agreement. "Can't think of a better person to be a deputy than you, Mitchell."

He let out a hollow laugh. "People in this town want my head. I'm the last person they'd want wearing a badge."

"Then it seems to me you better get to work helping your dad catch the real criminal, because he could sure use the help."

"How are you ladies so sure that I'm not the real criminal?"

Ms. Francine snorted. "Young man, if you were a real criminal, you wouldn't have come back to Red River. This little town isn't exactly prime hunting ground for crime."

Exactly the thing that had been needling the back of Mitchell's mind. There was no monetary gain in the fires or in the mugging. Mitchell's instincts told him Lorenda was the only common denominator. She was mugged for a suitcase of old clothes. She was at Middle Fork Lake when the fire broke out. And indirectly, she stood to lose from the rec-center fire because she didn't have a place to rehearse.

Shit. The pieces fell into place, locking together like a jigsaw puzzle. He'd known there was a connection, but he hadn't seen the big picture until now. Bart Wilkinson was the only other common thread. And Mitchell himself.

"Well, I'm going inside to watch my soaps." Ms. Clydelle used her cane to stand, then she swatted his thigh with it.

"Ouch." He rubbed his leg.

"Let us know if you plan to stay in town long enough to finish painting that house." Francine stood too.

Mitchell gave them an appreciative smile for encouraging him. It had been a long time since anyone in Red River had done so. And then he went to find his wife.

Chapter Twenty-One

By late morning, Lorenda found that juggling the Y chromosomes in her life was getting harder. They seemed to be multiplying.

Bart Wilkinson had called and asked her to stop by the school for a quick update on the music program. Mitchell would probably be upset that she'd gone alone, but she was a big girl and could handle Bart, no matter how much Mitchell's overprotectiveness might disagree.

Good thing she met with Bart, because he'd managed to convince a few of the parents to let their kids come back to the program. Rehearsals were back on, and so was the concert. So when Felix Daniels asked her and Dylan to meet at Joe's for a lunchtime interview about the music program, she'd been happy to accept.

Imagine her surprise when yet another male called asking for her time and attention later that afternoon. Daniel Summerall was coming into town and wanted to look at the cabin again.

More Ys than she could handle.

She walked into Joe's in black heels, a black pencil skirt, and a cream silk blouse. Her program was back on, and she was going to own it! She slung her hobo bag over a shoulder, and strutted.

The peanut shells under her feet made her black stilettos wobble off balance. She stopped. Smoothed her skirt and glanced around the crowded room to see who'd noticed. Every head turned in her direction, not a friendly face among them, and the chatter quieted.

So the stilettos may have been over the top.

She perched on the edge of a stool at the bar where Dylan was working. "Maybe we should've picked a more private spot for the interview?" She put her purse, phone, and keys on the bar.

"Don't let people chase you away from your dream. Trust me, I know." Dylan filled an order and placed it on a tray. "So what's our game plan for the interview?"

"Well, I just met with Principal Wilkinson. A few kids are reenrolling, so we can start rehearsals again on Monday. That doesn't give us a lot of time before the concert, but we'll work with what we've got. As long as the kids do their best, then the rest is on me."

Dylan wiped his hands on a towel and slung it over a shoulder. "For the record, I think what you're doing is great, Lorenda. Thanks for asking me to be part of it."

Her confidence soared a little higher. "That's exactly the spirit I want Felix to see. I want the whole town to see how music can change a kid's life."

Dylan gave her an understanding smile as Felix walked in wearing his trademark suspenders and black beret tilted just enough to one side to look suave. His white hair and Santa Claus beard were stark against his black flannel shirt. He sidled over to the bar and sat next to Lorenda.

"Thanks for coming on such short notice." Felix set a small tape recorder in front of her. "Honestly, between the two fires I haven't had much time to get this interview done. I'm glad we're finally getting together. There's nothing more I like reporting on than community projects." His look slid from Lorenda to Dylan. "So who wants to start?"

Dylan braced his elbows against the bar. "She's the boss. I'm just helping out."

"Okay, then." Felix pressed a button on the recorder. "Lorenda, what makes you want to start a free community music program for kids?"

That was the only cue she needed. She poured out her heart about how music had touched her life. Her heart. Her soul. Allowed her to reach into an alternate dimension and get lost in it. It soothed her when she was worried. Calmed her when she was upset. Cheered her when she was sad, and marked every phase of her life from the time she'd first picked up an instrument as a child to right now.

She stopped talking for a moment and listened to the C&W music that was streaming low through the speakers to entertain Joe's lunch crowd. Her eyes closed as she let the song seep into her innermost thoughts. It would forever time stamp this moment, this memory, into her heart, like music had done with so many other memories.

Music was the thread that stitched the many facets of her life together.

And suddenly, both the heaviness and the joy of falling in love with Mitchell pressed down on her. She was in love with him. One hundred percent heart and soul.

Probably a good thing since they were married.

"Wow," Dylan said, and Lorenda jumped. "Not much I can add to that."

Felix scratched his beard. "If the program is free for the kids, how do you plan to fund it?"

Good question. So far, all of the expenses were coming out of her pocket, but she couldn't do that forever. As the program grew, she'd need outside support. And the program wouldn't grow without better equipment and some money to invest in it. She needed Daniel Summerall and all of the connections he could provide. She also needed Principal Wilkinson's support to keep enough kids involved to make it work.

"I've got some irons in the fire when it comes to funding." One. She had a total of one iron in the fire, and that was Daniel Summerall. She glanced at the clock on the wall. "In fact, I have a meeting with a potential donor in a few minutes."

Daniel would be at the cabin soon for another showing, and hopefully he'd decide to buy it. Her commission would help keep the program alive for a while. She just hoped Daniel's support didn't have strings attached, because he still didn't know she'd gotten married.

She shook Felix's hand. "Thanks. I'm hoping the publicity from this article will encourage community interest."

Felix shut off the recorder. "I do have one question for you off the record."

"Okay, shoot," Lorenda said.

"Is someone in danger?" Minx murmured in her usual sensual voice. "Should I call nine-one-one?"

Lorenda snatched up the phone and turned off the power completely. Only way to get rid of her porn-star OS system. "Sorry. My phone has a mind of its own. Kind of scary, actually."

"The scuttlebutt around town is that some parents have concerns about danger that might surround the program because of your husband. Any comment on that?"

Lorenda's laced fingers rubbed furiously against each other. Finally, she pushed the recorder button on again. "Last time I checked, a person was innocent until proven guilty. People have every right to be concerned for our community. There's a criminal on the loose, but Mitchell didn't do it. Frankly, I have faith in the people of Red River and know they wouldn't try and convict him with no evidence."

She looked at Dylan. "See you Monday at rehearsals?"

He gave her an approving nod. "You bet."

Trying to look confident, she gathered up her purse and headed for the door to go meet her one iron in the fire.

She just hoped that iron in the fire didn't cause both her and the program to get burned. And she hoped her faith in Red River wasn't misplaced.

Lorenda held a leather-bound notebook in her left hand to keep her wedding ring hidden during the showing. If her mom and dad had given Mr. Summerall the impression that Lorenda was available, well, then, they could explain to him that she was married now. She wasn't responsible for misleading Daniel Summerall.

And Kansas wasn't flat.

They stepped out onto the hardwood deck adjacent to the downstairs den so he could take in the view one more time.

"I'll take it." Daniel slid a hand into the pocket of his expensive steel-gray dress pants that had probably cost more than Lorenda's hefty commission on this sale. His gaze settled on her.

"Great!" She gave him a brave smile, trying not to show the guilt rippling through her. "I'll draw up the contract and e-mail it."

He leaned against the railing with an elbow. "How are preparations for the concert coming along?"

She pulled in a breath. "Good. It's a small group. I expect it to grow over time." Or not. "The kids are showing so much enthusiasm." Their parents, not so much. "And we have a lot of support from the community."

Did her nose just grow? She flicked an index finger across the bottom of it.

"Were you going to bring it up?" he asked.

"Well . . . I . . ." She'd wanted to, she just hadn't been sure how.

"Lorenda, you have to go after the things you want." The color of his eyes shifted as his gaze drifted over her face. "Even if you might get rejected. Even if you might fail. Even if it might be humiliating, and even if it ruffles some feathers."

He was right. And his statement didn't just resonate with her because of the music program. She wanted to turn her convenient faux marriage into the real thing. Ask Mitchell to take her hand and jump with both feet. Only, she'd been avoiding the subject because she was a chicken.

Maybe she was scared of going long term with another alpha. Maybe she was scared of rejection. Maybe she was scared that she might fail at marriage again if they did make it real. It was easier to fail at something that wasn't supposed to succeed in the first place.

The look in Daniel's eyes said he was thinking of going after things he wanted too, and it wasn't just the cabin.

She drew in a breath and held it until she thought her lungs would explode. Badassery just wasn't on her list of talents. Neither was manipulating the truth.

She withdrew a printed document from the notebook. "Everything you asked for is here. Guidelines, a budget, and a mission statement." She held it up. "Even a rundown of what we have planned for the concert."

He tried to take it, but she held it out of reach. "First, there's something I have to say."

Something raced across his expression, but it was gone before Lorenda could identify it.

"Look, you're a really nice guy, Daniel, but I'm afraid my parents may have misled you." She chewed her lip for a second. Looked out over the green landscape. "Before you offer your support or buy this cabin, I have to clear the air about something." Not to mention clear her conscience. "I got married recently." She flipped her hand over and showed him the glittering wedding band. "It was sudden, and my parents weren't a hundred percent on board." Their approval ranked in the negative numbers, but that was beside the point. "They liked you and hoped that you'd ask me out. You haven't, but just in case you were thinking about it, I wanted you to know the truth so there is no misunderstanding between us."

There. She'd said it. God, it felt good to get that off her chest. Maybe her pulse would stop thundering now.

One corner of his mouth lifted, and he studied her. Finally he took in the view of the mountains. "I'd be lying if I said I wasn't disappointed."

Uh-oh. She may have just lost his support.

"I'd be lying if I said I didn't find you the most attractive woman I've met in a long time."

Oh. Okay. She felt a blush coming on.

"I'd also be lying if I said I didn't know you were taken from the moment I first met you."

What? She blinked. "What?" She blinked again. "I wasn't even engaged then."

He pushed off the railing and stood beside her, both hands shoved into the pockets of his dress pants, his shirtsleeves cuffed up on his forearms just enough to look casually stylish.

"But you were already in love. It was hard to miss."

She had no idea it had been so obvious.

He took the paper from her. "I'm not afraid to go after what I want, but I'm not stupid. I already knew I didn't stand a chance as long as my competition was still in the picture." He walked to the edge of the deck. "I wasn't sure if whoever you were in love with felt the same way about you."

Neither was she.

"I figured I'd get to know you and see where it led after I bought a cabin and, more importantly, made a decision about your program. So I waited to ask you out, hoping that glow in your expression that only happens when a woman is in love would fade."

Daniel was as talented with words as he obviously was with music. Of course she wanted the alpha war junkie who communicated best with "hooya!"

She had to give Mitchell credit, though. His communication skills weren't bad when using his hands. Or his mouth.

"The glow didn't fade, Lorenda." Daniel turned an expression on her that said he was more than a little disappointed about that. He stepped off the deck and flicked his car remote. The lights on his silver Beamer blinked. He turned around and walked backward a few steps. "Draw up the sales contract for the cabin. I'll see you at the concert." He reached the car and opened the door. "You still have to prove yourself as a music teacher and as a leader before I'll put my reputation on the line to support your program."

He climbed in, and the sporty engine roared to life.

His BMW disappeared before Lorenda realized her jaw was hanging open.

———————

Mitchell flew through the mountain pass on his way to the cottage, frantic to find Lorenda. She hadn't been at her office. His mom had called and said his dad was picking the boys up from school in his sheriff's car for a sleepover. He dialed Lorenda's cell again but got her voice mail.

What had his heart pumping with fear was that her safety app wasn't registering her location.

Next he called her parents. "Hi, Mrs. Brooks. Is Lorenda with you?" He tried not to sound alarmed, even though fear had every one of his muscles tensed into a ball.

"No, Mitchell." Her tone was stiff. "Is something wrong?"

"No, ma'am. Just trying to catch up with her."

Mrs. Brooks cleared her throat. "She had a client come in from out of town unexpectedly. Besides that, I don't know what she had planned today."

Dammit. He didn't know where Lorenda was or whom she was with. Or if she was safe. "Thanks, Mrs. Brooks." He hesitated. What the hell? "I appreciate all you do for Lorenda and the boys." Mr. and Mrs. Brooks had been Lorenda's safety net. Her fallback plan when Cam hadn't come through for her. "Is there anything I can do for you? You know, to show my gratitude?"

A beat passed in silence. "Just take care of my little girl. She's always been well liked. Had lots of friends to turn to. Now that circle of friendships is much smaller."

She left out how that was because of Mitchell. He had to hand it to his mother-in-law for trying to be diplomatic.

Mitchell slowed to take a sharp curve. "I promise I'll make this right." Somehow.

He ended the call just as he got to Lorenda's drive, slammed on the brakes, and fishtailed into the driveway. Her SUV was parked out front. The truck had barely stopped rolling when he bailed out and hightailed it to the house. A rush of adrenaline surged through him the same way it always had during those critical moments of a mission that determined success or failure. Life or death. He walked past her SUV and put a hand on the hood. It was still warm, which meant she hadn't been there long.

He burst through the front door, then skidded to a halt.

Lorenda, dressed in a tight black skirt that revealed every curve and just enough bare knee to make his prick roar to life, stood there with a bottle of champagne in one hand and two stemmed glasses in the other. Her cream silk blouse was undone two buttons lower than when he'd kissed her goodbye in the drive earlier, revealing a choker of amber beads and a lacey bra.

And those heels. Six-inch black stilettos with sexy red-painted toe-nails peeking through the tips that screamed *fuck me* louder than a heavy metal concert.

"Just in time." She smiled. "I was getting some things set up to celebrate."

Malarkey must've sensed Mitchell's tension, because he stayed curled in a ball on the recliner.

Relief slammed through Mitchell, the same way it did when a mission was over and his team had been extracted from the hot zone. He sagged against the door.

"Mitchell, what's wrong?" Lorenda put the bottle and glasses on the coffee table next to a grouping of candles and a box of matches that hadn't been there that morning. She hurried toward him, but he met her in the den with just a few long strides.

"Where have you been?" His words were much more demanding than he'd intended, but he'd been scared out of his mind.

She took a step back at his tone. "Felix Daniels interviewed me at Joe's, and then I . . . I had a client."

"You didn't answer your phone." Mitchell tried to stop gritting his teeth, but that hard edge was still in his voice.

"It was acting up again. I turned it off." Her jaw hardened too, but she grabbed her phone off the credenza and pressed the button. "There. It's on now." She tossed it back on the table.

"You should've called to let me know." Didn't look like the gritting was going to stop anytime soon.

Both manicured hands slid over her hips and came to a stop at her waist.

Mitchell's mind blanked.

"I'm a grown woman, Mitchell."

Was she ever.

"I'm well aware of that, Sparky." His gaze slid over her, starting at the icy-blue anger in her eyes, down her creamy exposed cleavage, over the valley of her slender waist and the curve of her mouthwatering hips, and along her long, bare legs, all the way to those shoes.

Jesus, those *shoes*.

"Then stop acting like an alpha ass." Her tone was as fiery as her gaze.

He trekked toward her, the flecks of fire in her eyes turning a little more to sparks of desire with each step he took.

"I don't know how to be anything but an alpha ass." He stopped a breath away from her. "Especially when it comes to your safety."

She stood toe to toe, nose to nose with him.

It was sexy, and he liked it. What he didn't like was her putting herself at risk and scaring him. And he knew just how to get her to back down and listen to reason.

"When it comes to protecting you, Jaycee, and Trevor, an alpha ass is what you're gonna get, babe. So get used to it, and don't expect an apology from me for protecting what's mine."

Her eyes widened. Lips parted. Sexy pink tongue slipped out to trace her lips, and he knew he had her.

He also knew he wanted her.

"I don't know whether to slap you or kiss you for that." Her tone was husky with lust, and her quickening breaths brushed over his neck and jaw.

"I don't know whether to toss you across my knee and spank that nice ass of yours for meeting a stranger alone." His voice was a gritty whisper. "Or tear every stitch off you and prove that you like an alpha ass a lot more than you think."

Her breath caught, lusty gaze dropping to his mouth. He leaned into her so that the sensual vibes pouring off of her circled and settled over him.

"I'd already met this client, so he technically wasn't a stranger. And this is my house," she whispered. "You can't discipline me like a child."

He brushed his nose gently against hers. "Then that leaves me no choice." He took the lapels of her shirt into his hands.

Her eyes narrowed to challenging slits of fire. "You wouldn't."

He lifted a brow as if to say *try me*.

She grabbed his hands. "I love this top."

"Then lose it." He loosened his grip. "Fast."

She met his gaze, then lifted her chin like she was not only calling his hand but raising the stakes. "Stay there." She pushed him back against the credenza that lined the back of the loveseat.

She stepped just out of his reach.

Her slender fingers went to the front of her shirt, and one slow, agonizing button at a time, the silk parted. When all the tiny pearl buttons were undone, she pulled it from her skirt and let it hang loose and open, revealing the creamy skin of her slender torso, a flat stomach, and an elegant, lacy bra.

It looked expensive. And sexy. And made him want to growl.

So he did, and a naughty smile spread over her pink lips.

She worked the buttons on the cuffs of her sleeve. "I have a lot of nice lingerie. It makes me feel pretty and feminine. It's my one vice." One cuff opened and she went to work on the other one. "Except for fashionable clothes. And shoes." She slid one foot forward and toed the floor with the tip of those fuck-me shoes. His prick turned to granite. "Okay, and ice cream too."

He crossed his arms and clamped his hands under his biceps to keep from tossing her over a shoulder like a caveman and hauling her upstairs. This was just too damn good to interrupt.

The second cuff fell open, and she swished her shoulders. The silk floated to the floor and pooled at her feet. "I've had to keep the lingerie to myself," she said in a sex-kitten voice. "Until now, the only men who have seen it are Ben and Jerry." Her hand went to the back of the twisty strings of amber and gold around her neck right where he wanted to sink his teeth.

"Leave 'em," Mitchell growled. His gaze dropped to her shoes. "And the shoes too."

"You don't like the lingerie?" She ran a fingertip along the top of one bra cup, then the other. The lace barely covered her nipples.

He swallowed. "I love the lingerie. I have to say, it's my favorite of all your vices. Nice as it is, though, it's going to get in the way of my mission in another minute or so."

"Really?" She unbuttoned the waistband of her skirt and slid the zipper down. She pivoted so that her backside was to him. "We'll see about that." She reached around to her back and unhooked the bra, letting it slid down her arms. With a fingertip, she held it to the side, and peeked over one shoulder with a wicked smile.

She let it go the way of her shirt, but she still didn't turn around so he could enjoy the view.

He frowned because, why would she be embarrassed now? He'd seen every inch of her up close. Over and over again.

She skimmed her thumbs inside the waistband of her skirt and let it glide over her hips to the floor. And, sweet Jesus, if he thought she was being shy, he'd been staggeringly wrong.

Thank God, because his closet sex-kitten wife was wearing a thong. A black lace one. At least the tiny piece of it he could see looked like lace.

He reached her in one stride and wrapped her in his arms so his front spooned against her back. With one hand, he angled her head to the side so her neck was exposed. The other hand found her breast, the nipple already tight and throbbing.

"On second thought, I don't think the lingerie will be a problem," he growled against her ear.

She arched back against him. "I didn't think so." She raised an arm over her shoulder to sink all five long, luxurious fingers into his hair and pulled his mouth to hers. Her kiss was urgent and scalding hot, scorching a trail of need through every nerve ending. She tasted sweet and spicy at the same time like the exotic foods he'd sampled overseas.

Her body was soft against his hardness.

She tried to turn in his arms to face him, but he stopped her. With his fingers working a nipple, he sank the other hand to her sleek abdomen and then took small steps forward to the wall. She followed his lead, and he threaded his fingers on top of hers and guided their joined hands flat against the wall. He braced their weight that way and slid his other hand under the tiny triangle of lace between her thighs.

Their lips and tongues still working that desperate kiss for all it was worth, she drew in a feathery breath when his fingers found her clit. He circled her sweet spot until it throbbed, then he pushed two fingers into her hot, wet center.

She cried out.

"Yes, baby." His whisper against her ear made her shiver.

"You're overdressed," she panted out.

That he was. He pulled off his shirt and kicked off his boots and pants with lightning fast movements. Completely naked, he stepped into her and covered her hand against the wall with his again. He moved the tiny black string to one side and bent his knees to enter her from behind. She was wet and ready and tilted one knee out to take all of him in.

The air around them became as thick and tense as his erection as he rolled his hips against her firm bottom and came up so deep that he filled her completely. Her head fell back against his shoulder, and he placed his mouth against her ear.

"You're so damn beautiful it hurts."

A shudder racked through her so fierce, so fast, so full of fire, that he had to grit his teeth to stop an orgasm from overtaking him. He found the pulsing nub between her thighs again and stroked it with his thumb in the same rhythm he stroked the most intimate part of her with the tip of his shaft.

One of her hands slid down to cover his, and she followed his movements. "Oh God, Mitchell."

The desperation in her voice drove him on, and his thrusts went deeper and faster until her body started to tighten around him. Just a slight tremor at first, then it grew and expanded until she exploded into an earthquake of quivering flesh that sent an orgasm thundering through him too.

When the last waves of it receded, she turned into his arms. This time he let her, and she went in for a soft, sweet sigh of a kiss. He wrapped his arms around her so tight that he could feel her heartbeat against his chest.

He never wanted it to end. Never wanted to let her go. Never wanted to leave her.

Never was a long time. But they had now, and maybe now could grow into forever.

His palms skimmed down her slender back and over the soft flesh of her ass. She squeaked when he lifted her, and her legs instinctively closed around his waist, her heels digging into his backside.

"Christ, Sparky, I already want you again." She did a nice grind against his groin, and he moaned. Loud.

"I didn't quite get that," Minx purred from Lorenda's phone. "Could you repeat?"

Oh yeah, he planned to repeat, but not with a cell phone monitoring him. "Grab your phone."

She did. "Now open the drawer." She did that too, and he let go of one of her cheeks long enough to snatch the phone and toss it in. He slammed the drawer and gripped her ass again. Her flesh felt so good filling his palm.

"I'm getting you another phone the next time I drive into a bigger town where they actually sell quality devices." He walked to the sofa. "With a service that doesn't spy on our love life like the NSA."

"I signed a contract for two years." She clamped her arms around his neck.

"I'll pay for both." If she kept him around that long. Right now, though, he didn't want to talk about the phone. "What are we celebrating?" He nodded to the champagne and candles.

She smiled and gave him a soft, contented kiss. "Besides the cataclysmic orgasm you just gave me?"

He laughed.

"I sold a big property today, and I plan to donate some of it to the music program."

He drew back, his brows pulling together. "I thought all the students dropped out?"

"Um . . . a few reenrolled." When she chewed her lip, and her eyes flitted away, Mitchell knew something was up, and he wasn't going to like it. His gaze raked her face. "What aren't you telling me?" Because this might be a problem, unless she planned on finding a new place to rehearse.

She gave him a knowing, naughty smile. "We can talk about it later. For now, we're celebrating."

He laid her back on the plush sofa. She stretched out. Both hands behind her head, strands of gold and amber glinting against the afternoon light that filtered through the blinds, small triangle of lace covering the sweetest piece of real estate on earth, and her long legs crossed at the ankles still sporting those fantastic heels.

Whatever she had to tell him could wait.

He found his jeans and slid them on. He zipped his pants but left the button undone, then walked to the coffee table. The tip of the match hissed when he struck it against the pack, and each candle flickered to life. He picked up the chilled bottle and peeled off the foil covering.

Lorenda propped on one elbow to watch, completely unashamed at the way she admired every inch of him from head to bare feet. Her wandering gaze made him go hard again.

Her eyes filled with raw emotion. The same raw emotion he'd been feeling deep in his soul. He'd thought it was gone forever after spending so many years in a foreign desert so far away from home. But Lorenda had somehow been able to tap into it, and he'd felt more human these past few weeks than he'd felt since he was an eighteen-year-old kid getting his head shaved on the first day of boot camp.

Forget the champagne. He just wanted her.

He slammed the bottle to the table and had her under him quicker than he could blink.

"There's something I want you to think about," she whispered against his mouth.

"Oh, I'm thinking about plenty right now." His mouth smothered hers again, and he went in for a deep, sensual kiss.

She started to protest, but he pressed his hips into hers.

"Oh!" She arched into him, her legs wrapping around his waist.

He groaned and then pulled a taut nipple between his teeth, sucking it into a hard peak.

She fisted the back of his hair and pulled his mouth to hers. "I want you to stay here. With me," she whispered against his lips.

Scalding desire rushed through him.

"Baby, I'm not going anywhere. Except down." He feathered open-mouthed kisses all the way down her center to that erotic triangle of lace.

The champagne stayed on the table, unopened and forgotten, but he made sure they celebrated in a whole different way.

Chapter Twenty-Two

Monday afternoon the seats Lorenda had set up in the gym were filled with students who had rejoined the music program. She and the kids had a lot of work to do to get back on track and prepare for the concert, which was less than two weeks away. Unfortunately, the bleachers were filled with angry parents who kept spearing Mitchell with dirty looks and then turning them on Lorenda.

This wasn't exactly what she'd pictured when she'd asked Bart to put his support behind the program and encourage the parents to let their kids come back.

Dylan passed out sheet music to the kids, and Lorenda adjusted her music stand.

As whispers buzzed through the crowd, Mitchell lounged in the back corner of the gym, arms and ankles crossed, trying to look inconspicuous. Inconspicuous was impossible for a well-built, good-looking bad boy like him. He'd added a pair of aviators to his standard-issue black T-shirt, faded Levi's, and combat boots. She suspected the aviators served as a shield against the hard scrutiny of the townsfolk. With his arms crossed, his thorny tattoo was taut over a large flexed bicep.

And the jeans? They hinted at his powerful thighs. Thighs she'd spent most of the weekend wrapped around.

She'd asked him to stay with her. He'd said he wasn't going anywhere. With the house to themselves until Sunday evening, they'd demonstrated in every way possible how they felt and what they meant to each other.

But his insistence that Bart was behind the mugging and the fires and Mitchell's refusal to let her out of his sight was too much. After getting no attention at all in her first marriage, Mitchell's concern was touching. It was also bordering on obsession and was crossing a line to domineering.

The angry buzz of whispers escalated a little more with each passing minute.

"Lorenda," Dylan said so only she could hear. "Maybe we should get started."

"Just a second." She picked up her phone and sent Mitchell a text. *Can you wait in the parking lot? I'll be fine.*

His phone must've dinged, because he retrieved it from his back pocket and his head tilted down like he was looking at the screen. He typed something back and then shoved his phone into his pocket.

Her phone vibrated.

No.

She glared at him.

His jaw hardened in response.

"What's he doing here?" One of the parents pointed to Mitchell.

That's all it took for an avalanche of complaints to come barreling at her from every direction. Lorenda held up her hands and tried to quiet them.

Wasn't happening.

She tried again, only to have the crowd's angry chatter turn to a low roar. Her gaze roamed the crowd as it spiraled further out of control.

A loud whistle ripped through the gym. Every mouth closed, and every head turned to Mitchell. He'd moved to stand behind her, and his fingers were still between his lips. "My wife has something to say."

"I . . . um . . ." She smiled at him, then turned to the crowd. "I invited the parents to observe because I thought it would settle your doubts. So please, give me a chance to work with your kids this week. I think you'll be pleased."

"We don't want him around our kids." A mother stared at Mitchell.

The timing couldn't have been worse, because Bart walked in before Lorenda could defend herself or her husband.

He stopped. Took in the audience. "Folks, give us a minute." He walked to Lorenda. "I need a word with you alone."

Mitchell eased another step closer. "Not alone."

Lorenda glanced over her shoulder, irritated at Mitchell for butting in. "What could possibly happen?"

He didn't back down. "Not alone, Sparky."

Bart's gaze bore into Mitchell. Finally Bart said, "This is why no one wants their kids in the program, Lorenda. I've tried to help you. They're here now because I called them like you asked, but there's nothing more I can do." He kept his voice low enough so only they could hear.

"You *asked* him to help you?" Mitchell said.

Her eyes slid shut.

"I'm the only one trying to make her life easier here, Lawson." Satisfaction glittered in Bart's eyes. "You've been making it harder since the minute you stepped back into Red River. You don't deserve her."

Mitchell's fists clenched, and he took a step toward Bart, whose eyes flew wide with fear.

The crowd gasped.

So did Lorenda. "Mitchell!"

"Whoa." Dylan stepped in between Mitchell and Bart. "You don't want to do that, buddy. Not with all these people watching, trust me."

"Lawson, I've allowed your presence here because of Lorenda, but you start a disturbance everywhere you go," Bart said. "I have to look out for the students, so you're no longer welcome on school property."

Lorenda had to do something to salvage the situation. "Bart, that's a little drast—"

"Then my wife can't be here either," Mitchell said. Like she wasn't even standing there.

"I can speak for myself," she ground out.

His stare, which had Bart zeroed, was lethal. "We've already talked about this, Sparky."

This had to stop. This wasn't the time and the place, but Mitchell's imagination was running wild and making an already difficult situation worse. She understood that he was accustomed to war, and being in a little town like Red River didn't provide the constant adrenaline rush he was used to, but this was bordering on delusional.

Tugging his arm, she pulled him away so they could have some privacy. "No, Mitchell, *you've* talked about it. I've listened, but I can't do that anymore. Your preoccupation with Bart needs to end."

"You're taking his side, Lorenda?" He didn't call her Sparky this time, and it made her pause.

"I'm not taking anyone's side."

"That's funny, because the only side I'm on is yours." Mitchell's words clipped out, like he was angry. Or maybe hurt. "I thought that might be worth something to you."

Lorenda knew he wasn't just talking about the music program. Cameron had never been on her side. Never been there for her at all. Now Mitchell was overcompensating with overkill protectiveness.

"Is that why you're acting so crazy and blowing the situation out of proportion? Because you're trying to make up for Cameron's lack of interest?"

A muscle in Mitchell's jaw ticked. "Is that what you think? That I'm acting crazy for wanting to protect you?"

"No!" She lowered her voice. "No, but I don't think Bart is capable of all the things that have happened."

"He's capable of far more, and even if you can't see it, I want you to trust me." He closed the small space between them. Leaned in so that his quick, angry breaths washed over her cheeks. "And none of this has to do with my brother, Sparky. I'm looking out for you because I—" He stopped.

Her breath caught, and she held it. Time slowed, and she waited . . . wanted him to say, "Because I love you."

"Because I wouldn't be able to live with myself if something happened to you," he finally finished.

Her heart dropped to her toes. More of his martyr heroics. She wasn't sure why she'd expected anything different. But somehow she had. She'd lost her heart to him, and he couldn't give all of his in return. Over the weekend, she'd convinced herself that he loved her.

Obviously, her imagination was working overtime just like Mitchell's.

"Bart got all of these parents to give me another chance. He deserves some credit for that." She stood her ground. Daniel Summerall had told her to go after the things she wanted, and she wanted the music program to work.

Mitchell stood his ground too. "He did it to stay close to you. Now he's trying to get between you and me so he has you alone and vulnerable."

"That's silly."

"Bart wants me out of the way," Mitchell said. "The question is, Sparky, do you? Because if you do, I can move back into the garage apartment."

Her pulsed kicked, and tears threatened. How could he make her choose? If he really did love her, would he be issuing an ultimatum? She'd given up enough in her life. She wasn't giving up anything else.

"This is my dream, Mitchell. The only way I'll ever be able to make a difference." She took a step back. "Bart is trying to help me with it."

Mitchell crossed his arms over his chest. "His goal is not to help you. Don't be naïve."

Fury bubbled up from somewhere deep inside. *Naïve?* Naïve was getting married at twenty years old to a man who put her at the bottom of his list. Naïve was marrying his twin brother—who had a martyr complex that could rival Joan of Arc's—under false pretenses.

Naïve was thinking Mitchell might love her just because their sex was so good that she'd darned near had an out-of-body experience.

She pulled her phone from her jacket pocket and held it up. "I've got the safety app you downloaded. If I need you, I'll call." She took a deep breath and squared her shoulders. "I don't want you to be at any more rehearsals." She swallowed. "Please leave."

Mitchell's posture had already been tense, but every inch of his perfectly formed frame seemed to solidify to stone.

"Are you going somewhere?" Minx purred. "I can . . ." Minx's voice sputtered, the service coughing out the last of her words. ". . . provide . . ." She cut out. "direc . . ." The screen on the phone flickered, then died out completely. Lorenda pushed the power button.

Dead as her music program had been until Bart breathed life into it again.

Mitchell retrieved his phone from his back pocket. "Use mine." He put it in her hand. "The boys are on the playground. I'll use one of their phones until I get you another one."

He studied her from behind those sexy aviators, and she almost caved. But she couldn't. Not when she was so close to success. So she resisted the urge to gnaw her lip, lifted her chin, and refused to look away.

He turned and walked out of the gym.

Chapter Twenty-Three

Thursday evening, Lorenda parked in Joe's back parking lot to join the mommy mafia and discuss last-minute details for the concert dress rehearsal over dinner. She pulled down the visor and looked at her reflection in the mirror.

Delta. Powder and makeup wasn't hiding the new shiner and swollen schnoz she'd accidentally given herself with a runaway champagne cork. Yesterday evening she'd been so happy with the kids' progress she'd decided to celebrate, snagged the bottle of champagne from the fridge that she and Mitchell had never gotten around to opening, and popped the cork to have a victory toast.

By herself, since Mitchell had moved back into the apartment.

The sting of sadness sliced through her. She'd known what she was getting into by marrying Mitchell, and she'd done it anyway. His overzealous need to protect her might have been in the right place, but it was also ruining her dream. And that dream was all she'd have left if . . . when he left.

She'd been on her own for so long, it surprised her how quickly she'd fallen into the habit of thinking of her and Mitchell as two halves of a whole. It was time to stand on her own two feet again like she always had.

She'd started by not checking in with him anymore. This was Red River. She could take care of herself without an alpha babysitter.

She forced the sick feeling of longing and loneliness out of her mind, even if it did still pound at the door of her heart. She'd been through it before and gotten over it. She could do it again.

She retrieved a powder compact from her purse, dabbing her nose and around her eye. The cork had caught her right where the two joined, blackening both of them.

"*Ow.*" She hissed in a breath when she tried to slide a pair of fashionable sunglasses onto her nose, going for the Garbo look. She pulled them off and found Jaycee's baseball cap in the back seat. Adjusted the bill so it hung low and shadowed the top half of her face.

Sierra. She flipped up the visor and stuffed Mitchell's phone in her purse, since she still hadn't gotten a new one for herself. It was getting dark. Maybe no one would notice. She snuck in through the back door just in case, and found her BFFs in a corner booth.

"What happened?" Miranda blurted.

"Shh!" Lorenda hissed out. "I'm trying to stay incognito."

"Looks like someone punched you," whispered Angelique.

Lorenda tried to angle her back to the crowd. "A champagne cork got away from me. It's nothing."

Langston walked over. "Ladies' night out, I see."

"Hey, Langston," Ella said. "We're just surveying the damage to your sister's face."

Lorenda turned a half smile on him.

"What the hell happened?" His voice was a near shout.

Every head turned.

Lorenda tried to pinch the bridge of her nose, but it hurt, so she looked toward the wall again to hide her face from the crowd. "I had an argument with an angry champagne cork. It won."

"Ouch. Must've been one badass cork." Langston took a swallow of his beer with a snort.

"Don't be a pansy," Lorenda said. "I've been through childbirth. Twice."

"I know. Mom and Dad never let me forget that the grandchild score is two to zero in your favor." He rolled his eyes.

"If you draw attention to my bruises again, I'm going to sit here all night and make you listen to our labor and delivery stories"—she gave him a sidelong glance—"in agonizing detail."

"Later, ladies." Langston walked away.

The waitress came over to take their orders. When it was Lorenda's turn she said, "I'll have the number three and water with a wedge of lemon." The server left, and Lorenda turned her attention back to her three BFFs. Who stared at her with open mouths.

"What?"

"Mm, mm, mm." Ella shook her head.

Miranda let out a low whistle. "The sex is that good, huh?"

Well. Yes, it had been. Until their argument in the gym a few days ago. But what did that have to do with her drink order? "What are you guys talking about?"

"You always order beer during girls night out. *Always*. It's the only time you drink because the kids aren't with you," Angelique said. "If you're content with water, then something else is filling that void."

Ella adjusted in her seat so she could look over Lorenda's shoulder. "And the thing filling that void just walked in."

Bruises forgotten, she turned to gawk at Mitchell, who glanced in her direction before sliding onto a stool next to his father and Joe. Totally not the trio she expected to see meeting up for a friendly drink.

All four of the mommy mafia kept staring. Mitchell must've sensed the attention because he glanced over a shoulder at them and did a double take.

Lorenda jerked back around. But not without taking notice of the dozens of eyes on her. A buzz started to circulate the room as people whispered. And stared at her. And whispered some more. Then started to shoot daggers at Mitchell with their eyes.

Foxtrot.

The waitress delivered their food and drinks.

"That's a lot of testosterone over on that stool." Miranda picked at her chicken and steamed veggies.

Was it ever.

"I'm glad you're obviously putting it to good use." Ella cut into her steak.

Lorenda would've blushed if she hadn't wanted to cry. She missed Mitchell, and not just because of the sex. She missed him being in her life. Being part of her, because she did feel like part of her was missing.

"What's going on?" Miranda asked. She knew Lorenda too well.

"Nothing I want to talk about tonight." Lorenda pulled a checklist from her purse. "Let's talk about the concert and dress rehearsal before our food arrives."

She ran through the list until she was satisfied that all the bases were covered. "Thanks, guys. I don't know what I'd do without you. The kids are making amazing progress, so we're going to be ready."

Lorenda just wasn't sure she was ready. She was finally getting a chance to teach music. But the cost might be more than she could bear.

Mitchell was worn out by trying to covertly keep up with Lorenda the last few days. He'd kept his distance just enough so she wouldn't get all huffy with him again. So maybe she wouldn't tell him to get out of her life completely, since she'd already told him to get out of her rehearsals.

Some husband he was. She'd gone to Bart for help, because Mitchell was the cause of most of her problems.

He sat sideways on the stool next to his father so his glances in Lorenda's direction wouldn't be so obvious. Dylan set drinks in front of them.

"Give us a minute," Joe said to Dylan, who moved to the other end of the long bar to wait on other customers. Joe and his dad, two old buddies who went way back, shot the breeze for a minute.

Mitchell had spent every night in the garage apartment since Lorenda had told him to leave the gym and not come back. Since she'd refused to answer his question about wanting him out of the way.

Which had silently answered his question anyway.

Just a week ago, she'd said she didn't want him to leave, until she'd realized that what he'd tried to warn her about all along was true. His presence in her life wasn't in her best interest.

Not sleeping in her bed where he could pull her against him, the possibility of not having a future with her had turned him into a bear.

Probably not the best time to visit his father and try to make amends with Joe for burning his restaurant down.

His father had wanted to meet at the station, away from the public eye, since Mitchell was supposed to be keeping a low profile. Once the security app showed him where Lorenda had gone, he'd insisted on meeting at Joe's. When it looked like his dad was ready to get down to business, Mitchell muted the cell he'd borrowed from Trevor.

"Thanks for hearing us out, Joe," his dad said.

"We've been friends for a long time, Larry." Joe took off his big cowboy hat and set it on the bar. "If you say we need to talk, then we talk."

"Son, tell Joe where you were the night of the rec-center fire and about your dog tags." It wasn't a request. Mitchell didn't speak. He weighed his options. Anything he said could be used against him. His dad had done it before, so maybe Mitchell should call Angelique over and have this meeting with her present.

"This is off the record, right, Joe?" his dad said, like he'd read Mitchell's thoughts.

"'Course." Joe nodded.

What the hell. Prison couldn't be that much worse than Afghanistan.

Mitchell ran a hand through his hair. "I was alone at Middle Fork Lake the night of the rec-center fire. No one can vouch for me, so I have no way of proving that I wasn't near the rec center when that fire started." He looked Joe in the eye. "But I wasn't."

Mitchell could've done another tour in the war zone in the time that Joe stayed silent. "Okay. And?" he finally said.

Mitchell's gaze slid to his father.

"Go ahead and tell him the rest, son."

Mitchell relayed the whole story of their camping trip, including finding his dog tags across the lake in the Wilderness Scouts camp.

Joe's bushy brows pulled together. "Why would anyone want your dog tags?"

"Honestly," Mitchell said, "I think someone wanted to leave a piece of evidence behind that would point to me. Only I found it before the investigators."

"Which means Mitchell didn't have to come forward with that information. No one would've known if he'd kept his mouth shut." Funny how the old man made a compliment sound like an insult.

Joe braced his weight against the bar with both elbows, thinking. Weighing. "You believe him, Larry?"

"Lord knows he's given me every reason not to over the years, but I do."

Gee. Another almost-Kumbaya moment.

For once, Mitchell kept his smart mouth and cocky comeback to himself.

"Mitchell's made mistakes, and he wants to make up for them, don't you, son?"

"Besides the fourteen years I spent fighting a war?" Mitchell couldn't help it. That time in hell had to count for something.

His dad leveled a cast-iron glare at him.

Mitchell rubbed the corners of his eyes. "Yes, I've been helping out some folks to make up for being a punk-ass kid. I'll do whatever you want, Joe, but mostly I want you to know that . . ." He wasn't sure how to finish, because he wasn't going to lie again and say he'd burned down Joe's. He didn't have to drudge up ancient history, but he was done lying. "I'm sorry your place burned down. I really am." That was the truth. "I know it was an accident."

His dad's brow wrinkled at the way Mitchell phrased that, so he skipped over it in a hurry.

"If I could go back in time, I'd make sure it never happened."

Before Joe could respond, an angry, familiar-looking man who'd had too many beers in him came over and poked his finger in Mitchell's chest. Pretty ballsy considering he was a foot shorter and probably hadn't seen his feet over his beer gut in a decade.

"You've got some nerve coming here," he growled. "My nephew was on that campout, and you could've got him killed. Or was that your intention?"

Mitchell stood, slow and easy.

"Son." His dad's tone held a warning. "Let it go." Then his dad turned to the man. "Walter, you've had too much to drink. Go home before you do something you're going to regret."

Walter Renfro. Mitchell remembered him from high school. He'd been a few grades older and rode the bench on the football team while Mitchell, Langston, and Talmadge did all the work.

A woman at a nearby table stood. "My son was there. You should be behind bars." She glared at the sheriff. "Now he's gone to beating his wife, and you're buying him a drink instead of arresting him!"

"*What?*" Mitchell seethed. "I've never hit a woman."

The entire restaurant went quiet, and everyone stared in his direction.

"Then why is her face all bruised up?" The woman wasn't really asking Mitchell. She was accusing him.

He scanned the crowd, but Lorenda wasn't in her seat. Finally, he spotted her darting around the dance floor toward them with her friends right on her heels.

Langston appeared at his side.

A few jeers rang out, and the negative energy in the crowd gained momentum quickly. A small crowd of sneering patrons surrounded them. Then Mitchell felt another jab to the chest.

"Back off, buddy." The sheriff stood.

"I'm not your buddy." Walter's words slurred from too much alcohol. Obviously the reason he had the cojones to take on someone Mitchell's size. Walter took a swing, Mitchell ducked, and Walter's fist landed on Langston's chest.

Langston didn't even flinch, because he was built like a tank, just like Mitchell.

Walter howled in pain, holding his hand.

A snarling crowd had formed around them, and Lorenda pushed through it.

"Who did this?" Mitchell took her arm, and pulled her to him. "I need to know whose ass to kick."

"I'll explain later." She glanced around the crowd.

"Don't lie for him anymore! He's not worth it," a woman yelled.

"That's enough," his father roared. "Go back to your tables or go home."

"We're doing your job, Sheriff, since you can't," someone shouted from the crowd.

"Or won't." Walter still held his hand. He looked at Lorenda. "How can you do it? Cameron was a good guy. A hero. How can you desecrate his memory by marrying his no-good brother?"

"Mitchell is a decorated veteran just like Cameron was." Tears glistened in Lorenda's eyes.

Mitchell growled at Walter. "Don't ever talk to my wife that way." He took a step toward Walter.

"Don't, son." The sheriff's voice was calm. A plea. The look in his eyes was that of a father. Mitchell had seen that look in his father's eyes when he was looking at Cameron. But never him, until now.

"Everybody clear out," Joe said. "Take your business elsewhere until you can cool down."

Mitchell's lips parted. Joe wasn't throwing Mitchell out. He was throwing out anyone who wanted to attack Mitchell.

"Sheriff, why haven't you arrested him? We want an answer!" a woman shouted, and verbal agreements rounded the crowd. She looked at Joe. "And you're going to ask us to leave?" She jabbed a finger in Mitchell's direction. "What about him? He burned your old place down years ago. Now he's back starting more fires and beating up a woman just because she stood up to him and asked him to leave the school the other day." The woman's hands went to her hips.

Everyone went quiet.

That seemed to give the woman confidence. "My son is in her after-school program, and I saw what happened Monday in the gym. Now she shows up all bruised."

Every set of eyes in the room turned on Mitchell, including his dad's and Joe's.

If Mitchell told the truth about Lorenda's misplaced trust in Bart it might make her look bad. He'd also be suggesting that her judgment wasn't sound, and the parents might lose faith in her. Plus, he had no evidence to outright accuse Bart, so Mitchell stayed silent. Again. Like he was guilty.

Seemed to be the story of his life.

"See?" someone shouted.

Lorenda started to speak, but the sheriff interrupted. "Mitchell hasn't been arrested because there's no evidence against him. He paid for his past mistakes in the military. Don't you think that's punishment enough?"

"He was given medals!" Walter said. "He should've been given a prison uniform. And he's still getting away with it because of you. I think it's time for your resignation, Sheriff. We don't trust your judgment anymore or your ability to do your job and keep Red River safe." Walter jabbed the sheriff with a finger, and a few people took a step back.

"Don't touch my dad again," Mitchell growled.

"Or what?" sneered Walter. "You'll break my nose like you broke your wife's?"

Mitchell reared back to swing, but Lorenda grabbed his arm.

"Mitchell! Please don't." She stepped between him and the crowd. "You people are something. This is Red River. We're supposed to take care of each other."

"That's what we're doing," said one of the women. "Watching out for each other by getting rid of him." She glared at Mitchell.

"Mitchell didn't hit me." She pointed to her face. "He wasn't even in the room when this happened."

Tears slid down Lorenda's cheeks when she turned to look at him, like she was saying she was sorry.

"Sparky," Mitchell murmured.

She didn't listen.

"Cameron started the fire that burned down Joe's, not Mitchell."

The crowd went silent.

Mitchell dropped his chin to his chest, closing his eyes against the harsh truth that had come out after so many years of keeping it locked down tight. His hand closed around her arm, and he stepped close to her, his chest brushing against her back, and let out a sigh of resignation that made her hair flutter. "Lorenda, don't. Let them believe what they want."

She shook her head. "No, Mitchell." She looked over her shoulder at him, her gaze smoothing over his face. "I loved Cameron, but I can't lie for him anymore. Especially not if the truth can help you."

Lorenda turned her full attention on his dad. "Mitchell never asked Cameron to stay in the military."

The sheriff's look of confusion turned to shock as her words sunk in.

"I begged Cameron to get out of the military when I got pregnant the second time. Mitchell tried to get Cam to see reason and come home to me and the kids." Her voice shook. "The truth is, he didn't want me, and he didn't want his kids either." She swiped at another tear.

Mitchell caressed up and down her arm.

"He stayed in the military so he wouldn't have to come home to us."

The sheriff's face turned red, and he blinked away the glaze in his eyes. "Son," he said, turning his glassy eyes on Mitchell. "Is this true? I forced you into the military for nothing? Your brother died because of me?"

His dad's hand went to his chest to clutch at his heart. His face turned almost purple, and his eyes rounded.

"Call an ambulance," Langston said and jumped into action.

Mitchell was right there with him. "He takes heart medication."

"Pock . . . et," his dad whispered as they lowered him to the floor. And then his eyes fluttered shut.

It was after midnight when Lorenda and Mitchell finally left the emergency room in Taos and drove back to Red River. The sheriff's EKG had shown no signs of a heart attack, and the doctor called it more of an episode.

They rode in silence with just the illumination from the dashboard and the whir of four-by-four tires filling the cab of the truck. Lorenda laced her fingers and stared straight ahead.

She pulled Mitchell's phone from her purse and sent her mom a text. Her mom texted back saying the boys were asleep and she'd bring them to school tomorrow. Lorenda put the phone away and cleared her throat.

Still an uncomfortable silence filled the cab.

They rumbled into her drive, and Mitchell had his hand on the door handle before the truck stopped rolling.

Lorenda wrapped her fingers around his muscled arm. "Mitchell, I'm sorry. The last thing I wanted was to cause more trouble for you and your parents."

Mitchell's heavy sigh reached through the darkness and whispered through Lorenda's heart.

"It's not your fault, Sparky." Mitchell voice was dull. Almost lifeless. "It's mine." He let his head fall back on the seat. "All of it is mine and Cam's. We set this whole thing in motion graduation night, and we're still ruining lives because of it."

"Don't say that. And stop being a martyr. It's ruining your life, Mitchell. No one else's."

"I'm toxic to everyone I touch."

"Mitchell." Lorenda slid her hand into his, and he rolled his head to the side to look at her.

He reached out to gently circle her neck with his fingers. The roughness of his hands sent a delicious shiver shooting from her core to the tips of her fingers and toes.

"I've ruined your life too, Sparky. You just haven't realized it yet." His thumb brushed her bottom lip, and it parted. "You had to go to Bart Wilkinson for help because of me. That pretty much proves that I'm a sorry excuse for a man." His thumb made another trip across her lip.

"You're a wonderful man. The best I've ever known." She placed a hand over his and guided the tip of his thumb to her lips. Drew it between them and licked across it with her tongue, just like he'd done hers on their wedding day when they'd cut the cake.

He hissed in a breath.

How stupid she'd been to make Mitchell feel like she'd chosen Bart's help over his. That hadn't been her intention. She'd been trying to stand up for herself and go after a dream she'd wanted for so long.

She'd been trying to hang on to something that would fill the hole in her heart if Mitchell weren't in this for love.

Maybe now it was time to go after something else she wanted so badly it hurt. Something so much more important than a music program.

The cool night air filled the cab, sending a chill over most of her body. The sexy man next to her filled her heart, sending heat rushing to the spot between her thighs. Mitchell was the only man capable of doing so.

She took his hand and placed their hands palm to palm. Then she threaded their fingers together.

"I've missed you." Her voice was a whisper. Definitely vulnerable. Hopefully sexy.

He let out a low growl.

"I want you, Mitchell. All of you. In my house, and in my bed."

Another growl, then he went in for an urgent kiss. No slow build, no words, no gentle nips. Just straight to the good stuff. She let him. Being without him the past few days had her wanting to skip a few steps.

"There's no place else I'd rather be." He pulled her as close as they could get with the console in between them. When he moved to her neck, she let out a moan. His lips weren't gently nipping and suckling like usual. His mouth moved the length of her neck like he was hungry, and he sunk his teeth into the crook of her neck with enough pressure for her to gasp.

His incredible fingers went to the hot, throbbing spot between her thighs and worked it.

"*Mitchell.*"

He placed a smoking-hot, openmouthed kiss in the same spot his teeth had just been, then an even hotter one on her lips. "I love it when you say my name like that."

Threading her fingers into the back of his hair, she pulled his mouth into hers for another deep kiss. Then she brushed her nose across his. "I love it when you do the things that make me say it like that."

He laughed.

First time she'd heard him do so in days. That had to be a good sign.

So she decided to roll the dice. Winner take all. "I love *you*, Mitchell."

He went rigid, and his breaths sped up.

She swallowed. Brushed her lips against his and gave him the soft kiss that said it was alright if he couldn't say it back. It hurt, but she'd rather he be honest, and that silence told her what she needed to know.

Her time with Mitchell would come to an end. When, she wasn't sure, but it would. She was doing the right thing by going after her dream so she'd have something meaningful to hang on to when she found herself alone again. But they had tonight. They had the here and now, while it lasted.

Chapter Twenty-Four

Mitchell parked the truck across the street from Brandenburg Park with Malarkey in the passenger seat, while Lorenda and her crew of volunteers prepared for a dress rehearsal. With an arm slung out of the window, he watched at a distance to give her some space.

So he wouldn't chase away the parents and destroy her hard work.

Hadn't mattered much to folks that he wasn't responsible for the fire when he was in high school. Hadn't mattered much that there was no evidence that he'd started the two recent fires. He'd still been a hell-raiser, and people thought he was the most likely suspect. Some of them even thought Lorenda was covering for him by blaming an innocent dead man. Cam. A fallen hero. A brother Mitchell loved and missed, and Lorenda's KIA husband.

They wanted Mitchell gone from Red River, and his dad gone from the sheriff's department.

Lot of good telling the truth had done.

The only positive thing to come out of it was the new respect his ailing father seemed to have for Mitchell. His dad had come home from the hospital the day after his episode, and Mitchell, Lorenda, and the boys had spent most evenings over at his parents' house.

The late-afternoon breeze rustled Lorenda's long, silky hair, and she hooked an index finger around a stray lock to brush it away from her face. She was so gorgeous it took his breath away.

She'd told him she loved him.

And he'd been too chickenshit to say it back. Why, he wasn't sure. She'd torn down every barrier he had. Every wall he'd constructed to block out the pain of his past.

She'd saved him in every way possible, and he couldn't tell her he loved her.

Even though he did.

Jaycee and Trevor bounded over and piled into the truck with him, and Malarkey jumped all over them.

"Can you teach us how to drive, Uncle Mitch?" Trevor's voice was so loud it seemed to echo.

"Your mom would ground all three of us." Mitchell tousled Trevor's hair.

"She's busy. She won't even know," Trevor's said with a little pout.

Sounded exactly like what Mitchell would've said at that age. Which was kind of scary.

Lorenda's crew bustled around the park. Lorenda set up chairs and music stands under the gazebo, and the rest of the crew lined up white folding chairs for the audience. Lorenda stopped what she was doing, pointed, and the crew started rearranging them.

Mitchell chuckled. His sexy, passive wife was becoming quite the commander in chief.

A few parents settled into the audience chairs to watch the dress rehearsal. Only a handful of kids took their seats under the gazebo.

Huh. That wasn't even half of the kids who had been in the gym last week.

Lorenda turned toward the audience, and Mitchell caught the deep frown on her face. She glanced at her watch and then took her place in front of the kids, raised her conductor's baton, and they started to play.

They weren't half bad, considering the on-again-off-again conditions they'd had to practice under, and now it looked like fewer than half of the kids had shown up for the dress rehearsal. They ran through four songs. Everyone clapped. As Lorenda stepped out of the gazebo to reach for a sheet of paper Dylan was trying to hand her, a skinny, stringy-haired guy came out of nowhere.

It was just like it had been that first day in the park. Time slowed as Mitchell processed what was happening. The same guy who had mugged Lorenda in the park sprinted toward her again. At a dead run, he clotheslined her with an outstretched arm.

Mitchell was out of the truck and running before Lorenda hit the ground. The kid didn't stand a chance. Mitchell was on him within seconds and had him pinned against the grass.

"Ah!" the kid yelled. "You weren't supposed to be here." He struggled against Mitchell's weight.

"Too bad for you I am. Who told you I wasn't going to be here?"

The mugger didn't say anything, so Mitchell tightened his hold on the kid's arms.

"Come on, man! I wasn't trying to hurt her. I was just supposed to scare her." The mugger turned his head so Mitchell could see his pasty white skin. A greasy film covered his face.

He was an addict needing a fix.

Mitchell had seen it so many times in the impoverished villages scattered around Afghanistan. Had seen soldiers break under the pressure and turn to drugs, only to become criminals themselves in order to support their habits.

Mitchell looked around for a way to secure the mugger so he could check on Lorenda. A crowd had gathered around her. They helped her to her feet and sat her in a chair. When he saw Lorenda hug Jaycee and Trevor, who'd run over to see their mom, Mitchell's eyes slid shut for a beat in relief.

"Jaycee! Trevor!" Mitchell yelled. "Over here."

They came running, and Dylan followed them.

"Jesus," Dylan said. "Who is this prick?"

"No idea, but it's time to find out." Mitchell hitched his chin up at the boys. "Remember how I said those survivalist bracelets might come in handy one day? Well, today's the day. Unwind both of them for me."

Jaycee's was unwound first, and Mitchell used it to secure the mugger's hands. Trevor's bound the mugger's feet.

"Now go back to your mom and stay with her." They did as they were told. "Dylan, stay here in case I need help." Mitchell pulled the phone from his pocket and dialed the sheriff's office number. Maureen answered on the first ring. "Tell whoever is working Red River for my dad to get over to Brandenburg Park. The same mugger attacked Lorenda again. We got him." The kid struggled again, and Mitchell dug his knee into the kid's back.

"Ow!" he yelped. "Police brutality!"

"I'm not the police, dumbass," Mitchell said.

"I'm a witness," said Dylan. "I haven't seen any brutality."

"You're lucky I haven't broken your jaw for hurting my wife." Mitchell cinched the rope around the kid's hands tighter. "The only reason I haven't is because I need you to be able to talk and tell us who's behind this."

"I got nothing to say without a lawyer," the kid snapped, and Mitchell put his hand on the back of the kid's head and pushed his cheek into the grass.

In the distance a siren blared to life.

"That hurts." The kid struggled more against Mitchell's weight.

"Oh, you'll tell me what I want to know," Mitchell promised.

"What are you gonna do? Beat me?" the kid spat.

Mitchell laughed for real. "Won't need to. You're a repeat offender. They'll hold you without bail this time." Mitchell had no idea if that was true, but it seemed like a good place to start. "You won't be able to get out and get your next fix."

The siren got louder, then a state trooper pulled around the corner and skidded to a halt at the edge of the park. Dylan waved both hands in the air, flagging him down.

"I'll call a lawyer!" the mugger growled.

"Go ahead. The only lawyer in town is my wife's good friend. You can call a lawyer from another town, but the wheels of justice tend to move slowly in these parts. By the time you get anywhere you'll be jonesing so bad you'll be crying for your mommy. But if you talk, maybe the authorities can get you some medication to help with the withdrawals."

When the trooper got there, Mitchell pulled the mugger to his feet and handed him off.

"Nice work." The trooper looked at the ropes.

"I'll be at the station as soon as I check on my wife."

The trooper unbound the kid's feet and hauled him to the car.

First Mitchell wanted to check on Lorenda. Then he was going to get that kid to give up the information they needed to catch whoever was behind this.

———

Lorenda still hadn't completely caught her breath by the time Mitchell got to her. The mommy mafia formed a tight circle around her, and the parents and kids were like an outer shell. Just like that first day in the park, Mitchell had tackled her mugger to the ground and held him there until the police arrived.

He weaved through the crowd toward her, and her anxiety faded a little more with each step.

"Back up and give her some room, folks." He knelt in front of her—face grim, body sexy. Her breathing sped up again.

"You okay?" he asked.

She nodded, her hand on her chest. "I think so."

His brow wrinkled.

"Yes, I'm fine. Stop worrying." She tried to put on a brave smile. Didn't work because the creases above his forehead deepened.

One of his large hands rubbed the length of her thigh. "I'm always going to worry about you." His tone wavered. So small, so fleeting, it was undetectable to the untrained ear. But Lorenda knew pitch from years of music lessons, and a hint of apology or regret or self-reproach twined its way through his words. He couldn't meet her gaze. "Maybe we should go to Doc Holloway's office and have him look at you."

"That's what I said," Angelique spoke up.

Lorenda shook her head. "I've got to keep working with the kids. The concert is in a few days."

"I'm sorry, Lorenda," one of the moms said. "I've kept my daughter in the program because he"—she glanced at Mitchell—"because I felt the gym was secure. Now I'm not so sure."

"That's right," a dad said. "A lot of parents pulled their kids again the past week, because of the, uh, controversy in your life." His gaze slid to Mitchell for a moment. "I've let my son stay in your little band because he loves the trombone, but I can't keep putting him in dangerous situations."

"That's why half the kids aren't here today?" Mitchell asked her. "Because of me? Their parents have been pulling them out even though I've stayed out of the gym?"

She hadn't told him. Didn't want him to blame himself and shoulder the responsibility like he always did. His look told her that was exactly what he was doing. A seed of sorrow sprouted in her heart.

"Mitchell." With her hand, she covered his, which still scanned up and down the length of her thigh. "Stop it. This isn't your fault."

"Dangerous situations seem to follow you two everywhere." This from another mom. "I'm pulling my kid too."

"Wait, you can't possibly blame Mitchell for this. He *caught* the guy." Lorenda saw her dream slipping away again. "I understand your concerns, but I've done everything I can to make this work for you and your kids. I've opened rehearsals to the parents." And had turned to Bart for help, even knowing how Mitchell felt about him. "Please. We're so close. Don't deprive your kids of this chance."

A few grumbles and murmurs floated through the crowd, but most parents turned and walked away with an "I'm sorry" or a "forget it."

"Well, that bites," said Ella.

Tears stung the back of Lorenda's eyes. She choked them down as she watched her dream walk away. "You guys have done enough," she said to her friends. "I can handle it from here." Because there wasn't much left to handle.

"You sure?" asked Miranda.

Lorenda nodded.

"We promised Joe we'd stop in for a guest musician who is playing tonight. That's where we'll be if you need us." Miranda gave her a hug, and the mommy mafia left.

When she looked at Mitchell, she couldn't help it, a tear streamed down her cheek, and she swiped it away. "No sense in me trying to go back to college if this is what I can expect."

"I'm sorry." He pulled her into his arms and placed a kiss in her hair.

That kiss gave her courage, made her feel loved and desirable and not alone anymore. She'd come to depend on the connection she felt every time she was in his arms.

"I'm a wuss. I couldn't stand up to these parents. At least not enough to convince them that this is good for their kids." She blew out a throaty laugh. "I can't even pull off a free music program." That made her both a wuss and a failure. Unless she could find more band students who knew the music and an audience to fill the chairs, her attempt at enriching children's lives with music was dead. She let another tear fall.

"You're one of the toughest people I know, Sparky."

"Daniel Summerall is expecting a concert. That usually entails students who play and an audience who watches. Without both, he won't have much to put his support behind."

Andrea's mom walked up behind them. "Mrs. Lawson?"

Lorenda straightened and wiped her eyes. Mitchell didn't move and kept stroking her leg.

"Yes?" Lorenda said.

"I don't know if you can still have a concert with one student, but I'd like Andrea to continue lessons with you."

That sprout of sorrow she'd had for Mitchell budded into hope. "You . . . you would?"

"I would." Andrea's mother nodded and put her arm around her daughter. "Andrea's always been a shy kid, but she's blossomed so much just in the few weeks you've been working with her."

If Lorenda could open the world of music to just one student, then it was worth a shot. "Andrea, if you're still in, then I'm in with you." This time Lorenda's eyes stung with happy tears. "The show will go on as planned, and you'll be the star."

Andrea beamed as her mom led her away.

She'd still have empty chairs, which probably wouldn't inspire Daniel Summerall to put his support behind the program, but she owed it to Andrea and Andrea's mom to give it her all.

"Come on. I'm dropping you and the boys off at your parents'," Mitchell said.

"My parents aren't home. They drove into Santa Fe to do some shopping for me. I need a few things for the concert that I can't get here in Red River." She sniffled away the last of her tears. "I asked them to get me another phone while they're there so I can give yours back."

"Then I'll take you to my parents' place." Mitchell offered his hand to pull her to her feet. "There's a criminal at the sheriff's office, and he owes me some answers."

Chapter Twenty-Five

On the way to the sheriff's office, Mitchell made a decision. Not the decision he wanted to make, but the one that was best for Lorenda. Everything in her life had turned to pure hell since he'd shown up in Red River. He'd come home to fix things. Instead he'd ruined her life in every way possible, nearly caused his dad to have a heart attack, and probably ended his dad's career.

That had to be a world record for number of screwups in such a short amount of time.

Mitchell had sealed his fate as an outcast in Red River long ago during his troublemaking youth. One thing was clear—no matter how hard he tried to set things right, some bridges couldn't be rebuilt. He didn't have to drag Lorenda under with him, though.

He didn't know how he'd go on without her, but he loved her enough to let her go.

He dialed Allen Carson's number.

A crusty voice answered on the third ring. "What is it?" Mitchell would've laughed if he didn't feel like such crap over what he was about to do. His ex-commander always sounded irritable, even when he was in a good mood.

"Hello to you too. It's Mitchell Lawson."

A beat of silence went by. "Hope you're calling because you finally came to your senses."

Mitchell stopped at an intersection on Main Street to let a group of off-season tourists cross. They waved a thanks. He returned it, and wished the residents he'd known his whole life could be as civil.

Some mistakes followed a person around forever.

And didn't that suck?

"You still got a job opening for me?" He rolled through the intersection when it was clear.

"I should say no," Allen groused.

Mitchell waited.

"Yeah, I've got a job for you. But if you ever leave me hanging again, you're fired."

There'd be no reason to leave his boss hanging again once Mitchell left Red River. The job was all Mitchell would have left. Lorenda was it. The only woman for him, and if he couldn't have her, he'd stay married to his work.

Maybe that's why he hadn't been able to tell her he loved her. Deep down he knew if he stayed, if he let himself love her totally and completely, he'd seal her fate right along with his. He couldn't live with that, and if he said the words out loud, it would be too hard to walk away.

"Deal." Mitchell pulled into the sheriff's office and parked.

"When can you report?" Allen asked.

"I have a few things to tie up here, then I'm all yours." Regret steamrolled through him. He shook it off, because the only way Lorenda could put her life back together and have all the things she deserved was for him to step aside.

"I'll give you a call when the paperwork is ready for you to sign," Allen said.

"Sounds good." Mitchell was about to end the call but stopped. "Hey, Allen. For now, call me on this number, not my old one." He still had Trevor's phone, and Lorenda still had Mitchell's.

"Will do." Allen hesitated. Finally he asked in a smart-ass tone, "What changed your mind? Can't settle down? Or did you just miss me?"

Mitchell ran a hand over his face. Settling down wasn't the problem like he thought it would be. He wanted nothing more than to stay in Red River and settle down with a certain gorgeous blonde, her two awesome kids, and her ugly dog. The thought of not staying to settle down with her exhausted him, and he had just made the decision less than five minutes ago.

"I'm poison to the people I care most about. They're better off without me." Mitchell probably should've owned up to that before agreeing to marry Lorenda and becoming Jaycee and Trevor's stepdad. But he'd wanted her from the minute she'd fainted into his arms that first day in the park, and she'd come up with the perfect excuse for him to have her.

He'd convinced himself that going along with her plan was for her protection. But it was also so he could be with her guilt-free, knowing all along he didn't have much of a future in Red River.

Now that he thought about it, he was an even bigger bastard now than he had been in his rebellious teens.

"Then you're joining the right crowd, because we're all in the same sinking boat. That's why we do what we do, Mitchell," Allen said.

Mitchell hung up and walked into the station. "Hi, Maureen. Where's the trooper on duty?" Mitchell asked without stopping as he passed her desk.

Her phone rang, and she reached for it. "He's questioning the suspect." She picked the receiver up and answered the call.

Mitchell headed to the interrogation room.

"Hey, you can't go in—"

Mitchell swung around to face Maureen again. "The trooper can arrest me if he wants, but I'm going to find out why this scum is targeting my wife." He drew himself up, puffed out his chest, and threw the door to the interrogation room open, walking in with a chip on his shoulder as big as a Humvee.

"Officer"—Mitchell looked at his name tag—"Anderson."

The state trooper actually looked a little scared of Mitchell. But Mitchell wasn't dialing it down. The intimidation factor could work to his favor, especially since the young trooper wasn't familiar with this kind of work. They mostly issued speeding tickets to unsuspecting tourists who were traveling through Northern New Mexico on vacation.

"Can I have a moment with him?" Mitchell notched his chin at the suspect. "I won't take long."

"Don't leave me with him." The perp was practically begging. He twitched like a junkie who'd been too long without a fix.

Mitchell nodded to the mirrored wall behind the mugger. The trooper hesitated. Mitchell inhaled, drawing himself up even more for effect.

The trooper stood. "A minute."

That's all Mitchell needed.

He turned to the mugger as the trooper left the room. "Unless you tell us who put you up to this, you'll go down for two counts of assault."

"I want a lawyer," the kid said.

"Sure. You can ask the trooper for one as soon as he comes back." Mitchell scratched his jaw. "I figure I've got a minute, maybe two, alone with you. Then several hours or even days before an attorney makes it way out here to this isolated little mountain town." He shrugged. "My dad's the sheriff, so I'm sure I can ask him not to transport you to the county jail as quickly as they did last time. Paperwork can get lost. Might take days to find it."

The kid's eyes went wide. His twitching got worse.

"I'm suspected for the rec-center fire, which I'm guessing you had something to do with. If you don't tell us what you know, we'll both go down." Mitchell braced his weight against the table, angling toward the perp. "And if I'm going to be charged for a crime I didn't commit, then I might as well add a few more felonies to the list." He leveled a hard stare at the kid so his veiled warning couldn't be misunderstood. "I'm also guessing your part in all of this had something to do with money to support your habit."

The kid twitched, looking away.

Mitchell's dead-on stare didn't waver.

In under ten seconds, the kid caved, and they had their man. Lorenda was finally safe.

And Mitchell could leave her to get on with her life without causing her more problems.

When Mitchell left the interrogation room, he stopped short. A crowd had formed in the waiting room just like on the day the mugger had attacked Lorenda. His dad, dressed in civilian clothes since he was still on sick leave, and Officer Anderson were waiting too.

"Maureen, call Felix Daniels from the paper and tell him to hightail it over here. I want to make an official statement to the press before too much gossip circulates," his dad said and then pulled Mitchell and Anderson into the hallway for privacy. "I saw the whole interview from the observation room."

"I already called for backup. State troopers are on their way to Bart Wilkinson's house now." Anderson lowered his voice so the growing crowd couldn't hear. "Crazy." He shook his head. "An elementary-school principal would go to those lengths to get a woman's attention?"

"It started that way, I'm sure," his dad said. "He wanted Lorenda to need him. He wasn't expecting a seasoned vet to show up and interfere with his plan." His dad gave Mitchell an appreciative look.

Mitchell nodded. "Bart's objective changed once we got married. Setting fire to the rec center so Lorenda would have to keep the music program at the school wasn't enough. He had to get me out of the way. Today's attack was obviously so he could swoop in and be her hero, while I still looked like the villain."

Anderson grabbed a pen and pad from Maureen and closed the door of the interrogation room behind him so the perp could write out his statement.

"That was good police work, son," his dad said. "You cracked him like a nut without much effort. That's one daunting look you have. It speaks a thousand words. All of them intimidating as hell to a suspect."

"I learned it from you." Mitchell smiled.

And this time his dad smiled back.

"What are you doing here, Dad?" Mitchell asked. "You should be home resting."

"I was taking a walk when you dropped Lorenda and the boys off at the house." He tapped his chest. "Doctor's orders. Says it's good for the ticker." He rolled his eyes. "Plus, your mother makes me do it." He hitched up his starched Wranglers that were already held up by a belt buckle the size of Wheeler Peak. "When I found out, I had to come down here and see what was going on. As an observer only."

He glanced over Mitchell's shoulder to the waiting room, which was brimming with people wanting to know if their town was going to be safe.

"Before I make an announcement, I wanted to tell you"—his dad's eyes glistened under the fluorescent lights—"your instincts were right. From the minute you rolled into Red River and tackled that mugger in the park, you've been right. I was wrong, son. Wrong about so many things." His dad's voice wobbled.

I'll be damned.

"So was I" was all Mitchell could get out of his closing throat. Because he'd been so wrong to antagonize his dad for so many years. Wrong for not telling his dad the truth on his graduation night. Wrong about so many more things in his life, both past and present.

Felix Daniels barreled through the door with an old-fashioned tape recorder.

His dad held out his hand, but when Mitchell tried to shake it, he was pulled into a big bear hug. That hug set at least part of Mitchell's world right. His father hadn't hugged him like that since he was a kid, and he'd missed it more than he'd realized. More than he'd ever cared to admit.

When his dad finally let go, Mitchell followed him into the crowded waiting room. Maureen handed him the phone, and his dad listened. "Good job. We'll see you in a few." He gave the phone back to Maureen. "It's done. The other suspect is in custody."

Mitchell's entire body relaxed, finally letting go the tenseness that he'd had since that first day in the park when he'd seen Lorenda hit the ground. Another little piece of his world fell into place.

The buzz of chatter in the waiting area died out, and Felix flicked on his recorder.

"The person who mugged my daughter-in-law twice is under arrest. He didn't act alone. A second arrest has just been made. My son was not involved at all. Not only do I owe him an apology, but this whole town owes him one for all the wrongs we've doled out." He turned to Mitchell. "What can we do to make this right, son?"

Mitchell scrubbed a hand over his face. "I want every chair filled at the music concert tomorrow."

His dad frowned. "What else?"

Mitchell shrugged. "That's it." It would make Lorenda happy, and if she were happy, then he would be too. And that made something click in his stupid male brain.

If Lorenda loved him and he left her, would she be happy?

Only one way to find out.

"You heard him, folks," his dad said.

Mitchell didn't stay to listen to the rest. He walked out of the sheriff's office to go find the last piece of his world that still needed to be set right.

Chapter Twenty-Six

Lorenda sat in a swing on the back porch of her in-laws' cabin-style home, which backed up to several acres of land and had a nice stream running through the south side of the property. Jaycee and Trevor cast fishing lines into the stream, the soft sound of the running water soothing her. Brought peace to her after a very trying and troubling day.

Sierra. Her entire life had become trying and troubling.

She heard the shrill ring of a landline echo from inside the house and Badass Becky's muffled voice as she answered it.

Lorenda kept swinging. Kept listening to the babbling stream. Kept watching her two wonderful boys fish. Kept waiting for Mitchell to call.

He didn't.

Becky appeared at the screen door. "I just got word from Maureen at the sheriff's office." Her mother-in-law walked onto the porch and took a seat in the swing next to Lorenda. And it dawned on her that Becky looked more at peace than Lorenda had ever seen her.

"What's up?" she asked.

That's all it took for a dam of tears to break in the strongest woman Lorenda had ever met. Decades of a mother's worries came flooding out as relief took hold, and Becky told her the whole story about Bart and the mugger and Mitchell finally being free. Which meant Lorenda was safe and so, so wrong to dismiss Mitchell's instincts.

Becky pulled Lorenda into a hug. "Thank you, hon, for finally telling us the truth. For clearing Mitchell's name, so he can finally find himself. Cameron was a good boy, but he was a kid, and kids make mistakes. Mitchell's been carrying around a burden for all of us since he was very young. It was time to put an end to it."

Lorenda needed to find him. Tell him how wrong she'd been about Bart and how sorry she was. "Becky, can the kids stay here for a little while so I can go talk to Mitchell?"

"Of course." She wiped her eyes.

Lorenda found her purse and got into her SUV. Before she could pull out of Becky's drive, her cell rang, and a strange number from Washington, DC, popped onto the screen. She frowned at it and answered.

"Uh." A strange male voice came through.

"Can I help you?" she asked.

"Uh, yeah. This is Allen Carson. I'm looking for Mitchell Lawson." His tone sounded confused. Then a muffled cuss word sounded in her ear. "I forgot he told me not to call this number."

"I'm Lorenda Lawson, Mitchell's wife."

Several beats of silence went by. "Mitch . . . Mitchell's wife?" Allen asked. "I'm sorry, I didn't realize he got married. Congratulations."

"Thank you. Can I take a message?"

His sigh was heavy. "Look, I really shouldn't be talking to you about this, but now some things make more sense." He cleared his throat. "Mitchell was set to take a high-paying job with my security company, where he'd be in charge of his own team." He paused. "In Afghanistan."

Fear ricocheted through her. "I see. Go on."

"He'd put off taking the job for family reasons." More throat clearing. "Until today."

Lorenda blinked. Several times, letting that soak in. Her heart pounded so hard she could actually feel it beating against her chest. "If you're telling me all of this, then there must be a reason."

"There is." Allen's tone was coarse. "Mitchell might get pissed. Might even want to kick my ass, but marriage and this job don't always mix. Probably why he didn't tell me about the change in his marital status when he called today. I'm guessing by your reaction you didn't know about the job?"

"No, I didn't." She tried to keep her voice from shaking. Wasn't happening. "So I need you to tell me what he said."

Apparently Allen drew in a breath, because it came through the phone loud and clear. "Something about him being poison to the people he loved, and they were better off without him."

Lorenda hoped she was one of the people he loved, but he still hadn't said it.

"This job is high stress. I've seen it take its toll on a lot of marriages." Lorenda could vouch for that.

"That's why I'm not married. Obviously you and Mitchell have some talking to do before he reports. If you two decide this job is right for him, then tell him to call me."

"I will." She backed up, put the car in drive, and spun out. She headed to Joe's, because that's where she could be sure to find the biggest audience, which would spread what she needed to say as quick as lightning. And she had a pretty good idea why Mitchell thought he was poison to the people he loved. It was because this town, including her, had made him feel like poison. "And, Allen," she said. "Thanks."

"Sure thing. I hope everything works out."

Lorenda ran two stop signs and broke at least three traffic laws before skidding to a halt in front of Joe's. She didn't even stop to close the door of her SUV before taking the wood steps two at a time and crashing through the front door.

The place was packed, and the musicians were setting up in the corner on the far side of the long bar.

"Hey, Lorenda." When Dylan saw the look on her face, he stopped. "Everything okay?"

"No. Nothing's okay. I plan to make it right, if I can." Time to find that backbone she'd never had the courage to use.

Miranda hurried over. "What's wrong? You look like you're ready to take on the world."

"Do your whistle thing, and get everyone's attention," Lorenda said, because Miranda had a way of bringing an entire town to order with her authoritative whistle. "I've got something to say to everyone in Red River, and, God as my witness, I'm going to say it today, even if it's the last thing I do in this town."

Just like the BFF Lorenda knew she was, Miranda put two fingers between her lips without asking for an explanation. A loud, sharp whistle ripped through the restaurant, bringing the entire establishment to a halt. Every last head in the place turned in their direction.

Lorenda so needed to learn how to whistle like a badass.

She cleared her throat. "I assume you've all heard the news about the man who attacked me and who put him up to it." It wasn't a question, because everyone in a four-state radius had probably heard. "I'd already told you that Mitchell didn't start the fire that destroyed Joe's, and now you know the truth about the recent fires."

A lot of guilty expressions looked back at her from the crowd.

"I kept saying he was innocent, but most of you wouldn't listen." She fought off the sting in her eyes. "I'm just as guilty as the rest of you. I didn't listen when my husband said I was in danger and that Bart had something to do with it."

She swallowed, tears welling in her eyes at how she must've made Mitchell feel just as alone as everyone else had. Like the entire world was against him. He'd put everything on the line to protect her and the boys, and she'd repaid him by dismissing his concerns. She'd even called him an alpha ass.

Maybe an alpha ass—the very thing she'd been avoiding since her first marriage ended—was exactly what she needed. Exactly what she wanted.

Mitchell. He was what she wanted and needed, and she'd move heaven and earth to show him.

"I'm ashamed of myself. I'm ashamed of this town, because we're better than that. Or we should be. Mitchell is one of ours, and he should've been treated like it. If we can't *all* start treating him the way he deserves, then I don't think I belong here either."

She had a choice to make, and she was choosing Mitchell. Anyone who didn't like it could bite her.

Murmurs floated through the room.

Now all she had to do was go find her husband and ask him once and for all if he wanted to be with her for real. No more faux marriage. No more great sex without a long-term commitment to make it work. She was in it forever, and she wanted to know if he was too, even if that meant spending their forever somewhere other than Red River.

Because her home was with Mitchell, and she wanted his home to be with her. Not a town that didn't see him for the wonderful man that he was.

She swung around to go find him.

And bumped right into a hard wall of muscled stealth.

"Ooff!" She tried to step back, but Mitchell's arms circled around her waist and hauled her against him.

"You going somewhere?" His tone was soft. Sentimental. Sexy.

A fire started down below. The good kind that simmered through her veins and set her girl parts to a flaming heat.

"Funny." She tilted her head back to look into his smoldering eyes. "I was going to find you so I could ask you the same thing. I talked to your *boss*."

"So did I. He just called me and filled me in on his conversation with you." His eyes searched hers. "I told him Afghanistan wasn't on my list of most desirable places to work." His fingers caressed the small of her back. "So, I was thinking about settling down. Becoming domesticated. Maybe getting a wife, and a dog, and a couple of kids. Know anyone who might be interested?"

"The only person I know who might be remotely interested wants someone she can depend on. Someone who will always be there for her." The color of his dark eyes grew even more intense, filling with emotions that made her heart expand and fill too. "You were going to leave me."

His breaths were fast and hard like he'd run all the way to Joe's. "I was." His honesty and his regret showed in the tightness of his jaw. "But then I remembered something important you said."

"What would that be?" Hopefully not the alpha ass part.

"You said you loved me."

"I did say that. I do love you."

"I love you too, babe." He glanced over her shoulder, looking around the silenced room. "I don't know if that's good for you and the boys or not." He ran his hand up her back.

The love in his words and in his expression stole the air from the room.

"Life doesn't have to be perfect," she whispered, because it was hard to speak. "We want to be with you, no matter where that takes us." She swallowed. "Even if we can't stay here in Red River."

"Does that mean I don't have to sign up with an online dating service to find a wife?" he teased. "Because Minx could probably help me out with that if I can fix your old phone. She already tried to sign us up a few weeks ago."

"That little hussy can stay broken, because you're taken," Lorenda teased.

He brushed Lorenda's hair back over her shoulder with a tender touch. "I don't know what I'll do for a job. We'll have to discuss our options, but I want you to be part of that decision. No more making decisions about our future without your input, I promise."

Two scratchy female throats cleared somewhere behind her.

"Ouch!" Joe said as Clydelle poked him in the leg with her cane. Francine raised her ginormous purse like she was threatening him. "Okay, okay." He lumbered toward them, mumbling something about two old hens. "Mitchell, I don't know about everybody in Red River, but I know some of us feel real bad about everything." He turned back to look at Clydelle and Francine. They gave him a *go on* motion. "And well, we were thinking that the sheriff sure could use some help." Joe gave Mitchell a sincere look. "There's no one better qualified than you."

Some applause and a lot of "amens" rounded the room.

For the first time that Lorenda could remember, Mitchell looked choked up in a good way. He glanced around the room. "Only if people in Red River want me as their deputy. I won't take the job if all I'm going to get is resistance from the people I'm supposed to serve. I had enough of that in the military." His gaze found hers again. "And only if my wife agrees, after we've have a chance to talk about it."

She kissed him then. Soft and sweet. When she broke the kiss, he pulled her into his neck. She nuzzled the ropey muscles, and he placed a kiss at her temple.

"I think this is where I'm supposed to ask the woman I love if she'll marry me, but we're already married," he whispered so no one else could hear. "So instead I'll ask you to make it forever."

"Forever is a long time," she whispered back, and he tensed. "So let's go home and get started on it."

Chapter Twenty-Seven

Brandenburg Park had transformed into a magical fairy-tale setting by Saturday night. Twinkling white lights draped the gazebo and most of the trees. All of Lorenda's music students had returned to the program and filled their seats to participate in the concert, and Andrea was ready to perform her flute solo.

Every seat in the audience was full, with the overflow crowd spreading blankets on the grass to listen to the kids.

Daniel Summerall sat front and center, a leggy blonde on his arm.

Lorenda scanned the crowd. Her pulse revved when her gaze landed on Red River's sexy new deputy standing at the back of the park, holding up a large tree. He still wore Levi's and combat boots, but his trademark black T-shirt had been replaced by an official department-issue deputy shirt. His badge was anchored to his belt, and his holstered Glock made him look even more badass.

Lorenda's mouth watered, and she licked her lips.

One side of his mouth curved into a naughty, knowing smile, like he could read her thoughts all the way from the back of the park.

Lorenda turned to the kids and had them tune their instruments to the oboe player.

The crowd quieted, and as if the heavens had opened up, the kids played to perfection. Okay, so not really to perfection, but it was like angels singing to Lorenda's trained ears. Because they were kids, learning the joy of music. Learning the skill of playing music, which would challenge their brainpower and open up a whole new world to them.

When the concert was over, Lorenda had the kids take a bow and then directed the audience to enjoy refreshments served by her best friends.

As she walked off the gazebo steps, Daniel captured her arm. "Great job, Lorenda. You've got my support." He looked around the park. "I've rarely seen this much community interest. If you can pull something like this off so well, then I'm in."

"Thank you, Daniel." She shook his hand, and he went back to his bombshell date.

Lorenda went to find her husband.

She scanned the row of trees that lined the back of the park where he'd been standing, but he was gone. She kept walking, looking, searching. Until strong arms reached from behind a large oak and snatched her up, hauling her behind it into the shadows.

"Hi." Mitchell covered her mouth with his.

"Hello, Deputy," she whispered between his soft, sweet kisses.

"You did great." He nuzzled her neck. "I'm so proud of you."

"The kids did great, not me." Her breathing picked up speed as his hot mouth got familiar with her neck. "And their parents deserve credit for letting them come back to rehearsals. Daniel Summerall is going to endorse the program."

"I knew you could do it." His eyes anchored to her mouth, and he dipped his head to pull her bottom lip between his teeth for a nip.

Her hands slid around his waist and landed on his cuffs.

A shiver of anticipation raced through her.

"If I ever commit a crime, promise you'll be the one to arrest me, Deputy. Cuffs and all."

He moaned so deeply against her ear she was afraid someone might've heard. "I promise."

"I hope you know you're really rocking that uniform." She speared her fingers into the back of his hair and pulled his mouth to hers.

After a long, deep, sensual kiss that blew Lorenda's mind, he pulled away. "I'm on duty. I don't want to let the folks of Red River down my first day on the job. Not after they had an emergency city council meeting yesterday and all but forced the uniform into my hands." He threaded his fingers with hers and pulled her from behind the tree and toward the crowd.

Her mom and dad walked over with the boys.

"There you are, sweetheart." Lorenda's dad gave her a kiss on the cheek.

"It was spectacular!" Her mom beamed.

Jaycee and Trevor surrounded Mitchell, staring at his badge and gun.

Lorenda's heart stuttered.

Mitchell must've read her thoughts. "I have a concealed carry permit. That's the only reason the sheriff's department allowed me to carry one right away, and it will stay locked up in a safe when I'm not wearing it." He turned his attention to the kids. "You hear me, boys?"

They nodded, still staring at the badge.

"I want to be a deputy like you and Grandpa," Trevor said.

"Me too," said Jaycee. "Except I want to be the sheriff."

"We can talk about that when you're adults. Until then, I have something for both of you." Mitchell pulled two sets of dog tags from his pocket and draped one around each of the kids' necks. "One tag on each chain is mine, and the other is your dad's."

The kids' eyes rounded in awe as they studied them.

Lorenda's throat closed.

The boys ran off to show their friends.

The look of pure love and probably a lot of lust must've shown on her face because her parents started to fidget. Lorenda didn't stop staring at her sexy, strong husband, and her parents finally wandered away quietly.

"Thank you."

"Of course." He smoothed the back of one finger down her cheek. "I don't ever want them to forget their dad."

She swallowed. "And thank you for inspiring me."

His brows drew together.

"I registered for spring semester. It'll be a long drive back and forth to the university, but I think I can work my classes out so I only have to go in three days a week. They offer some online classes too."

He brushed his lips across hers. "A little driving doesn't seem like a lot since we've got forever." His lips covered hers, and she melted into his kiss, his body, his arms. "When you get home from classes every day," he whispered against her mouth, "I'll be waiting for you with open arms."

She smiled up at him and felt it to her soul. "I'm counting on it."

Acknowledgments

I owe a huge shout-out to Stan and Karen Sluder. Thanks for the guinea pig story. As always, I have to thank my BFF, Kim R., for all the years of friendship and laughter. Life wouldn't have been nearly as much fun if I hadn't met you. Thank you to my editors, Maria Gomez of Montlake Romance and Melody Guy. The entire Montlake team rocks. Hard. Thank you to my agent, Jill Marsal of the Marsal Lyon Literary Agency. A huge thank you to my critique partner, Shelly Chalmers, who makes my books so, so, so much better. Thank you to the town of Red River for being my muse and my favorite weekend getaway. And thank you to Fritz Davis for being a real-life character.

About the Author

Photo © 2014 Frank Frost Photography

Shelly Alexander is the author of *It's In His Smile*, *It's In His Heart*, and *It's In His Touch*, earlier titles in the Red River Valley series. A 2014 RWA Golden Heart finalist, she grew up traveling the world, earned a bachelor's degree in marketing, and worked in the business world for twenty-five years. With four older brothers, she watched every *Star Trek* episode ever made, joined the softball team instead of ballet class, and played with G.I. Joes while the Barbie Corvette stayed tucked in her closet. When she had three sons of her own, she decided to escape her male-dominated world by reading romance novels and has been hooked ever since. Now, she spends her days writing steamy contemporary romances and tending to a miniature schnauzer named Omer, a tiny toy poodle named Mozart, and a pet boa named Zeus.

WITHDRAWN